28/8/22

WAT

Please renew/return items by last date
shown. Please call the number below:

Renewals and enquiries:  0300 1234049

Textphone for hearing or
speech impaired users:  01992 555506

www.hertfordshire.gov.uk/libraries
L32

**Hertfordshire**

# HITLER'S TASTER

V.S. Alexander is the author of nine novels, whose rights have sold in nearly a dozen countries in Europe and South America. Hitler's Taster, Alexander's second novel for Kensington Publishing in America, has been optioned for film, and translated into several languages. The Taster, which Booklist has called a 'powerfully moving novel', also is available from Harper Collins UK. Other books include The Magdalen Girls, The Irishman's Daughter, and The Sculptress, which is slated for release in March 2021. Two more novels are in the works.

# HITLER'S
# Taster

## V.S. ALEXANDER

**avon.**

Published by AVON
A division of HarperCollins*Publishers* Ltd
1 London Bridge Street
London SE1 9GF

www.harpercollins.co.uk

This paperback edition published in Great Britain
by HarperCollins*Publishers* 2020

First published in the United States as *The Taster*
by Kensington Publishing 2018
Published in Great Britain as *Her Hidden Life*
by HarperCollins*Publishers* 2018

A catalogue copy of this book
is available from the British Library.

ISBN: 978-0-00-844467-9

Typeset in Bembo by
Palimpsest Book Production Limited, Falkirk, Stirlingshire
Printed and bound in UK by CPI Group (UK) Ltd, Croydon CR0 4YY

To James E. Gunn, who lit the fire

# PROLOGUE

Who killed Adolf Hitler? The answer lies within these pages. The circumstances surrounding his death have been disputed since 1945, but I know the truth. I was there.

Now I'm a childless old widow left alone in a house filled with memories as bitter as ashes. The linden trees in spring, the blue lakes in summer, bring me no joy.

I, Magda Ritter, was one of fifteen women who tasted Hitler's food. He was obsessively concerned about being poisoned by the Allies or traitors.

After the war, no one, except my husband, knew what I did. I didn't talk about it. I couldn't talk about it. But the secrets I've held for so many years need to be released from their inner prison. I don't have much longer to live.

I knew Hitler. I watched as he walked the halls of his mountain retreat, the Berghof, and followed him through the maze of the Wolf's Lair, his headquarters in East Prussia.

I was near him in his final day in the tomb-like depths of his Berlin bunker. Often he was surrounded by an entourage of admirers, his head bobbing like a buoy on the sea.

Why didn't anyone kill Hitler before he died in the bunker? A trick of fate? His uncanny ability to avoid death? Assassination plots were hatched and, of those, many were aborted. Only one succeeded in injuring the Führer. That attempt only reinforced his belief in providence – his divine right to rule as he saw fit.

My first recollection of him was at a 1932 Party rally in Berlin. I was fifteen at the time. He stood on a wooden platform and spoke to a small crowd that grew larger by the minute as word spread of his appearance at Potsdamer Platz. Rain spit from gray clouds that November day, but each word he spoke exploded in the air until the crowd glowed with heat and rage at the enemies of the German people. With every beat of his fist to his breast, the sky shook. He wore a brown uniform with a black leather belt stretched across his chest. The red, white and black swastika patch was prominently displayed on his left arm. A pistol hung at his side. He was not particularly handsome, but his eyes held you in their powerful grip. Rumors circulated he wanted to be an architect or an artist, but I always imagined he would have been a better storyteller; if only he would have let his imagination play out in words rather than in malevolence.

He mesmerized a nation, inducing euphoric riots among those who believed in the shining new order of National Socialism. But not all of us worshiped him as the savior of Germany. Certainly not all 'good Germans.' Was my nation guilty of aiding the most notorious dictator the world has ever known?

A cult has grown up around Hitler, in death as large as when he was alive. Its members are fascinated by the horror and destruction he cast upon the world like the devil. They are either fanatical worshipers of the Führer or students of human psychology who ask, 'How could one man be so evil?' Either way, those followers have helped Hitler succeed in his quest to live forever.

I have struggled with the horrific actions perpetrated by the Third Reich and my singular place in history. My story needs to be told. Sometimes the truth overwhelms and horrifies me, like falling endlessly into a darkened pit. But, in the process, I have discovered much about myself and humanity. I have also discovered the cruelty of men who make laws to suit their own purposes.

Life has punished me and nightmares hound my sleep. There is no escape from the horrors of the past. Perhaps those who read my story will not judge me as harshly as I've judged myself.

# THE TEAHOUSE

## THE BERGHOF

# CHAPTER 1

A strange fear crept over Berlin in early 1943.

The year before, I had looked up at the sky when air-raid sirens sounded. I saw nothing except high clouds, streaming like white horses' tails above me. The Allied bombs did little damage and we Germans thought we were safe. By the end of January 1943, my father suspected the prelude to a fiery rain of destruction had begun.

'Magda, you should leave Berlin,' he said at the onset of the bombing. 'It's too dangerous here. You can go to Uncle Willy's in Berchtesgaden. You'll be safe there.' My mother agreed.

I wanted no part of their plan because I'd only once, as a child, met my aunt and uncle. Southern Germany seemed a thousand miles away. I loved Berlin and wanted to remain in the small apartment building where we lived in Horst-Wessel-Stadt. Our lives, and everything I'd ever known, were contained on one floor. I wanted to be normal; after all, the war was going well. That's what the Reich told us.

Everyone in the Stadt believed the neighborhood would be bombed. Many industries lay nearby, including the brake factory where my father worked. One Allied bombing occurred on January 30 at eleven in the morning when Hermann Göring, the Reichsmarschall, gave a speech on the radio. The second occurred later in the day when the Propaganda Minister, Joseph Goebbels, spoke. The Allies had planned their attacks well. Both speeches were interrupted by the raids.

My father was at work for the first, but at home for the second. We had already decided we would gather in the basement during an air raid, along with Frau Horst, who lived on the top floor of our building. We were unaware in those early days what destruction the Allied bombers could wreak, the terrible devastation that could fall from the skies in whistling black clouds of bombs. Hitler said the German people would be protected from such terrors and we believed him. Even the boys I knew who fought in the Wehrmacht held that thought in their hearts. A feeling of destiny propelled us forward.

'We should go to the basement now,' I told my mother when the second attack began. I shouted the same words upstairs to Frau Horst, but added, 'Hurry! Hurry!'

The old woman popped her head out of her apartment. 'You must help me. I can't hurry. I'm not as young as I used to be.' I rushed up the stairs to find her holding a pack of cigarettes and a bottle of cognac. I took them from her and we found our way down before the bombs hit. We were used to blackouts. No Allied bombardier could see light coming from our windowless basement. The first blast seemed far away and I was unconcerned.

Frau Horst lit a cigarette and offered my father cognac. Apparently, cigarettes and liquor were the two possessions she would drag to her grave. Bits of dust dropped around us. The old lady pointed to the wooden beams above us and said, 'Damn them.' My father nodded halfheartedly. The ancient coal furnace sputtered in the corner, but it couldn't dispel the icy drafts that poked their way through the room. Our frosty breaths shone under the glare of the bare bulb.

A closer blast rattled our ears and the electricity blinked out. A brilliant orange light flashed overhead, so close we could see its fiery trail through the cracks surrounding the basement door. A dusty cloud swirled down the stairs. Glass shattered somewhere in the house. My father grabbed my mother and me by the shoulders, pulled us forward and covered our heads with his arched chest.

'That was too close,' I said, shaking against my father. Frau Horst sobbed in the corner.

The bombing ended almost as quickly as it had begun and we climbed the darkened stairs back to our apartment. Frau Horst said good evening and left us. My mother opened our door and searched for a candle in the kitchen. Through the window, we saw black smoke mushrooming from a building several blocks away. My mother found a match and struck it.

She gasped. The china cabinet had popped open, sending several pieces of fine porcelain, given to her by her grand-mother, to the floor. She bent down and scraped the shards into a pile, trying to fit them together like a puzzle.

A cut-glass vase of importance to my mother had smashed to bits as well. My mother grew geraniums and purple irises in the small garden behind our building. She cut the irises when they bloomed and placed them in the vase on the dining room table. Their heady fragrance filled our rooms. My father said the flowers made him happy because he had proposed to my mother during the time of year when irises bloomed.

'Our lives have become fragile,' my father said, looking sadly at the damage. After a few minutes, my mother gave up her hope of reconstructing the porcelain and the vase and threw them into the trash.

My mother pinned her black hair into a bun and walked into the kitchen to get a broom. 'We must make sacrifices,' she called out.

'Nonsense,' my father said. 'We are lucky to have a daughter and not a son; otherwise, I fear we would be planning a funeral not far down the road.'

My mother appeared at the kitchen door with the broom. 'You mustn't say such things. It gives the wrong impression.'

My father shook his head. 'To whom?'

'Frau Horst. Our neighbors. Your fellow workers. Who knows? We must be careful of what we say. Such statements, even rumors, could come down upon our heads.'

The electricity flickered on and my father sighed. 'That's the problem. We watch everything we say – and now we have to deal with bombs. Magda must leave. She must go to Uncle Willy's in Berchtesgaden. Maybe she can even find work.'

I had flitted from job to job in my twenty-five years, finding some work in a clothing factory, filing for a banker, replenishing wares as a store clerk, but I felt lost in the world of employment. Nothing I did felt right or good enough. The Reich wanted German girls to be mothers; however, the Reich wanted them to be workers as well. I supposed that was what I wanted, too. If you had a job, you had to have permission to leave it. Because I had no job, it would be hard to ignore my father's wishes. As far as marriage was concerned, I'd had a few boyfriends since I turned nineteen – none of them serious. The war had taken so many young men away. Those who remained failed to capture my heart. I was a virgin but had no regrets.

In the first years of the war, Berlin had been spared. When the attacks began, the city strode like a dreamer, alive but unconscious of its motions. People walked about without feeling. Babies were born and relatives looked into their eyes and told them how beautiful they were. Touching a silky lock of hair or pinching a cheek did not guarantee a future. Young men were shipped off to the fronts – to the East and to the West. Talk on the streets centered on Germany's slow slide into hell, always ending with 'it will get better.' Conversations about food and cigarettes were common, but paled in comparison to the trumpeted broadcasts of the latest victories earned through the ceaseless struggles of the Wehrmacht.

My parents were the latest in a line of Ritters to live in our building. My grandparents had lived here until they each died in the bed where I slept. My bedroom, the first off the hall in the front of the building, was my own, a place I could breathe. No ghosts frightened me here. My room didn't hold much: the bed, a small oak dresser, a rickety bookshelf and a few items I collected over the years, including the stuffed toy monkey my father had won at a carnival in Munich when I was a child. When the bombings began, I looked at my room in a different way. My sanctuary took on a sacred, extraordinary quality and each day I wondered whether its tranquility would be shattered like a bombed temple.

The next major air raid came on Hitler's birthday on April 20, 1943. The Nazi banners, flags and standards that decorated Berlin waved in the breeze. The bombs caused some damage, but most of the city escaped unscathed. That attack also had a way of bringing back every fear I suffered as a young girl. I was never fond of storms, especially the lightning and thunder. The increasing severity of the bombings set my nerves on edge. My father was adamant that I leave, and, for the first time, I felt he might be right. That night he watched as I packed my bag.

I assembled a few things important to me: a small family portrait taken in 1925 in happier times and some notebooks to record my thoughts. My father handed me my stuffed monkey, the only keepsake I had retained throughout my childhood years.

The following morning, my mother cried as I carried my suitcase down the stairs. A spring rain spattered the street and the earthy scent of budding trees filled the air.

'Take care of yourself, Magda.' My mother kissed me on the cheek. 'Hold your head up. The war will be over soon.'

I returned the kiss and tasted her salty tears. My father was at work. We had said our good-byes the night before. My mother clasped my hands one more time, as if she did not want to let me go, and then let them drop. I gathered my bags and took a carriage to the train station. It would be a long ride to my new home. Glad to be out of the rain, I entered the station through the main entrance. My heels clicked against the stone walkway.

I found the track that would take me to Munich and Berchtesgaden and stood waiting in line under the iron latticework of the shed's vaulted ceiling. A young SS man in his gray uniform looked at everyone's identification papers as they boarded. I was a Protestant German, neither Catholic nor Jew, and young enough to be foolishly convinced of my invincibility. Several railway police in their green uniforms stood by as the security officer sorted through the line.

The SS man had a sleek, handsome face punctuated by steely blue eyes. His brown hair folded underneath his cap like a wave. He examined everyone as if they were a potential criminal, but his cool demeanor masked his intentions. He made me uneasy, but I had no doubt I would be allowed to board. He looked at me intently, studied my identification, paying particular attention to my photograph before handing it back to me. He offered a slight smile, not flirtatious by any means, but coyly, as if he had finished a job done well. He waved his hand at the passenger behind me to come forward. My credentials had passed his inspection. Perhaps he liked my photograph. I thought it flattered me. My hair was dark brown and fell to my shoulders. My face was too narrow. My dark eyes were too big for my head and gave me an Eastern European look, presenting a face similar to a Modigliani portrait. Some men had told me I was beautiful and exotic for a German.

The car contained no compartments, only seats, and was half-full. The train would be packed in a few months with city tourists eager to take a summer trip to the Alps. Germans wanted to enjoy their country even in the midst of war. A young couple, who looked as if they were in love, sat a few rows in front of me near the middle of the car. They leaned their heads against each other. He whispered in her ear, adjusted his fedora and then puffed on his cigarette. Blue clouds of haze drifted above them. The woman lifted the cigarette occasionally from his hands and sucked on it as well. Soon thin gray lines of smoke trailed throughout the cabin.

We pulled out of the shed in the semi-darkness of the rain. The train picked up speed as we rolled away from the city and past the factories and farmlands south of Berlin. I leaned back in my seat and pulled out a book of poems by Friedrich Rückert from my suitcase. My father had presented it to me several years ago thinking I would enjoy the Romantic author's poems. I never took the time to study them. The gift meant more to me than the verses inside.

I stared blankly at the pages and thought only of leaving my old life for a new life ahead. It troubled me to be going so far from home, but I had no choice thanks to Hitler and the war.

I found the inscription my father had written when he gave me the book. It was signed: *With all love from your Father, Hermann.* When we'd parted last night, he seemed old and sad beyond his forty-five years, but relieved to be able to send me to his brother's home.

My father walked with a stoop from constant bending during his shift at the brake factory. The gray stubble he shaved each morning attested to the personal trials he endured daily, among them his dislike for National Socialism and Hitler. Of course, he never spoke of such things; he only hinted of his politics to my mother and me. His unhappiness ate at him, ruined his appetite and caused him to smoke and drink too much despite such luxuries being hard to come by. He was nearing the end of the age for military service in the Wehrmacht, but a leg injury he suffered in his youth would have disqualified him anyway. From his conversations, I knew he held little admiration for the Nazis.

Lisa, my mother, was more sympathetic to the Party, although she and my father were not members. Like most Germans, she hated what had happened to the country during the First World War. She had told my father many times, 'At least people have jobs and enough food to go around now.' My mother brought in extra money with her sewing, and because her fingers were nimble, she also did piecework for a jeweler. She taught me to sew as well. We were able to live comfortably, but we were not rich by any means. We never worried about food on the table until rationing began.

My mother and father did not make an obvious display of politics. No bunting, no Nazi flags, hung from our building. Frau Horst had put a swastika placard in her window, but it was small and hardly noticeable from the street. I had not become a member of the Party, a fact that caused my mother some consternation. She believed it might be good because the affiliation could help me find work. I hadn't given the Party much thought after leaving the Band of German Maidens and the Reich Labor Service, both of which I lazed through. And I wasn't sure what being a Party member actually meant, so I felt no need to give them my allegiance. War churned around us. We fought for good on the road to victory. My naïveté masked my need to know.

I continued thumbing through the book until the train slowed.

The SS man at the station appeared behind my right shoulder. He held a pistol in his left hand. He strode to the couple in front of me and put the barrel to the temple of the young man who was smoking the cigarette. The woman looked backward, toward me, her eyes filled with terror. She seemed prepared to run, but there was nowhere to go, for suddenly armed station police appeared in the doorways at both ends of the car. The SS man took the pistol away from the man's head and motioned for them to get up. The woman grabbed her dark coat and wrapped a black scarf around her neck. The officer escorted them to the back of the car. I dared not look at what was happening.

After a few moments, I peered through the window to my left. The train had stopped in the middle of a field. A mud-spattered black touring car, its chrome exhaust pipes spewing steady puffs of steam, sat on a dirt road next to the tracks. The SS man pushed the man and woman into the back of the car and then climbed in after them, his pistol drawn. The police got in the front with the driver. As soon as the doors closed, the car made a large circle in the field, cut a muddy swath through the grass and then headed back toward Berlin.

I closed my eyes and wondered what the couple had done to be yanked from the train. Were they Allied spies? Jews attempting to get out of Germany? My father had told us once – only once – at the dinner table about the trouble Jews were having in Berlin. My mother scoffed, calling them 'baseless rumors.' He replied that one of his co-workers had seen *Juden* painted on several buildings in the Jewish section. The man felt uncomfortable even being there, an accident on his part. Swastikas were whitewashed on windows. Signs cautioned against trading with Jewish merchants.

16

I thought it best to keep my thoughts to myself and not to inflame a political discussion between my parents. I felt sad for the Jews, but no one I knew particularly liked them and the Reich always pointed blame in their direction. Like many at the time I turned a blind eye. What my father reported might have been a rumor. I trusted him, but I knew so little — only what we heard on the radio.

I looked for the black sedan, but the motorcar had vanished. I had no idea what the couple had done, but the image of the woman's terror-filled eyes burned itself into my memory. My reading offered little comfort as my journey continued. The incident unsettled me. I wondered who might be next and when it all might end.

# CHAPTER 2

The Berchtesgaden train station was smaller but grander than Berlin's. The Nazi banners hung in strict vertical rows, offsetting the large columns inside, giving the building a formal Roman look. Off to one side, a gold door glittered. It appeared to be reserved for dignitaries. A black eagle perched on a swastika was rendered in bas-relief on its surface. Perhaps it was the entrance to a reception room for important people visiting the Führer; after all, this was the final stop for those invited to his mountain retreat.

I looked for my uncle Willy and aunt Reina and saw them standing near the entrance. We exchanged Nazi salutes. My uncle seemed happier to see me than my aunt. He was a pear-shaped man with a potbelly, who still retained the red hair and freckles of his youth. Some of the spots had blossomed into brown blotches that spread across his face. He held his police cap in his hand. My aunt's smile seemed forced, as if I were the unwanted stepchild who had come home for a visit. She was elegant and cultured, compared to my more affable uncle. My father had told me that he found my aunt and uncle a strange match. I was young then and never questioned their attraction, but now as I stood before them their differences showed clearly.

After we swapped greetings, my uncle loaded my bags into their small gray Volkswagen. I took my place in the backseat. I could see little of the mountain scenery as my uncle drove, with the exception of dark peaks that shot up through the broken clouds into an ebony sky. I had only been to Berchtesgaden once when I was child.

My aunt and uncle lived in a three-story Bavarian-style chalet wedged between a small restaurant and a butcher shop on a crowded street not far from the town center. The Alpine influence was everywhere. Their home was tall, but not as wide as a chalet you would find perched on a mountainside. I got out of the car and breathed in the crisp mountain air. It was hard to believe I was in the same country as Berlin.

We took off our coats and left my luggage near the door. Uncle Willy was dressed in his local police uniform with the swastika on his left arm. Reina wore a cobalt blue dress with a fastened collar. A diamond brooch in the shape of a swastika was pinned above her heart. A large black-and-white portrait of the Führer hung over the fireplace where his solemn, solid figure brooded over the dining room. My aunt had sewn a table runner covered with swastikas. Reina was Spanish and a supporter of Franco, and Italy's Mussolini as well. Everything in their house was fastidious according to the Nazi ideal of Germanic perfection. Nothing was out of order. The furniture was polished to a brilliant shine and symmetrical in its placement. I felt as if I had stepped into a fairy tale, something out of the ordinary and surreal in its effect. It was like being at an art exhibition – beautiful, but not home.

The evening was cool, so my uncle stoked the fire. Aunt Reina served a beef stew and bread, and we enjoyed a glass of red wine. The stew was light on meat and vegetables, more broth than anything, but it tasted good. I was hungry from the trip. The meal was heartier than the vegetable dishes my mother cooked these days. Eggs and meat were scarce all over Germany, especially in the cities.

We talked about my parents and our relatives. We spoke briefly of the war, a topic for which Willy and Reina had only smiles. Like my mother, they were convinced we were winning and Germany would be victorious over our enemies, particularly the Jews. My life had been so sheltered, with people of my own kind, my own few friends, that I had never thought much about the Jews. They were not part of my life. We had no friends, no neighbors, who were Jewish. No one we knew had 'disappeared.'

Uncle Willy said the right to our Lebensraum was as indelible as our heritage. When the Jews and the Bolsheviks were removed, the land would be Germany's to populate. The East would produce the food, the minerals and the raw materials the Reich needed for its thousand-year reign. His face beamed as he talked.

Aunt Reina surveyed her perfectly laid table like a queen. 'This crystal came from my home in Spain.' She tapped the side of the glass with her nails. 'When it's safe to travel, I will take you to my birthplace; it's such a beautiful country. The Allies are doing their best to flood us with propaganda. Despite that, we know the Führer cannot be wrong.' She glanced at the portrait over the fireplace and smiled. 'We will be victorious. Our men will fight until the final battle is won.'

I nodded, having no taste for the topic, because I was an ordinary German girl with little of the sophistication of my aunt. She was unlike any woman I had ever met – more opinionated than my mother, and with a soul of tempered steel. Nothing I could say or do could influence my aunt's and uncle's thinking or the outcome of the war. Even my few girlfriends were more concerned with their jobs, making money and getting along. We hardly ever talked of the war except to note, with longing, the misfortune of boys being shipped off to battle.

After my aunt and I cleared the dishes, we sat up for another hour in the living room until Uncle Willy nodded off. Reina declared the evening at an end when my uncle began snoring. I carried my bags to my second-floor bedroom, which looked out over the street. The third floor housed the attic, a room my aunt used for storage.

The town lamps were out, but a few muted window lights shone underneath the blackout shades. Past the buildings a mixture of dark and light fell on the terrain. The mountains displayed varying tones of black: the rock dun and dense, the forest lighter in its darkness. The clouds swirled overhead and sometimes a shaft of light shot through them like a luminous arrow. I couldn't tell if it came from the ground or the heavens, but it momentarily lit the clouds as if an electric torch had been placed inside them. I stood at the window and found it hard to pull myself away from the view. Magic and myth filled the air in the Obersalzberg. No wonder Hitler had decided to construct his castle on the mountain above Berchtesgaden, his Berghof.

I unpacked a few things and then sat on the bed. As much as I admired the beauty of Berchtesgaden, I was a stranger in my aunt and uncle's house. I went to bed thinking of my comfortable room in Berlin and my parents. They would be in bed now, the shades down, the lamps out. Frau Horst would still be awake, smoking a cigarette and sipping her cognac. She never went to bed without having a drink.

The silence in my room was eerie. In Berlin, particularly before the war, when the wind was right, I heard trains and their lonely whistles. I always wondered where they were going, but I was content to stay in my bed, rather than dream about travel. Cars rumbled by, horns blared, at all hours. The city hummed. I would have to get used to the quiet. Quite unexpectedly, I missed my tree-lined street and the hellos and small talk from our neighbors.

By the next morning, all pleasantries with my aunt had dissipated.

'You must get a job if you want to live here,' Reina told me in a voice filled with the heaviness of iron. The comforts of the previous evening evaporated as she served me a bowl of porridge with a little goat's milk. There was no butter on the table and I didn't dare ask. 'We can't afford to feed another mouth, and your parents aren't in a position to send money. You must work or find a husband. The Reich needs strong male babies for future service.'

I was shocked by her demands, but they weren't entirely unexpected. 'What would you have me do?' I said. 'I can't walk the streets looking for a man.'

Creases formed around Reina's mouth. 'I am not suggesting you be a whore,' she said matter-of-factly. 'Wanton women damage the Reich and pervert our soldiers. A man's seed should be saved for children. You must find a job – something you can do, or have talent in. Do you have any talent?'

I thought hard before answering. I'd never had to do much around my parents' house except clean and mend. Sometimes I cooked, but rarely. My mother commanded the kitchen. 'I can sew,' I finally replied.

'Not enough money. And work here would be scarce. All Berchtesgaden women know how to sew, probably much better than you.'

My aunt's lack of confidence in me stung. However, her tactic was succeeding. I sank into my chair and questioned my own lack of initiative. My parents had never forced me to work and I assumed that the small jobs I did around the house paid for my keep. Perhaps I was wrong.

'What good are you to the Reich?' My aunt placed her hands on her hips and stared at me. 'Every citizen must be productive. You should be ashamed and so should your parents for raising such a worthless girl. Perhaps it would have been better if you'd stayed in Berlin. Your father is such a worrywart.' She shook a finger at me.

Whatever fondness I held for my aunt was rapidly diminishing. We had spent little time together and the prospect of more than a few days portended disaster.

'I will look for work after breakfast,' I said.

My aunt's eyes brightened. 'That's a good girl. There must be something you can do.'

I was not convinced.

I helped my aunt with the dishes, then took a bath and unpacked the remainder of my things, although I felt no certainty about staying. Wanting to look smart, I picked out my best dress. I hadn't applied for a job in several years and felt woefully unprepared. My aunt presented me with a writing pad and pen, both covered in swastikas.

The clouds had cleared overnight and the sun's rays bore down in full spring strength; still it was cool enough to wear a jacket. The mountain air and dazzling light quickened my step after the unpleasant conversation with my aunt. I looked to my right and was thrilled to see the Watzmann, whose beautiful serrated peaks loomed over the valley like shark's teeth protruding from the earth. The white snows of winter still clung to the heights of its rocky face. Everywhere I looked there were forest and mountains. Berchtesgaden was so different from Berlin, where everyone felt on edge.

I wandered down the street, past shops with empty windows. Many were shuttered or boarded up completely. I even stopped to read a local broadsheet for employment news, but no jobs were listed. How did my aunt expect me to get a position with so many shops out of business or selling only rationed goods and services? No window signs seeking job hunters were visible, except for the butcher's next to my aunt and uncle's. A few measly bird carcasses hung on hooks behind the counter. The butcher wanted a helper with strong shoulders, to help clean and lift. I couldn't see myself gutting birds or cleaning up bloody messes. Besides, it only made sense that the shop owner would want a man who could haul heavy slabs of beef, as scarce as they might be.

My parents had given me a few Reichsmark to pay for necessities. They expected my aunt and uncle would feed and house me at no cost. That, of course, was wishful thinking and only partially true. I guessed it was my uncle Willy, the head of the house, who allowed me to come to Berchtesgaden over the objections of my aunt.

I stopped at a restaurant and looked at the menu. Sausages, which probably came from the local butcher shop, looked good to me. The savory meat was a special treat and was hard to get anywhere now. I sat at an outdoor table and wondered whether I should use my parents' hard-earned money for such an extravagance. I needed something to cheer me up, so it didn't take me long to decide. The owner took my order for one sausage and fried potatoes. The sausage was served bubbling in its own juices on a warm plate. The smell of the fried potatoes reminded me of the way my mother used to cook.

After I ate, I was unsure what to do. In two hours, I had scoured most of the town with no luck. I walked aimlessly for a while, enjoying the scenery until I saw my uncle walking toward me.

'Have you eaten?' he asked, and rubbed his belly.

I pointed to the restaurant where I'd had lunch. 'The sausage was excellent.'

He pulled me aside into the shade of a shop's awning. 'I talked to your aunt after you left.' He frowned. 'Don't pay attention to her. She can be gruff at times. She's trying hard to protect us from the war.'

I nodded. 'I'm grateful for what you've done. Otherwise, I would have no place to go.'

He lifted a finger as if he were about to lecture me. 'I've called upon a few people this morning. Being a policeman and a Party member opens doors. Apply at the Reichsbund and I'll take it from there.' He tilted his head toward a building down the block draped with Nazi flags. 'Don't be shy. Go on. I'll work my magic.' He gave me a peck on the cheek.

I left him, smiling, and walked to the Reichsbund, an office of the civilian service. I stared into a window crowded with books, banners, placards and Nazi publications.

Beyond the window, a woman dressed in a gray uniform sat at a desk. She looked up from her work as if she'd sensed my presence. Uncle Willy's courage bolstered me. I stepped inside to see what positions might be available. The woman's blond hair was pinned back in a rather strict style, but she was otherwise pretty, with high cheekbones, blue eyes and a thin nose. She was the kind of person you wanted to like. I supposed that was why she was in her position.

I inquired and she asked me to take a seat in an oak chair in front of her desk.

'I'm from Berlin living here with my aunt and uncle, but I need work.' I blushed at my inadequacy.

She stopped writing in her book, placed her pen in its center and closed the cover. 'May I see your identification papers? Are you a Party member?'

I wondered why I had not joined the Party long ago. If I thought about my loyalties, I fell in line with my father, who was non-committal at best, a silent critic at worst. Still, I needed work or I might be forced to return to Berlin. 'My papers are at home with my aunt and uncle. I'm not a Party member.'

She eyed me rather suspiciously, but then, sizing me up, she must have judged I was no threat to Nazi politics. 'Who are your aunt and uncle?'

'Willy and Reina Ritter. They are Party members and live near here.'

She clasped my hands like a schoolgirl chum. 'I know them very well. They're fine upstanding people, a credit to all loyal Germans. What's your name?'

I told her and she listened raptly to my history. As I talked she took out another book, making notations on what I said. When I was through, she asked me to stand in front of a black screen near the back of the room. She took several pictures of me with a flash camera. These, she said, would go to her superior when they were developed.

'Is there anything I can do – that I would be qualified for?' I asked.

'There's nothing in this district,' she said. 'You're not qualified as a bookkeeper, or as a gardener, for construction, or a locomotive engineer. Many women already serve the Reich, so positions are limited.'

I sighed. Reina would not be pleased.

The woman saw my frown and said, 'But that doesn't mean this interview was for nothing. The Reich always has work for its people whether or not you are a Party member.' She looked at me like a patient teacher. 'If you were as supportive as your aunt and uncle, we could look upon you more favorably.'

I rose from my seat. 'Where can I join?' I asked as sincerely as I could, yet something inside me rebelled at the thought of being a Nazi. My mother had once admonished my father for not being 'stronger,' a man who thought more like the Party leadership. In order to get a job, I would have to adopt my mother's thinking.

She pointed to a desk across the room. 'Herr Messer will be here Saturday. Come see him.'

I walked out of the Reichsbund somewhat encouraged,

although I didn't want to face my aunt, because I still had no job prospects.

Reina was in the kitchen when I arrived, so I sneaked up the stairs to my room and put my feet up rather than face her.

About forty-five minutes later, I heard my uncle open the door and greet my aunt.

I found them sitting in the living room. Reina was shocked that I was home, but greeted me with a smile. 'Willy told me the news. I'm sure something good will come of your interview.'

Uncle Willy lit a cigarette, exhaled and said, 'I'm certain of it.'

That night at dinner, we talked of my aunt's childhood in Spain and how she and my uncle had met at a hostel in the Italian Alps. Willy had lodged there for a political gathering; Reina was staying overnight with a group of hiking friends. They saw something in each other that members of my family couldn't see.

The conversation died the same time as the fire and we went to bed about ten. I spent several hours worrying about work until I finally fell asleep. The next morning I went out again, but found nothing. Again, I dreaded coming home with no job. When I arrived, I found my aunt and told her the bad news.

She stood with her hands clasped in front of her, oddly calm considering her fervor for my search. 'The Reichsbund called this afternoon. They want you to report in the morning. Apparently, they have a job for you.' She hugged me and kissed me on the cheek with her cold lips. Later, I asked Willy if he knew what the position was, but he shook his head.

That evening, we celebrated with wine. My aunt allowed me to call my parents to give them the good news. Frau Horst and my parents shared a phone in the building. My mother seemed pleased. I couldn't tell what my father was thinking. I told them I was planning to join the Party. My father replied, 'Do what you must to survive.'

His words cast a pall over my celebration.

I wasn't a fortune-teller, but I wondered how dire my circumstances might become as a worker in the Reich.

# CHAPTER 3

I reported to the Riechsbund the next morning. Instead of being greeted by the woman who'd taken my information the day before, an SS officer met me. He smiled pleasantly and asked me to take a seat in front of the desk. As I studied his face, handsome with Nordic features, I made a connection I had not considered before. Most SS men were young and similar in facial structure. The Führer wanted them to be Aryan. They were thinly muscular, usually blond and blue-eyed and driven by their adoration for their leader. They wore black uniforms when the Party first came to power, but recently they dressed only in gray. This young man was clothed in black and I understood later he was a member of the Führer's Leibstandarte, his personal protection corps at the Berghof.

I asked the SS man what job I would be doing. He gave no specific reply, only that I would have to wait and accept service without hesitation. He opened a file on the desk that had been marked with the Reich's seal and spread the photos of me across the desk.

'You're not a Party member?' he asked, and then lit a cigarette.

'No.'

'Why not?' Smoke flowed like a white ribbon from his mouth.

'There was no need.' My answer was simple and direct. Young women need not join unless they were motivated by politics — a highly unusual profession. I was not the only one who thought that way. A few of my girlfriends were as unconcerned about the Party as I was. We all felt the same. For a man, the feeling was different. It was a badge of honor, a matter of pride, to serve the Reich and go to war.

'Germany has changed.' He pursed his lips, gathered the photos in his hands and studied each before tossing them one by one on the table. 'You are not what the Führer would typically request. You are too dark, too Eastern looking. One might question your loyalties — your heritage.'

I lowered my gaze, taken aback by his effrontery. After a few moments, I raised my head and looked him in the eye, more out of spite than anything else. 'No, I am not a Party member, but I am proud to be a German. There is nothing in my background, or heritage, to give you concern.'

He smiled. 'That's more like it. Show some spirit.' He leaned back in the desk chair and puffed on his cigarette. 'We have contacted your aunt and uncle, your parents in Berlin, even a few friends and neighbors. Your record is in good standing. You understand we must be careful.'

Over the next hour, he questioned me about my education, work habits, hobbies, even whether I had plans to have children, every personal question the Party could possibly dredge up. I answered his questions truthfully and he seemed satisfied. He then gave me a battery of tests on mathematics, arts and sciences and politics. I believed I did poorly on most of them, particularly the political questions, which had much to do with Germany's history and the Nazi rise to power. I finished before twelve and he dismissed me.

I stopped at the door and turned. 'You said I was not what the Führer would typically request.' A lump rose in my throat, but I got up enough nerve to ask the question. 'Am I to work for the Führer?'

His lips parted in a thin smile and his eyes met mine. 'I have nothing to do with your assignment. I'm only here to make sure you are not deficient in any area required by the Reich. That's all I can say.' He stood and bowed slightly. 'Good day, Fräulein Ritter.'

I closed the door. Through the office window I saw him place my examinations and photos back in my file. I didn't smoke and I rarely drank, but at that moment I wished I had some vice to indulge because my nerves thrummed like a plucked violin string.

Over the next two weeks, I trained for my unnamed position. I rose early and arrived home late, but my schedule created little hardship for my aunt and uncle except for the disruption of having me as a houseguest. During training, the Party served us breakfast, lunch and a small supper. My aunt did not have to cook for me. That suited her.

One of the things I enjoyed most was my group's excursions into the countryside surrounding Berchtesgaden. The staff judged us in calisthenics. The tests were conducted in a serene Alpine field near the Hoher Göll mountain. My lungs acclimated to the rarified air and I soon realized I was more coordinated than some of my new friends. I ran fast, particularly in sprints. My long legs served me well. Every night I fell exhausted into a dreamless sleep. After an initial soreness, my muscles grew stronger and tighter. I lost weight. I never got around to joining the Party. Frankly, I didn't want to.

After my training was over, I had one day of rest and relaxation at Willy and Reina's before beginning my mysterious new post. The woman who had interviewed me at the Reichsbund called to say I should be ready to depart at 5:45 the next morning with my bags.

My aunt and uncle talked later than usual after supper. Willy was excited about my new job; his freckled face beamed with pride. We said our good-byes and I promised to call them once I arrived at my new duties.

Pink clouds streaked the sky the next morning. My uncle stood at the door, dressed in his police uniform. My aunt, in her long blue housecoat, looked over his shoulder. A black Mercedes touring car pulled up in front of the house and an SS chauffeur got out. SS corps flags fluttered above each headlight. Without a word, for he must have known me from my pictures, the driver placed my luggage in the trunk and held the door open for me. I took my place in the plush leather backseat. I will always remember the look on my aunt's face – it was one of happiness mixed with jealousy. Now she knew my job was important. Other civilian servants were not treated in such a royal manner.

I waved as the car pulled away and the driver turned east toward the Obersalzberg. I had no idea where we were headed. We drove through the pleasant valley that cradled Berchtesgaden and passed the tidy farms surrounding the town. The driver said little to me as we headed higher into the mountainous terrain; the deciduous trees became fewer as stands of fir and spruce carpeted the hillsides. The valley spread out below and I could see the church spires of Berchtesgaden.

Eventually, my curiosity got the better of me and I asked the SS driver where we were headed.

He took his eyes off the road for a moment, looked into the rearview mirror and said, 'The Berghof.'

I'd heard of Hitler's 'mountain court' from my parents and my aunt and uncle. Before the war, it had become a tourist attraction after the Führer had taken up residence. People had gathered on the long driveway outside the main house to catch a glimpse of him. Often he stepped out to greet the adoring crowd and shake hands with well-wishers.

My heart raced at the thought that I would be working at his secluded retreat. My feeling arose more from excitement about my post rather than any admiration for Hitler. I imagined seeing the diplomats, the foreign visitors, the important Party members: Bormann, Göring, Speer, Goebbels, many of whom visited the Berghof almost daily.

Soon we came to an area cleared of forest as the road climbed upward. Through the driver's windscreen a rustic-looking gatehouse appeared beside a gated archway. The rough-hewn structure rested on a rock base. Several SS men peered through a window as our car approached. One of the guards stepped out and pulled back the gate. He must have known the driver, for they exchanged nothing more than a wave. Another guard stood in the gatehouse doorway, his weapon strapped over his shoulder. They barely gave me a look, unimpressed with my presence. They were used to seeing kings, princes and diplomats from all over the world.

As we drove past the gate, I caught sight of the Berghof. It sat perched on the hillside, like an eagle preparing for flight. Its chalet style had been modified to monumental architecture, yet the sloping wings of the roof gave it an inherent lightness. Perhaps the mountain air made it seem delicate and airy, unlike the fortified home of a leader at war. The sun glinted off the white exterior giving it a welcoming look. I watched in awe as it slipped past my eyes. The car rounded a corner near a linden tree and headed toward a small driveway that split off from the one we were on. The driver was taking me to the entrance of a long building on the east side of the structure. He stopped the car and opened the door.

'You are to see Fräulein Schultz, the Führer's cook. I will take your luggage to your quarters.'

'The cook?' I was dumbfounded. Although I had experience preparing meals for my family, I hardly felt qualified to cook for the leader of the Third Reich.

'Those are my orders.' He shifted his head toward the door and a guard stepped out of the shadows. 'Take Fräulein Ritter to the cook.' The driver got into the car, turned it around and drove toward the main entrance of the Berghof.

The guard stepped forward, opened the door and led me through the halls to the kitchen. Although it was early, a large staff had already gathered for meal preparation. The room was well appointed with modern equipment. Several stoves and ovens were set against the walls, as well as racks of dishes and cookware. Cookbooks lay scattered across a large table. Men and women dressed in service uniforms were kneading dough, preparing eggs and cutting fruits and vegetables. A tall woman with an oval face and wavy brown hair stood out from the crowd. She projected authority in her dark dress covered by a white apron. She was talking with a man at a black stone sink. When she spotted me, she stopped her conversation and walked over.

'You must be Fräulein Ritter,' she said.

'I am.' I shook her hand. 'You are Fräulein Schultz?'

'Yes. The Führer's dietician and cook.' She looked at me with concern. 'What have they told you about your position?'

I shrugged. 'Nothing.'

'Come with me to my office off the kitchen. You'll be staying here in the east wing so you can be close to me, the kitchen staff and the other tasters.'

I didn't understand. We went into the hall past the kitchen to a series of doors. Hers was the first. She opened it with a key and we stepped inside the small room. She took off her apron and sat at her desk while I took a seat in the guest chair. A window faced north, the same direction as the Berghof, looking out upon the sprawling view of the Untersberg. She turned to me with her hands folded in her lap.

'You have been chosen,' she began, 'by me and Captain Karl Weber, the SS officer who oversees the security of my staff. You are one of fifteen.'

I shifted in my seat. 'Fifteen what?'

'Tasters who work for the Führer at his headquarters.'

'Tasters?' I had no idea what she was talking about. 'Perhaps you could explain what that means.'

She looked at me like a teacher who was irritated with a student. 'You, and others, taste the Führer's food. Your body is offered in sacrifice to the Reich in case the food is poisoned.'

My breath fled, horrified as I was at her words. The cook must have recognized the distress in my face, for she reached across and held my hand.

'There's no need to panic,' she said. 'I will tell you frankly, he is obsessed with being poisoned. He thinks the British have it in for him – it's all very Shakespearean if you ask me. Why would they resort to such medieval tactics when one well–placed assassin's bullet would do? His personal physician could poison him as well, but we don't taste his medicines. Your chances of being poisoned are slim. After all, we all sample the food as it's prepared.' And with a sly glance she said, 'Still, I suppose there's always a chance. I suppose you may not be ready for such candor, but you need to know the truth.'

'This is why I was chosen for civilian service?'

She withdrew her hands and returned to her businesslike demeanor. 'Yes. Apparently, the Reichsbund felt you were qualified for this position. It's a great honor.'

I didn't know how to respond, so I said meekly, 'I suppose it is.' I thought of my uncle Willy and wondered if he would be proud of my position. His recommendation had gotten me here.

'You will be working with me,' she explained. 'If you do a good job, I have other duties you might pursue, such as bookkeeping for the kitchen. That's an important task as well. We have full growing capabilities for food – greenhouses you will become familiar with.' She paused and studied my face. 'You're pretty. There are plenty of attractive men here, enough to keep a flirtatious girl busy. I discourage intimate fraternization with officers and other staff. We have movies, dancing sometimes, but you must remember you are in service to the Führer. Your personal life is of no consequence.'

I shuddered. *My life might end here.* Not even the bombings in Berlin had forced me to face my mortality in such a brutal way. The thought that I might die for Hitler stunned me. An unwitting trap had been set and closed over me. My parents had sent me away, Uncle Willy had pulled strings and now I was in a position that might lead to my death. My mind raced, thinking of ways that I might get away from the Berghof. But where would I go?

She stood and I felt dwarfed by her figure. Apparently, she could read my thoughts, too. 'I wouldn't be hasty in your conclusions. If you reject your position there could be serious consequences. You might never work again. As I said, the risk is slight. When the war is over, your service to the Reich will be rewarded.' She picked up her apron. 'I must get back to the kitchen.' She lifted the hair that fell across my left cheek before she opened the door. 'Captain Weber was right. You are pretty – in a different way. Perhaps that's why you were chosen. He wants to talk with you. Wait here.'

She left me sitting alone in the office. I bent over, covered my face with my hands and waited for the SS officer. In a matter of days, my life had changed from that of a common German girl to one of importance in the Reich. My head spun from what fate had thrown my way so quickly. The thought of dying, let alone for Hitler, had rarely entered my young head. Like a trapped animal there was nothing I could do. To back out would place shame and derision on my family, perhaps even open them to questioning. I could only wait and hope for the best.

The handsome officer came a few minutes later.

'You are prettier than your photos,' he said after he had

a chance to look at me. His words were offered in a factual tone with no sexual innuendo intended. I thanked him, but with little enthusiasm. After all, what did my looks have to do with tasting food?

Fräulein Schultz had called him 'Captain.' The insignia on SS uniforms meant little to me. There were two patches on each side of his collar. One contained two silver bolts that looked like lightning.

His blondish-brown hair, parted on the right, swept back from his forehead. His mouth was sensuous, not cruel; the bow in the upper lip carried a distinctive cleft. His hazel eyes were topped by long brows that curved like arches to either side of his nose – a pleasing feature in its own right – strong and chiseled to a fine point. Perhaps his ears were his only flaw. They were large for the size of his face. Nevertheless, they didn't detract from the officer's overall appearance. I was drawn to him, but what woman wouldn't have been? I knew, of course, that such an attraction was dangerous. He could have me shot as easily as he might take me in his arms.

'You have been chosen for a dangerous job,' he said.

I watched as he took a seat in the cook's chair and withdrew a pack of cigarettes; but, finding no ashtray, he replaced them in his jacket pocket.

'I didn't ask for it,' I said. 'I had no idea what my job would be until ten minutes ago.'

He settled back. 'You can always leave. The Führer is not an impossible man. Many have come and gone here.'

'That's not my wish,' I said, hoping to overcome my own doubts. What else would I do? Reina would not be happy if I ended up on her doorstep. 'I need to work. And, besides,

I've been told that finding any work might be impossible if I leave the Berghof.'

He offered his hand. 'I understand.' His eyes shifted from business, as if he understood my plight. 'My name is Karl Weber. I'm an officer in the security detail assigned to oversee the kitchen and dining. Not exactly an exciting job, but I suppose I've earned it. I fought in Poland and France. The fighting was pretty rough, but not as rough as our troops on the Eastern Front have had to endure.'

'Were you wounded?'

'No, I was lucky.'

We sat for a moment and I was unsure of what to say. My fate had been sealed by the Reichsbund and there was little I could do about it. To leave would bring disgrace upon my parents. My aunt might throw me out on the street. I remembered I needed to call Willy and Reina to let them know what I was doing. 'May I make a phone call? Do I have that privilege?'

He laughed. 'You're not a prisoner. Of course you can make a call. However, every telephone conversation at the Berghof is monitored. You have no privacy here. Whom do you wish to call?'

'I told my aunt and uncle I would let them know where I was.'

'Don't bother. They and your parents have been informed you're in the Führer's service. They were all pleased; however, they don't know what you will be doing. I wouldn't recommend telling them. Also, it's best now that you have limited communication with those outside the Berghof.'

'I have few friends to talk to, but I should ignore my mother and father as well?'

He studied me and leaned forward. 'Fräulein Ritter, please understand a few things about your job. One, you are under my and the cook's command. More important, you serve the leader of the Third Reich. Two, your life from this point on will never be the same. Three, if you wish to leave you must do it now because there will be no turning back once I leave this room.' He looked at me intently. 'You're not a Party member, are you?'

I shook my head. Being a Party member was apparently something I couldn't escape.

'Perhaps you should be.' He looked out the window toward the mountains whose colors were shifting in the morning sunlight from purple to dark green. Still facing them, he said, 'I was the one who chose you. Cook wanted another girl, but I insisted.'

'Cook?'

'Fräulein Schultz. She had another in mind, but I recognized something different in you. I couldn't explain it. She wouldn't have understood my reasoning. But now that I've met you, I realize I was right in my assumption. Otherwise, I would insist that you leave.' He turned to me.

I twisted in my chair. 'Should I be flattered?'

His jaw clenched. 'No, you should be frightened for your life. But I know you are fit for this job. I understand you, and, in time, we will get to know each other.'

He stood at attention before me and raised his right arm stiffly toward the wall. 'Sieg Heil!'

I got to my feet but didn't salute and said nothing. Oddly, I felt distracted and somewhat soiled, as if I had been hoodwinked by the Reichsbund and Captain Weber. The officer gave me a look, but it was thoughtful, not one of anger or

41

defiance. He showed little emotion, seeming to accept I had no use for politics or war.

'You will use the salute when it is needed,' he said matter-of-factly. 'I'm sure you know how.' The salute was used everywhere. He opened the door and left me alone.

For several weeks, I learned the kitchen routine. I scrubbed and washed pots, helped carry food to the servers, cleaned the stoves and refrigeration units and watched with interest as the cooks prepared the meals. Cook laughed when I asked if Hitler was in residence. 'Of course,' she said. 'Why would we go to such trouble otherwise? Not for Bormann or Göring. They have their own chefs. And certainly we wouldn't work this hard for some minor bureaucrat.'

Captain Weber checked on my progress almost daily. The kitchen was small enough that we saw each other quite often. Many times he stood nearby watching me and Cook, until she became irritated and with a scolding look ushered him out of the room.

'You have better things to do than waste time with us,' she said.

He smiled back and told us he wanted to make sure everything in the kitchen was up to the Führer's high standards.

I knew this was only a ploy on his part to get close to me. My head and heart turned to him when he was in the room. It was hard to concentrate on work when the handsome Captain stood nearby. I enjoyed his attention.

Cook also issued instructions: I should never wander alone in the Berghof, only speak when spoken to and never disturb or interrupt a conversation, particularly one involving the Führer – if I ever encountered him, which according to

Cook would be a rarity. She also told me that the SS were everywhere and knew everything we were involved in, including our personal habits. This unsettled me so much I had an uneasy feeling every time I went to the bathroom. I searched the walls and ceiling for a microphone.

An SS officer I only knew as a Colonel in the Leibstandarte often lurked nearby. He had a pleasant face with round blue eyes, a square jaw and a prominent cleft in his chin; however, a veneer of icy impenetrability masked any warmth he might have carried. Everyone in the kitchen kept their distance unless they were serving him.

'Stay away from him,' Cook warned. 'He would turn on his mother.'

I wasn't sure why she had warned me. Perhaps a member of the kitchen staff had gotten in trouble with the Colonel. I didn't ask. I heeded my aversion to the man and kept my distance.

My roommate was a young woman from Munich by the name of Ursula Thalberg, who had worked at the Berghof for several months. Ursula had an oval face framed by blond curls. She also exhibited an outgoing and buoyant personality. Her face was often lit by smiles when she talked. Like most of us, her politics were fueled by what we knew of the Party through the Reich papers and radio broadcasts. Ursula was more concerned with the 'Faith and Beauty' program, a voluntary plan espoused by the Reich to make us into model German women, than with politics. I knew of the program, but had little use for it. For the most part, Ursula and I were content to take mountain walks and practice our outdoor gymnastics in pleasant weather. Ursula also was a taster.

Our room was small but comfortable, with two single beds, a desk, a chair and a phone. A few books and mementoes lined the shelves, and a tiny closet held our uniforms and civilian clothing. My stuffed monkey found a home on my pillow.

Ursula smoked, but only when she had no fear of being caught. Cook had said Hitler strongly discouraged men and women in his service from using tobacco. One night, not long after we had met, Ursula turned off the lights, opened the window and exhaled the smoke under the sill as we talked. I hadn't taken up my position yet and was full of questions.

'Aren't you scared of being poisoned?' I asked.

She chuckled. 'Not really. I'm much too young to die. Besides, the Führer is so well protected, who could possibly poison him? The traitor would be found out immediately and die a horrible death.'

I was amazed at her nonchalance. 'What's it like being a taster?' I was determined to find out more about my job, despite the ugly possibility of being poisoned. The more I knew, the less chance I had of dying.

Ursula puffed on her cigarette, parted the floral-print curtains and blew the smoke out the window. 'There's not much to it, really. The cook spoons out a serving from each dish. The serving is taken from various points in the dish – not from one spot. Several of us taste the food and then we wait. Sometimes we drink as well, if a bottle has been opened. We have to eat an hour before the Führer, in case . . .'

'No one has died?'

'No, but several tasters have gotten sick.' She laughed and then added, 'But I think their illnesses were caused by the soldiers they kissed the night before. There's nothing wrong with the food. You've seen it. Only the best comes from the greenhouses, and it's always prepared in the most delicious manner. If you think about it, we're lucky we don't have to deal with rations like the rest of the country.'

I settled on my bed and cradled my stuffed monkey in my arms.

'You look ridiculous with that toy,' Ursula said.

I flipped the monkey in the air and caught him in my arms. 'I know, but he reminds me of home and my family.'

'I don't miss Munich. I love it here.' Then her mood darkened and she lowered her voice. 'How much do you know about the war?'

I shook my head. 'Little – just what we hear on the radio and read in the papers.'

Ursula took another puff. 'The soldiers here talk, especially if you're pretty, even though they're not supposed to.' She winked. 'I know we will win the war, but there are rumors going around that the Allies and our Eastern foes are gaining ground. Some say it's only a matter of time before Germany falls.' She shook a finger at me. 'Don't spread that around.'

I believed we might come to a stalemate with the Allies, but losing the war was something I'd never considered despite my father's negative feelings. The suggestion of having to deal with the enemy horde chilled me. It was too much to think about in one evening. Ursula saw my uneasiness as I shrunk back against the wall.

'How does the Colonel feel about such talk?' I asked.

'He's a dangerous man,' Ursula said. She reached under the bed, pulled out an ashtray and snuffed out her cigarette. The smell of burned tobacco filled our room. Ursula waved her hands, trying to get the smoke out the window. She peered out. 'If he caught me smoking, he'd report me in a second.'

'I'm beginning to feel like I'm in prison,' I said, having no idea what a real prison would be like.

She shrugged. 'Don't worry. You'll have your class in poisons soon. It's most interesting. Cook explains it well. You learn to identify them by sight, taste and smell.'

'Taste?' I asked, wondering how such a process could exist.

'A pinprick of a taste. A lick of the fingertip. Not enough to harm you – at least for most poisons.'

I shivered and yearned to shift the conversation to another topic. I'd learned enough for one evening. 'Would you like to do something tonight? I feel restless.'

Ursula's eyes lit up, making me wonder whether she had secretly wanted to go out all along. 'I was going to read, but let's take a walk instead. It's too late to go to a movie at the Theater Hall, but the SS barracks are up the hill.' She fluffed her hair and looked at her face in a compact mirror.

We put on our coats and walked through the east wing of the Berghof. A guard stationed at the door where the driver had dropped me off nodded as we passed. Ursula said, 'Good evening.' She was familiar with many of the soldiers. Because we were in the immediate area surrounding the residence, we did not need to show passes. Ursula said that if we had wanted to visit anywhere outside the perimeter the SS would question us.

The SS barracks stood on the hill to the southeast of the Berghof. The four main buildings were constructed around a central field used by the corps for drills and inspections. Ursula said many of the men would still be up and she would introduce me to a few of the officers. We strolled around the barracks and peered into the field. The buildings were darkened by the blackout blinds. Now and then the breeze would lift a blind and a warm buttery light would pulse out, only to be extinguished as quickly as it appeared. Ursula and I walked in the milky light of a quarter moon, which shone through the silky clouds.

After a little while, we came upon a group of soldiers standing near the corner of the southern barracks. We spotted them by their dark silhouettes and the orange flare of their cigarettes. They were laughing and quite unaware of our presence. Two of them were without shirts and shoes, wearing only pants hitched up by suspenders strapped over their bare shoulders. As we approached they gave us a friendly greeting and salute, and one of them reached out to Ursula and gave her a kiss on the hand, much to the delight of the others. She introduced me to the soldier, Franz Faber. He was blond, with a wide smile, and a few inches taller than Ursula. A scar ran down the left side of his face. Ursula and Franz were so familiar with the group they forgot that I knew no one. The other men drifted away and left me standing awkwardly with the couple. I didn't want to be uninvited company, so I ventured farther into the courtyard. That was when a man called out my name.

I turned and saw Captain Weber. He was one of the men without a shirt and shoes, but I hadn't recognized him in the crowd. I flushed with embarrassment because Ursula and I had interrupted their gathering. I wrapped my collar tighter around my neck.

'It's a beautiful evening, isn't it?' He held out his hand.

I shook it politely and nodded. 'I'm walking with Fräulein

'Thalberg.' I looked at my watch. 'We should be getting back to the Berghof. I'm sorry to disturb you.'

'Nonsense.' He rubbed his hands together. 'It's too chilly to stand out here under the moon. Won't you come inside for a moment?'

'Cook wouldn't like that. I believe she would refer to it as "fraternization."'

He laughed. 'Don't worry about Cook. I can handle her.'

I had never been in a barracks and wasn't sure I should be, but how could I resist the Captain's invitation? I had nothing to go back to but my lonely quarters. Ursula and her companion stood where I'd left them. I waved my arms until I got her attention and then pointed to Karl. She immediately understood and waved back. The officer directed me to the barracks entrance. His private room was only a few feet away. He opened the door and we stepped inside.

His quarters were small, similar to what Ursula and I lived in, but, unlike me, Captain Weber lived alone. The window, shielded by its blackout curtain, looked toward the central field. The room contained a bed, a desk and enough wall space and shelves to display the certificates, medals and trophies awarded during his education and from the Reich. His uniform jacket hung on the back of the door. His polished black boots rested at the foot of his bed.

I looked out of the corner of my eye, relishing the chance to peek at his body before he pulled on a white shirt and buttoned it up about halfway. His stomach was lean, his chest and shoulders broad. He motioned for me to sit on the desk chair while he sat on the bed. He reached for cigarettes and then reconsidered. 'I'm trying to give them up. They're bad for you.' Smiling, he leaned back as if we were the best of friends.

'I wouldn't think the men would be allowed to smoke outside.' I pointed to the ceiling. Our neighbor, Frau Horst, had told me that bombers could target the light from cigarettes. At the time, I thought she was being silly.

'I look the other way. Who knows how long any of us will be around? Besides, the Allies don't fly near here – not yet.'

I stared at him, unsure what to say.

'How are you enjoying the Berg?' he finally asked, breaking an uncomfortable silence.

'The Berg?' I was unfamiliar with the term.

'Everyone on the staff calls it the Berg, especially if you're fond of the "boss."'

'It's just a job.' I placed my hands in my lap. 'I haven't tasted yet. I'm a little nervous.'

'Don't be. How are you getting along?'

'Fine. I've met most of the staff. The Führer has a number of cooks.'

'Yes. There's one he likes in particular – a man he snatched from a sanatorium. Cook is jealous of him, but Hitler loves the way he prepares eggs.'

It surprised me that the Captain called the Führer by his name. It sounded so informal and disrespectful, but I ignored the thought and said, 'I've seen Fräulein Braun and her friends taking a walk with her dogs.'

'Yes, her Scotties, Negus and Stasi. They're in the Great Hall at midnight with all the invited guests, while Blondi has to wait elsewhere. Hitler begs Eva to let Blondi come into the room, but she won't allow it as long as her pups

49

are there. I heard Eva kicks Blondi under the table.' He snickered.

'She kicks who?' I couldn't imagine what Karl was talking about.

'Blondi. Hitler's German shepherd dog.'

I laughed now that it all made sense. I'd seen the dog when Hitler's valet took her for a walk. She was a handsome animal who was friendly to most people. She got to ride in the Volkswagen Cabriolet reserved for the Reich's leader.

Karl peeked out the blind for a moment. 'Ursula and Franz are still talking. Actually, it's more than conversation, but I don't want to pry. They've known each other since they were children in Munich. They're in love.' He propped his pillow against the wall and stretched out on the bed. His eyes sparkled in the lamplight. I felt they were looking through me, not past me, boring a hole into my soul. I shifted in my seat, uncomfortable being alone in a room with an officer who seemed interested in more than conversation. 'What do you think of Eva?' he asked, and then added, 'Do you know who she is?'

I shook my head. 'A friend of the Führer?'

'We all think she's more than that, but most Germans don't know who she is.'

I hesitated to answer his question about what I thought of her because I was afraid he might be a secret admirer of Hitler's companion. I didn't know the Captain well enough to know why he was asking me these questions. Everyone needed to be careful when they talked to an SS officer; at least that's what I believed, particularly after what I had learned since the incident on the train. My father had said words were as precious as gold these days and should be meted out with equal care. My mother displayed a certain fervor in toeing the Party line and with it a healthy respect for saying the right things. I gave an innocuous answer. 'I hadn't heard of her before I came here. She's pretty and wears stylish clothes that suit her well. Her jewelry seems expensive.'

Karl smirked. 'She changes her outfits almost hourly, while the rest of Germany—' His face reddened and he looked away from me. For a long time, he didn't speak. I wondered whether I should leave.

'I'm sorry,' he said. 'I should keep my opinions to myself, but it's hard sometimes to maintain a positive attitude the way things are going.'

'Why?' I asked. Nothing I had heard, except Ursula's comment earlier, gave me any reason to be concerned about the war; it was odd that the Captain had brought up the issue at all.

'You don't care for politics, do you?'

I shook my head. 'Not really.'

'You can be honest with me. What we speak of will go no farther than this room.'

I studied his eyes, observed the depth of them so I might judge the truth of his words. All I saw was sincerity, but I still felt I should be guarded in my comments. 'Frankly, I'm more concerned about my parents than myself. At first the war didn't mean a lot to me, any more than it did to other girls in Berlin. We heard how the people in the East were our enemies. But now things have changed, the Allied bombings have begun and food is in short supply. Life is hard.' I looked away, afraid to ask my next question. 'Are we losing the war?'

I heard him shift on the bed. When I looked again, he was sitting up, staring at me. 'Are you aware your question verges on treason?'

I was astounded by his reaction. 'I asked because I wanted to know. I suppose we should never speak of losing the war. You told me I could trust you. Besides, if I were a traitor, would I be the Führer's food taster?'

He rose from the bed. 'Which answer do you want? The Reich's or the truth?'

'The truth.'

He smiled. 'I *was* right to choose you. But you'll have your answer later. It'll be lights-out soon. I should escort you to your room. I've already taken a chance, having a woman in here.' He lifted the blind and peered out. 'Ursula and Franz have disappeared.'

'I can walk by myself.'

He shrugged and offered his hand. I shook it.

'I'm not sure that coming here was a good idea,' I said, and opened the door to the dimly lit hall.

Karl touched my shoulder. 'Let me take you to a movie in the Berghof. Eva picks out the films. We see them before the public does. Often we get them from America. Hitler doesn't watch them because he thinks the Reich's leader shouldn't enjoy himself while the country suffers. The only films he watches are dreary repeats of his speeches, so he can learn how to be a better speaker.'

I was surprised. 'That's what he does best.'

The Captain nodded.

I thought for a moment about his offer of a movie. 'I'd be happy to accept your invitation. I think Cook would allow that.'

'Of course she would.' He stood close to me as we walked down the hall. When we got to the barracks door, he bowed slightly. 'I would remind you that even an SS officer is human. Good night, Fräulein Ritter.'

My heart beat a little faster as I stepped out on the practice field. Had the Captain professed an interest in me? I dared not think it. My physical attraction was no reason to trust him.

The moon had shifted higher in the sky and the temperature had dropped a few degrees. A chilly breeze stung my cheeks as I hurried back to the Berghof. The same guard who had let us out was still on duty, but another SS man stood in the shadows. As I got closer, I recognized him as the Colonel whom Cook and Ursula had warned me to stay away from. He stepped toward me and said, 'May I see your pass?'

'I don't have it with me,' I said. 'I was told I wouldn't need it.'

'You should keep it with you at all times, Fräulein Ritter,' the Colonel said. 'Open your coat.'

'You know me?' I asked, and then complied with his request.

His cold hands patted down my body. Satisfied, he waved me on toward the door. 'Of course.' His tone was as dark as the shadows on his face.

I returned to my empty room and got ready for bed. Franz and Ursula were obviously smitten with each other. I briefly imagined kissing Karl before I convinced myself the thought was ridiculous. I needed my job. There was no turning back now. No charming man could force me to break rules that might cost me my position, despite how 'human' he might be. I thought of the SS officer who had taken the couple off the train. How human was he? Did he go home that night and make love to his wife? Did he tuck his children into bed and kiss them good night?

These thoughts swirled through my head as I tried to sleep. Was the war really going badly?

Sometime after midnight, Ursula returned to the room. She didn't turn on the light to undress. She slipped into her nightgown, got into bed and sighed like a girl who had spent a rapturous evening with a man.

I envied her.

# CHAPTER 4

My hands trembled as Cook busied herself with various mushrooms, vials and small bowls containing powders. Her thin arms hovered over the oak table. My first class in poisons occurred early one morning in a corner of the kitchen while the rest of the staff went about their business.

I had no appetite for breakfast and my stomach churned as I looked at the items laid out before me. I sat because I felt too nervous to stand.

'We will deal with four areas,' Cook began. 'Mushrooms, arsenic, mercury and cyanide. We can't possibly cover everything today, but this will be our starting point.' She pointed to the mushrooms. 'One of these is safe to eat, the other isn't. Can you tell them apart?'

Dread crept over me. I had no idea. They looked the same to me. She pointed to two white spheres that looked like puffballs. 'Come now, which of these is poisonous?'

I shook my head.

'I can see we have a long way to go.' She pulled on a

pair of rubber gloves and held one of the funnel-shaped mushrooms in her hand. 'This is *Omphalotus olearius*. It grows in Europe. It's rarely deadly, but can cause severe illness. It looks similar to *Cantharellus cibarius,* a Chanterelle, which grows here as the Pfifferling. It has a peppery taste.' She broke off a small piece of the Chanterelle and held it on the tip of her finger. 'Go ahead. Taste it.'

I took the yellowish-orange meat between my fingers and was about to put it into my mouth.

'Wait,' Cook cautioned. 'Smell it first.'

I felt silly smelling and tasting mushrooms, but this was to be part of my daily routine.

I put the piece to my nose and sniffed. 'It smells like an apricot.' I popped the bit into my mouth and let it slowly dissolve until the peppery taste was too much. I swallowed it and swished my tongue trying to get out the taste, worrying that Cook was playing a horrible trick. Did she want to poison me?

'Look at the *Omphalotus*. It grows in America and Asia as well. It has unforked gills and the interior is orange – not like the Chanterelle.' She split the two mushrooms in half to demonstrate the difference in color. 'The Führer rarely eats mushrooms. He doesn't really like them, but see how easy it would be to grind, chop or mince the *Omphalotus* and slip it into his egg and potato casserole. You must be aware of the colors and smells of the poisonous foods and be on the lookout for their evidence.'

Cook then explained the difference between the two puffballs that lay on the table. One was deadly, the second not. My eyes must have glazed over, for other than the size and the amount of soil on both, the mushrooms looked strikingly similar. I could not tell the difference. Cook shook her head as if chastising a lazy student for her stupidity. 'You will learn,' she said in a firm voice.

*Or die.*

We moved on to arsenic. Cook took a small amount of the powder and heated it in a pan. It smelled like garlic. She also took a piece of the grayish-white granules and struck them with a hammer, causing friction and heat. The odor of garlic filled the air. 'The poisoning causes symptoms very similar to cholera: diarrhea, vomiting, cramps and convulsions,' Cook said. 'That's why it was easy to hide such poisoning hundreds of years ago. Cholera was prevalent. The pain from arsenic is acute. Real garlic is an antidote against a slow poisoning.' She ordered me to put on gloves and sniff the arsenic, which smelled metallic rather than like garlic. My hands shook when she told me to taste a small particle. My jaws clenched shut. Cook gave up, pried my mouth open and placed the tiny piece on my tongue. It tasted faintly of iron, hardly enough to notice.

She then held up a brown bottle of Mercury Chloride. 'This was used to treat the syphilitic disease of sexual inter-course, but it can kill as a poison. It causes profuse sweating, high blood pressure and rapid heartbeat. No need to taste it – it has no taste.' Cook handed me the small bowl of white salts and had me examine it. A faint smell of chlorine wafted from the bowl, but I may have imagined it, the odor was so weak.

Finally, we dealt with cyanide. This was the poison, Cook said, that would most likely be used against the Führer. The white granules had a faint smell of bitter almonds. Cook was pleased when I noticed the odor. 'Some can't smell cyanide. It's a genetic trait. You're lucky you did; otherwise, you might have had to find other work.' I was shocked at my own misfortune. If I had lied about the smell, I might have been assigned as the kitchen bookkeeper or to another less dangerous task. Instead, through my ignorance of poisons, I'd secured my job as a taster.

Cook swirled her gloved finger in the granules. 'Cyanide salts are exceedingly poisonous. It knocks you unconscious and you can't breathe; your skin turns blue.' She pointed to a metal vial on the table. 'Unfortunately, a few of our officers have already committed suicide in this manner. Breaking a cyanide capsule with your teeth will cause death in a matter of minutes. Nothing can be done once the poison's in your system.'

The liquid looked harmless enough, almost colorless, but I was surprised at how quickly death could come. I would take Cook's word as to the assessment of the poison.

My head spun with all that had been shown to me. One of the other cooks needed to see Fräulein Schultz, so she stepped away for a few minutes. I held the cyanide vial in my hands and looked at the thin glass ampoule. I replaced the vial on the table and looked around the kitchen. Cook was supervising Hitler's breakfast preparations. I could only wait. As I sat in my chair, I marveled at how such a small glass capsule might change the course of history, if only someone had the courage to carry out a plan. Hitler was no hero to me, but I dared not speak what I thought.

Captain Weber asked me to a movie the first night I tasted food for Hitler. Karl arranged our date through Eva Braun. Apparently, his looks and standing in the SS were important enough to get himself positioned occasionally within Eva's circle. Since Karl and I had talked in his quarters, I had seen Eva several times in the kitchen. Her presence was a special event that disrupted the cooks and orderlies, for she demanded that attention be paid to her wishes. Cook told me Eva was the Führer's companion and the social mistress of the residence. She appeared in fine dresses that flattered her figure even as she walked about inspecting the ovens and stoves. Mostly, she wanted to know what the staff was preparing for her invited guests, not for Hitler. She talked to each of the cooks and even asked to taste a lamb dish as it was being prepared. This caused much consternation to Cook, who scolded Eva without insulting her, and stated that she could not guarantee her safety if she continued such unorthodox actions. Eva tossed her head, shaking her curls, and laughed. She exuded an air of invincibility, as if no disaster could ever befall her.

Cook had told me that Hitler professed to be a vegetarian, but rumors circulated that he ate meat: squab, some fish and even chicken. When I questioned her, Cook said Hitler never ate anything but eggs, fruits and vegetables. Eva ate meat and enjoyed it, as did most of her invited guests. Hitler didn't impose his eating habits on others, but he made sure the meat-eating guests at the table were uncomfortable. He often talked about butcher shops and slaughterhouses and how horrible they were. Cook said some officers left the table because these luncheon and dinner stories were so filled with blood and envisioned entrails that stomachs turned.

I had not seen the Führer, so everything I knew about him I learned from others. Much of the Berghof's gossip was spread in shadow. One never knew if the Colonel was around the corner with his ear pressed to the wall.

One late morning, after Eva had visited the kitchen, Cook pulled me aside and whispered, 'The Führer thinks Eva is too skinny. He likes a woman with more meat on her bones. You'll see what I mean, if you get to know him. He always pays attention to women with curves.' She chuckled. 'God forbid Eva should change the way she looks. She put her hair up once and he hated it. He told her he didn't recognize her. Eva never did it again, although he complimented one of his secretaries when she did the same.'

I wanted to laugh, but the irony caught in my throat. The rumors of Germany's defeat were in opposition to what I saw and heard at the Berghof: the nonchalance of Eva Braun, who strolled the grounds with her guests and dogs; conversations about dresses and hairdos; the bucolic scene of Albert Speer's children in the kitchen asking for apples. Even Hitler, Cook said, was a gentleman host, more of a mountain prince than the leader of a war machine. Everything was peace and plenty in the rarified atmosphere of the Berghof.

I was so inquisitive, I asked Cook what the Führer was really like. I'd seen nothing of Hitler's rumored rages at his officers or the cold, calculating persona that terrified those weaker than he.

'He's like your grandfather,' she said, and I laughed at the thought. 'I've never seen him mad,' she continued. 'Upset, yes, but furious, no.'

The Colonel appeared at the kitchen door, all spit and polish, looking the picture of the perfect SS man.

'See him,' Cook said, and looked his way. 'It's typical for him to show up out of nowhere. He's watching us now.' She discreetly put a finger to her lips. 'Be careful what you say around him. I would never get in his way because I don't trust him. He protects the Führer better than Blondi. The Colonel has repeatedly told me that if there are setbacks in winning this war, they aren't the Führer's fault. The Allies have caused our misfortunes, he says, but I wouldn't be surprised if he blamed the German people.'

The Colonel walked past us into the kitchen, surveying the sinks, the counters, the tabletops, like they were his own domain. He made me nervous. The rumors circulating through the mountain residence made it seem as if the Berghof were resting on a slowly melting iceberg while everything around sparkled in sunshine.

Hitler always ate about 8:00 p.m. in the dining room. Around seven, Cook lined up the dishes for me to taste, as well as the food for his guests. Ursula had been given the night off to attend to a family matter in Munich. Normally we both tasted the food. The other girls worked at breakfast or lunch or were at the other headquarters. Cook had given me a few more lessons in poisons, including other mushrooms and salts. I studied them as much as I could, but was not convinced of my ability to save the Führer from being poisoned.

Cook placed the Führer's meal in front of me: a plate of eggs and diced potatoes scrambled together, yellow and fluffy; a thin porridge; fresh tomatoes sprinkled with olive oil and pepper, a green salad with peppers and cucumbers, a plate of fresh fruit sprinkled with sugar. The tomatoes, along with the salad vegetables and fruits, had been grown in the Berghof's greenhouses.

I looked at the food and thought this could be my last meal. A tight grip of fear shot through my arm as I lifted the spoon. My indecision showed.

Cook's voice sounded sharply in my ears. 'Think what you're doing! Don't just taste the food.'

I considered what she meant. 'Of course. I'm sorry.' I lifted the plate to my nose and sniffed. The odor was completely normal; the warm, comfortable smell of scrambled eggs and fried potatoes wafted into my nostrils.

'Go ahead,' Cook said. She urged me to action with a sweep of her hands. 'We haven't got all night.'

The other cooks stared at me, as if I were a lunatic. Ursula was used to tasting, but I found it hard to rid my mind of the fear of taking my last breath. Cook crossed her arms, so I steeled myself and put the food into my mouth.

The dish was delicious. There were no smells or tastes out of the ordinary. I relaxed a bit and made my way down the table, sampling the food. The cooks and orderlies returned to their preparations and ignored me. I tasted asparagus, rice, cucumbers, tomatoes, a melon and a piece of apple cake, Hitler's favorite dessert. Soon I had eaten enough for a meal.

'Now what?' I asked Cook.

'Now you wait.' She said these words simply and without emotion, as clinically as a heartless physician telling a patient she only had a short time to live.

I took a seat at the small oak table in the corner and watched as the dishes were placed on their serving platters in preparation for the evening meal. It struck me that any of the cooks or the orderlies, as they served and delivered the food, could administer a poisonous dose to Hitler. However, only one cook and a few orderlies were allowed to touch the food I'd tasted. This was a form of life insurance. If something happened to the Führer then most of the kitchen staff would be exonerated – only those who had the responsibility of serving would be suspect.

After the last plates were taken away about eight, I was allowed to leave the kitchen.

'See, there was nothing to worry about,' Cook said.

Her blasé attitude concerned me. She didn't taste food like I did, although I had seen her dip a spoon into dishes now and then. My fate rested in my own hands – more the reason to be prudent when tasting.

I returned to my room, changed clothes, fussed with my hair and tried to read a book.

Karl knocked on my door about ten. My heart fluttered a bit when I saw him. His hair was neatly combed, uniform sparkling and pressed, boots polished to a slick shine. He smiled and then bowed slightly.

I closed the door and placed my left arm through the arch he created with his right. We walked toward the Great Hall, the large sitting room I'd heard about but never been in. Before we reached it we came to a flight of stairs that led downward. 'Dinner conversation was dull as usual,' he said. 'Eva talked about her dogs and Hitler carried on about Blondi. Then Bormann got to talking about his children.' He rolled his eyes. 'That was fascinating. I can outline each of their school careers and his plans for them. It's so much more pleasant when Speer is here. At least he's not a boor.'

'Where is the Führer?' I held on tightly to Karl as we descended the stone steps.

'He's in the Hall with his generals for his evening military conference. Fortunately, I'm not part of that. That will go on until midnight, or later, when we may be called in for tea. That usually lasts until two, sometimes longer.' He put a finger to his lips as if to tell a secret. 'That's why he and Eva sleep so late. The rest of us must tend to our duties.'

'I'm lucky I'm only the taster.'

Karl released my arm and stopped on the stairs. 'Your job is important, perhaps one of the most important in the Reich. You stand between Hitler and death. You must always remember that.'

An uncomfortable shudder swept over me as I pondered the immensity of my task yet again. Was I really all that stood between Hitler and death? There were fourteen others who were in the same position. Did they feel as I did? My task didn't fill me with a grand sense of importance. In fact, in the past several weeks I'd preferred to think of it as only a job. Knowing the Führer's fate was intertwined with mine was too much to bear. I changed the subject. 'What movie is being shown?'

'*Gone with the Wind*. Everyone is excited to see it. Eva said it's very romantic. Most American films are.'

He took my arm again and we reached the bottom of the steps. A long hall with several doors on each side stretched out before us. Karl opened the one nearest us and laughter danced on the air. The room was filled with men dressed in suits and women attired in fine dresses. Eva and her friends sat in chairs lined up in the front row on either side of the projector while other guests sat behind them. Negus and Stasi, Eva's dogs, were nestled at her feet. We were in a small bowling alley constructed under the main rooms of the Berghof. A screen had been placed at the far end of the lanes. Two young men I knew from the kitchen took orders and then returned with trays brimming with drinks.

Karl and I sat near the rear in plush high-back chairs.

They were somewhat stiff, and I wondered if they'd be uncomfortable to sit in through an entire movie. When the alley went dark, Karl reached across and touched my hand. Warmth spread through my fingers and up into my arm. The shock touched my heart and I struggled to catch a breath.

'Is something wrong?' Karl asked.

'No,' I whispered. 'I tasted tonight for the first time. Perhaps it's a reaction to the food.'

Karl twisted in his seat and took my hands. 'If you're sick, I will get the Führer's personal physician.'

I leaned back. 'Please, Karl, I'm fine. Let's enjoy the movie.'

He nodded and relaxed somewhat. The lights flickered, the music swelled from the speakers and we turned our attention to the film. I made sure to keep his hand in mine. He squeezed my fingers as Scarlett teased the Tarleton twins. I had the same reaction when, later in the film, Scarlett kissed Rhett Butler.

About one in the morning, a telephone call interrupted the film. We were only about two-thirds of the way through, but the picture was finished for the evening. Those who wanted to see the ending would have to wait for another time. Karl escorted me back to my room, kissed my hand and disappeared down the hall. I got into bed and dreamed that night of making love to him.

Over the days, my fear of tasting lessened. One afternoon, I called my parents for the first time since arriving at the Berghof and told them I was working with Hitler. The Reich had informed them previously of my service. However, I did not tell them what I was doing. I could tell my father was not pleased with my new position because his silence gave away his thoughts. I also knew someone, probably an SS man, was listening to our conversation. I suspected my father did as well.

My mother was more effusive and pressed me about my job. I told her I was in service to the Führer and left it at that. It was best not to give either of them any more information. When I hung up, it struck me how much I lived in a world of distrust and fear. Perhaps my father's cold replies amplified what I was feeling. At the Berghof, we lived in a monastic world: secluded, insular, broken off from the realities of the war. Hitler and his generals bore the psychological brunt of the fighting. We never saw or heard the reported rages, or experienced the tensions that apparently permeated this mountain retreat. We only heard rumors. We could either choose to believe or not. I didn't like feeling this way because I wanted the world to be 'normal.' After the conversation with my parents, I realized how far and how fast I'd slipped away from the everyday. I wondered whether everyone in Hitler's service felt the same. I was being seduced by the singular drama in which we played. We were all Marie Antoinette asking the world to eat cake while the earth burned to ashes around us.

After about two weeks, I finally tasted a meal without some degree of shaking. Ursula and the cooks had teased me, so unmercifully, in fact, that eventually I forced myself to relax. They assured me that no poisons would get by them. The 'last meal' became a joke around the kitchen. Despite their assurances, I still suffered from a nervous stomach now and then.

Captain Weber and I spoke often when we passed each

other in the halls and sometimes we enjoyed leisurely conversations in the kitchen. Cook raised as much of a fuss as she could, but it was Karl's right to oversee as he saw fit. One night he suggested we go to the Theater Hall for an impromptu dance. I, of course, accepted with Ursula's urging.

Karl called for me at my room and accompanied me up the slope to the Hall. The air was fresh, the night chilly, as we walked. A small dance floor had been formed by pushing chairs aside to the walls. The lamps were dimmed, barely enough to light the room. Records, mostly waltzes, crackled out of an old table phonograph. The music flowed into the room from a gold-colored, blossom-shaped speaker. Two other couples were dancing. A few of the men, lacking women, danced together, not touching each other except for their hands. They shot looks of envy our way when Karl pulled me close and swung me into a waltz. We flowed naturally into each other.

The night melted into stars and warmth. I loved being next to Karl and, judging by the content smile on his face, he loved me as well. We danced for several hours, hardly saying a word. If love was an energy, a force, it passed between us that night. When I finally left his arms, my body tingled.

As we were leaving the Hall, we heard a cough. Karl grabbed my hand tightly and guided me out of the building. I looked back. The Colonel walked out of the shadows, cigarette in hand, the smoke drifting through the dim light. His gaze followed us as we left.

'How long has he been watching us?' I asked Karl.

He did not look back. 'All evening,' he said.

One afternoon in late May, I accompanied Karl and Ursula on a trip to the Teahouse. It was my first visit. I had seen it once from the terrace that ran along the north and west sides of the Berghof. I sneaked a peek at its round turret rising through the trees below when no one was about but an SS guard enjoying the air. He recognized me and didn't mind that I shared the view.

The mountains to the north were often misty and veiled in clouds, but the first day I saw the Teahouse the sky was crisp and blue. Looking out upon the scenery, I realized why Hitler had chosen this particular spot as his own. He'd purchased the property – claimed it, some had said – and begun renovations a short time later. The view gave its owner the psychological superiority of one who might believe he was a god. To look upon the magnificent rocky peaks was to feel on top of the world while those below were mere specks, dirt beneath his feet. Hitler was indeed master of all he surveyed.

Karl, Ursula and I set off to the Teahouse shortly after one o'clock. The blue sky above the Berghof held today as well, but a band of high clouds was approaching from the northeast. We walked down the driveway and then cut off on a trail that descended through the forest by way of a wooded path. At one magnificent bend, rails of hewn logs kept the walker from tumbling over the precipice of the Berchtesgaden valley. A long bench had been constructed there so Hitler could ponder the magnificent view to the north. Karl told us that Eva and her friends liked to use the rails as a kind of gymnastic bar, balancing upon them and pointing their legs over the cliff, at least for the sake of photographs. She was always posing and using her new film camera, he said. Hitler was often uncomfortable with her filming, but grudgingly obliged her hobby.

The Teahouse, less than a kilometer from the Berghof, soon came into view. It was like a miniature castle planted on a rocky hillside. The path ended at stone steps to its door. Karl had a key because the kitchen staff was so often called to serve there.

'I really shouldn't be doing this, but I want you to see it,' he said. 'It's quite charming. Hitler relaxes here and invites others to join him. He'll be down later.'

Karl opened the door and Ursula and I peered inside. A round table decorated with flowers and set with silk table-cloths, sparkling china and polished silver sat near the middle of the room. Plush armchairs decorated in an abstract floral pattern of swirling bellflowers added to the medieval atmos-phere of the turret. A kitchen and offices lay behind this large circular room. We stepped inside and Karl urged me to sit in one of the chairs. I did and luxuriated in its soft cushions.

'That's where *he* sits,' Karl said.

I jumped out of the chair.

Ursula laughed. 'Scaredy-cat,' she said. 'He's not here.'

'Why did you tell me to sit there?' I asked Karl, irritated by his prank. 'I don't want to get into trouble.' I felt foolish.

'You won't. Sit and enjoy the view.' I returned to the seat and looked out the windows that encircled the front half of the tower while he and Ursula whispered in the doorway.

'What are you two plotting?' I asked.

Karl turned to me, his face sullen. 'Nothing. I'm talking with Ursula about her mother — she's been ill, you know.' The night Karl and I had gone to see *Gone with the Wind,* Ursula had been called to Munich.

I sat for several more minutes as they continued their

secretive discussion. Finally, I got up, explored the other tables and chairs and then stood behind them. They abruptly stopped their conversation when I got too close.

'We should be getting back,' Karl said. 'We can't hang about here too long.'

As we walked, I wondered why we had come in the first place. I didn't have a good feeling about our visit to the Teahouse. Something gnawed at my stomach and I knew my discomfort centered on Karl and Ursula. They were up to something.

# CHAPTER 5

Karl informed us that Hitler often stayed at the Berghof for only a short time before leaving for another headquarters or hiding place. When Hitler was in residence, a giant Nazi flag flew over the grounds. As it turned out, he wasn't even at the Berghof for about two weeks in May. I wasn't sure where he went, but Karl, on the sly, told me it was to the 'Wolf's Lair.' To foil assassination attempts, the Führer kept his travel schedule secret and often switched trains or flights at the last moment or showed up early or late for appointments. He'd used this tactic for years, and it had served him well, particularly since the war broke out.

A rumor circulated that Hitler was holding a reception at the Teahouse for kitchen staff before he left on his next trip. It would be the first time I had a chance to meet the leader of the Reich. I asked Karl about this and he confirmed it was true.

After breakfast the next morning, everyone was in high spirits and anticipation about 'tea' with the Führer. A light rain fell, but it did not dampen our gay mood. Cook wanted me to take inventory from the greenhouses and record food items, in addition to my tasting duties, so I was late getting back to my room.

'Eva has instructed everyone to wear traditional Bavarian garments,' Cook told me. 'There will be a costume on your bed.'

'Why is dressing up so important?' I asked her.

'Because Heinrich Hoffmann, Hitler's personal photographer, is here. He and Eva thought it would be a good opportunity to capture the benevolent spirit of the Führer as he entertains and thanks his staff.' She chuckled. 'Eva loves to dress up. That's really why we're doing it.'

When I went back to my room, I interrupted Ursula. She was already dressed in her Bavarian costume. I really had no fondness for the hose, petticoats, the flouncy dress and puffy sleeves of the garment. Ursula sat on her bed, sewing her apron. She turned quickly away from me when I entered.

'You'd better get ready,' Ursula said, looking back over her shoulder. Her fingers trembled and the needle slipped from her hand.

'Are you all right?' I asked. 'Is there a problem with your apron?'

She shook her head. 'I'm shaky because I haven't eaten. I need to get to the kitchen for some food.' She began sewing again and stitched across the apron's left pocket.

'There's not much to eat now. The staff is preparing lunch, but I wouldn't be concerned about me getting ready. I'm sure it'll be after four before we're called to the Teahouse. We've got plenty of time.'

Ursula sighed. 'Yes, plenty of time.'

She went back to her work as I inspected my dress and its trimmings. 'I don't have an apron. Do I need one?'

Her eyes dimmed. 'I don't know. You might ask Cook. This one was given specifically to me.'

I stretched out on my bed with a book. 'The weather is so nasty it's a good day for reading.'

Ursula threw the apron and needle on her bed. 'Can't you take a walk or find something to do?'

I sat up, shocked at her harsh tone. 'What's wrong? I've never seen you so upset. Is it your mother?'

She buried her face in her hands and cried. I crept over to her, sat behind her and cradled her shoulders. This made her sobbing even worse.

'Yes,' she said between gasps. 'I have no family now. Both of my brothers are dead because of the war. My father is already dead and my mother is dying. I don't care if we lose this war – I've already lost everything. My brothers were all I had.'

I turned her so she faced me, and wiped her tears with a handkerchief. 'You must be strong and not let your troubles overcome you.'

Ursula pushed me away. 'You say that so easily because you still have your family. Wait until they are gone. Then you'll see how hard it is.' She collapsed on the bed.

Saddened by her mood, I got up and stared out the window. The mountains were lost in the silver mist and fog. On days like this, the Berghof's air of invincibility vanished. 'I'll leave you alone, but you only have to ask if you need my help.' I found my poetry book on the shelf. I knew Hitler was still eating breakfast and after that he would meet with his military staff for a few hours in the Great Hall. I had no idea where to go. 'I'll be back later to get ready.'

Ursula continued working on her checked apron. A few flecks of white powder shone on the red fabric. I closed the door, not thinking much about what I'd seen.

I sat at a table on the corner of the terrace. No one else was around because of the cold rain. The wind blew mist under the sun umbrella, making reading uncomfortable. After a few minutes, I gave up and found a vacant chair in a hallway. Eva happened to walk by with her two Scotties. The dogs were used to guests at the Berghof but still insisted on sniffing me. Eva stood before me, looking bored and out of sorts; she wore a dark blue bellflower skirt with a matching bolero jacket. I admired the diamond-encrusted bracelet on her left wrist.

'The Führer gave me this.' Eva jangled the bracelet and laughed casually; however, there was no humor in her voice. She leaned down as if to whisper in my ear. 'If you promise not to tell anyone, I'll let you in on a secret.'

I was astounded at her intimacy with me – someone she barely knew. I didn't know what to make of it. She must have been lonely and in need of a friend. Cook and others in the kitchen had hinted at Eva's personality. Somewhat flighty, haughty when she needed to be, entitled, but also flirty and fun with her friends. Because I'd had so little contact with her, I wanted to make up my own mind.

'What's your name?' she asked.

'Magda Ritter.'

She continued her conversation, asking me where I was born, questioning me about my parents, my schooling and how I came to work at the Berghof.

I answered everything truthfully. She shook my hand, but

didn't give her name. Obviously, I was expected to know who she was.

She studied me with her blue eyes. 'I've seen you in the kitchen. What do you do?'

'I'm a taster for the Führer.'

She beamed like a benevolent member of the clergy. 'Ah, a wonderful position. You are protecting the life of the most important man in the world. You don't know how he depends on his staff to guide him through these terrible times.'

I smiled because she knew so little of me and tasting. No matter how magnificent the meal, you wondered if it was your last. 'I would never expect the Führer to know who we are.'

'Of course he does. People like you lift him above the fray. If there was any threat to the Berghof, he would be the first to throw himself at the enemy. He would protect his staff until all danger had vanished.'

I nodded, uncertain of what she was getting at, but clearly Eva wanted to paint him as a kind and congenial man. Cook had told me stories about his loving interactions with Blondi, his dog, his fond dealings with Speer's children and Eva's guests. His closest associates believed the Führer could do no wrong.

Eva knelt in front of me and patted the Scotties. They sat patiently at her feet during our conversation. 'Why are you reading here?'

'Because my roommate is in no mood for company.'

She turned her attention from the dogs and put her hand upon mine. 'I know how you feel. The Führer often ignores me, sometimes for days at a time, because he is so busy. When he leaves for other parts of the Reich, I go to my little house in Munich. Life can be lonely and boring there, too.'

It was hard for me to feel sorry for her with the world at her feet while others suffered, but I sensed that even as wealth and power lay within her reach she wasn't happy. Her dejected expression added to her sudden melancholy mood.

'Well, I've said too much and I need to get ready for the reception this afternoon,' she said. 'You will be going? If so, I hope you enjoy the dress I provided.'

'Yes,' I said, 'it was nice of you to do so.' I studied her clothes. 'You look beautiful now. Why would you change?'

She rose to her feet and the dogs jumped up as well. 'It's one of the few pleasures I have. Dresses, makeup and jewelry. When I look beautiful, he is happy.'

She walked away and I called out, 'What about the secret you were going to tell me?' I regretted my silly words as soon as they left my lips.

Eva turned, her skirt swirling around her. 'But I've already told you. I'll see you later.' She took a few steps and faced me again. 'Why don't you read in the sunroom? No one's there and you shouldn't be disturbed. If anyone asks, tell them I gave you permission.'

I thanked her and watched as she disappeared down the hall with the dogs at her feet. The companion of the most powerful man in Europe was lonely – that was her 'secret.'

I walked to the sunroom, which was pleasant for reading even though its namesake was hidden by the clouds. It was in the original part of the old house and was furnished with lounge armchairs, a table and four rather uncomfortable slat-back chairs. I sat in one of the plush armchairs and spent most of my time looking out the wide picture window rather than concentrating on my poetry. Even though Eva said I could be there, I felt out of place on this side of the Berghof, away from my quarters.

In mid-afternoon, I returned to my room. Ursula was gone. I put on my costume and looked in the small mirror attached to the wall. There was nothing glamorous about me; in fact, I felt like a clown in an outfit that would be ridiculed outside of a beer hall. But Eva had ordered it and I felt compelled to comply. My costume didn't include an apron. Karl rang my room about three and said he was on his way to the Teahouse and would see me there about four. Hitler was notorious for missing appointments. We expected it might be five before he even showed up.

Several members of the kitchen staff joined me when it came time to leave. Our mood was light and jovial. We even stopped at the overlook, but the valley was obscured by clouds, so there was little to see.

Gradually, the Teahouse came into view out of the mist like something from a fairy tale. Nazi flags and bunting festooned its turret, and a banner above the door proclaimed: *Thank You for Your Service.*

Inside, candles lit the room and a cheery fire in the hearth chased the damp away. Most of the kitchen staff were gathered inside and sat around a few small tables. The massive one with the view of the mountains was reserved for Hitler and his guests. Bavarian crèmes, cookies and apple cake, the Führer's favorite, were displayed on fine china. Orderlies stood ready to serve the treats to the crowd. Fine champagne sat in ice buckets at each table within easy reach of the guests.

Karl observed the crowd from the kitchen entrance. Ursula was nowhere to be seen. I wondered how we could all cram inside the Teahouse. If it became too crowded, I decided, I would join Karl in the kitchen.

Franz Faber, the young officer Ursula disappeared with the night we went for a walk to the SS barracks, joined Karl. They talked for a time until Karl saw me. He left Franz and, sporting a broad grin, whispered in my ear, 'You look rather silly.'

I scowled and then laughed. 'I agree. I'll be upset if Eva and Hoffmann are not here with their cameras.' I looked around the room. 'Have you seen Ursula?'

'She's making tea.'

I glanced through the turret windows. There was no sign of Hitler, Eva or their guests. The rain had let up, so Karl and I walked outside and stood near the steps leading to the entrance, stealing a few moments together. Our quiet was interrupted by the sudden, frenzied barking of a dog. That was followed by shouts and a general commotion.

Karl sprinted up the steps.

I followed and peered inside the door, careful to stay out of the way. Karl, Franz and the Colonel stood near the kitchen entrance. Behind them, I saw the pale, stricken face of Ursula. She wore her costume and the apron she'd been working on. The Colonel clutched a furiously barking black shepherd. The crazed animal snapped and growled at Ursula.

Over the uproar, Franz shouted, 'It isn't possible.'

The Colonel brushed him aside, gave control of the dog to Karl and then pulled Ursula from the kitchen into the circular room. She held a silver teapot in her right hand.

The Colonel took the teapot from Ursula and ordered

her to take a cup from one of the small tables. Her hands shook as she obeyed his order.

Franz rushed to her and said to the Colonel, 'I'm sure this is a mistake. Fräulein Thalberg would never poison the Führer.'

'Shut up,' the Colonel commanded. 'Get away from her.'

Karl stared at me. Horror spread across his face. My heart pounded as I leaned against the door frame. The Colonel, still carrying the tea, grabbed Ursula roughly by the arm and pulled her down the steps of the Teahouse. He ordered her to hold out the cup; then he poured the hot liquid into it. He sniffed the steam as it rose in milky wisps in the air.

'Drink it,' he said. His lips formed a vicious smile.

Franz stood frozen in the doorway. Karl, still restraining the barking dog, stared in disbelief.

Ursula looked blankly at the Colonel. She lifted the cup to her lips and drank it in one draught.

The Colonel took back the cup and waited.

Nothing happened for a few long minutes as Ursula focused her gaze upon the ground. Then, slowly, her body convulsed. Her eyes rolled back in her head and she collapsed on the path. Franz started to run to her, but Karl and a member of the kitchen staff held him back.

Down the path, conversation and laughter filled the air. Hitler, with a walking stick in hand, strolled ahead of his entourage. He was accompanied by Eva and the guests, no more than fifty meters from the Teahouse. She carried her camera in her quest to get photographs of the Führer. She darted ahead of him at one point to snap pictures.

I watched in disbelief as Ursula, her skin and lips turning blue, lay unconscious on the ground. The Colonel did nothing. Cook had told me about the body coloration as one of the symptoms of cyanide poisoning. It led to an unconscious state and respiratory failure – a lack of oxygen. The convulsions, her gasps, continued until her mouth gaped open. With one final breath, her body shook and then her arms fell lifeless by her sides.

Karl ordered the staff to stay inside, although the whole event could be seen through the Teahouse windows.

Heinrich Hoffmann, Hitler's gray-haired photographer, rushed up and snapped a few pictures of the body. Hitler stopped the procession and motioned for the Colonel to come to him. With the teapot and cup in hand, he approached the Führer. I couldn't hear their conversation, but after a short time Hitler turned and said something to the group. Amid looks of astonishment, they retreated and disappeared into the mist.

The Colonel poured out the contents of the pot on the trail and addressed Karl. 'You should have better command over your staff, Captain. Get a couple of men to take the body to the doctor's office for an autopsy.' He grabbed his dog's leash. The animal wanted to sniff Ursula's body. 'You and Faber – in my quarters in an hour. In the meantime, make sure the Teahouse is cleaned up. No one should eat or drink anything. Keep only the items that are sealed.' He handed Karl the teapot and the cup.

He raised his right arm in salute. 'Heil Hitler.'

Karl and Franz came to attention and saluted as well. The Colonel turned toward the Berghof, pulling his dog with him. As soon as he was out of sight, Franz's eyes brimmed with tears. Karl held his friend back while two SS men took the body away.

'Go back to your room and remain there,' he told me when I approached. 'None of us is above suspicion.'

The thought shook me. I took one last look inside the Teahouse with its magical furnishings. I remembered the fairy tales my mother had read to me when I was a child. They were often brutal tales ending in destruction or death. I was coming to realize how much the Reich was like a fairy tale. Death was never far away.

# CHAPTER 6

I returned to a ransacked room. Ursula's things had been removed. Our small closet stood open . . . Books and papers from the shelves had been scattered about. Shivering, I cleared a place on my bed, sat down and cried.

I cried for myself as much as Ursula. Fear crept over me. Was there no one I could trust? What about Captain Weber? A thought jolted me. What had Karl and Ursula been talking about in the Teahouse when we visited it? Could he have known about the poison? It made no sense to me – how could Ursula have been so foolish? Was Karl an accomplice? My gloomy questions distressed me. Ursula had ended her life and put mine in danger. She was mad to think she could have ever succeeded – but I dared not think about the attempt!

Someone knocked on the door. I wiped my tears and composed myself. I had no time to answer before I heard the turn of the doorknob. The door swung open and Cook stepped into the room. She was in great distress: her face crimped in pain, her hands clenched. She lurched about in the small space between the beds, more agitated than I'd ever seen her.

'Did you know anything of this?' She slowed her steps and paced back and forth near the door like a caged tiger.

'Of course not,' I said, and looked away. I couldn't imagine she expected me to answer 'yes.'

'Look at me! Never avert your eyes when the SS or the Gestapo question you.' Her face reddened. 'You might as well admit your guilt. If you give them any indication you're lying, they will beat you until they have what they want to hear.'

I sobbed at her harsh words. 'I don't know how this happened. How could Ursula do such a thing?'

Cook sat next to me and her voice softened. 'I believe you knew nothing of this, but you must prove your innocence. I know Ursula suffered because of her brothers' deaths – but to attempt such an insane act! How could she be so callous? In an attempt to poison the Führer she has ended her life and dishonored her family. The Gestapo will question all of us.' She wrung her hands. 'What a stupid woman.'

I looked at her, not knowing what to say. I had proclaimed my innocence, yet I could tell no one about the powder I saw upon Ursula's apron. To do so would implicate me.

'Captain Weber has called for a new taster, but she won't be here until tomorrow,' Cook said. 'Tonight you must taste all the food. Be in the kitchen by seven.'

She left and I changed out of my Bavarian costume into my work clothes. In a fury, I threw the Bavarian dress on the bed, disgusted by the event it represented. I wanted to tear it to bits and toss it into the hall as a reminder to Eva of her ridiculous idea.

Soon another knock, loud and firm, interrupted me. I opened the door and was shocked to see the Colonel. He pushed past me, sat on the desk chair and eyed me suspiciously. I took Cook's advice and looked into his eyes as he questioned me.

At one point, he asked, 'Have you stopped smuggling poison into the Berghof?' I caught his trick. Either answer, negative or affirmative, would have incriminated me.

'I never brought poison into the Berghof for her or anyone else. I had no idea Ursula was carrying out such a plan.'

He stared me down and asked where Ursula might have gotten it. I told him I didn't know; it was absurd to ask me.

He seemed satisfied by my answers, but asked me more questions about my habits. He wanted to know who I knew at the Berghof, what I felt about the Reich.

My stomach turned when I answered questions about the Reich. For the first time in my life, I was lying to *save* myself. Only anger and pain about Ursula's death, Hitler and the war filled me. The Colonel told me, from now on, to report any suspicious behaviors directly to him. The kitchen and staff would be under special watch. He said good-bye, stood and saluted the Führer. I had no choice but to do the same.

That night, in the kitchen, two SS guards watched the staff's every move. I didn't know them because my contact with the Leibstandarte had primarily been limited to Karl and Franz. One of the guards, a rat-like man with greasy blond hair, observed my tasting. My nerves were on edge. I wondered if Ursula had spread cyanide in the food as well as the tea. The kitchen door slammed and I dropped a spoonful of an asparagus dish destined for Hitler. The SS man was quick to act. He pointed menacingly and commanded me to take another bite. Cook glowered at him, but it did no good. Tensions were running high. I managed to make it through the tastings, but I trembled with every bite as dread shook me.

The next morning, Cook gave me a list of vegetables and asked me to record the number of those plants in the green-houses. I gathered the inventory books and walked up the grassy slope to the glass and metal structures that glinted in the silvery morning haze. The air felt fresh and dewy against my skin; the sunlight had that magical, ethereal effect, painting the surrounding mountains in muted pastels. It was like walking in a watercolor.

The greenhouses were two tiered, both about 150 meters long. Most of the fresh food for Hitler was grown here. There was also a 'mushroom house.' Cook had told me that the Führer rarely ate them, but apparently others did in enough quantity to warrant a special growing area.

I opened the door to the lower greenhouse and stepped inside. Even though the morning was cool, the greenhouse was warm. I took off my jacket and draped it over a metal stand. A patchwork quilt of plants lay on the floor as far as I could see. I grabbed my book and pen and walked past the square plots until I got to a plant I recognized on my list – cucumbers. I bent down and began counting the staked plants festooned with their starry yellow flowers. The door opened behind me.

Karl stood at the entrance. He put his right hand over his eyes to shade them from the light and stared at me. I waved. He called my name and walked quickly toward me. We were the only two people in the greenhouse.

When he got to me, he stopped and looked the greenhouse

over from top to bottom. He whispered in my ear, 'Be careful what you say.'

'I can only talk a few minutes,' I said. 'I have a job to do for Cook.'

I picked up my jacket and left the inventory books on the stand. We walked down the paved road in front of the greenhouses. Karl breathed easier when we got to a safe spot. Below us, the Berghof glowed in the sun.

'How did it go with the Colonel?' Karl asked.

I looked at him, trying to gauge the intent of his question, wondering whether I should trust him. There was something about him – a kindness, a willingness to listen – that made me want to trust him, to feel comfortable enough to talk honestly. 'I answered his questions,' I said, trying to be non-committal.

He reached into his pocket and pulled out a gold cigarette lighter. He fidgeted with it and turned it over in his palm a few times. 'I'm still trying to give them up.' He pointed to the lighter. 'At least it gives me something to do.' He chuckled and then asked, 'Did you notice anything unusual about Ursula before you went to the Teahouse?'

I shook my head.

Karl's face tensed and his gaze narrowed. He put his arm around my shoulder; his face was close to mine. 'I told the Colonel you knew nothing about the incident yesterday, despite what you may have seen.'

My heart raced.

'I protected you in every way I could,' he continued.

'Why?'

'Because – ' He drew away and looked at the lighter in his hand. 'This is hard for me to admit, but since you've

86

come to the Berghof, I've been unable to think of much else besides you.' He turned away, as if he was afraid of what I might tell him.

I put my hand on his shoulder. 'I've thought about you as well.'

He turned, his face flushed. 'Really? I'm very happy to hear that.'

I laughed. 'You don't have to be so formal, Karl. This is as new for me as I suspect it is for you.' I pulled him to me and gave him a kiss on the cheek.

'Thank you.' He looked around. Far up the hill a group of SS officers were walking down from the barracks. Karl took my hands in his. 'We don't have much time. I want to share something with you, Magda. It's important to me. That's only part of it – there's much more. It concerns the war. Do you want to know why it's important to me?'

I nodded.

'Then I'll come by your room tonight when it's safe. You must trust me as I trust you.' He kissed me. 'Go back to work. I have to go.'

He walked quickly toward the Berghof as I headed back to the greenhouse. The SS officers smiled and nodded as they passed by.

I knelt next to the cucumber plants and started to count again, but couldn't help but wonder what Karl had to tell me that was so important. However, more exciting for me was the thrill that lingered from his kiss.

A soft knock on my door woke me at two in the morning.

I pulled on my robe and opened the door a few centimeters. Karl stood in the dim hall, his face ashen in the gray light. His eyes were puffy with dark circles underneath them. He pushed the door open and slipped in through the narrow opening. My room plunged back into darkness. I had gone to bed thinking he wasn't going to come.

'Light a candle,' he said.

'Are you certain this is safe?' I asked, aware that it was dangerous for an SS officer to be in my room at this hour. 'I don't have a candle. I'll get one from the kitchen.'

'Please, but be careful. A guard is on duty outside the entrance. I made up the story that additional investigations regarding Ursula and the poisoning were being conducted under cover of night.'

'At this hour?'

'I told him it was of utmost secrecy.'

I put on my slippers and stepped from the room. The Berghof was in blackout; fortunately, I had walked the hall so many times I knew where I was going. Candles and matches were stored over one of the sinks, kept there as accessories for Hitler's evening dinners. I opened the cupboard like a thief, took them and then crept back to my room. I wondered if the Colonel was hiding under a table waiting to catch me in my nocturnal wanderings. Fortunately, neither he nor anyone else stopped me.

I found Ursula's ashtray pushed against the wall under her bed, placed the candle in it and lit the flame. A warm yellow light flared outward in a small circle. Karl sat on my bed, his head cupped in his hands. He finally looked up, withdrew an envelope concealed in his uniform jacket and placed it beside him. He motioned for me to sit on the bed next to him.

I did so. Then he kissed me with a sudden warmth and passion.

I didn't push him away. His lips drifted to my neck where his soft breath sent tingles down my spine. I regained my composure and broke away from his embrace even though I didn't want him to stop. My heightened emotions made his affection too uncomfortable.

'What is this about?' I asked. 'Why put us both in danger?'

He caressed my face and said, 'I told you when we met that I recognized something different in you. I still believe that's true.'

I looked at him, unsure what to say.

He took his hands away. 'Franz was distraught this afternoon. He could barely answer the questions the Colonel asked him. He lied about his relationship with Ursula. Franz told the Colonel they were only friends. I know they were more than that. He told me so himself – you know how men brag.'

'Why are you telling me this?'

'Because you think for yourself and you don't want the German people to suffer any more than I do.'

'Of course I don't.'

'Tell me, are you in love with Hitler?'

I almost laughed, the question was so ludicrous. I was quick to answer. 'In love? Not at all.'

'Do you believe in him and the dream of the Third Reich?' He paused as if pained by his words. 'I'm saddened for Germany.'

I thought of my father because Karl's words were exactly like something he would say. 'I don't admire the Führer,' I said. 'My father says he surrounds himself with bullies who do his dirty work while he enjoys life. That kind of man earns no respect. I agree with that.'

Karl picked up the envelope he'd placed on the bed, opened it and withdrew several photographs. 'These are hard to look at, but you need to see them. Hitler is wrong about the war; he is lying about how the Reich deals with Jews and prisoners of war. The lies must be stopped.' He handed them to me. 'My life is in your hands.'

I tilted the photos toward the candlelight. The first series showed SS officers shooting naked men, women and children perched atop a ravine. You could even see the smoke erupting from their rifles. 'Where is this?' I asked, horrified by what the photos portrayed.

Karl bowed his head. 'Near the Eastern Front.'

It was shocking enough that our soldiers were shooting unarmed men – but women and children as well?

The second set of photos was even more gruesome and I blanched at the sight of corpses entwined in death. There were so many you could not tell where one body ended and the next began. The photos showed mounds of luggage, shoes and eyeglasses, followed by mountains of decomposing flesh. I was stunned. In the final picture, a naked man lay dead on a slab in front of an opening that looked like the door to an oven. A prisoner – nearly a corpse himself – stood by his side, presumably to make sure the body was cremated.

'Is this propaganda from the Allies?' I asked, not wanting to believe what lay in front of me.

Karl shook his head. 'No, the photos are real. They came from an SS officer at Auschwitz. You must keep what you've seen to yourself.' He replaced the photos in the envelope and slid them back in his jacket. 'There's an underground network of officers who believe National Socialism must be stopped – for the good of Germany. We are determined to make sure this happens.'

I didn't want to hear his words – not because of Germany, but because I was selfish. Karl's life was in danger. Anyone who defied Hitler was doomed. 'Only a few men know about this? You're taking a huge risk.'

Karl nodded. 'A risk worth dying for.'

I trembled as if an icy wind had raced over me, my body full of conflicting emotions. On the one hand, I recognized my growing attraction for Karl and I admired his strength, courage and conviction. Not every man would place his life in a woman's hands, or ask that she join him in keeping such a powerful and dangerous secret. The pictures he had shown me were already seared into my memory. What kind of tyrant could order these kinds of deaths? Shouldn't all of Germany rise up to stop such atrocities? But so few people knew and what use would it be to start a revolution? The Reich, and its powerful officers, would crush anything in its way. Then I pictured Ursula dead upon the ground. She had sacrificed herself for her brothers. How could I dishonor her and Karl by ignoring the photographs? Karl studied me, awaiting my response. Finally, I asked, 'What do you want me to do?'

'Offer your strength,' he said, grasping my hands. 'Don't betray me. I'm not alone, but few can be trusted.' His breath caught and he stroked my hair. 'It's too much to ask, but perhaps one day you'll return the love I feel.'

I wanted to draw away because his words overwhelmed me. The only man who had ever professed love for me was my father. 'Why should I love you when you may die? There's no future in death.'

'If Hitler continues to lead there will be no future for anyone.' He rose from my bed and looked down upon me. 'I must get back. Think about what I've said.'

He started to leave, but I gripped his arm. 'Did you know Ursula was planning to poison the Führer?'

'Only through her hints, but she talked about it as if it were a joke. That's what we were whispering about at the Teahouse the day we went. I cautioned her not to be so brazen, but I had no idea she had taken it upon herself to poison him without anyone's help. She was so bitter about her brothers' deaths. I was trying to comfort her — in fact, squelch such talk about Hitler.

'Poisoning the tea was a foolish thing to do. She would have killed everyone who drank at his table. It was a suicide mission. If she hadn't been identified as the perpetrator, all of us might have been executed.'

I hesitated, but then admitted, 'I saw the poison on her apron. I didn't know what it was.' Pangs of sorrow stabbed at me. 'Maybe I could have stopped her if I had known, but would I want that knowledge? What would become of my parents if the SS thought I was involved? I don't want them to die. They're all I have in the world.'

'Ursula loved her brothers more than her own life. She died for them. The madness gripping us demands stern sacrifices. That's the truth. If you decide to join me, either of us might be killed. Your parents might be in danger as well. The Gestapo and the SS have ways of making death quite unpleasant. No one wants to be a hero, but consider what we've talked about.'

He bent down, kissed me on the cheek and then quietly walked out. My head swam with emotion as I crawled into bed. Was I willing to risk my life, and perhaps my parents' lives, for Karl? The pictures he had shown me ran through my head as the hours dragged by. Could the world be saved from such horrors? I tossed and turned.

After a few hours of fitful sleep, I awoke. My view had shifted. Calm descended upon me. Ursula had sacrificed herself for the love of her brothers. Could I sacrifice myself in order to shorten the war? My heart told me that Karl and his love for me were true. I tried to ignore the feelings building inside me, but something greater than myself was urging me on. I had to trust my intuition.

I was no longer the sensible Magda who had entered the civilian service only for a job. Now I was Magda Ritter, a woman who could be a traitor, a co-conspirator in the Führer's death and – if I followed my heart – a lover of Captain Karl Weber.

# THE WOLF'S LAIR

## RASTENBURG

# CHAPTER 7

Hitler disappeared in early July 1943. Preparations started in late June, and he vanished within three days as did nearly everything connected with him. The Berghof housekeeper and her husband remained, as did those charged with keeping the residence in readiness should Hitler return. Martin Bormann stayed for a few days, but his brother Albert was gone, presumably with the Führer. Speer sped off to Berlin and we were told that Göring had vacated his home, which was located on a rise above the Berghof.

Karl slipped an envelope under my door in the middle of the night, addressed to me, to say he had been called by the Führer to Rastenburg and the Wolf's Lair. He did not want to wake me. I was dismayed he had taken the risk because there would have been trouble had someone else gotten hold of the note. No one was supposed to know where Hitler was headed. After I read it, I burned it in Ursula's ashtray and ground the ashes into the earth on a walk to the greenhouse. I was sad Karl had to leave, but I understood the nature of his job.

Cook had said little about Ursula's poisoning, but I could tell she was upset. Her normally mild and cheerful demeanor turned cold and pallid in comparison to earlier days. The attempted poisoning had sent shock waves through the Berghof. Cook watched everyone with an eagle eye and supervised all the food preparation even though Hitler was no longer there. She wanted no mistakes, and, by implication, suspicion to fall upon her.

She lectured me one day about what a great loss it would be if the Führer were assassinated. 'There would be no Germany,' she said. 'We must stand by him to the end. Every sacrifice must be made.'

I only nodded and thought of the terrible pictures Karl had shown me – proof no one could deny. Yet, according to Karl, only a few officers knew about them. To distribute them to the German people would be folly. I wondered if the populace would even believe they were real. Most, under the Reich's constant propaganda barrage, would think they were manufactured by Jews or Bolshevists. Goebbels would use such a tactic to his advantage to stir up the people. Dirty Jews or communist swine had produced these photos to ferment dissension, he would preach from his political pulpit. He was a master at his art.

In my first few days without Karl, my thoughts were filled with misgivings and apprehension about any attack on Hitler. To follow Karl might mean my death and, most likely, a similar fate for my parents. My heart longed for his love, but a careful, rational look at our situation brought fear and doubt. I could not abandon my parents to the Gestapo and their tactics; even Uncle Willy and Aunt Reina might be persecuted. What if my love affair with Karl blossomed into a full-fledged relationship? Any misstep, any informant, any error in judgment could cost him his life. What if we were married and I became pregnant? Could I carry a child through the horrors of war, bear it and bring it into a world of despotic criminals? These conflicts tore at my mind until I was exhausted from thinking.

One evening in early July, after a halfhearted tasting and meal, I walked to the terrace to enjoy the air. An SS officer stood on the far side taking in the view. We were alone and I was happy because I didn't want company. The chairs and sun umbrellas were piled in a corner – most of the furniture had been shoved aside because Hitler was no longer there. I sat on the stone railing and looked out over the valley. The long shadows of the setting sun cut purple swaths across the mountains. The green forests were turning gray in the fading light. The air was pleasant and carried a summer scent of grass and meadow flowers. I was absorbed in the beauty in front of my eyes when someone tapped my shoulder. The touch startled me and I turned to see Eva Braun.

She wore a simple black dress, but she looked elegant, as if she had dined with the Führer. There was a touch of red on her painted cheeks and her hair looked freshly done. I detected that slight sadness that nearly always lingered in her eyes.

'Magda, isn't it?' she asked.

'Yes.' I was surprised she remembered me.

'You're not reading tonight.' She sat down beside me and looked out across the broad expanse. 'It's a lovely evening.'

'Very lovely.' I looked away, in no mood for delicate maneuvering. What did she want?

'We seem to be of like spirit tonight,' she said. 'Is there anything I can do to make things better?'

I shook my head. I couldn't tell anyone, certainly not Hitler's confidant, what I was going through. I made up an excuse, one I thought she would want to hear. 'I miss the excitement the Führer brings to the Berghof. It's very dull now that everyone is gone.'

Eva nodded. 'I'm off to Munich tomorrow to be with my parents and friends. The dogs are coming with me. I don't suppose I will see Adolf until he comes back in . . . well, whenever he returns. He is so busy.'

I knew she couldn't say when Hitler would return. It would be as much a blunder as Karl telling me the Führer was on his way to Rastenburg.

Another SS man appeared on the terrace with Eva's two Scotties leading the way. She said nothing to him as he handed her their leashes. 'Negus, Stasi, sit!' The spunky black dogs did as they were told and sat looking at her with their pink tongues hanging out. The SS man saluted and turned on his heels.

Eva smirked. 'They're so formal. I suppose they have to be.' She paused and then asked, 'Do you have a boyfriend?'

I knew anything I'd say would get back to Hitler. If I gave her Karl's name, it might make it easier for us to see each other; on the other hand, the connection would bond us together for either good or bad. I'd been told that one of Hitler's private secretaries had married an SS officer because the Führer enjoyed seeing them together. He'd played the role of fatherly matchmaker and the two had eventually given in. I hoped my answer might make things easier for Karl and me. 'Captain Weber took me to your showing of

*Gone with the Wind,* and we've been on walks and to dances.'

Eva smiled. 'Oh, Captain Weber. A fine officer and handsome man. The Führer depends upon him. He would be an admired and respected husband.'

I fought to keep from blushing. 'We have no marriage plans. We barely know each other.'

Eva petted one of the dogs and said, 'That could change. When the war is over, everyone who served will be honored. Karl and you will have a happy home and many children for the Reich.'

I looked away wanting to finish the conversation about my private life.

'Wasn't it horrible about the other taster?' Eva asked.

Her eyes snared me and I knew I must be cautious in my response. I remembered Cook's words about what to do under questioning. I looked at her and said, 'Yes. She must have gone mad to do such a thing. I never suspected.'

'That's why the Führer has people like you and Karl working for him. We must protect him; otherwise, all is lost.' She smiled, but panic also flashed in her eyes. Perhaps she sensed, or knew, the war was going badly. 'Why, even young women are suspect. One was captured and tried in Munich in February for handing out leaflets that maligned the Führer and the Party. A word of advice, Magda – never trust anyone. You cannot be too cautious. Remain loyal – but what am I saying? I know you will be.'

I hesitated, but then asked, 'What happened to the woman?'

'Her head was cut off.' Eva gave an uncomfortable laugh, rose from the railing and pulled on the dogs' leashes. 'Adolf despises such nasty business.' She held out her hand. 'I suppose it will be a while before we see each other again.'

I nodded and shook her hand; it was cold to the touch. She said good night and I did likewise. The SS man was still in the corner. I wanted to find out if Eva was telling the truth about the woman who had been beheaded, so I decided to ask the officer. My question would be risky, but I reasoned I would get an answer if I told him I was trying to find out for Eva. He had certainly seen her on the terrace with me.

He barely gave me a glance as I approached. Apparently, he was a sentry assigned to look out over the grounds and the SS guardhouse below. He had taken a seat on the stone railing. His shoulders were hunched with boredom; there was little to guard when Hitler was away. Even the skies were clear from threats. A few Allied planes had flown over recently. The air-raid sirens sounded, but no bombs were dropped.

'Excuse me,' I said. 'I was talking with Fräulein Braun. She heard about a woman who was arrested for handing out leaflets in Munich. Eva wanted me to find out more about her.' I used her first name to make it sound as if we were friends.

The officer looked at me oddly, as if sizing me up, but answered my question to be rid of me. 'Sophie . . . Sophie something or other. She was tried and convicted of treason, as were her brother and a few other conspirators. They worked for an underground organization. I don't remember the name.' He stared out over the valley, bored with my intrusion.

'What happened to them?'

He turned, his blue eyes ablaze. 'What happened to them? What should happen to all traitors – they were guillotined. That I remember. Good riddance.'

He must have caught the look of horror in my eyes, for he shook his head as if to pity my weakness. He turned and stared at the dark mountains. I thanked him and left the terrace.

That evening as I lay in bed, I longed for Karl and wondered about the young woman who was executed for handing out anti-Nazi tracts. Hitler only accepted blind obedience to the Party. If Karl and I dared step out of line, we would be killed. A terrifying thought struck me: *Karl and I have already crossed that line.*

The next morning at breakfast, Cook relayed orders that we were to be in Rastenburg in three days. The communication came directly from Hitler. It was a two-day trip by train. I was happy about seeing Karl again, but somewhat surprised that Cook and I had been summoned.

'He likes my cooking,' she said in response to my questioning. 'You'll join the other tasters at the Wolf's Lair.'

'All of us?'

She shrugged. 'It's not up to us to question the Führer's orders.' She leaned close and whispered, 'I think it has to do with the size of the staff in Rastenburg and the incident here with Ursula. He and Captain Weber are being cautious.'

I imagined the food lined up on a table with each woman tasting a single dish. If one died then another would take her place, perhaps within the hour, like a deadly assembly line. Each death would be counted as a victory for the Führer, a sacrifice for the good of the Reich.

'You may leave after breakfast,' Cook said, and handed me a small gold book with few pages in it. The Reich eagle was emblazoned in black on its front cover. 'Keep this with you at all times. It verifies that you work for the Führer.'

I opened it and one of the pictures taken of me in Berchtesgaden stared back. The book stated I was 'to be granted all special privileges,' as a member of Hitler's staff. I was free, under his orders, to travel in Germany, or any territory of the Reich.

I'd been thinking about going home to Berlin for some time because I hadn't seen my mother and father in months. My job and blossoming relationship with Karl had consumed my time. An extra day away from the demands of the Reich was a gift to be savored. 'I'd like to visit my parents,' I told Cook.

'As long as you're at the Wolf's Lair in three days you can do as you like, but tell no one where you're going.'

After breakfast, I said good-bye to the staff who remained and quickly packed my things. The bare room looked forlorn and, for an instant, I had a memory of Ursula reclining on her bed, lighting a cigarette, blowing smoke out the window so she wouldn't get caught. I admired her courage, but faulted her planning. She took on Hitler and failed. As Karl had pointed out, hasty actions, like those of Ursula, ended badly. One had to proceed with caution and an abundance of planning. I pushed such notions from my head. The very thought of bringing Hitler down seemed impossible.

An SS car took me to the train station in Berchtesgaden. I had no time to visit Uncle Willy and Aunt Reina; I was in no mood to talk with them anyway. I wanted no questions about Hitler, or their encouragement about how wonderful it was to serve the Führer.

I arrived in Berlin late in the evening. The city surprised me with its vibrancy. I had gotten used to the quiet mountain solitude of the Berghof. The lights, the chug of motorcars, the hundreds of smells – each inviting a memory – made Berlin seem oddly new to me. It was as if I were seeing it for the first time.

I made my way to my parents' apartment. Their street was quiet, away from the bustle, and, other than the blackout, the war seemed far away. There had been no major Allied bombings since Hitler's birthday. The trees were in full leaf and their boughs cast dark shadows on the surrounding buildings. Slivers of light traced the outlines of a few windows. Sometimes the curtains would undulate in the breeze and a block of light from someone's apartment would splash upon the sidewalk, only to be dissolved in an instant. A phonograph played in one house. The tune was melancholy but sweet, a lovely female voice praising the soldier who had gone to war for the Reich. The world seemed peaceful, and its serenity filled me with a sense of calm that had escaped me for months. I realized then that my job had taken its toll. My first hint was when I enjoyed a meal on the train. I was happy to be away from tasting, to just enjoy food and not worry that every bite could kill me.

I pushed the buzzer and waited. I hadn't called because I wanted my visit to be a surprise. After a few more rings, my father came to the door in his robe. The hall was dark. His eyes scrunched up in a squint. The look of dismay on his face turned to a smile as soon as he recognized me. He swept me into his arms and nearly knocked the breath out of me with his hug.

'Magda, Magda,' he said with tear-filled eyes. 'My God, how your mother and I have missed you.' He released me from his grip.

I stood on the stoop holding my bag. 'May I come in?'

He took a few steps backward and said, 'Of course, how silly of me.'

My mother appeared at the bedroom door, her eyes half-closed from sleep. She rushed toward me without saying a word and embraced me like my father had. After we exchanged kisses and hugs I was allowed inside.

'Are you home for good?' my father asked warily. The tone of his question made it clear that he still wanted me out of Berlin.

I put my bag on the floor next to the coat stand. 'Only overnight; then I have to catch a train by noon tomorrow to—' I couldn't tell my parents where I was going.

'Come to the kitchen,' my mother said. 'I want to hear all about what you're doing. We have two tea bags left for the week. I'll make a pot. I'm too excited to sleep.'

My father nodded and we walked to the kitchen. My mother lit a candle and then my father and I sat at the small oak table while my mother made tea. She fidgeted with the kettle and the water and then turned to me with wide eyes. 'What is he like?' Like most Germans, she was fascinated by the Führer, a man she had never seen.

'Lisa,' my father said. 'You're not the Gestapo. Did you stop to think that Magda might not be able to talk about him?'

My mother's eagerness faded with a scowl. 'No.' She went back to the tea.

'I've never met him,' I said. 'I've seen him a few times at the Berghof and once near the Teahouse.'

'He has a teahouse?' my mother asked, astonished that such a thing existed.

'He has afternoon tea and apple cake there with his guests,'

I said, feeling that such information could cause no harm. 'It looks like a castle turret set into the forest. I've even talked to Eva Braun several times.'

No hint of recognition flickered in my parents' eyes. How stupid of me to mention her name. Of course, they wouldn't know who she was. Eva was a secret known only to a few. I dropped the subject.

My father settled in his chair. 'What do you do?' He asked the question casually, as if he expected the answer of a 'normal' job, such as a bookkeeper or accountant.

My stomach turned over – I didn't want to create needless anxiety by telling them I was a taster and that my life was in danger every day. Living in Berlin, my parents had enough to worry about. 'I work in the kitchen. I'm responsible for the food inventories and kitchen supplies.' It was a partial truth.

My mother returned to the table with three porcelain cups. While waiting for the kettle to boil, she sat next to me and held my hand. 'I'm proud of you and so relieved. Such a good job, isn't it, Hermann?'

My father nodded, but I could tell by his frown he was less than enthusiastic about any job connected with National Socialism. I asked about Frau Horst and our neighbors to shift the conversation away from me. Until we went to bed, we talked about my parents' work and the mood in Berlin.

My mother was cleaning breakfast dishes by the time I got up the next morning. My father was sitting in the dining room drinking a cup of tea before he left for work.

'I was about to wake you up,' he said, 'to say good-bye.' His eyes were dim, as if life had become an insufferable chore, a series of days strung together to be barely tolerated. 'Thank you for not telling your mother,' he said softly.

My heart skipped a beat. 'I don't know what you're talking about.'

'Of course you do.' His tone was flat, unemotional. 'Uncle Willy found out what you do through his connections to the SS. Berchtesgaden is a small place.' He cupped his hands round his teacup. 'He and Reina, of course, are ecstatic about your position. They couldn't be happier. I begged him not to tell your mother because I don't want her to worry.' He took a sip of tea and then put his cup on the table. 'To them there is no sacrifice too great for the Führer.' He put his hands in his lap and looked toward the kitchen.

I whispered for fear my mother would hear, 'I had no idea what my position would be. It was the job they gave me.' It felt good to share this with my father. I now understood why he cried when he saw me.

He sighed. 'Your mother, who thinks washing dishes is still important while the world burns, believes the Reich will win the war. She has no idea about the rumors that circulate. I fear the worst for us all, Magda. It's like we live in some manufactured world that's shrinking day by day. I can feel the walls tumbling on Germany, on Berlin, on us.'

I trembled, afraid to look him in the eye. 'What rumors do you hear?'

'That we have lost great battles in the East, that the tide has turned and that the easy victories Hitler forged in the early years are over. I would never speak to your mother of such things. She would throw me out of the house.' He laughed. 'You cannot depend upon the *Volkischer Beobachter* for an accurate reporting of the war. The Party paper is not fit to line the canary cage.'

'You must never tell anyone what you've told me,' I said

firmly. 'Keep your politics to yourself, and don't stir the pot. I, too, have heard rumors, and I know things I can't tell you. Believe me, there are people who want to end this war for the good of Germany.'

He smiled and his eyes showed a spark of life for the first time since I'd arrived. Perhaps I had given him the small hope that things might change for the better.

'I want to breathe in your words,' he said. 'There is so little for me to believe in.' He reached across the table and clutched my hands. Outside the window, the world looked sunny and cheerful, but like everything else, the pleasant weather was illusory, a distraction from the truth. He gripped my fingers. 'Please be careful.'

I assured him I would, but my father's fears infected me. My small respite from Hitler and the Berghof felt like a deceit. We were trapped in a make-believe world propagated by the Reich while all around us battles were being fought, troops slaughtered and innocents butchered. Our sense of well-being and safety was shrinking, and only a fool would believe that our way of life could continue. However, there were many fools still to be convinced. The Reich was doing its job well. People still believed in Hitler and his fiery rhetoric – to fight for Germany to the end, until the last man, woman and child had died for the Reich. I couldn't hold on too long to that thought, for I felt the world might collapse around me.

My father kissed me and my mother good-bye and left the apartment. My mother and I sat at breakfast and, as my father predicted, we talked about the things in life that got her through the day: food, laundry, housecleaning, growing a garden. In normal times, these were innocuous but pleasant subjects. However, our days were far from normal. Conversations about food and rationing took on monumental importance.

With my father's sense of a collapsing Germany closing in on me, I said farewell to my mother in the afternoon and boarded a train for the Wolf's Lair in East Prussia. She, also, shed a few tears as I departed. I told her I would return when I could, but I had no idea what lay ahead. As I boarded the train, I wondered whether I'd ever see my parents again.

# CHAPTER 8

I left Berlin about five in the evening bound for Rastenburg. The conductor awarded me a sleeping car when he saw my 'in service to the Führer' identification papers. The overnight trip was uneventful except for one long stop in the middle of Poland when the train halted because of a threat from Allied bombers. The night porter knocked on every door and explained the situation. I lifted the blackout curtain in my car and wondered how any bomber could target the train on a moonless night. Black woods surrounded us; we were no longer rolling through the fertile plains of eastern Germany. I slept fitfully, with one eye open the rest of the night, despite the train's concealment by the deep forest.

We arrived about nine in the morning. It was a rather desolate station surrounded by trees and little to recommend it in the way of scenery or pomp. I gathered my suitcase and descended the steps to the platform. Two other young women stood nearby, looking as lost as I did. Both had dark blond hair, but one was taller than the other and seemed to be in control of her shorter companion. The taller one craned her swan-like neck, as if looking for something. I barely had time to put my bag on the ground when a stout SS officer strode toward me, grim and composed.

'Fräulein Ritter,' he said in a commanding tone.

I was surprised he knew who I was.

'The cooking staff is expecting you,' he continued. 'You will take the courier train to the Wolf's Lair.' He left me and then addressed the two young women on the platform. He directed us to another train on a railroad siding, and, after a few minutes' wait, it pulled away into the forest. I introduced myself to the women who sat across from me, for on this train the benches ran along the side of the car. The taller woman was named Minna; and the shorter, Else. They were new tasters from Berlin and had been chosen for service with Cook by the SS, with the approval of Hitler.

Minna settled against the brocade seat with an air of authority and smoothed her skirt with her hands. Her lips shone slickly through bright red lipstick and her eyebrows were penciled in severe dark lines — far more dramatic than most women would require. Cruelty emanated from her full mouth. She would be trouble, a woman who hung on every word spouted by the Reich and more than willing to die in service to the Führer. On the other hand, Else was pretty with round eyes, a petite mouth and a shy demeanor. Whether she intended to, she looked upon Minna as her guide. Else, I decided, would follow anyone who made up her mind for her — a perfect candidate for the position of taster. If the Gestapo asked her to swallow poison, she probably would.

'What is *he* like?' Minna asked with a sideways glance of superiority.

I did not want to coddle her. 'I've been asked that question many times. You'll be lucky to catch a glimpse of him, let alone have a conversation.'

Minna glowered. 'I'll talk to him. In fact, I'm certain I will know him quite well.' She swung one well-shaped leg over the other.

She had no idea about Eva Braun and Hitler's relationship. I wanted to laugh, but I felt I would be giving away too much. Instead, I sat back and tried to enjoy the forest scenery as it passed by in dark green patches of pine, birch and oak.

Else asked, 'Are you scared when you taste?'

Even though I had only been in the job a few months, I could at least trumpet my seniority. 'It's a dangerous job. I was nervous at first. You never know which meal will be your last.'

Else gulped and stared at me. Minna laughed and then smiled in a high-handed way.

'Don't be silly, Else,' she scolded. 'You will never have to worry. From now on you will lead a charmed life. You will enjoy the best rooms, secure and safe from harm. You will eat the best meals, with no fear of being poisoned because who would dare raise a hand against the leader of the Third Reich? You will revel in the company of the Führer himself. What woman could ask for more? We will live like queens while the rest of Germany defends the Fatherland. If the Wehrmacht falls, we will be protected by the Führer. Let the German people eat cake, as Marie Antoinette would say.'

Else, afraid to contradict Minna, stared at her companion like a scared puppy. A slow fire burned within me and I wanted to slap sense into this boastful woman. But I could not in any way betray my feelings. I had bigger worries –

Karl, my parents, the lingering specter of death – to be concerned about than that of a braggart consumed by pride and stupidity.

Soon our journey ended at a little station in the woods. The portly SS man who had taken us to the train appeared in the door and instructed us to depart. I stepped onto the platform. I knew we were at the Führer's headquarters, but no buildings were visible. Another train sat on a siding nearby. The station was surrounded by a thicket ripe with trees and bushes. Bugs swarmed around our heads in the clammy air. The officer led us down a wooded path where small bunkers and huts, hidden by camouflage, appeared among the vegetation. In a few minutes, we reached a checkpoint where a young guard asked the SS man for a password. The guard then studied our identification papers, told us to drop our bags and turn in a circle. We did so and he seemed satisfied. I imagined he was looking for bulges in our clothing where we might conceal a weapon. He searched our purses and bags. Confident that we had no weapons, he handed us a small passport for the Wolf's Lair and ordered us to keep it with us at all times. Then we passed through the gate of an electrified fence.

We moved on, following the SS man, through the woods until we came to a section where the bunkers were more visible. These low, fortified structures extended into the forest on both sides as far as I could see. Camouflage netting hung over everything, a protection against air attacks. The camp also supported a few buildings made of wood and concrete that looked more like meeting halls with windows.

At last we came to an unpleasant structure. It had small windows on its façade, which was buttressed by a heavy iron door. As marginally inviting as the outside appeared, the inside conjured thoughts of hell. My lungs sucked in warm and humid air in the cramped space. I felt as if I were breathing through a damp towel.

The officer directed us down a narrow hall that reminded me of pictures I'd seen of steamship interiors. He opened a second enclosure and a series of smaller wooden doors appeared ahead on both sides. The last room on the right was ours. He flipped a switch. A single bulb covered by a green metal shade cast a triangular patch of light on the floor. Four beds, two on each side of the room, were positioned against the walls. A locker sat next to each bed. The accommodations made my room at the Berghof seem like a palace. The room here contained barely enough space for the beds, let alone four women. There were no windows. I took a deep breath and fought against the sickening claustrophobia that jabbed at me from all sides.

'These are our quarters?' Minna asked the SS man with obvious distaste.

Again, I wanted to laugh because the first of her illusions had been shattered. The bunker's living conditions were far from what Minna had described to Else as the 'best accommodations.'

The officer glared at her. 'You're lucky to be here. Don't complain if you have any sense.' With that admonition, he left. I inspected the room. Except for the beds – four small-framed cots covered with gray blankets – and the lockers, the room was empty. One of the beds was already taken. The sheets were neatly folded down. A leather bag sat under its middle.

Air circulated with a whoosh through a vent located in the room's ceiling. This annoying mechanical feature kept us alive underneath thick layers of concrete and earth.

Else threw her bag on a bed and began to cry.

'Hush up,' Minna said. 'Weeping will do you no good.'

'I can't live here,' Else said. 'No one told us his headquarters would be like this. I expected it to be like the Reich Chancellery.' She collapsed on her bed. The Berlin Chancellery was vast and opulent, with the finest furnishings, paintings and carpets. Open–air gardens surrounded the buildings. Here, we were reduced to living like subterranean animals.

I claimed the bed nearest the door and put my bag under it. Even I was dismayed at the conditions we were being forced to live in. 'I'm sure we'll spend a lot of time away from this room – for our own good.' I felt emboldened by my seniority. 'I'm going for a walk. No one said we had to remain inside.'

Else looked at me as if I were deserting her. She leaned forward on her cot. 'May I go with you? I don't care if there are bugs. I feel sick.'

I didn't want her tagging along because I hoped to run into Karl, but the door opened and my plan was interrupted. A pallid young woman who looked as if she had spent too much time inside the bunker stepped into the room. She had a thin nose and large eyes. She could have been pretty, but in the harsh light she looked tired and washed out. I could tell her hair had been lightened by coloring.

'I'm Dora,' she said, and extended her hand to me because I was nearest to her. I introduced myself while Minna sized up Dora in her bird–like way. Else smiled and wiped at her tears, pleased to see another woman who might be a friend.

'Who are *you*?' Minna asked, seating herself like a queen on the remaining bed.

Dora's eyes narrowed. She had the same reaction to Minna

that I did. 'Dora Schiffer, the Head Taster at the Wolf's Lair.' She looked at Minna and Else. 'You two must be the new girls. You are to come with me to be introduced to the cook and the rest of the staff. Magda, you will be in the kitchen at seven to taste. You have the rest of the day free to do as you wish.'

Minna scowled. 'We take orders from you?'

Dora folded her arms. 'Yes.'

'We shall see,' Minna muttered.

'There's nothing to see,' Dora said, 'because I outrank you in every way. You are under my charge. This is my room and it's up to me to make sure you do your duty.' She reached into a pocket on her dress and pulled out a book similar to the one we'd been given at the gate. She passed it around the room. Dora was an SS member. According to the markings in her book, she had previously been assigned to a place I didn't recognize – Treblinka.

'Do we have time to freshen up?' Minna asked.

'Make it fast,' Dora said. 'The bathroom is at the end of the hall.' After Minna and Else left the room, Dora stood in the doorway and looked at me. 'So, I have at least one troublemaker to deal with. Enjoy the day, but be careful not to venture beyond the fences. There are three perimeters around headquarters. Guards with dogs are posted every thirty meters. They will ask you for your papers.' She brushed a finger across her lip. 'Land mines surround the Wolf's Lair. Be careful. A foolish mistake could cost you your life.' She studied me as if she were interrogating me.

I stared back.

'Heil Hitler.' She closed the door and left me alone.

I gave them plenty of time to find their way out. Apparently, this residence was for women only. I found a bathroom with shower stalls not far from our door, and an office and small library that had been constructed near the entrance. The latter had windows that looked out on the headquarters grounds. The view was limited to the forest, but the windows were screened and open. No hint of a breeze came in through the mesh.

I sat in one of the cushioned library chairs and pondered my fate. Sweat formed on my face and arms in the late morning heat, even though the sun was muted by the netting and leafy trees. It was as if a green pall had been cast over the headquarters. Only the buzzing of the mosquitoes and flies that pressed their black bodies against the screens entered my ears. Still, I imagined sleeping here would be better than in my cramped room.

I got out of the chair and perused the books on the shelves. Most were German history and mythology; others, on topics of science. I wondered if they were Hitler's or had been placed here by someone else. One title in particular attracted my attention: *The Origin of Species* by Charles Darwin. Faint recollections from my schooling flitted through my mind. I didn't remember much of what the book was about, so I opened it and turned to the overleaf. The page was stamped in black ink with the Nazi eagle and engraved: *Given to the women of the Wolf's Lair by the Führer.* Hitler had signed his name below the inscription. I put the book back on the shelf and left the room.

I walked quickly down the path outside my quarters, swatting at the flies that buzzed around me. One could hardly enjoy the day outside with such pests. They landed on my arms, my face, any exposed skin, nearly covering me. The humid scent of the woods filled the air. As I stood, unsure of which direction to go, it became clear to me why Hitler had chosen this particular spot for his eastern headquarters. Unlike the scenic majesty of the Berghof, the Wolf's Lair was a swamp in a godforsaken land. No enemy of the Reich could reach it except through fierce fighting in the inhospitable terrain — if they could find it.

It was almost eleven and my stomach growled. I had eaten two small meals on the train, but it had been many hours since I'd had food or drink. I headed east and skirted the fence that enclosed our area in the woods, the inner perimeter Dora referred to. Members of the RSD, an SS security force, were stationed at checkpoints around the fence. Many high-ranking SS men walked through along the path, but I saw no women. I stopped at a checkpoint and asked the guard for directions to the mess hall. He asked me for my papers and, satisfied that I belonged within the compound, told me how I could find it, which was several hundred meters away.

I walked past several buildings until I reached it, constructed of concrete and stone, low to the ground, although not a bunker. It had windows, and was more pleasant inside than my quarters. Long tables and chairs were lined up in three straight rows. The large kitchen in the back bustled with activity. An orderly opened a double door and gave me a peek at the gleaming stoves and other appliances inside. Minna and Else were nowhere to be seen, but I recognized a man, a cook from the Berghof.

Fruit and oatmeal sat on the hall serving table, so I helped myself and topped them with milk and honey. The men and women at the Wolf's Lair, like those at Hitler's mountain residence, were well fed.

I sat by myself at one of the long tables, for breakfast was long over for most of the staff. I was enjoying my food when someone tapped my shoulder. It was Karl.

I wanted to jump up from my seat and kiss him, but he kept his hand firmly pressed upon my shoulder. 'Don't smile or act as if you are friendly with me.' His voice was tight and controlled.

I ate another bite of oatmeal and kept my face forward while he stood behind me. 'It's a pleasure to see you again, too, Captain Weber.'

'Please, Magda, don't joke. The situation is more dangerous than you can imagine. Meet me at ten tonight by the cinema and I'll explain.'

'Dora Schiffer is keeping track of us. She seems a strict disciplinarian.'

After a brief silence, Karl sighed and then said, 'Oh, you've met. Tell her you're going to the movie and you'll be back when it's over.'

I nodded and turned my head to catch a glimpse of him as he strode through the door. I finished my food, took my dishes back to the serving table and left the mess hall. I walked back to my quarters, but couldn't force myself to go into my room. I sat in the empty library and thought of my father's words about how Germany was shrinking because of Hitler's actions. It was true. I felt more and more like a captive, even though I worked for the most powerful man in Europe. I worried about Karl as well. Melancholy shrouded me like an immense dark cloud. I fidgeted in the chair and studied the book titles on the shelves until I dozed into an uneasy sleep. When I awoke, Dora Schiffer was standing in the doorway smiling at me.

'I wish to talk to you about Ursula Thalberg's poisoning,' she said, and my heart leapt into my throat.

Dora was well acquainted with interrogation techniques. Like the woman in Berchtesgaden who worked for the Reichsbund, Dora asked me every question on a list prepared by the Reich, and also a few of her own. Most of them I'd answered before, but some I hadn't. She was particularly curious about the relationships I had with the staff at the Wolf's Lair. I told her the truth, but I did not embellish my answers: I knew Cook and Captain Weber from my work at the Berghof, and many of the kitchen workers who were transferred here to serve the Führer. Dora asked me about Ursula – the second time I'd been questioned at length about my former roommate and her poisoning. She concluded her questioning by telling me I should be wary of Minna. The new taster, she said, was a woman who was out to work her way up through the Reich by finding favor with Hitler – of that, Dora was certain. Any misstep and Minna would find herself out of a job and back in Berlin. After listening to Dora, I believed that Minna could find herself in far worse circumstances than out of a job. Before she left, she reiterated her order for me to be at the kitchen before seven, the same one I'd been in earlier in the day.

After she had dismissed me, I returned to my room, stored my things, showered and changed into fresh clothes. Minna and Else were missing, and I wondered if Cook was already instructing them on poisons.

When I arrived at the kitchen, I found the two women sitting against the wall still dressed in the clothes they'd worn on the train. They looked exhausted from their day spent

121

with a cook named Otto, whom I had seen at the Berghof. Hitler liked the way Otto prepared eggs and had snatched him from a sanatorium where he worked. I asked about Cook and was told that she was not feeling well and wouldn't be working tonight.

Minna and Else said nothing, only stared at me, as Otto set up the dishes to be served to Hitler. The July fruits and vegetables were in season. Most of them had been shipped from the Berghof greenhouses. A steaming egg and potato dish sat at the center of the table. Otto nodded for me to begin. First I smelled the food and then tasted it. I ate fresh cucumbers and tomatoes, green beans and boiled potatoes with parsley before I came to an egg dish. A mushroom sat next to it. I wasn't sure whether it was poisonous, but I didn't want my lack of memory or courage to slow my work. I lifted a large spoonful of the egg dish and smelled it. An inviting, creamy scent filled my nostrils; I decided it was safe to eat. It tasted delicious: warm, buttery and fulfilling.

I continued down the line tasting strawberries, apple cake and an iced cake I'd never eaten before. After I was through, Otto took the dishes away, but left the mushroom on the table. As was the case after most tastings, my stomach felt full. I sat next to Else and she gripped my hand. I turned to look at her. Her bead-like eyes flickered with fear.

'The egg dish contained poisonous mushrooms,' she whispered.

I wanted to laugh. How ridiculous would it be for a cook to poison a taster? 'He wouldn't do *that*.'

'Of course he would.' Minna stared smugly at me.

A few moments later, Dora Schiffer propped her thin frame against the kitchen door. She waved her long arms at

Minna and Else and they got up to follow her. Dora returned a short time later and asked, 'How are you feeling? You look a little pale.' She towered over me like a tall bean stalk.

'Fine,' I said, beginning to wonder if I had been wrong.

'Remain seated, just to be safe.'

I watched as the staff transferred many of the dishes I'd tasted to serving platters and then took them away for Hitler's eight o'clock dinner. Soon a sweat broke out on my brow and my heart pounded fiercely. Overwhelmed by nausea, I clutched my chair.

Dora noticed and came to my side. 'Something's wrong,' I told her. I reached for the table but, instead, slipped off the chair onto my knees.

Dora clapped her hands and Otto ran from the kitchen. He leaned over me. 'Feeling poorly?' he asked.

'What did you do to me?' I groaned and doubled over in pain.

'I think you've learned your lesson,' Otto said. 'You should take nothing for granted.'

My head swam in a vicious circle and I retched on the floor, unable to control my stomach. Otto's round face stared down at me. He seemed more interested in my reaction to the poison than helping. I collapsed in a heap and the world went black.

# CHAPTER 9

A man stood by my bedside when I awoke in the head-quarters medical facility. The room blazed with light from the overhead bulbs. I wondered how long I'd been uncon-scious. My stomach ached and my parched throat longed for water. I blinked and Karl's blurry form came into focus. He smiled at me piteously and then sat in a chair next to the bed.

'What time is it?' My voice hardly carried above a whisper.

'Almost noon,' Karl said. He handed me a glass of water. 'Take a drink – it will do you good. You've vomited everything out of your body. They used a stomach pump as well. I came as soon as I heard. I've been here all night.' He punched his fist against his thigh. 'I should kill that thug for what he did to you.'

I sipped the water. The cool liquid soothed my throat.

'He deliberately poisoned you,' he said. 'Otto put poisonous mushrooms in the dish – not the kind that can kill, only make you ill. It was a game for him. His clue was the mushroom near the food. Cook was furious when she found out. She went directly to the Führer. He was less than sympathetic. He told Cook he understood the pain you must be going through, but such actions were for the good of the Reich and the protection of its leader. He said such tests were a valuable training tool. They taught the other tasters not to be complacent.'

In an odd way, Hitler was right, although I hated to admit it. 'Have I lost my job?' I tried to lift my head, but the room spun in a circle.

'No. You're still on staff, but you'll be doing inventory for a few weeks until you recover. That bastard cook – he's a street brawler like the rest of them. They have no morals, no compunction against killing their own citizens. They'll destroy everything.' Karl's voice rose as he talked. I had enough sense to lift a finger to my lips. What he was saying was dangerous, even though we seemed to be alone.

He clutched my hand and his fingers felt warm against mine. I wanted to kiss him.

'I have to leave. I'm happy that you're better.' His eyes took me in from head to toe. 'We need to talk, but it's better to wait until you're stronger.'

I patted his hand and he said good-bye. I didn't see him again for several days, until I got out of the hospital and back to the kitchen.

Over the next few days, Karl made it clear he did not want to talk to me. He only nodded when we passed in the mess hall. If I initiated a conversation he would cut me off with a curt, 'I can't talk now, Fräulein Ritter.' I was lucky if he smiled at me. I believed a plan, some secret operation, must be in the works and it scared me. Karl was distancing himself. Our relationship had been much more loving at the Berghof.

Else and Minna limited their contact with me as well, apparently because I had failed them on their first evening in the mess hall. Else hated her position as a taster, but she was still under Minna's thumb. She would approach me, as if she wanted to talk, but then retreat out of caution. I avoided Otto. If the Führer supported his foul trick, it would do no good to confront him.

Several weeks went by and Hitler was called away to Berlin for a few days. Cook and three of the other tasters I knew only in passing accompanied him. Minna and Else stayed behind. Because I was now charged with keeping food inventories and helping in the kitchen, rather than tasting, my evenings were free.

One afternoon Karl stopped me on the path to the mess hall and asked me to meet him that evening at ten outside the cinema, a plan similar to the one he had proposed the night I got sick. I mentioned to Dora I was attending a film and might take a walk afterwards. I suspected she would think nothing of it because all of us were eager to spend time out of our cramped quarters.

The evening was cool, but humid. Low clouds hung over the Wolf's Lair. Occasionally rain pattered against my shoulders. There was little light to guide me, but I'd been here long enough to find my way around. The faint sounds of stringed instruments and theatrical voices emanated from the cinema. The movie was in progress.

I turned the corner on the north side of the building and saw a figure under a stand of trees. The orange glow of a cigarette flared briefly. My nerves tightened. Karl had given up smoking. As I got closer, I called out his name. A dark figure waved to me.

'Is that you?' I asked. The man didn't answer and I thought of running away.

I repeated my question. He stood silent for a time and then crushed out his cigarette.

I was about to turn when he whispered my name. It was Franz, Ursula's boyfriend and an SS officer like Karl.

He held out his hand. 'It's good to see you again, Magda.'

I grasped it. 'I didn't know you were here.'

'I arrived a couple of days ago. I'm here for a few weeks, then I'm headed to the Eastern Front, to command a panzer division. Some of the generals have consented to talk to those of us who are about to give our lives for the Reich.' He chuckled.

I peered through the black stands of trees, searching for Karl, but didn't see him.

'He's coming,' Franz said, soothing my fear. 'He was delayed a few minutes by orders from Berlin.'

I couldn't understand why Franz was invited to a meeting between Karl and me, but I dared not ask.

Franz leaned against a tree and reached into his jacket for another cigarette.

'Isn't it dangerous to light them at night?' I asked. 'Bombers can see the flame.'

Franz laughed. 'I doubt the Allies can see through all this netting. Anyway, to hell with it. Hitler isn't here and I could give a damn what happens. The whole place could be bombed to pieces as far as I'm concerned. Besides, the smoke keeps the bugs away.' The bitterness in his voice underscored his pain. I suspected much of it had to do with Ursula's death.

My curiosity got the better of me. 'What's going on? Why isn't Karl here?'

Franz lit the cigarette, took in a deep breath and let the smoke seep from his lungs. The scent of burning tobacco hung heavy in the damp air. 'Karl will tell you what he can.' He leaned forward and whispered, 'There isn't much time left to save Germany. I won't be at the Wolf's Lair long and neither will Karl if our plan works. For your sake, don't get too attached to either of us, Magda. We know what needs to be done and we might not come out alive.'

His words struck me like bullets.

'My world crumbled when Ursula died,' Franz said. 'She was a wonderful woman who loved her family more than she loved life. She sacrificed herself to save Germany. Hitler and the rest of them can go to hell. Ursula and I were to be married.'

'I'm sorry,' I said, shaken by his admission. 'I didn't know. Ursula never told me.'

'We kept our plans secret because life—' His voice cracked. 'Life is so uncertain, so unkind, it's hardly worth living.' He groaned. 'Every day I ask myself why I should endure this torture. I suppose I do it for Ursula.'

'How—'

'—Please, Magda, the less you know about this the better. Don't force Karl to tell you.'

A chill swept over me. I was about to respond when he said, 'Quiet. Someone is coming.'

I turned. Another figure approached us through the gloom. The man, dressed in a dark uniform, walked swiftly, brushing past the trees. It was Karl. He put his hand on my shoulder and addressed Franz. 'Everything is in readiness. When the time is right, I'll act.'

'What are you talking about?' I asked. 'You're frightening me.'

Karl ignored me.

'I will be there,' Franz said. 'We are brothers.' He shook Karl's hand and then saluted him by holding his hand over his brow. Franz grasped my hands and kissed my cheek. 'Good-bye, Magda. It's unlikely we will ever meet again. Good health and happiness.' He crushed his cigarette underfoot and walked away.

Trembling, Karl collapsed against the tree.

I begged him to tell me what was wrong. For a long time, he wouldn't speak. I held his hands and listened to his breath slip in and out of his body. I looked to make sure no one was near. We were barely visible in the feeble light. I drew him close. He placed his head next to mine and his tears ran down my cheek.

'Karl, please tell me.'

His lips brushed against my throat and a jolt like an electrical charge skittered over my body.

'Kiss me,' he said.

I pressed against him and our lips met, playing out our passion. I placed my hands in the small of his back and pulled him toward me. He held me close and showered me with kisses. Suddenly, he jerked away.

'No, no, this is wrong,' he said, and leaned against the tree. 'There's no time for us. It's over.'

'Why?' I asked. Sorrow welled up within me. 'Are you going to die?'

'Perhaps.' He kissed me, opened his jacket and then a few buttons on his shirt. He guided my hand to his heart. 'Do you feel it beating?'

His heart pounded with strength and power under my fingers. I wanted to find a secluded spot in the forest and make love until we were spent from ecstasy. I let my fingers caress his skin.

He clasped his hand over mine, stopping me from exploring his body. He kissed me again. 'I want to make love to you, but more than that I want you to love me. Forever. If only I could predict the future.'

'No one can do that.' I snuggled closer to him. 'Not now.' His words had stoked my passion. 'I want to make love to you, too. Forever doesn't matter.'

'But what if we had a child?' he whispered, his face close to mine. 'How could we bring it into this world? It wouldn't be right. I asked you to come tonight because I want you to know why it's impossible for us to be together.'

I shook against him.

'But you must stay strong whatever happens,' he continued. His tone shifted, as solemn as the darkness that surrounded us. 'In a few days, there will be a military display at the Berghof. Franz and I will be there with Hitler. The course of history must be changed.'

I pressed my head against his chest. 'Tell me this isn't happening – now that we've discovered love and a chance for happiness.'

'You're wrong, Magda. There'll be no happiness until this evil is eradicated.'

'Then let someone else do it. Let Franz – or let me.' As awful as my words were, I meant them.

He sighed. 'Don't be silly. Your parents are still alive. Mine are gone. Hitler can't hurt anyone I love – except you.'

Karl's profession of love warmed me, but my joy was short-lived. Through the haze of my feelings, sounds filtered out of the cinema: subdued voices, the scraping of chairs. The doors opened and people shuffled down the path.

'We must get back,' Karl said. 'You go first.'

'I love you.' The words were out of my mouth before I knew it. They felt powerful and natural. I'd thought about love many times, but had never said the words aloud to Karl. Now I loved a man plotting to kill Hitler.

I walked away, but turned briefly. Karl nodded, encouraging me to go ahead. I stepped into the crowd leaving the cinema. As I walked toward my quarters, I saw Minna on the other side of the building, in the corner opposite where Karl and I had been talking. I wondered whether she might have been spying on us or overheard our conversation. She waved when she saw me, lit a cigarette and leaned against the cinema wall. I continued on as if I hadn't seen her.

I sat in a library chair rather than going to bed. Minna walked past me, without a word, about a half hour later. I awoke the next morning about six. I showered and then went to my room for a change of clothes. I switched on the lamp. Dora and Else were gone, but Minna lay stretched across her cot. She pulled the sheet up across her breasts. The annoying vent whooshed overhead. The humid room smelled of Minna's stale lavender perfume. 'How was your evening?' she asked lazily.

I had no desire to answer her question.

'Where are Else and Dora?'

She yawned. 'Else is working breakfast and Dora has gone to supervise the other girls. Did you enjoy the movie?'

I stared at her. 'How did you know that? Did you ask Dora where I was going?'

Minna said nothing.

'I didn't go after all,' I said, suspecting she'd seen me outside the cinema.

'You didn't miss much. It was a boring silent film about the First World War.'

I dropped my towel and reached for my undergarments.

I felt her eyes traveling over my naked body. 'You've got bug bites on your legs. Before you go outside, you should put on rubbing alcohol like I do. It keeps the bugs away.'

'Thank you. I'll keep that in mind.'

She rolled on her side as I dressed. I held up a small mirror to check my face. It reflected Minna's devious face as she said, 'There's a very interesting SS Captain here by the name of Karl Weber.'

I combed my hair and tried to mask my irritation. 'Yes?'

'You know him, don't you?'

'We met at the Berghof. I've seen him a few times. We went to a movie together.'

'I think you have more than movies in common.'

I turned, the mirror clutched in my hand. 'What are you getting at?'

'Dora would be interested to know about your liaisons with Captain Weber. What are you two up to?'

I pulled a dress and shoes from my locker. 'That's none of your business.'

'It's very much my business if it involves the Reich.'

'You're imagining things. I have to get to work.'

She sat up on the cot with the sheet draped across her. 'Funny, last night I heard something about evil being eradicated. You said you would be prepared to die.'

My blood ran cold. I sat on the bed. Minna glared at me, smug under her flimsy cover. I tried to calm my wildly beating heart. What if she was a Gestapo agent? How much had she really heard? I hoped that her vanity outweighed her intelligence. 'You must have misunderstood. Maybe it was words from the movie.' I pointed at her. 'And what right do you have to spy on us?'

She shook her head and her eyes focused on me like a bird of prey. 'I wasn't spying. Don't think you can get away with anything by threatening me.' She admired her fingernails and then smiled sulkily. 'I was talking a walk. I happened to overhear a conversation – that's all.'

'We were talking about the Allies. Captain Weber is certain he will be shipped off to the Western Front soon.' I placed the mirror on the bed beside me. 'I'm not happy about it.'

Minna craned her long neck toward me. 'You should tell Dora about your concern for your Captain. She might ask the Führer to grant him a special favor. Or better yet, maybe I'll tell Dora about your trysts. I'm sure she will be interested.'

I slipped into my dress. 'Don't bother. No favors are necessary.'

'Don't be silly,' Minna said. 'We must all stick together.'

I wanted to wring her neck, but I had to remain calm. I put on my shoes, said good-bye and walked quickly to the officers' mess. Along the way, an anxious sickness stabbed at my stomach. I had to talk to Karl. Minna knew much more than she should have and that was dangerous. We had to decide what to do.

He wasn't in the hall. I went to the kitchen and told Cook the fetid air of the dormitory was making me sick. A walk might help clear my head. She agreed and said I could come to work later. I casually asked if she had seen Captain Weber. She replied that he'd been called to a situation conference at eleven. That meant he was in a building near Hitler's bunker, an area I had never been in. It was several minutes past ten.

I walked west past my quarters to a road that turned north. I didn't have far to walk until a guard post appeared in front of me. The man on duty was older than most, and he observed me like a teacher greeting a new student rather than an obvious threat. A black-and-tan German shepherd sat next to him. The dog's brown eyes followed my every move. The guard asked for my papers, which I produced, and he then asked me what business I had in this area. I told him a lie about delivering a message from Cook to Captain Weber – a plausible story because of Karl's association with the kitchen staff. He said nothing more and let me go on my way.

The trees clumped densely here making it difficult to see more than a few meters to the left or right of the path. I was keenly aware of being alone. The footpath curved and an immense concrete bunker loomed into view. Intuition told me it was Hitler's. A single lamp hung over a small door.

As I walked, a few other low buildings appeared in the green forest light like ships emerging from a fog. I stopped, unsure of which way to proceed. I must have given the impression I was out of place, uncertain of my direction, because a sonorous voice called out to me.

'Are you lost, my child?'

My breath caught and I jumped.

The Führer glided like an apparition out of the forest. He was dressed in dark pants and a fawn-colored double-breasted jacket. A single medal was pinned to its left lapel. I had no idea what it signified. He also wore a military cap with a circular red headband. Blondi, his shepherd, trotted ahead of him, her tongue hanging over the side of her jaw.

My face must have given away my surprise. His eyes captured mine. A powerful hypnotic power emanated from his intense gaze. He studied me, taking in my shock, deciding whether he wanted to bother with conversation. Finally, he asked my name and I answered.

He stepped closer. 'What do you do?'

I cringed as I gave the Nazi salute, and said, 'I'm a taster and bookkeeper in your kitchen.'

He ignored my obsequious performance and ordered Blondi to sit. 'You protect me from the poisons that come my way. There was an unfortunate incident recently at the Berghof. Were you there?'

'Yes.'

He walked closer, with a slight stoop, and offered his hand. Blondi sat obediently, but I could tell she wanted to sniff my legs. A glint popped into Hitler's eyes. 'Are you the taster who was poisoned by Otto?'

I stiffened. 'Yes, I'm the one. His little test made me sick for days. Cook was very upset about the whole affair and the time I missed from work.'

'I shall order him never to do it again.' A few sickly rays of light fell across Hitler's face when the breeze shifted the branches above. Cook had told me Hitler didn't like the sun. He moved back into the shade. 'Where are you from?'

'Berlin, my Führer.'

His question and my response opened a torrent of comments about the city. He spoke of his plans for the capital, to be carried out by Albert Speer; and, dismissing Berlin, he told me how much he preferred Munich and the Obersalzberg to the city.

I looked at my watch. It was nearing ten thirty. Hitler saw my concern and said, 'Blondi will never forgive me if I don't finish her walk. Why are you here?'

I repeated the lie I had fabricated. 'I have a message from Cook for Captain Weber.'

'Oh, Weber. He should be in the conference room with the other officers. You'll find him at the guest barracks hut.' He pointed to a low building with windows I'd seen in the gloom.

'Thank you, my Führer.' I saluted again.

'You and Weber should join me for tea sometime.' He tugged on Blondi's leash and he walked toward the large bunker I thought was his.

My pulse quickened. I stepped off the path and headed for the conference room. A strange thought struck me as I approached a group of officers huddling a few meters away from the door. Hitler had seemed so normal, almost like a grandfather. Could this be the same man who had ordered the destruction of thousands of innocent men, women and children in the East, as Karl's pictures had shown? Hitler hardly seemed the demon I imagined him to be. I shook the thought from my head. Karl must be right. I had given my trust and heart to him.

I was nearing the men when a second SS guard with a dog stopped me. I presented my papers again and explained what I was doing. Rather than let me go on my way, this

136

guard walked to the officers and asked for Captain Weber. One of the men entered the hut and several minutes later came back with Karl. Karl thanked him and then walked toward me. He showed no sign of concern until he came to a stop in front of my face.

'What *are* you doing here?' he asked in a fiery whisper. 'Are you out of your mind? Why did you take such a risk?'

I looked past him toward the others — none of them seemed interested in our conversation. 'Minna — one of the tasters I work with — overheard us last night. She threatened to tell Dora Schiffer. In fact, I think she will. If she does, we're finished.'

Karl's face blanched and he clasped his hands together. After a few moments, he regained his composure. 'How much did she hear?'

'Too much. I told Minna we were talking about the Allies, but I don't think she believed me.'

His eyes flickered in nervous thought as he paced in a small circle. 'My God, what to do? Damn. Everyone knows everyone else's business in the Reich.'

'Please, Karl. The others will suspect something. I know exactly what to do.'

He stopped and faced me, his jaw set and his eyes fixed as stones.

'Give me until one this afternoon,' I said, 'and the problem will be solved.'

He shook his head. 'You must not do anything rash. Promise me.'

'I just met the Führer.'

Karl's face slackened. 'That's the kind of trouble I want to avoid. What did he say?'

'He wanted to know who I was and what I was doing here. It was a pleasant conversation. And he knows about us – someone must have told him, maybe Eva or Cook.'

'Promise me you won't . . . we've talked far too long. Don't put yourself in danger.' He turned toward the officers.

But I knew as he walked away that nothing he could say would sway me from my plan.

After another stop by the SS, I finally made my way back to the mess and the kitchen. Else was hunched over one of the preparation tables. She'd tasted the breakfast offerings. The other tasters were now involved with lunch, which would be served to the Führer, and invited guests, in the mid-afternoon.

Else and I had not talked much since I had been taken off tasting duty, but I suspected she still loathed the position and was miserable under Minna's suffocating wing. I said good morning.

Else greeted me with a bright smile. 'I was hoping to talk to you.'

'Really? Why?'

'I want out of this job – maybe do bookwork like you.' She clutched her throat. 'I can't stand the pressure of not knowing whether I'm going to – '

I finished the thought for her. 'Be poisoned? Die?'

She nodded.

'You heard Minna. The chances of being poisoned are small. Now that you've been through class and performed the job, you must feel more assured.'

'Yes, but not as much as you and Minna. I don't even know why they have me taste in the morning. The Führer only has a glass of milk and an apple. He's obsessed with apples. Apple this and apple that.'

'Where is Minna? Is she tasting lunch today?'

Else's smile soured as she looked around the room for our companion. 'Yes, she should be here soon.'

'Have you seen Dora? I have a question to ask her.'

Else pointed to the kitchen. 'She's been with Cook all morning going over books.'

'Which reminds me, I need to get to work.'

'Magda,' Else called out as I walked toward the small desk I used. 'Thank you for being so nice. I'm sorry Otto poisoned you.'

'Thank you. I'm stronger for it.'

Inside I felt like a shivering fool. The poisoning had indeed made me stronger — it had strengthened my resolve to fight against a lawless Reich. But I needed to win another battle without giving myself away. It was a risk I had to take.

I knew where the poisons were kept — under lock and key in Cook's office. I went to my station and rifled through a few books to look as if I were working. I peered into the kitchen and saw Cook, Dora and Otto. Otto was preparing food at one of the stoves while Cook and Dora talked. He saw me and smirked. I had not talked to him since his 'trick.' Cook and Dora seemed absorbed, but I interrupted them anyway. I asked Cook for the keys to her office under the pretense of finding an inventory book I needed. She handed them, hung from a large metal ring, to me and returned to her conversation. Dora barely gave me a glance. I asked in an offhanded way if either of them had seen Minna. They shook their heads. That was the answer I wanted.

I opened the door and stepped inside. The room was filled

with cookbooks, kitchen equipment and logs, much like Cook's office at the Berghof. A medicine cabinet on the back wall glinted in the light. A black skull and crossbones stared out at me from the frosted glass. I found the key to the padlock and popped it open. All the poisons I had studied in my classes at the Berghof, and more, were inside. I was unsure which to take. Mercury Chloride and arsenic were too slow to act and required a larger quantity than was in the cabinet. It seemed my only choice was cyanide, either the granules or the capsule. I decided upon the capsule. I had seen its effect on Ursula: quick and nearly painless. The trick would be how to break it and get the liquid mixed in with the food. I knew the consequences if I was caught. I would be executed. Either way, the trap had been laid by Minna. If I did nothing and let her live, she might report Karl and me to the Gestapo. If I killed her, I would become a murderer. That thought, abhorrent as it was, filled me with a creeping dread. But what could I do? It was either Minna or us.

I dropped the capsule into my pocket, secured the cabinet and found an inventory log to carry out. Else, looking forlorn, still sat at the table waiting for Minna. Otto was bringing out the lunch dishes. I returned Cook's keys, making sure she spotted the book I was carrying, and then returned to Else. I looked at the dishes spread out on the table and decided on the potato casserole. Enough runny liquid had settled over the dish that the cyanide might not be noticed.

Else sighed. 'I wish Minna would get here. I don't want to taste lunch, too.'

'She'll be here soon.' I brushed against one of the spoons and knocked it off the table, sending it skittering across the floor.

Else got up to retrieve it.

I only had a few seconds. 'I'm sorry,' I said, and turned quickly. No one from the kitchen was looking, and, fortunately, no SS officers were in the room. I broke the capsule against the bowl's rim. The poison slid down the side into the potato dish. I thrust the two halves of the capsule back into my pocket. Else walked back with the spoon in hand. The faint odor of bitter almonds drifted above the dish. I turned quickly, apologized again and asked her if she would return the inventory book to the corner desk. As she walked away, I stirred the dish while my heart fluttered in my chest. The cyanide was infused into the food and the aroma faded. I covered the dirty spoon with my hand and took a few deep breaths to calm myself.

Cook summoned Else into the kitchen, and just as quickly sent her back. 'I have to taste lunch with some of the other tasters,' she said with a frown. 'Minna hasn't shown up. They're looking for her. And I'm already full.' She patted her stomach.

Panic surged through me. 'This spoon is dirty. I'll get a clean one.' I walked to an empty sink and washed the utensil. I left it in the sink and dried my hands with a cotton towel. Turning away from the other kitchen help in the room, I wiped any trace of my fingerprints off the capsule fragments and wrapped the towel around them. A few potato peelings lay nearby. I picked them up with the cloth. There was a waste receptacle near Otto. I unfolded the towel over the wastebasket and dropped the peelings and the capsule into it.

My heart was nearly in my throat. Where was Minna? If she did not come to work, how could I save Else? I didn't want her to be poisoned.

Else chastised me as I walked past her to my station. 'You forgot the spoon.'

I laughed halfheartedly, but it was too late to get another one. Dora had left the mess hall. Otto and Cook stood across from Else to watch the tasting. Cook told Else to begin.

'Let me,' I said from across the room. 'Else has been on duty all morning and I'm ready to resume my service to the Führer. I've been away too long.'

Otto snickered. 'You are the brave one – after the lesson I taught you.'

Cook and Else objected, but Otto waved me on. I picked up a fork and started with the salads and vegetable and fruit dishes at the right end of the table, knowing a casserole full of poison awaited me in the center. My stomach churned as I tasted down the line. I smelled each dish carefully before tasting and commented on how excellent each was. In fact, I tasted nothing except the dryness of my mouth.

When I came to the potato dish, I picked up the bowl, lifted it slowly and then sniffed the contents. My nose twitched and I smelled it a few more times.

Otto's eyes narrowed. 'Is something wrong?'

'Is this dish intended for the Führer?' I asked.

'Of course. It's one of my specialties and a favorite of the Führer's.'

'Do your special dishes always contain poison? I smell cyanide.'

Otto lunged toward the table. 'Impossible! I made it myself. And I did not poison it as a test for the taster. Not today!'

'What is this about?' Cook asked. 'Is this a joke on us again?'

I put the dish back on the table. 'This is no joke. There's poison in this casserole.'

'Else, do you smell it?' Cook asked.

Else hesitated, fear shining in her eyes. I urged her on.

She leaned forward and sniffed the dish. 'I can't tell. It smells off. Something's wrong.'

Cook immediately called for an SS guard. A contingent of them rushed into the kitchen. 'Test this for poison and search the kitchen. We'll get to the bottom of this. Meanwhile, Magda, taste the other dishes. Else, I'll bring out another sample of the casserole. Taste it.'

We did as Cook instructed. I knew Else was safe. The SS rummaged through everything: the drawers, the utensils, the wastebaskets. It would only be a matter of time before they found the broken capsule in the trash. Trying hard to hide any display of nerves, I glanced at them as they worked.

As we watched – for we were instructed not to leave the mess hall – Else leaned to me and said, 'My God, Magda, I could have been poisoned. Otto could have killed me with one of his tricks.' Her face turned pale. 'I must get out of this job.'

I patted her shoulder. 'Calm down. I have it from the Führer that Otto will no longer be conducting these tests.'

Dora, dour and shaken, appeared at the doorway. She stood silent for a moment and then announced, 'Minna is dead – strangled with one of her own stockings.'

Else gasped.

I was shocked, too, but I had a strong suspicion who killed her. Karl had murdered her. Who else could have done it? My body went numb. Karl a murderer? I didn't know what to think. He had saved us, but had he also damned us to a worse fate?

The SS found the ampoule in the trash near Otto's station. His corpulent face turned crimson and he vehemently denied to the Colonel he had poisoned the dish. Else and I were questioned as well by the officer. He scrutinized me more severely, scowling the whole time, but my companion and Cook vouched for my integrity and loyalty to the Reich. They asked him, 'Why would she poison herself? She's already been poisoned once in her service.'

After more than two hours, Else and I were released. The Colonel led Otto away for more questioning. I was sure Hitler would pardon him and he would be free by the Führer's dinnertime. Cook ordered me to be on hand for an evening tasting. I was concerned – if Otto was released, he might really try to kill me.

The dinner tasting was without incident, however. Cook reported with satisfaction that Otto was no longer in the service of the Führer and that he had been ordered to a barracks on the Eastern Front.

Karl was waiting for me outside the mess hall when I finished about ten. No one was around. He grabbed my arm and led me into the forest.

'That was very, very stupid,' he said. 'I know what you did. Who else would do it?'

I pulled away from his grip. 'What *I* did? You killed Minna. The SS will be on high alert now.'

He scoffed. 'They are always on high alert at headquarters.' He leaned closer to me. 'I didn't kill Minna, but I'm fairly certain I know who did.'

Karl turned and looked into the dark woods. Nothing stirred as I waited for his answer.

'Franz killed her,' he said sharply. 'He, too, saw her behind the cinema as we were leaving. I told him what Minna said to you. Franz believed she was dangerous and had to be . . . eliminated.'

As much as I hated the thought running through me, I was glad Minna was dead. She had heard too much and I knew she would use any means to work her way into Hitler's favor. She was no longer a threat. I was also relieved that Karl hadn't killed Minna; however, the war was taking its toll on me. How could I be happy that a woman had been killed and that we were at least partially guilty of her murder? My soul seemed blighted and I was disgusted at my own inhumanity. I was unprepared to deal with such feelings.

The severity of our situation struck me like a hammer blow. First Ursula and now Minna. Two women had died because of plots to overthrow Hitler. More deaths were sure to follow. A hollow feeling opened inside me as I contemplated our uncertain future. 'Do you think anyone suspects Franz?'

'The damn SS is so concerned with keeping the Führer alive, they may not give Minna's death more than a passing thought.' Again, he looked over his shoulder to the path, which lay in darkness. 'But what if they suspected Minna of trying to poison the Führer? Perhaps they'll think that was why she was killed. Your little trick actually might have helped us.' Karl shook his head in disbelief. 'No, no, it's too insane. Magda, you must never try anything like that again unless a plan is in place. So much could have gone wrong. As it is, with Minna's murder and the attempted poisoning, the Colonel will be out for blood. She may be a small fish to them, but the situation is still dangerous. I only hope he takes a day or two to investigate and then closes the case – unsolved. Otto's in deep trouble, too, thanks to you.'

A violent shaking wracked me and my back scraped against

the rough bark of a tree. The square-jawed face of the Colonel appeared in my mind, his teeth gritted in anger.

Karl took me in his arms and the heat from his neck drifted across my face. I wanted him to make love to me, to ease my fear, but what would it matter? We were doomed, if not through our actions, then by the uncontrollable events of war. He kissed me. 'Let me take the chances from now on. Don't be a martyr.' He kissed me again and then backed away. 'We need to get out of here before we both do something we might later regret. You go first. If anyone stops you tell them you were out for some air.'

I reached out, pulled him close, unwilling to let go. His skin was moist and hot and our embrace added to the night's warmth.

We clung together for a few minutes before he gently released me. 'Go now. Tomorrow is the day. Avoid the field to the east of the Wolf's Lair. It's not safe to walk near the outer perimeter because of the land mines. Treat the day like any other.' He gave me a lingering kiss.

I walked away without turning back and soon was on the path to my quarters. I walked slowly, as if in a dream, even as mosquitoes swarmed around me. How could I treat the day like any other? I clutched my stomach, which was knotted with fear, took a deep breath and tried to calm myself. I had to put on a brave face for Karl.

When I arrived at the dormitory, Minna's bed and locker had been cleared. Else, her eyes red, sat on her bed. I said hello and she burst into tears.

'I'm going to kill myself,' she said between sobs. 'I can't go on. I've been here all evening, paralyzed – afraid someone will murder me.'

I sat across from her and offered what little comfort I could. 'It's truly awful. We live in a terrible time. Perhaps your job here is finished. Another girl will be here soon and you can move on.' I wanted to lift her spirits by adding that Minna's murderer would be caught and justice meted out, but, in truth, I didn't want that to happen.

I was too upset to talk anymore. I undressed and crawled under the sheet on my cot. The vent hummed as the bunker's claustrophobic walls closed around me. Dora arrived after midnight. Else sniffled in her bed. I tossed and turned, wide awake, thinking that today could be Karl's last day on earth.

# CHAPTER 10

Dora got up early and dressed in full SS uniform. Her hair was pinned back and she wore a regulation cap. She fussed with her skirt and shoes, walking incessantly between the washroom and our quarters. I couldn't imagine why she was so concerned with her appearance unless something important was happening. Else had none of Dora's energy. She only managed a meager smile as she got dressed for her breakfast duties. I tried to assure her that other tasters would be there in addition to a new girl who would join us shortly.

I wasn't on duty, but I had no desire to sleep in in our cramped quarters. One idea for the morning came to mind: offer my bookkeeping services to Cook in the officers' mess hall. She could always use a hand when it came to inventory. At least work might keep my mind off Karl. Dread had been my constant companion since Karl had told me that today would be the day. I wanted to beg him to abandon this deadly mission, but I knew I couldn't change his mind. Sorrow and fear threatened to overwhelm me. I shoved the frightening thoughts aside as I began my day, but they were always there, lurking.

I showered, dressed and made my way to the hall. The August day was sunny and warm with excitement on the breeze. I couldn't see it, but it crawled over my skin as I walked. The air crackled with tension.

When I arrived, I was surprised at the number of SS officers, including generals, and other important staff members crowded inside. One in particular stood out. He was a large man with a big belly. He looked like a king holding court. From pictures, I recognized him as Hermann Göring, the Reichsmarschall. He smiled and puffed out his chest whenever he spoke, as jolly a Party member as I had ever seen. Albert Speer, the Armaments Minister, was there, looking somber, yet dapper, in his field jacket and knee-length black boots. I recognized him from the few times I had seen him at the Berghof. He kept slicking his hair back with his hand. Hitler wasn't there, but he couldn't have been far from the hall. The Bormann brothers stood apart, as was their custom, eyeing each other from across the room. A number of men turned their attention to a smartly dressed older man in a business suit.

I walked to the kitchen, intending to ask Cook if I might help out, but she was waving her arms and shouting orders to anyone who would listen. Apparently, the officious crowd had worked her into a tizzy. The smell of baked apples lingered from the ovens. Else and three other girls from a different dormitory sat on stools near the tasting table. I assumed they'd finished their jobs and were awaiting additional orders. Dora orchestrated the whole scene like a conductor.

I moved back to the hall. Karl, in his dress uniform, stood near Speer. While they talked, Karl gave me a look. We caught each other's gaze with a quick glance. The signal that crossed between us was one of mutual avoidance. I took a seat at a vacant table near the kitchen.

A short time later, a high-ranking officer, apparent from all the medals on his jacket, entered and gave the Nazi salute. Everyone snapped to attention. The officer pointed to the small windows on the front of the hall. Hitler, dressed in his double-breasted field jacket, dark pants and cap, stood waiting on the path with his hands clenched behind his back.

'Gentlemen, this way for the demonstration,' the officer said.

The older man in the business suit led the way. The crowd poured out the door, like dogs on the hunt, and turned to the east. Karl was one of the last out the door. He picked up a knapsack that had been resting near his feet. I hadn't seen it when I first entered the hall. He stopped briefly near the door, turned and smiled. His smile, full of melancholy sadness, sent shivers down my spine. It was like looking at a skull, death itself staring me in the face.

When the procession of officials and officers had disappeared, I got up from the table and followed them down the path. They disappeared into the thickness of the green forest. Soon I would be swallowed by it as well, but I knew which way the men were going. Their voices carried on the air.

The path led onward for many meters before it ended and became a trail. Ahead of the men, I saw a fence that I couldn't get through. Two SS guards stood near a gate. I veered off onto a smaller trail that led into the woods. The muddy ground squished around my shoes and bugs flew up from their moist hiding places. Karl had warned me about land mines, so I followed the narrow track already set into the earth.

A cleared field beyond the gate crossed into my view as I maneuvered through the vegetation. Hitler and his party stood in a circle around a large black machine – a tank as far as I could tell. A branch snapped behind me and I jumped.

'What are you doing here, Fräulein?'

I turned and faced an officer with a black patch covering his left eye. His shoulders were stooped from injury. He stood next to me, using a walking stick for support. He was a handsome man despite his disfigurement.

My mind went momentarily blank. After I regained my senses, I blurted out: 'I'm carrying a message. I wasn't sure which way to turn.' My excuse sounded as false as my words.

'A message? To whom?' He smiled, but his expression was more a smirk than a sign of kindness. He tapped the ground with his walking stick.

I didn't want to link myself to Karl, so I replied, 'To the Führer,' and immediately regretted my hasty stupidity.

'Then I will give him your message,' he said.

I shook my head. 'It's confidential.'

'I'm Colonel von Stauffenberg. I saw you veer off the path. You must be very bad at following people, or very interested in goings-on that aren't your business. Give me the message.'

He was a different man from the Colonel who had given me such grief at the Berghof. Still, I gulped. I had trapped myself and I saw no easy way out of it. 'Please tell the Führer he will have the most delicious apple pie tonight. Magda, his taster, will make sure of it.'

Von Stauffenberg chuckled. 'Yes. I can see your message is confidential. Of course, "apple pie" is the secret code for the Reich's latest invasion plan.'

I pushed past him, but the Colonel braced his cane against a tree and stopped me in my tracks. 'I don't know what you're doing here, but I'm not going to report you.' His lips narrowed and he looked at me like a hawk eyeing a succulent rodent. 'You realize the outer perimeter of the Wolf's Lair is filled with land mines. You could be blown apart with one fatal step. Many unfortunate animals have ended their lives here.'

'Thank you for your advice,' I said. 'I must get back to the kitchen.'

He lifted his cane and asked, 'What is your name?'

'Magda Ritter.'

'I will remember you, Fräulein Ritter. You can be sure of it.'

He followed me back to the path. I turned west, the way I'd come, as the Colonel continued toward the field. I looked back before the trees blocked my view. Hitler and the man in the business suit were standing on top of the machine. Göring and the others were crowded around like adoring lambs. Von Stauffenberg ambled toward them. *How unfortunate,* I thought, *that a high-ranking officer would make it his business to remember my name.*

The whole day my nerves were on edge. I couldn't sit still as I waited for an outbreak of chaos at the Wolf's Lair, or the horrible news of Karl's death. Every effort to clear my mind failed. I paced the library, picking out books to read, but ended up throwing them on the table. As the hours dragged by, I convinced myself the worst was over and prepared for my tasting. During work, I tried to put on a good face although Cook and the other tasters weren't convinced by my display of pleasantries. Cook, in particular, knew me well enough to know that something was wrong. She asked me several times if I was ill. But as the hours passed, my fear lessened. Surely if something horrible had occurred the news would have spread across the Wolf's Lair.

Later that evening, after hours of not knowing what had happened, Karl found me on my walk home and slipped an envelope into my hand. I almost collapsed from relief.

'Read it and then burn it,' he whispered. 'Make sure the ashes are destroyed. I'm writing this letter because it is dangerous to be seen together.' He walked quickly away.

I folded the envelope and tucked it into my pocket. Reading the letter in my bedroom was risky, so, once again, I took refuge in our dormitory's library.

As I thought, no one was there. I switched on a small lamp, took a book of German history from the shelf and settled into the overstuffed chair. I was away from everyone and for that I was thankful. I took out the letter, folded it in half and inserted it in the center of the book. I pretended to be reading history but, instead, focused on Karl's letter:

*Dearest Magda,*
*I am reluctant to be around you. Even handing you this letter comes with great risk. You hold my life in your hands. In fact, more than my life — the fate of Germany lies within this writing. I trust you will destroy any trace of it and I'll know where your heart lies. If not, I will be executed for treason. Either way, you see I'm prepared to die for what I believe.*

*This afternoon, I carried a knapsack loaded with a bomb. The explosion was meant for Hitler, Göring, Porsche and the rest. However, the plan was interrupted by von Stauffenberg, who was not scheduled to be here today. I cannot tell you more, but he and I are part of a movement to rid our country of the evil destroying it. Fortunately, I had not yet armed the bomb and I was able to dispose of it after the demonstration.*

*You might ask why we don't shoot the Führer and get it over with. Believe me, such a course of action has been discussed many times. Von Stauffenberg and the others are convinced any attempt to bring down the Reich must include as many of its leaders as possible, not just Hitler. To kill only him might lead to worse circumstances than those that already exist. This is not a decision made lightly.*

*I'm alive tonight because von Stauffenberg decided to make an unannounced trip to the Wolf's Lair. It was not my intention to kill a fellow collaborator. He is convinced the British have made plans as well and are waiting for the right moment. I doubt these include poison, but please be careful, my dearest. I want you to live whether or not I am alive. We will have no future until we can make it safe for our children.*

*Please destroy this letter and confirm my faith in you. Many lives besides our own hang in the balance. We will meet soon.*

*Yours in love,*
*Karl*

With trembling hands, I put the letter back in the envelope. Children? Any hope for the future? I marveled at his faith in me. If von Stauffenberg had not been there in the afternoon, the world would have been rid of a tyrant and many of his officers, and the man who professed his love for me would be dead.

I searched the library for a cigarette lighter or matches but found none. I stepped outside and saw a girl walking by who lived in the quarters opposite mine. I asked if she smoked and she nodded. I also asked if I might borrow her lighter. She pulled it from her pocket and we talked for a few minutes. She said to return it to her in the morning, because she was going to bed.

As soon as she left, I ran to the woods behind the dormitory, an area safe from mines. The words from Karl's note raced through my head. He was a hero, a man to respect and love. Although no stars were visible through the trees, my eyes swam with them. A strange, giddy excitement overtook me and I walked briskly, oblivious to the mosquitoes hovering around my head. Then the dark closed around me. How could I fall in love with a man who *wanted* to die? He wanted me to live, but how could I go on without him, shattered by his death? Despair and euphoria fought to control me. I shuddered to a stop near a rock outcropping, frozen in place, and listened. The night insects buzzed in my ears. I opened the lighter and the pungent odor of Naphtha wafted into my nose. I brushed my thumb against the wheel, the flint sparked and a yellow flame split the darkness. I held the note with two fingers and lit the bottom edge. The paper curled in a brown wave and was consumed so quickly I dropped it on the rock. The letter burned to shards of gray dust. I took the ashes in my hands, dropped them on the muddy earth and crushed them into the ground until they disappeared. I was certain no one would find them.

I crept out of the forest, making sure I hadn't been seen. When I arrived back at the dormitory, I washed my hands, returned to the library and stared at the bound volumes stacked so neatly in the cases. I couldn't force myself to read. Neither education nor entertainment could satisfy my heart as I sat curled in my favorite chair. Slowly, the excitement of Karl's admission left my body and I wept over our uncertain future – a future that might include death.

One thought consumed me: *Our fate is sealed.*

Hitler loved to take Blondi for a walk in the morning. Sometimes his valet took the dog, but usually the Führer walked her around the wooded area near his bunker.

Like a cancer invading my brain, I began to think of ways to kill him, speculating about his walks with Blondi, or how it might happen during a meal. These insane thoughts centered on me saving Karl. I wanted to die in his place.

Then my mind would calm and I would convince myself I was being foolish. How could I bring down the head of the Reich? I couldn't poison him without poisoning others who might be innocent. And what if I was captured? I would be killed and my parents probably arrested. I had no pistol to shoot him, and what would it matter if I did? Karl was right. With Göring, Goebbels, Bormann or Himmler leading the state, Germany might be worse off. I'd become a madwoman, with murderous thoughts buzzing in my brain. I thought my head would burst.

Near summer's end, Hitler invited Karl and me to evening tea. When I'd first met Hitler, when he was walking Blondi, he had made that suggestion. The invitation came to me through Cook one night after tasting. Nothing could be

156

done about it. One did not decline tea with the Führer, but I couldn't help but be wary of what was to come.

Franz was waiting for me when I stepped out of the dormitory one morning. I hadn't seen him since the night in the woods when he told me he was being sent to the Eastern Front. I greeted him and he walked beside me. He withdrew his cigarettes from his jacket and tapped one against his gold holder. Sunlight split the leafy canopy above and he squinted at me. He lit his cigarette and said, 'I hear you've been invited to tea with the Führer.'

'Yes.' I was happy to see Franz, but uncomfortable at the same time. A sense of carefree danger always seemed to surround him and meeting like this reinforced that feeling. 'I thought you'd been sent to the Front.'

Franz chuckled. 'I've been called back, so I can brief Hitler on the state of our war machine. It's in sad shape. We're losing ground and morale is low. Some of the troops are beginning to wonder what they're fighting for, but too many of them still believe the propaganda spewed by their officers.'

I looked into his face, now thinner and creased with lines. 'Why are you here? Do you have a message for me?'

He grabbed my arm and forced me to a stop. 'I did what had to be done to Minna. You must be pleased about that. I saved both your lives.'

'We should keep walking.' I continued on the path. We walked past the mess hall and toward the field where Karl had intended to deploy the bomb. 'Of course I'm grateful,' I whispered. 'Minna was a fool. But our position is too precarious and I want—' A lump formed in my throat.

Franz put his hand on my arm. A group of officers passed us, but none gave us more than a greeting and a glance.

'You love Karl, don't you?' Franz asked.

I nodded.

'Then you'll be happy to know his position within the group has been reassigned. Von Stauffenberg knows what you did in the kitchen, how you tried to poison Minna at great risk to yourself. He and the others, including myself, are grateful. In fact, I think your little stunt completely befuddled the SS. Otto got the blame.'

No one was around, so we stopped.

'Karl had his chance and, lucky for you both, von Stauffenberg got in the way,' Franz continued. 'The timing wasn't right. With these things you never know what will happen.' He puffed on his cigarette. 'Karl's been "retired," so to speak. He's to focus on reconnaissance here at the Wolf's Lair and at the Berghof. Von Stauffenberg is taking over in every aspect. That's what I was sent to tell you.'

Relief flooded through me; however, it faded quickly as I considered our circumstances. Far too many fears filled my head. I thanked Franz. We shook hands and then he turned and headed back the way we had come. As he disappeared from view, I thought how much he had aged in the few months I had known him. His blond hair seemed darker; his wide, bright smile had narrowed; his creased face showed the stress of battle. One thing I knew for certain: Von Stauffenberg would now figure prominently in the life, or death, of Adolf Hitler.

Karl and I had no chance to talk before meeting at Hitler's for tea. I made my way to the bunker, after freshening up from the evening's tasting. An SS guard on patrol stopped me and asked for my papers. When I told him I was having tea with the Führer, he walked with me. I knew he was only doing it to verify my story. Karl was standing near the door when we arrived about ten. The guard left after Karl had talked with him.

The Führer's bunker was more impressive at night than during the day. It sat like a black monolith on the sodden earth and, even though it was not as large as some of the others on the grounds, it rose up like a derelict Mayan temple covered by the forest surrounding it. A single bright light shone over its iron door. Karl greeted me formally and then spoke to the armed men at the entrance. They escorted us through the narrow opening into a large corridor lined with doors where we were met by a valet. I recognized him from the Berghof, where he had also been in Hitler's service. Tall, with a broad chin and thin lips, he was solidly SS: upright, strict, formal, a man's man, obsequious to the Führer. He led us farther down the corridor until we found ourselves in a cramped tearoom furnished with a round table that seated about six comfortably. Several painted landscapes adorned the walls. Two rustic lamps in the corners shone a warm light through their beige silk shades. One couldn't get over the feeling, however, of being in a bunker, no matter how hospitable the atmosphere. The fans whirred overhead. I fought the feeling that the walls were closing in around me. We said little to each other because we didn't know if our conversation might be overheard.

I'd chosen a simple black dress, black shoes and two small gold earrings for the evening. I could never be another smartly dressed Eva Braun for Hitler.

Karl tapped his fingers against the table.

'Calm yourself,' I said. 'You have no reason to be nervous.'

He placed his cap in his lap. 'Why has he invited us? Why tonight?'

I put my hand upon his and he relaxed with my touch. I wondered myself why Hitler had invited us. Did he have information regarding the officers who were plotting against him? Had someone given our secrets away? Did he know I had tried to poison Minna, or that Franz had killed her? Perhaps he wanted to question us about her death. Such useless speculation only fueled my anxiety.

The door opened after a quick knock and the valet appeared, followed closely by another. The valet I recognized from the Berghof held a bouquet of red long-stem roses, which he presented to me. 'These are from the Führer,' he said. 'He will be here soon.' He then ordered the other man to wheel in a cart loaded with coffee, tea, plates of cookies and slices of apple cake. I laughed to myself because I had tasted all this food earlier. The valets left us and a short time later the door swung open again.

Hitler appeared with Blondi by his side. Karl clutched his cap. We both rose and gave the Nazi salute. Hitler motioned for us to sit down. We, like Blondi, obeyed. Hitler looked more relaxed than I had ever seen him. A slight flush of color infused his cheeks, which were generally pasty because of his aversion to sunlight. His valet pulled out the chair next to me and the Führer sat. For a time, he said nothing, only looked at us with his riveting blue eyes. One could sense the fire burning underneath them. Rasputin's eyes must have had the same effect upon his followers.

Once again, I felt overwhelmed by Hitler's presence as if some powerful force emanated from him. What was it – the sheer force of his will? I could see how easy it would be, like the rest of the nation, to be swept up in the endless flow of his propaganda on radio and in films. What power he held over the German people!

A circular medallion was pinned on his black jacket. It consisted of a gold wreath on the outer layer bordered by a white band, and an inner red band with *NSDAP* written upon it, all of this encircling a black swastika on a white background.

Karl and I dared not speak until he had spoken to us.

'I am happy to see you,' he said, breaking open the conversation. He spoke in that deep baritone voice I had heard so often when he addressed the Reich. His speech pattern carried its own cadence, a rhythm that was in itself hypnotic. 'I hope we can enjoy the evening – I treasure what free time I have, for I am always called away from moments like these for some nasty business, unless I tell my adjutant not to disturb me.' He motioned for his valet to serve tea.

Blondi curled up near Hitler's feet and looked at me with her soft brown eyes.

'My Führer,' Karl said. 'We are delighted you have invited us to tea, but Fräulein Ritter and I are somewhat perplexed by your invitation. How can we be of service?'

Hitler held up his hand. 'That's noble of you, Weber, but you must leave your concerns outside the room.' He put both hands on the table, leaned forward and studied us. 'I want no talk of war, or battles, or strategy tonight. In the tearoom we talk of art, architecture and music. We celebrate German culture and history, and tonight we are here to celebrate love.'

'My Führer?' Karl asked, caught as much off guard as I.

The valet served me tea, then took my beautiful red roses and placed them in a crystal vase in the center of the table, so all of us could enjoy them. Their sweet fragrance soon filled the room, a welcome change from the musty, damp odor that permeated most of the bunkers.

Hitler smiled and held up his cup. 'I must thank the taster who suffered under Otto's hands.' He paused and my nerves tightened. 'But there is more to discuss.' Karl's leg brushed against mine and I sensed the tension in his body.

Hitler took a sip of tea and patted my hand. 'I try to greet everyone, to say hello, to have a kind word for all who serve the Reich, but I am a busy man. I don't have much time. You should convey my thanks to all in the kitchen. Several new young women have started recently. I promised Dora I would meet them.'

His eyes flashed with a spark of what I would call 'good will.' I had no doubt he would come to the mess hall and greet the new staff. At the moment, he seemed the picture of the kindly father who wanted his 'children' to be happy, to do well in a world under his guidance. From his mood, it appeared he believed no one on his staff would ever think of harming him. This attitude of benevolence was more than posturing. Hitler was sincere, but I also knew that any crime against the Reich would be punished in the most severe manner possible.

'Cook has told me,' he continued, 'that you two spend a great deal of time together.'

The blood rushed to my head and I blushed, more out of anxiety than embarrassment. So, it was Cook who had revealed our relationship.

'Magda and I have struck up a friendship,' Karl said.

I was dumbfounded by how easily he admitted it.

'We have our jobs to do,' I said, trying to earn some distance between Karl and me. 'Fate has thrown us together because we both happen to work in the same area.'

'Yes, but it has been noted,' Hitler said. 'Therefore, I wish to give you my blessing.'

Karl went white and I gasped. 'My Führer, that is not necessary,' I said.

He waved his hands in protest. 'Of course it's necessary. I have given so many blessings, it's like a second job; my secretaries, my staff, have all benefited. I encourage my officers to find young women of quality.' He took another sip of tea and nibbled on a slice of apple cake. 'Eat up; you haven't touched the delicious desserts made especially for you.'

'My Führer,' I said. 'I tasted them this evening.'

He smiled in mock surprise and laughed. 'In that case you can enjoy them knowing they are not poisoned.' He paused and then said, 'One issue remained, but I solved it.'

Karl and I looked at each other.

'You are not a Party member, Fräulein Ritter,' Hitler said, 'so I have made you one.' He withdrew a box from his jacket and handed it to me.

I took off the lid, unwrapped the paper inside and uncovered a medallion like the one he wore.

'The number on it signifies your place in the Party membership. Mine is "one."' He pointed to the medal on his jacket.

'Thank you.' Uncertain whether to put the medallion on, I closed the box and placed it on the table.

Hitler then turned the conversation to Bavaria and the Alps, rhapsodizing upon the mythology surrounding the Obersalzberg. Karl and I sat, unsettled, for the rest of the evening while

Hitler talked about Speer and his plans for the capital and the state of German art and film. Hitler even invited us to his study to listen to a recording of Wagner. It was after midnight when we were dismissed.

We stood for a time outside the bunker door not knowing what to say. An early fall chill had crept into the air and the cooler temperature felt good against my skin. Now that we were 'blessed' there seemed little need for pretense. I held Karl's hand tightly as we walked down the path. I silently marveled that I'd had tea with the leader of the Third Reich. I understood now, in Hitler's presence, how persuasive, how forceful, he could be. No wonder the German people followed him like sheep. My father had told me of a film called *Triumph of the Will*. He said its only point was to glorify the Party. I'd never seen it, but I could understand how such a powerful presence could be transferred to the screen and what a great impact it might have.

We stopped in a clearing on the path between the bunker and my quarters. Karl wrapped his arms around me and pulled me close. I felt warm and safe against him as he kissed me. I nuzzled my lips against his neck and he sighed.

'Imagine the Führer having the time for such details,' Karl said between kisses.

I started to speak, but he held his fingers against my lips and pointed to the box I was holding. After a few moments, I figured out what he wanted me to understand. The medallion. Karl pointed to it and then to his ear – as if the medal might be an object for spying on us. The thought hadn't crossed my mind.

'It's a beautiful pin,' he said. 'You should be very proud that the Führer has taken such an interest in us.'

'I'll let you look at it tomorrow,' I said. 'For now, let's savor the evening.' I pressed against him, offering more kisses.

He stopped me and lifted my chin with his fingers until my eyes were aligned with his. 'Perhaps we should be married,' he said.

My breath caught in my throat. 'Married?' In a different world, I would have jumped at the chance, but our future was so uncertain. I turned away from him, not wanting to share any disappointment. 'We should talk about this tomorrow.' Making plans seemed so absurd, I almost wanted to laugh. 'After all, now that the secret is out, there's no reason to rush things.'

'He'll want us to be married soon,' Karl said. 'He'll dote upon us like a kindly old grandfather.' He touched my shoulder. 'Let me take you home. I have to be up early tomorrow. We have plenty to consider.'

We left the clearing and soon we were at my door. Karl kissed me once more and we said good-bye. My head filled with thoughts about our questionable future and I didn't feel like going to sleep. I wasn't working in the morning so there was no reason for me to get up early. Once again, I sat in the library and waited for sleep to overtake me. I took the medallion out of my purse and turned it over and over in my hands. Nothing about it looked suspicious, but Karl would have to examine it to make sure it was safe. In the meantime, I would have to wear it and any negative thoughts about Hitler or the Reich would remain unsaid. I couldn't even talk to myself. How could I hold in everything I was feeling inside? I was more isolated than ever and in no mood to be a bride.

# CHAPTER 11

Karl and I were engaged in the fall of 1943. Hitler continued to press for us to be married, not directly, but through Cook and other SS officers. His actions did not come as a surprise, for he had done the same for one of his personal secretaries earlier in the year. Karl and I continued to make excuses, usually regarding the 'danger' of my position, but we knew we would have to be married soon – time was running out. In response to our delay, the Führer ordered me off tasting duty, but Cook's protests were strong enough I was allowed to stay on in the kitchen as a bookkeeper and also as a backup taster if needed. Despite his feelings about our future marriage, Hitler willingly conceded his complete control because Cook trusted my judgment as a taster.

Shortly after our tea with the Führer, Karl inspected the medallion. He thought it might house a miniature microphone; but, it was only a pin, nothing more. From that point on, I wore it every day when I was out, although I detested the Party and what it stood for.

During the fall, our existence at the Wolf's Lair became routine. I grew weary of 'bunker fever,' the claustrophobic prison of our cramped quarters, which now that the weather was growing cold became even more unbearable. Else and I took walks when I wasn't with Karl. We needed to get outside and take in fresh air, even on damp, rainy days. By mid–October the clouds were spitting snow and the bunkers seemed to turn into blocks of ice. I wrapped myself in sweaters and coats and put on gloves to keep warm.

I kept away from Dora and the other tasters because I didn't want to answer questions about my personal life. Hitler continued his occasional travels to and from the Wolf's Lair. Karl and I never knew the locations of his trips until he was safely back at headquarters. Then we heard, in great detail from those who accompanied him, the usually mundane saga of his trips. A rumor spread across headquarters that we would spend Christmas at the Berghof. One could rarely trust such whisperings. It was rumored the holiday would most likely be unpleasant, unlike those of former years. Cook anticipated food and merriment would be in short supply. Some of the dampness of spirit, she thought, would come from Hitler, who saw excessive festivities as wasteful and arrogant as Germany suffered, suffering he had drawn down upon it. The few times that Karl and I could be alone without someone hovering nearby, we discussed plans for Hitler's assassination, but not in brazen words. Our language became coded; any hint of conspiracy was too dangerous to mention even in passing. I asked Karl one day why 'our goal' could not be accomplished sooner. 'Patience,' was all he said, and whenever I broached the subject, the same word would be muttered.

In mid-November, I was in Cook's office going over the food list when one of the orderlies interrupted me for a phone call. It was my mother. My father was seriously ill and in a hospital in Berlin. She wondered if I might be able to come home for a few days to help her take care of him. I agreed and immediately asked for the time off. I packed a few things, leaving most of my belongings at the Wolf's Lair. The next morning, I was on a train to the city.

My mother met me at the station on a bright November day. We took a taxi directly to the hospital, where the halls were filled with the smell of antiseptic and the fleshy odors of the ill and infirm. I later came to know these smells as 'death.' The hospital stunk, from the ravages of influenza to the horrific wounds of the soldiers who happened to be lucky enough to end up in Berlin. Although this was not a military hospital, many rooms were filled with soldiers. A few were swathed from head to toe in bandages and breathed through tubes inserted in the small slits of their dressings. My mother had warned me that my father had the grippe and we would have to wear gowns and masks to visit him. She'd been with him for several days and was badly in need of rest herself. The staff had warned her not to stay too long in the room because her lengthy visits increased her exposure to the disease.

A nurse met us near the wing where my father was housed. My mother and I dressed in our medical gear and proceeded down the hall to the room. At first I couldn't see my father because he was in a bed near a window, which looked out upon a courtyard. A cool gray light fell through the blinds. The blackout curtain had been lifted. Naked branches formed an intricate web of dark lines against the whitewashed surface of the opposite wall. We passed by the bed of an older man whose complexion was as gray as the light entering the room. My father was asleep and I signaled my mother not to disturb him. We retreated to the hall. I was relatively rested from my journey, so I told my mother to go home – I would join her later in the evening and she could return in the morning.

I pulled up a chair near the window and soon drifted off in the quiet room. My father's coughs awakened me. His face flushed crimson with fever.

'Either I'm hallucinating or my daughter is here,' he said in a rough whisper as he pulled off his mask.

'I'm here, Papa.' I rose from my chair, stood beside him and pointed to the mask. 'You should put that back on.'

'Your mother is not to be trusted,' he said. 'I told her not to send for you.'

'She needs a rest from taking care of you.' I put my gloved hand on his arm.

'How are you, Daughter? I'm glad you're here.' His hair had turned almost gray since I'd last seen him several months earlier. The lines on his face had deepened into dark folds.

'I'm fine. We can talk later. I'm here for at least three days. You should be discharged by then.'

He sighed. 'I hope you're right because I can't afford to be sick. Reichsmark are hard to come by these days. I know many men who would like to take my place at the factory.' He pulled on the mask and hacked violently into it. Pain contorted his face until the coughing spasms subsided. A nurse appeared at the door. She administered a shot and soon my father fell into a deep sleep.

I left the ward and wandered until I found the dining

hall. I had only eaten a small breakfast on the train. When I returned to the room an hour or so later, my father was awake, eating his supper. He picked at the boiled potatoes and a small cut of meat covered in a thin brown gravy. The meals here, served to those who were sick, were so different from those served to the Führer and his staff. I felt ashamed of my good fortune.

My father looked at me and smiled. I returned the smile under my mask and wondered what to say. I couldn't talk about work because of the sensitivity of my job, and I debated whether to tell him I was engaged. I was afraid he would disapprove of my relationship with Karl. My mother soon showed up and put an end to any chance of a prolonged conversation. I promised to visit the next day. My mother and I stayed until ten.

'I'm engaged,' I told my mother when we arrived home, confident she would be pleased. 'I'm a member of the Party now and engaged to an SS Captain. His name is Karl Weber. You would like him.'

My mother showed little emotion. She sat across from me at the kitchen table, her hands in her lap, her eyes down-cast upon the cotton tablecloth. The woody odor of tea wafted up from our two cups. We shared a tea bag. 'I only have five bags left. Do you know what a tea bag costs these days? I'm saving some of these for your father when he comes home.' She covered her eyes with her hands and burst into tears.

'Mother?' I was unaccustomed to seeing her in such an emotional state. I got up from the table and stood behind her, holding on to her shoulders. 'Everything is in short supply.' My words were a half-truth. Supplies were short in Germany, not at Hitler's headquarters. 'I can send you some money if you and Father need it.'

She sobbed, shaking in her seat, then uncovered her eyes and stared at the wall. 'It's not the money. There's no happiness in Berlin. There were bombings a few nights ago. What are we to do? I'm beginning to believe, like your father, that the Führer is a madman driving us to destruction.' She wiped her eyes with the backs of her hands. 'I'm happy for you, Magda. At least you are safe with the Führer. You will be protected.'

I didn't want to cause her further distress, so I didn't express my feelings. Soon I feared we would be no safer at the Berghof and the Wolf's Lair than in Berlin.

'I hate to say it, but I've envied you. It's not good for a mother to envy her daughter. Wherever you are, you're protected. You eat delicious food, you never worry about going hungry. You don't worry about bombs falling from the sky, or the Gestapo taking you away in the middle of the night.'

I returned to my seat and took a sip of the weak tea in my cup. Everything my mother said was true, but it was also a lie. I worried about being poisoned, about bombs raining their destruction. The Gestapo could easily take Karl or me away during the night. 'Maybe you and Papa should live with Uncle Willy and Aunt Reina. It may be safer in Berchtesgaden.'

My mother shook her head. 'Your father would never agree to it. He would never toe the Party line like his brother and we couldn't appear like peasants on their doorstep. Reina is the queen of that household. The atmosphere would be stifling.'

I nodded, for I knew the truth in her argument. 'Should I tell Father about my engagement?'

'Let him recover first. I'm not sure how he'll take the news.'

My mother was wise. I longed to tell my parents about my relationship with Karl and what he intended to do for Germany, but that was impossible. We finished our tea and talked about the neighborhood. Sometime after midnight, I lifted the blackout curtain covering the kitchen window. The world seemed strangely quiet and I thought I heard the buzz of bombers overhead.

My mother and I were sitting in the kitchen the next evening when the air-raid sirens began their unearthly wail. We had taken shifts at the hospital during the day and were slumped in our chairs from exhaustion.

Mother looked at the ceiling as if in prayer and then stared at me with eyes wide with fright. The ceiling shook from an explosion and the kitchen light swayed as if dancing to a discordant rhythm. A fine shower of white plaster dust fell from a crack and settled on the floor.

'I hope it's nothing,' my mother said.

I was less hopeful. The air sparkled with electricity and the bombers droned overhead. 'We should go to the cellar,' I said in a panic. I shot up from the table, ready to grab a few things I might drag downstairs.

Another blast detonated closer than the previous one. The walls and furniture rattled. The intensity increased second by second and soon the house began to shake as if it had been struck by an earthquake. Searing billows of fire split the night while the white traces of flak roared heavenward from German anti-aircraft guns.

'Hurry – there's no time,' I screamed over the blasts that pounded our ears. The bombs hammered around us.

The more I considered the deafening apocalypse outside our window, the less I thought we should go to the cellar. I grabbed my identification papers and secured them in my belt. I took my mother by the arm and led her down the stairs to the front door. As we stood sheltered behind it, a gigantic orange fireball flashed down the street. The gutter flared with flames from dead leaves; some of the trees burst into flames. We were saved by the stone façade of our building.

I wrenched open the door and started down the steps, making sure my mother followed. When we reached the sidewalk, I looked east and gasped. As far as I could see, Berlin was burning. To the west, several blocks were on fire and a maelstrom of wind and flames swirled into the sky. I was unsure what to do, which way to go for shelter.

My mother stopped me from taking another step. She clutched me and yelled, 'Frau Horst. She'll burn to death!'

In my panic, I had forgotten about the old lady who lived upstairs. 'You stay here. I'll go for her.'

A bomb whistled in the air and exploded not less than a block away. The houses shivered on their foundations and then came to rest with creaking moans. Mounds of dirt and debris fell around us. I sprinted up the stairs to the top floor of our building. I pounded on the door, but there was no answer. Another bomb fell close and shafts of orange light shot up the stairs. I slammed my fists against the wood and then, in a moment of unearthly quiet, I heard a feeble voice say, 'Go away.'

I tried the knob, but it was locked. I screamed at Frau Horst again.

There was no reply.

The air fractured like glass around me and the concussion knocked me to the landing. The ceiling curled in red and yellow flames like paper held to a candle. Burning embers fell upon my skin and dress. I brushed their stinging bites off my arms and head and fled down the steps. I had no choice. Outside, waves of fire trembled in the sky. I called for my mother, but she was nowhere to be seen. One of her shoes lay next to the curb. I yelled until my voice cracked, but I couldn't find her. I fled west; it was cooler and the air was less smoky. I looked back to see my home consumed in the fiery tempest. I ran until I was far away; then, sat on the stoop of an unfamiliar house and cried. The bombing seemed to go on forever. I waited on the stairs until it stopped. The fire, smoke and ash from the neighboring blocks rose high into the air. The flames crackled as hellish heat swept over the city. The sound of the inferno was punctuated by screams and the thunderous crash of falling buildings.

I don't remember how long I sat there. People shuffled by me with burned flesh sagging from their bones. Men and women moaned while the children cried out in pain or for their parents. I could do nothing for them. I imagined my father in the hospital, filled with the dying and injured, while the Führer, sipping tea, sat far away in his bunker protected from the bombs.

Not even dawn could assuage my rage. I left the house after someone gave me a cup of water. I had no conscious thought of where to go, so I wandered for many hours until I arrived at the hospital where my father was being treated. Fortunately, the building was only slightly damaged in the bombing. The spirits of the staff seemed as broken as the city. The nurses had given up protecting visitors against the grippe. Rows of beds lined the halls. Patients had been wheeled there for protection against breaking glass.

My father was near his room, his bed against a wall. Dread filled his eyes when he saw me. I caught sight of myself in a mirror. My face was streaked with ash, my hair caked against my skin, my clothes pitted with holes from the embers.

I collapsed against him and cried until I could shed no more tears. 'The bombs,' I muttered, and could say no more.

My father knew what had happened without asking. He patted my hand as his face turned blank and ashen. He shed no tears. Anger and grief seethed inside him.

An all clear sounded and nurses moved the patients back to their rooms. I fell asleep in the chair by the window and slept well into the afternoon. My father and I talked only briefly. I told him I would have to return to my job. I didn't mention Karl or where I was; it was not the time for revelations or predictions of happiness. I had no home to go back to, so I begged the nurse to let me stay the night so I could leave on a train the next day. My luggage and money had been destroyed; however, I had my identification papers with me. Because I served the Führer, I was certain I would have no problem getting passage to Rastenburg.

That night, as I sat in the hospital with my father, a second round of bombs fell. This time they sounded farther away. Still, the hospital shuddered with the blasts, which broke a few windows and carved spidery cracks in the walls. My father walked to the hall in his mask and I huddled against him. The hours dragged by as we rode out the attack. For most of the night, I held his hand.

The next morning, I told my father I was leaving. 'Where will *you* go?' I asked him. 'Our house was destroyed.'

'I will find some place,' he said. 'Or perhaps I will live with my brother.'

I wasn't convinced that he could find an apartment in Berlin, let alone in our district, and I was certain that living with Willy and Reina would make him miserable.

'Let me see what I can do,' I said, hoping to enlist Hitler's help.

His face turned red and he puffed up in a rage. 'Never! I will ask no favor from that . . . man!'

I held his hands. 'You don't understand. I can make your life easier.'

He jerked his hands away. 'You do and you will be no daughter of mine. I will go back to my job and find a place to live on my own.'

I sighed. 'Of course, Papa. Whatever you want.' I took his hands again and leaned in close to his face. I was no longer afraid of catching the grippe. 'I'm on your side,' I whispered, and then kissed his forehead. 'Please believe me.'

His eyes sparkled in their dark sockets and he seemed to understand. 'Do what you must to survive. I know you'll do what is right.'

I left the hospital and hitched a ride on a horse cart. I got off near the old neighborhood and walked through the crumbled stone and mortar, jumped across the burned timbers that had fallen into the street, some still smoking from the fire. People were sweeping up, piling the remains of their homes near the curbs. A few families had settled into burned-out buildings, having no place to go. Their faces looked wan and war-weary with vacant, searching eyes and no hint of a smile. Berliners had come to know how much misery could by meted out by the Allies. At the moment, I was as lonely and forsaken as they were. I could do nothing but stumble along with them.

My mother's shoe was still lying where I had seen it two nights ago. I picked it up and turned it over in my hand. There were no bloodstains, no remnants of flesh. I asked a few neighbors if they had seen her, but no one had. I suspected she had perished in a firestorm, but I didn't want to believe it. That she had sought shelter or found a home with a friend were false hopes. There was a slim chance she was in a different hospital from the one my father was staying in, but to find her would take days of searching.

Only the burned-out frame of our home was left. The roof had been incinerated, the remaining floors collapsed downward, one upon another. A sooty gray smoke rose in pigtail curls from the basement. The entire building – tons of debris – had collapsed on top of it. I walked as far as I could on the crumbling frame and called out for my mother. She did not answer. My voice cracked as I called out again and again. Only the pop and hiss of the lingering fire rose from the basement. In my heart, I knew she and Frau Horst were dead.

I said good-bye to a few people who wandered like ghosts through the neighborhood. Most acted like shell-shocked automatons. However, in some I saw a burning fanaticism for revenge – the destruction, the deaths, the Allied attacks, would be avenged. Little could be done, however, by those bombed out of their homes. Such retribution was wishful thinking, as unlikely as stopping the falling bombs.

I trudged away from my neighborhood. My stomach

churned with each step as I thought of my mother, most likely dead, and my father, who had no home to return to. I stopped people I recognized and told them to watch for my mother. I couldn't tell them where I worked, so I asked them to contact the Reichsbund in Berlin if they had any news.

Eventually, I arrived at the train station. I must have looked a fright in my tattered dress. However, we had all suffered the same fate, and nothing was said about my appearance. Horror and destitution had found homes in Berlin. I told the SS guard it was imperative that I return to the Führer. As I suspected, once I showed my papers I was whisked onto the train. The conductor gave me a blanket to keep warm. The train and the tracks had escaped damage from the bombs.

As the train traveled east toward the Wolf's Lair, I had plenty of time to think about what needed to be done. Karl and I had a responsibility to act, and that urge burned brighter in me than it ever had before. I was certain others in the Party felt the same way.

# CHAPTER 12

The next afternoon, I arrived at Rastenburg to bitter cold. The day felt like winter, with the sun passing low on the southern horizon. Pinkish-red rays streaked the clouds and the icy smell of snow was in the air, but the crisp scent was tainted by the smell of decay from the foul swamp. The pervading dampness spread across headquarters. I found Dora at the dormitory and told her my story. She said she would find clothes to replace those destroyed in Berlin. I had left my few belongings at the Wolf's Lair, but clothing was now in short supply. I stood next to a heater while I waited for her. A few women lay huddled under layers of blankets on their beds. Dora returned with four dresses and a winter coat. I showered, put on a small amount of makeup and then set out to find Karl.

I caught sight of him passing through the guard gate into the second perimeter. He was in his gray field uniform. His eyes were focused on the ground and he did not see me until I called his name. He looked up, broke into a run, swept me into his arms and kissed me.

I dissolved into tears as he pressed my head to his chest and stroked my hair.

'I was worried sick,' he said. 'I had no idea whether you or your family was alive. I knew your neighborhood had been bombed because Göring's generals informed us in the situational conferences with Hitler. He is furious about what is happening in Berlin and places the blame squarely on the air force. Göring is in deep trouble.'

'Karl,' I said, sobbing, 'my mother is dead.'

He squeezed me tighter. 'I'm so sorry, Magda. How cruel this war is.' He put a finger to my lips. 'Weep, but be strong. It's the only way we can survive.'

I pulled away from him — my inability to control our circumstances stoked rage within me. 'I don't care who knows,' I cried out. 'Hitler, too. My mother is dead and my father is homeless. In Berlin, thousands are dead and hundreds of thousands are without homes. I've seen the destruction with my own eyes. For what? His Reich?'

Karl pulled me off the path past a stand of bare trees. We stood concealed behind them. 'Please, Magda, think before you speak. The operation is in place. I'm not sure when it will occur, but you must be patient. When it's over, Germany will be a free nation again.'

I stepped back, ready to fight anything blocking my fury, including Karl. 'I would kill him now, if I could.'

'Think of your father — think of the innocents who would die because you killed the Führer. It's a delicate operation that has to be planned. The Wehrmacht has to fall in line behind us. The officers have to support us; otherwise, we are lost. Please understand how complicated this has been . . . and if one man betrays us . . .' His eyes

180

grew cloudy and their edges turned pink with tears. 'And what would I do without you? How could I go on? Please, don't do anything rash. I couldn't stand to lose you, like Franz lost Ursula.'

His words calmed me enough that I considered what he was saying. He kissed me again and I welcomed his touch. 'Come to my room at ten.'

'What about the other men in your quarters?'

'I have the room to myself tonight. Would you like to be alone with me?' He brushed his fingers against my cheek.

I nodded and we embraced. Large snowflakes began to drift down through the trees, falling lightly upon our shoulders.

'It's cold,' Karl said. 'I don't want you to catch your death. We should go inside.'

We walked hand in hand to my dormitory and then parted. 'Until tonight,' he said.

I couldn't forget. I kissed him and wondered whether it was wise to go to his room. I barely had time to ask myself the question before my heart answered. *Yes.* I wanted to make love to Karl. Time was running out and I was unsure how much happiness the future held for either one of us. My mother was dead. My father, I thought, would be proud of my decision to fight Hitler. My love for Karl deserved to be fully expressed. I could no longer deny what few moments of joy were within our grasp. Damn the consequences. When I returned to my room, I knew my love for Captain Karl Weber would be consummated.

I met him on the path to his quarters at ten. We tried to avoid other officers, but we passed a few outside. They gave me a sideways glance and then looked away. The officer corps was a tightly knit organization. Apparently, it had become well known across headquarters that Karl and I were a couple.

His bed was turned down and a candle burned on his desk. Its yellow light flickered and spread ochre shadows across the room. We said little. He told me to sit on the bed and then he kissed me. We took off our clothes piece by piece until we were naked on the sheets, a blanket spread across our shoulders. Karl asked me if I was a virgin and I told him, 'Yes.' I think he was pleased to know I'd not been with another man. I asked him if he had ever been with a woman. He told me he had, several years ago, and had paid for her services. He swore it was the one and only time. My hymen had broken years ago while participating in girls' athletics, but I felt no need to explain that to Karl. He wouldn't have minded either way.

He put on a condom, entered me and made love in slow thrusts until we both relaxed into a natural rhythm. We swayed as our bodies clung to each other, molding ourselves as one, until we were consumed and spent by our mutual passion.

We lay in bed, nestled against each other, until early the next morning. We dressed and Karl escorted me back to my dormitory. Neither of us expressed any regret for the evening, but we knew we had to be cautious. Making love every night, even every week, was impossible. Hitler wanted those he had paired, in his wisdom, to be married for the benefit of the Reich. Sexual intercourse without marriage was akin to an act of treason. Our sexual relationship was a danger to the state. Both of us knew we must forsake our mutual pleasure – too much was at stake.

The fall days dragged by as thoughts of revenge consumed me. I kept them to myself, not even sharing with Karl because I knew he would never allow me to act on them.

In early December, I received a letter from my father. He had been released from the hospital, returned to work and taken a spare room in the home of a co-worker, a man with a wife and two children. The family had doubled up its sleeping arrangements, allowing my father to rent the room. Housing and incomes were scarce in Berlin. He wrote little about my mother, but his grief came through the letter in a somber and stoic tone. Still, I was happy to hear from him and learn that he was safe.

A week later, Cook informed me that Else, four other girls and I would be transferred to the Berghof for the holiday season, possibly longer. No one ever knew the length of Hitler's stays; sometimes he remained until spring or early summer before returning to one of his other headquarters. I was disappointed until I learned that Karl was coming as well.

That night, with the others, I boarded a train headed southwest to the Berghof. Else and I chatted on the long trip and played cards, but it took three days to reach Berchtesgaden because we traveled mostly at night. Hitler, ever fearful of Allied bombings, ordered the trains to roll under cover of darkness. The second night, I was invited to have dinner with the Führer. I had to hide my feelings of revulsion as he sat there in his appointed seat in the dining car. How I wanted to end his life there. I trembled at the thought of thrusting an insignificant weapon, a dinner knife perhaps, into his heart. As usual, his conversation was about anything but the war. Cook had warned me that any mention of it was met with a stern look and dismissal from the dinner table. Instead, he talked about art and culture and bombarded us with stories about his youth before returning to one of his favorite topics.

During dinner, he continued to proclaim his disdain for meat eaters. 'Do you realize how meat comes to the table?' he said with the air of a pontificate. 'Corpse upon bloody corpse strewn across the ground. You can't imagine how disgusting it is until you've seen it.' He reached down and patted Blondi, who lay at his feet, and then lectured us about the slaughterhouse.

I lost my appetite because of his graphic descriptions and the hatred in my heart for my host.

Else was awed by the majestic vistas of the Alps when we arrived in Berchtesgaden. She'd never been so far south. After we'd climbed into the entourage of cars waiting at the train station, we motored up the mountain road. Soon Hitler's retreat loomed ahead of us, luminescent under the brilliant December sun. After passing through the guardhouse, the car pulled into the entrance I'd first seen a half a year before. In a strange way, I felt as if I had come home after an abysmal absence. The sun, the beautiful morning light, the mountain air, revived me after the oppressive stay at the Wolf's Lair. The atmosphere here was much more relaxed than in Rastenburg. Else also noticed the difference immediately. She said her cares seemed to drop away – she might not even mind continuing on as a taster here. I showed her to our room with the view of the Untersberg, the same room that Ursula and I had shared. That small part of my history seemed a lifetime ago.

Because I was a senior member of her staff, Cook assigned me to taste the evening supper. Else was to taste for lunch, also an important meal in Hitler's schedule. I showed Else around the grounds so she'd be familiar with the greenhouses and the other buildings at the compound. We were back at the Berghof, admiring the view from the terrace, when Eva Braun showed up with her two Scotties. She remembered me and shook my hand. She and Hitler had been apart for several months and she seemed pleased to have company again. I introduced her to Else. Eva was cordial to me, but her measured tone with Else convinced me that one needed to gain Eva's trust in order to be invited into her circle.

'I fear there will be little for you to do this year,' Eva said to us. 'The Führer has ordered that any celebrations should be muted.' She sighed. 'I do wish the war would end soon, so our lives could get back to normal. Adolf . . .' She paused, blushing from her casual use of his name. 'The Führer is so absorbed in his duties that I worry about him. I don't want him to be in a bad mood. He may not even allow a tree this year, but he'll probably give his usual gift of chocolates to his staff.' She leaned down and petted the dogs. 'At least there's something to look forward to.' She cupped her hands around their jowls. 'Right, Negus and Stasi? And our holiday teas, of course.'

'When are those?' Else asked innocently.

Eva laughed, straightened up and drew together the lapels of her fur coat. 'Oh, they're not for you. They're for the invited guests of the Führer. I imagine you'll be the tasters for them.'

After a stiff good-bye, she turned and walked away leaving Else and me in the sun.

'Who was that woman?' Else asked.

'A companion of the Führer's. She rules the Berghof. Keep on her good side.'

We walked back to our room. Something had struck me as Eva talked to us – Hitler's teas. How better to poison the Führer than at one of his intimate gatherings by the fire in the Great Hall? Still, such a plan would be risky and might result in many deaths, including those who had let the poison slip by. The thought numbed me like a dip in a cold lake.

Many nights I tossed and turned as I formulated my plan to kill Hitler. I shared these thoughts with no one, especially Karl. I didn't know how seriously to take them – they became obsessive – like a madwoman who can think of nothing but murder. The anger, the murderous machinations, grew so intense I could barely sleep. Every time I decided upon the perfect plot, I thought about my father and what might happen to him, or Karl's words would come back to me. *Killing the Führer should be part of a master plan,* he scolded me in my head. What would be the consequences of killing Hitler? Of course I would be a hero to the Allies, but in Germany my family and I would be branded as traitors by the Nazis and punished by death. My anger and frustration were maddening.

But what if I could murder Hitler without anyone knowing? Perhaps I could slip into his room while he was asleep and slit his throat, or pour poison into his ear like

Claudius did to the king in *Hamlet*. There had to be a way to rid Germany of the tyrant. The only way my father, Karl and I would survive the assassination would be to commit the perfect crime. I had no good solution. I was not by nature a murderer.

During my work at the Wolf's Lair and the Berghof, I'd noticed that SS officers paid strict attention to their weapons. Rarely would they part with their guns. Sometimes they would take off their holsters at lunch and place them on the table, or by their sides, or cradle them on the floor next to their boots. The weapons were always close by. And only once had I seen an officer walk off without his gun. Stealing one was out of the question. It would immediately be missed. I suspected there was a weapons cache at the SS dormitory at the Berghof, but I dared not ask Karl where it was located, or make a foolish attempt to break into it. I was sure to be captured.

Poison wasn't particularly a good choice, either, although it was the most convenient for me. I had learned my lesson from trying to poison Minna — too many innocent people could be killed and suspicion cast upon those who survived. Otto, the cook, had paid the price for my plot against Minna.

Otherwise, a variety of objects could be used as instruments of death: a knife, a sword, an ax, a cane. Piano wire. A stocking, as Franz had used on Minna, or a necktie. A man could be murdered in a variety of ways, but none of them came easy for a woman in my position. Hitler's security forces, the Führer's natural reclusiveness, even the snow on the ground, which made it all but impossible to follow someone without leaving footprints, added to the problem of murder. I'd read long ago that it was difficult to kill a man and harder still to dispose of the body. I believed that to be true. Murder was a messy business with too many ways to bungle the job.

Killing Hitler seemed an impossible task. I had a fantasy of pushing him off the walking trail he loved so much that led to the Teahouse. The Führer and I would take a late morning walk together with Blondi and when we came to the overlook I would push him over the side to his death. But many people often walked with him. How could I arrange a solitary stroll with the Führer? Impossible! And, if I did, the blame would land on me. What if he didn't die from the fall? What if someone followed us? Too many questions filled my mind.

I realized one morning that I was going quite mad over my mother's death. The rage I felt was directed at Hitler and I couldn't quell my murderous emotions.

Karl met me that afternoon on the terrace. The December day was bright and cold after an evening snowfall. The magnificent mountains were mantled in white and transparent wisps of clouds flew over us on a crisp north wind. The sunlight fell in brilliant splashes on the terrace. Many gathered there at noon to take advantage of the warmth: Eva and a couple of her friends, attired in fine dresses and winter furs; SS officers in their snappy uniforms proudly surveying the scenery. I knew what they were thinking: *Germany can never be defeated because Hitler would never allow it to happen. We are invincible. Look at what we behold!* They were as mesmerized by the view as Hitler.

Karl and I walked to a corner of the terrace where we could talk far away from the others. Knowing that nothing would come of them, I told him of my many fantasies to kill Hitler.

His eyes narrowed in concern. 'Never act on these thoughts,' he whispered harshly. He grabbed my shoulders, turned my back to the others and stood behind me. He continued talking into my ear in a soft voice. 'One of our group has received intelligence from the British. They are operating in this area because they hope to assassinate Hitler in a sniper attack. We're trying to stop them. We agree in theory, but their plan will only present more problems if it is carried out.'

I looked down, dismayed, because I knew the question that haunted Karl. 'Who would take over if Hitler was killed?'

'Precisely.'

He stepped in front of me, held my hands and stood so close his body warmed me. 'Operation Valkyrie is in full swing, but you must give it time. The bomb on the Führer's plane did not go off.'

'What?' I stared at Karl, incredulous that attempts had already been made on Hitler's life.

Karl smiled, but I knew it was only an attempt to fool those on the terrace into thinking we were having a pleasant conversation. 'Operation Spark. It failed. A bomb was placed in a box that supposedly contained cognac bottles on Hitler's plane last March, but for some reason it didn't go off. We think the explosive cap froze in the cargo hold. There have been other attempts.'

I was stunned.

'You shouldn't know everything,' Karl said. 'It's not wise. The less you are aware of what's going on the better. We're constantly on guard. We never know when some rogue officer is going to attempt to assassinate him. Valkyrie is our best hope of saving Germany. There are others who believe as I do.'

Tears stung my eyes at the mere possibility of Hitler's death. I wanted to cling to Karl, but such a display of emotion would have been too hard to explain. I brushed the tears away. 'I feel so tired and defeated. Our situation seems hopeless. Is there nothing I can do?'

He sighed. 'Magda, you must get these thoughts out of your head. Don't drive yourself mad over something you can't accomplish.' He looked across the terrace. 'I have a plan, but we can't talk here. It's too dangerous. Put on your boots. Let's take a walk to the Teahouse.'

Karl and I agreed to meet at the front steps of the Berghof. I went back to my room and changed out of my shoes and into boots. Else was curled up under the covers, taking a nap after working the morning shift. I tiptoed around the room in order not to wake her. I closed the door quietly and walked down the wide hallway where Hitler often welcomed his guests to his mountain retreat. I opened the doors of the portico, which led to the broad stone steps, descending like the stairs of a Greek temple, to the driveway below. Mussolini, Chamberlain and countless other foreign dignitaries had climbed these steps to meet the Führer. The invited Party dignitaries, Speer, Göring, Goebbels, did the same when visiting. Hitler, his arm stiffly raised in a corresponding salute, towered like a god over them. From his vantage point at the top, he was the victor, the conqueror of those ascending from below.

Since I'd begun my work at the Berghof, I'd seen the newsreels and photos. The protocol was always the same. Hitler, dressed in his most regal military garb, often white, would stand at the top as the visitors arrived below. The guests always climbed the stairs to honor the leader of the

Reich. They arrived at this place to offer a gift or, as many had done, deliver a sacrifice. A nation would do as well as any offering.

Karl smiled when he saw me standing at the top. The evening snowfall had been plowed into neat rows on each side of the drive. The thick white piles glittered with sparkling stars in the sunlight. I took Karl's hand. We walked down the drive, patchy with ice, followed its U-shaped turn until we reached the trail that led to the Teahouse. We were the only ones out. I said little, but the sadness I felt earlier had eased and my spirits lifted underneath the evergreen canopy. If only we were not at war! If only a madman were not in charge! How different the world would be. Karl and I could be married, have children and start a life together. But my wishes might as well have been smoke, as transitory and fleeting as the wind that flowed around us.

When we came to the overlook, Karl stopped, swept the snow off the railing and stood silent. I started to speak, but he held up his hand.

'Listen,' he said.

I did, but heard nothing. He turned and brushed his lips across my cheek. My legs struggled to hold my weight; I felt light-headed as he caressed my face. 'I don't hear anything.'

'Nothing,' he said, and cocked his head. 'Nothing but the wind brushing against the trees, the flutter of snow falling from branches. How quiet and how beautiful the world can be.' He stepped away and put his hands over his face. His shoulders buckled and he broke into sobs. When he took his hands away, his face was red with rage. He shuddered to stifle his anger. 'Millions are dying because of one man! Think of it, Magda! Think how wonderful the world could be if there was peace. At this time of year we need to be reminded of peace. Hitler will stop at nothing to get his way, to fulfill his vision of what the world should be. He will kill and keep on killing until nothing is left but the Reich.'

I put my arms around him and drew him close. A tear fell upon my face. He pointed across the valley to the forest below and then to the mountain peaks spread across the horizon. 'See how easy it would be for the British to position a sniper below, say in the forest – anywhere they could get a clear shot.'

I tried to imagine Hitler standing at the overlook, perhaps with Blondi by his side. One bullet through the head. One bullet through the heart. The thoughts made me shiver, crazed with rage.

'How easy that would be,' Karl said, 'but how unfortunate for Germany. I hope the British realize the folly of their plan.'

'When you were going to—' I couldn't finish the sentence. 'How did you get the bomb into the Wolf's Lair?'

He leaned against the railing. 'It's easier than you might think. The officers and soldiers have developed a trust with one another. It's a strength and weakness for the Reich. Explosives can be slipped into a valise, or almost any object, for example, a cognac bottle. The guards rarely check a commanding officer unless they have some reason to be suspicious. When I knew my attempt was doomed by von Stauffenberg, I buried the bomb in swampy ground. Within hours the explosives would be useless.' Karl took hold of my shoulders. 'Magda, you must do something for me. It's very important . . .'

He hesitated as if he were searching for the right words.

'I'm asking you to do something that will assure your safety and possibly mine if it's carried out successfully. However, it's not without danger. But your life after Operation Valkyrie could depend on it.'

My pulse quickened. 'Go on.'

Karl steadied me. 'I want you to poison Hitler.'

I stared at him. How could he ask me to do such a thing when he'd wanted me to have no part of an assassination attempt?

'I'm not sure I heard you correctly,' I said.

'You must poison him, but then you must save him.'

The rage Karl had displayed a few minutes before had disappeared. Now only love showed in his eyes.

# CHAPTER 13

On the walk back to the Berghof, Karl convinced me that I should display my allegiance to Hitler, for if any part of Valkyrie went awry, suspicion would be deflected from me. Naturally, the Gestapo and the SS would consider me a collaborator because of our relationship. The best way to avoid that conclusion, he pointed out, would be for me to save Hitler's life. He had come to this realization within the past few days. As we walked, we came up with a plan.

'Austerity' was the holiday word at the Berghof as Cook had proclaimed. There were no parties, no Christmas tree and little joviality. The war on the Eastern Front was going badly, the Berlin bombings had taken their toll on the German people and the generals were concerned with the Allies' plans in the West. Of course, I would have been as much in the dark about these matters as the rest of Germany if it hadn't been for Karl. Only those directly affected, like the Berliners and the soldiers, knew the horrors of the war. The remainder of the Reich labored on, believing the lies spread by the Propaganda Minister.

But Eva Braun hosted a tea party every few days, as she had mentioned to Else and me on the terrace. The more Karl and I thought about it, the more we felt it would be a good idea if we both were invited to one of her teas, just as she had invited Karl to the showing of *Gone with the Wind*. That way, we could both be present for the poisoning.

The tea occurred a few days before Christmas. The snow fell heavily for hours and low clouds obscured the mountains as darkness descended upon the Berghof. Because of the weather, Eva scheduled her social event in the Great Hall after the Führer's situational conference, rather than in the Teahouse. I had never been in the room, but I had heard stories about its huge window, several meters in width and height, that looked out upon the mountains. Karl and I arrived after four in the afternoon and Eva and several of her guests were already nestled in the large couches and chairs that surrounded the red marble fireplace. I was immediately taken by the room, which consisted of two separate elevations. The south side, where we entered, was higher than the rest of the Great Hall. With its tapestries, oil paintings and sculptures, its wide expanse reminded me of a museum built around a sitting room. The heavy wooden ceiling was carved into ornamental squares that supported a round chandelier. Furniture groupings were scattered about the room in comfortable seating arrangements. Everything the leader of the Reich needed to conduct his business was in the Great Hall: a massive conference table, an extraordinarily large globe on a wooden stand, cabinets, a grandfather clock, even a piano. But the showpiece of the room was the gigantic rectangular window. I got only a vague notion of its grandeur because of the bad weather. Karl told me it could be lowered into the basement on warm days to give an unobstructed view of the Untersberg. Certainly the window fit the psychology of the Führer. With this touch as well, he had constructed his retreat to fit his view of the world – master of all he surveyed.

Two ladies in fine dresses and a large man in a suit sat on a wide couch facing the fire. The man wore a monocle over his right eye. The group looked uncomfortable on the couch because it was so big they had to lean forward with no support for their backs. Otherwise, they would look like stuffed dolls with their legs hanging over the lip of the couch. One large chair sat angled next to the fire. I assumed this chair was for Hitler. Eva sat to the right of it with the Scotties at her feet. There was another large chair to the left with a small table in between.

'Sit in that chair,' Karl whispered to me, and pointed to the vacant chair to the left of the empty one. 'I'll distract Eva. She loves it when men flirt with her.'

I took my seat. Not one of the guests recognized me or said hello. They all continued their private conversations. I watched as Karl went to Eva and bowed. Her eyes lit up as he complimented her dress and appearance. I heard him say, 'How lovely you look . . . as radiant as the winter stars . . .' He heaped on the flattery. She ordered a valet to rearrange the chairs so Karl could sit on her other side.

I had chosen a black dinner dress with long sleeves, offered to me by Cook when she learned of my invitation. I made sure my Party pin was prominently displayed. To complete my outfit, I had also been given a centuries-old 'poison ring' by Karl. He had purchased it in an antiques shop in Munich. The ring consisted of a silver band with a black opal on its top, which concealed a secret compartment. In it were a few granules of cyanide.

As we waited for Hitler, some of the guests looked my way and asked a few ingratiating questions. I struggled to keep my hands from shaking. Karl and I had rehearsed our plan for several days. He said it was crucial that I remain calm at all times. I wished the evening were over – the experience with Minna had tempered my enthusiasm for intrigue. The only way I could keep my hands still was to grasp my fingers and keep them planted firmly in my lap.

Eva was captivated by Karl. She laughed and smiled and threw her head back as he chatted with her. She was the picture of a woman in the throes of flirtatious infatuation. His ploy worked so successfully that a shiver of jealousy settled upon me for an instant. However, it was ridiculous to feel jealous of Eva Braun. Hitler would have her tossed out of the Berghof, or worse, for any sexual indiscretion.

A tap on my arm startled me. A young woman, who wore a fine cream-colored dress dripping with accent jewels, stared at me. The neckline was fitted with an ermine collar. 'I was admiring your ring,' she said to me. 'May I look at it?' She reached expectantly toward my right hand.

I was taken aback by her request and I instinctively withdrew my hand. Karl noticed and his eyes caught mine. He nodded casually and continued his conversation with Eva.

'Of course,' I said, and held out my hand. 'But please be careful, it's very old – it was a gift from my great-grandmother.'

'Oh, I won't touch it,' she said. She grasped my fourth finger and bent down, examining the ring for several moments. 'It's stunning. I love stones of all kinds. This is one of the most beautiful black opals I've ever seen. I do wish I could try it on.'

My heart jumped, but I managed to say, 'I wish you could, too, but the band is very fragile. I only wear it on special occasions, such as tonight. Tea with the Führer! I don't often get the chance.'

She released my hand. 'I see. What do you do?'

'I'm in service to the Führer. I stand between him and death. I taste his food.' I imagined that my job would shock this lady, whoever she was, and that the description of my position might cause a reaction. It did. She suppressed a low moan, put her hand to her stomach and returned to the couch. A few minutes later, I caught her looking at me and whispering to the finely attired woman next to her. No introductions would be necessary now.

The south door opened. A valet entered and stood stiffly by it. Hitler, followed by several of his adjutants, entered the room. We all rose and saluted when he entered. He was wearing a black double-breasted suit. He seemed a little older, his face more careworn than the last time we had met. Blondi was by his side on the leash. As soon as the shepherd entered the room, Eva's dogs barked and howled. She commanded them to stop, but they paid little attention to her. Hitler frowned and handed Blondi back to his valet. The door closed and the dog was gone. We continued to stand until Hitler had made his way around the room, bowing to the women, kissing their hands, shaking hands with Karl and the other man before sitting in the chair next to me.

The leather crackled as he sat. He didn't speak for several minutes; he brushed his brown hair back from his forehead several times and stared into the fire. The intensity of the blaze was mirrored in his eyes. I had been warned not to speak unless he had spoken to me. I fidgeted in my seat while the other guests fell silent waiting for the Führer to speak.

Finally, he said, 'Go on with your chatter. Give me a few minutes to myself.'

Eva and the other guests immediately broke into conversation, laughing lightly, all the time watching Hitler out of the corners of their eyes. He appeared to be in bad sorts, as if the situational conference he had held earlier had not gone well. Karl and I had heard no shouting during the afternoon, but that didn't mean anything. Hitler's fury could have been silent, as deadly as a sniper. He might have even ordered executions. I looked casually at my lap and saw the black opal glinting up at me in the firelight.

Hitler leaned toward me and I jumped in my chair.

'I'm sorry,' he said. 'I didn't mean to startle you.' His voice dropped so low I could barely hear him. 'I don't want the others to know, especially these bloodsuckers Eva brings along, but I prefer my guests to hers; if it wasn't for Mussolini I think I would have no friends at all.' He looked at the fire, where the gigantic logs hissed and popped on the andirons. 'This fireplace will be here as long as the Reich stands. It's made from red marble from the Untersberg. Mussolini has given me a fireplace, at the Eagle's Nest.'

I had never been invited to the Eagle's Nest, an even higher mountain retreat constructed for Hitler by Martin Bormann. 'The fireplace is beautiful, Führer.' I stopped, carefully analyzing what I would say next. Karl and I had tried various scenarios over the weeks, but we knew we couldn't prepare for every possible situation. 'You bear the weight of the world upon your shoulders.'

He turned to me and smiled. Any ferocity in his eyes vanished. 'The burdens I carry are for the Reich. None other, and so it shall be until the day I die.' He tapped his fingers on the arms of the chair. A valet came with a silver tea service and placed it in the center of the large table that our chairs surrounded. 'But there should be no talk tonight of war. Tell me, how are your wedding plans coming?'

I bowed my head, embarrassed by his question. 'We've moved forward somewhat.' I hoped my answer would appease him.

He reached across the small table and grabbed my right hand. 'Tell me the date, my child. I want to be part of it, for I know I've been instrumental in your match.'

My heart pounded in my ears. He had hold of my hand and with it the poison ring. My mind begged him not to look at it.

A log popped and a spark skittered across the fireplace rug. The valet scurried to the ember and swept it up quickly into a dustpan. I took this diversion as an opportunity to withdraw my hand. Then the valet returned and poured tea into a porcelain cup for Hitler. The Führer placed the drink on the small table next to us and looked at me expectantly.

This was the chance I was waiting for. I knew there was no turning back. The timing must be perfect, otherwise Karl and I had agreed not to take the risk. Eva and the others were engaged in conversation; tea was being poured for the guests. I pulled out a handkerchief I had placed in my sleeve and dabbed at my eyes. 'I am so overjoyed, my Führer. I can tell you we have planned a summer wedding.'

Hitler nodded with joy, placed his arm on my shoulder and pulled me toward him in a gentle hug. I accepted his embrace of congratulations, a rarely given token of affection. As I leaned toward him I covered my right hand with the handkerchief. I could not see it – nor could anyone else – but the ring was positioned over his teacup. I was about to release the catch on the opal with my thumb when Hitler looked down at the table. I had overlooked one fact. He hated germs – a stupid mistake on my part – my handkerchief over his cup must have upset him. His eyes flashed in disgust.

Our embrace was brief and he withdrew from me almost as quickly as he had drawn me forward. As the others were served and Hitler eyed the desserts, I stuffed the handkerchief back in my sleeve. The poison would have to wait for another time.

While the others drank, Hitler eyed the cup as he lifted it from the table. I was certain he would reconsider drinking from it, considering his phobia about germs.

The faint smell of bitter almonds wafted toward me from the steaming tea. I screamed and knocked the cup to the floor. It crashed on the rug and Eva's dogs bolted toward it.

'Magda, what's come over you?' Karl shouted.

'Keep the dogs away!' I lunged for the cup. 'The tea has been poisoned.'

A collective gasp filled the room, not the least of which came from the valet who'd served the tea and now looked upon me with wide, terrified eyes. The man on the couch spit out his tea and the others gulped and put their cups down. I took out my handkerchief and began to blot up the liquid. Eva collared the Scotties and dragged them back to her chair.

Hitler rose like a stern judge before a courtroom and said calmly, 'Don't touch the cup.' He looked over my shoulder. 'Don't ruin your dress. How did you know?'

I rose, expecting to see anger and hatred in his gaze, but his eyes were quiet and studied, as if he could read my thoughts. 'I smelled cyanide. Cook says it's a genetic trait.'

'I'm afraid we need to call for more tea,' Hitler said, 'but first I'll summon security.' I knew what that meant. The SS Colonel would be here soon to question all of us. 'It seems someone is trying to poison me. I would have suspected Otto, but he's no longer here.'

The woman who had examined my ring cried out, 'For God's sake, smell the teapot. We all drank from it.'

I lifted the pot and took off the lid. There was no smell, but I took several sniffs until I could be sure they were satisfied of my attention to duty. 'I smell nothing.' The ladies sank back on the couch in relief.

'Who handled the tea?' Karl asked the valet.

The young man quaked before Karl's question. 'Only me, sir,' he said. 'I swear no one touched the drink except me. It was tasted by one of the girls in the kitchen.'

'Then there can only be one answer,' Karl said. 'The cup was laced with cyanide. Is this the cup you planned to serve to the Führer?' He pointed to it, still on the floor.

'No, sir, I paid no attention to the cups and saucers. I swear it.'

'Someone in the kitchen is responsible,' Hitler said. 'Let me talk to the Colonel.' He pointed to the valet. 'He should start with you.'

'I will get him, Führer,' Karl offered, and left the room.

I returned to my chair and we all sat looking at one

202

another as the room grew still. Hitler stared into the fire as if nothing had happened. No one dared speak a word.

A few minutes later, Karl appeared with the Colonel and a few of his officers. They spread out across the room. One of them took the valet away for questioning. They also took the cup and my soaked handkerchief, which I'd left near it.

Eva tried to smile and be happy, but fear shone through her face. Hitler was not so concerned. 'Once again, providence has saved me,' he said to Eva. 'How many times have I told you that my destiny shall be fulfilled? The evening is not ruined. We shall just begin again.' Hitler instructed the Colonel to wait until tea was over; then he could question everyone in the room as he pleased. 'In the meantime, I shall order another pot of tea and coffee and a plate of fresh desserts.' He turned in his chair and looked me in the eye. 'And Magda shall taste them for us before we begin.'

The fresh food and drink were not poisoned, but the fact that I had nothing to do with the attempt shook me. With every sip and taste I wondered whether it would be my last. I took more care in tasting than I had in months. The tension in the room forced me to admit that I had become lax in my job.

Hitler, Eva and the other guests stared at me as I tasted the new plates brought out of the kitchen. They followed each bite with eyes like cats following a bird. I wondered who could have poisoned the cup. Karl must have believed I had done it, but he was wrong.

When the conversation resumed, Hitler droned on about Wagner's music until Eva gave him a cold, hard stare. He reluctantly stopped his lecture and the room drifted into silence. Eva attempted to steer our banter toward photography, the hobby she loved the most, but the other guests seemed to know or care little about it.

I had no appetite as the evening progressed. Hitler even fell asleep in his chair for a time, and Eva hoarsely whispered to her guests, 'I've had enough. I'm sorry this has been so disappointing.' She got up and walked to the door. The SS Colonel stood stiffly outside waiting for us. The commotion awakened Hitler and he proclaimed the tea at an end. His dinnertime, followed by another late night conference, was approaching, so he excused himself. Before he did so, he took my right hand – the hand with the ring – and kissed it. 'Thank you for saving my life,' he said. 'I shall remember this night and your service to the Führer.'

I wanted to wipe his kiss from my hand, but I knew that his memory of this evening would serve me later in some capacity. However, I found his gesture of affection revolting. It turned my stomach.

The other guests, Karl and I were left in the Great Hall. Karl had heard my exchange with Hitler and looked at me approvingly.

I turned away from the door so the Colonel could not see my face. 'I had nothing to do with it,' I whispered to Karl. 'You must take the ring, put it somewhere the Colonel will not suspect.' Under the pretext of holding hands, Karl slipped it off my finger. As we walked toward the door, I could tell he was frantically trying to figure out who had poisoned the cup and what to do with the ring.

The Colonel stopped me at the door and asked Karl to wait outside. Eva and her guests were told they would be called upon later, or in the morning. I knew Eva would never be questioned.

Two SS men followed the Colonel. I sat in the chair I'd been in all evening. The Colonel, in his gray uniform, sat on the couch across from me. One of the officers carried a pad to take down my words and sat near the table so he could write. The other stood nearby passively looking on. 'Find me an ashtray,' the Colonel said to the officer who stood. The man nodded and then left.

The Colonel's cruel eyes traveled over me. Chills raced over my skin under his fierce gaze. I hid my fear as best I could. He arched an eyebrow and sank back against the cushions. He did not look as small on the large couch as Eva's guests.

'You seem to attract trouble,' the Colonel said. The other officer scribbled on his paper.

'What do you mean?' I asked.

'Tonight you saved the Führer's life, but this is not the first time you've encountered poisons.' The other officer returned with an ashtray and stood by his superior. The Colonel withdrew a pack of cigarettes from his jacket and lit up. He threw the match into the ashtray and exhaled a long stream of smoke.

'The Führer does not like his officers to smoke,' I said.

The Colonel smiled with smug conviction. 'You're very assured for a servant.'

I found his insult childish. 'It's true I'm in service to the Führer. If you wish to classify my position as a servant to the Führer that is your concern.'

He motioned to the officer who was writing. The man withdrew a file from his clipboard and handed it to the

Colonel. He placed his cigarette in the ashtray and the smoke rose in white circles until it was sucked away in thin streaks by the fire's draft. He read from the file: 'You were dormitory mates with Ursula Thalberg, who attempted to kill the Führer with cyanide; you were sickened by a cook at the Wolf's Lair as a test of your abilities; you discovered poison in the food at the Wolf's Lair as it was being prepared for the Führer. That led to the dismissal of the cook who tested you.' He put the file on the table. 'And now tonight.' The Colonel blinked and took another puff on his cigarette. The SS officer who was writing looked at me for my reply.

I chose to focus on the Colonel. 'You're reciting nothing but the hazards of my job. I'm very good at what I do. Ask Cook.'

'Do you have access to poisons?'

I leaned forward and addressed him squarely. 'Everyone in the kitchen has access to poisons, or knows where they are. If you are implicating me, you might as well arrest the whole kitchen staff.'

He laughed. 'Do not tempt me, Fräulein. Sometimes nothing clears the air like a good housecleaning.' He pointed to me. 'Please stand up.'

I was shocked by his order. 'Why?'

'Do it.'

I shrugged and stood as the three men in the room watched me like I was a prisoner ready to be stripped. Another SS officer, this one a woman, entered the door to the Great Hall. She seemed somewhat familiar, but I had not met her. After all, the Führer was surrounded by nearly two thousand people at his various headquarters. She circled me, stopped and stood stiffly in front of me. Her eyes were unmoving; no hint of emotion showed in her face.

'Search her,' the Colonel ordered.

The woman came forward without a word and placed her hands on my shoulders and then moved her fingers down to my breasts. She squeezed them through the fabric and then moved her hands lower, across my genitals, until she finished her job at my shoes. She ordered me to take them off and then turned me around and completed a similar hand search down my back. She even examined my Party pin. I was glad I had given the poison ring to Karl, but I worried whether he was able to hide it in time.

'Nothing,' the woman said brusquely after she had completed her task.

I turned to the Colonel, my cheeks flushed with anger. 'See? You shouldn't have been concerned about me.'

'I am not convinced.' He took a final puff on his cigarette and then rubbed it out in the ashtray. 'Be aware that you and the kitchen staff are being watched. We will find the perpetrator of these crimes.' He pointed a thin finger at me. 'The criminal will be punished.'

'May I leave now?' I said, still angered by his implication. 'I'm tasting the Führer's dinner. I have work to do.'

His mouth curled into a haughty smirk. 'Go about your business. I have the Reich's business to conduct.'

I took one last look at the Great Hall as I shut the door. The three men and the woman were looking at me as if they knew what Karl and I had planned for Eva's tea party. The stares coming from their eyes shook me. Darkness had fallen and the extraordinary picture window on the north wall was black as the night, suiting my mood. Again, I felt helpless, under the crush of Hitler's hand and the scrutiny of his forces.

Karl and I didn't see each other until the next morning. We walked down the drive at the Berghof, then wound our way up the hill on a path that had been cleared through the deep snow toward Göring's residence. At one point we stepped off onto the short ski trails cut by Eva and her friends the day before. No one was out. The clouds had scattered, but the temperature was bitter under the hard blue sky.

'I was worried,' I said to him. We clung to each other as we tramped through the snow. 'I was afraid you'd get caught with the ring.'

'I dropped it in my underwear,' he said. 'I thought the SS would stop short of putting their hands down my pants. I don't know what I would've done if the Colonel had asked me to strip. He could have ordered me to.'

I couldn't help but laugh, although the circumstances weren't funny. 'The woman who searched me certainly wasn't shy. She searched almost every crevice.'

Karl nodded. 'Yes, I know *of* her. She's a beast and not to be fooled with. You are lucky she didn't order you to take your dress off. I've heard – never through firsthand experience – that some resistance operators hide contraband where it can't be seen. It can only be found by probing fingers.'

I shook my head. 'Imagine that those of us who want to live freely must resort to such tactics.'

Karl stopped and turned to me. We stood on a slope, half in sunlight, half in blue shadow. The frosty plumes of our breaths mixed as one and then disappeared into the air. Karl kissed me and then said, 'What's the old saying? "All's fair

in love and war"? We do what we must, no matter the price.'
He guided my head toward his shoulder.

'Nineteen forty-four will be here soon,' I said. 'Surely we can celebrate something.'

He kissed me again. This time his lips lingered on mine and my heart stirred with longing. It had been several weeks since we'd made love.

'Yes,' he said with determination. 'We can celebrate our union and pray that this year the Reich will come to an end.'

I put my arms around his neck and pulled him close. 'I hope you're right. Germany is in need of good news.'

We stomped up the snowy hillside until we were in the blinding sun. Instead of continuing toward Göring's house, we turned east toward the SS barracks. As we neared, Karl slowed. 'Listen.'

A faint melody drifted in the air, men's voices carried on the wind. I recognized the tune, one I had known from Christmases past, in happier times when Berlin was not shattered by bombs and death had not gripped the land. It was 'O Tannenbaum,' which my father had sung to me many times when I was a child. I remembered the silent nights of Christmas when all was calm and bright and there were no worries, no terrors of war, no horrors thrust upon the world. Times of peace were always brief, it seemed. Those times had ended and war, like a plague, enveloped us. I turned to Karl and sang softly to the melody. He cupped my face in his hands as the tears streamed from my eyes.

# CHAPTER 14

Christmas 1943 and New Year's 1944 dragged by like the ticking of a sad clock. The monotony of winter set in with its mostly gray days, dismal afternoons and long nights. Since Karl and I had arrived at the Berghof we'd experienced little joy, none of the pleasures that anyone leading a normal life would have expected during the season. But when I asked myself what 'normal' was, I could come up with no good answer. The world was being ripped apart. How could I complain when so many were suffering? Every time I wanted to cry or grouse about my circumstances, I thought of those with no food or shelter in the midst of winter, perhaps with nothing at all but a lean-to propped against the harsh, cold winds.

I saw little of Hitler during the early months of 1944 and that suited me fine. He traveled back to the Wolf's Lair leaving a few of us with Eva. The officers who confided in Karl told him the Führer was now impossible to get along with no matter his location. He was surly, irritable, and always directed blame away from himself to those beneath him. Hitler, the infallible, could do no wrong. Karl said the Führer had the uncanny knack of refusing the sound advice of his generals and then excoriating them for losses of men and matériel. They were doomed by *his* failure to listen, *his* belief in his omnipotence. He was also a disastrous statesman, a tyrant over the lands he had conquered. His puppet governments were little more than killing machines against those who resisted his iron hand.

We never found out who laced Hitler's cup with cyanide. Neither did the SS. So many splintered pockets of resistance were arising it was impossible to tell who might be responsible. The Colonel ordered that the poisons be taken out of the kitchen and Cook's classes for new tasters be discontinued. 'I'm more concerned about the Führer than a taster,' he told her. 'If they die, they die.' Cook was furious, but her protests had no effect. At first I suspected someone from the kitchen, perhaps even Else, had tried to poison Hitler, but when I studied her kind face and subservient demeanor I knew she would never attempt such an act. On the other hand, those loyal to the Führer, like the Colonel, remained staunchly so and above suspicion. They would fight to the death for the Reich. Karl and I decided we should keep to ourselves during the winter and not press our luck. The times were too dangerous and too much suspicion had been cast upon the kitchen staff. Karl assured me the plot we'd been waiting for would be put into motion soon. Therefore, we should exercise patience and caution.

After the holidays, Karl and I expected we would be called back to the Wolf's Lair. However, no orders ever came. Hitler returned to the Berghof in late February 1944.

The foul mood in the house was unchanged by the intermittent thaws and shoots of grass poking through the snow. Although the days were growing longer and the sun stronger, heavy clouds of melancholy hung over the mountain retreat. Eva and her friends, the SS staff, Göring, Bormann, Speer and others would sometimes bask on the terrace during the increasingly warm days. Most of the time they were like paper cutouts, as shallow and useless as the governments Hitler had set up in his conquered lands. I imagined these officers and dignitaries came to the Berghof to listen to Hitler, bow and scrape and then execute his orders whether or not they believed in them.

By late March, the British had made no move against the Führer, nor had any other governments. Karl hinted that attempts on Hitler's life, besides the one he was involved in, might be in the works from other SS officers. The SS and its divisions were fractured by a lust for power; the chain of command was Byzantine and Machiavellian. Its leaders often were not aware of what their fellow officers were doing. Hitler issued conflicting orders to the officers and expected them to be carried out no matter the cost. If the men asked for clarification, they would be labeled as idiots or traitors who were dragging down the war effort. Astonishingly, Karl told me that Hitler's generals were whispering about an attack the Allies might be massing for on the Western Front. Hitler knew of these rumors and scoffed at the idea. France was impenetrable, he thought.

Our mood brightened on June 6, 1944, when news of the Allied invasion at Normandy arrived at the Berghof. Karl disguised his delight in the company of the other officers, but with me he was euphoric. He sensed that Hitler could not win a war on two fronts. The Red Army was pushing to the west, the British and the Americans would push to the east and they would meet in the middle – in Germany.

Hitler, Karl reported, was 'white as a ghost and looked as if he hadn't slept in weeks.' He spent much of his time in the Great Hall hunched over, his hand shaking as he attempted to draw with colored pencils on his array of maps.

'Hitler will have no choice but to surrender,' Karl said to me a few days later. We sat in my room after I'd tasted. Else had gone out with one of the other girls for a walk. He whispered in my ear, cautious that he might be overheard. 'Valkyrie may not even be put into motion.' He clasped my hands. 'Wouldn't that be wonderful? The Allies may be here in a matter of days.'

I looked at his face and saw that he was searching for any good news to come out of this war. He could not hide the exhaustion that lurked underneath his skin. I wanted to build him up for our sake, but this evening I couldn't. That task was as difficult as the change of winter to spring – the promise was there, but there was no certainty when it would happen.

I withdrew my hands from his and spoke in a low voice. One couldn't be too cautious. 'It would be wonderful . . . but we are dealing with a madman.' I turned away, afraid to look at him for fear I would cry. 'I don't believe he will surrender. Germany will go down to defeat in ashes.'

When I turned, Karl's face was pale and wracked with pain. His voice shook. 'Please, Magda, tell me you don't believe what you're saying. For God's sake, tell me you believe we will live.'

I sighed. 'I only know I love you.' I brushed my hand against his cheek and said, 'Let's be married. Let's live before it's too late.'

He stared at me, his eyes clouded with emotion. He kissed me and whispered, 'Yes, as soon as we can.'

Eva came to me a few days before my wedding and helped me pick out a suit from her vast wardrobe. She invited me to her private apartment, adjacent to the Führer's. Her living room was nicely coordinated in blue and white furnishings with a matching couch along one wall. A white writing desk sat opposite, in addition to chairs and a small table. Two rustic windows let in light.

I sensed she was as excited about my nuptials as I was – perhaps even more so. Eva, like so many devoted followers of Hitler, had the sense that nothing could go wrong as long as he was in charge. The man she adored would, in the end, conquer all the lands he desired. My faith in that future was by no means as assured.

She took me into her bedroom where a large burled walnut wardrobe covered one wall. She pulled open the doors and said, 'Choose whatever you like.' I was astonished at her collection of beautiful dresses, shoes, furs and scarves. I handled the dresses carefully, deciding upon a smart navy suit, one of the least expensive Eva owned, but with modern styling. 'I'll loan you my pearls,' she said. 'They'll look wonderful with that outfit.' She sat on the edge of her bed and looked at me. 'I don't think we wear the same shoe size. You'll have to fend for yourself.' She laughed, but the sound came out small and bitter.

I was taken aback by her laugh. 'Have I done something wrong?'

'Oh no, Magda, not you. You've been above reproach. You've even saved the Führer's life. I'm forever grateful.' She stopped and lifted her hands, examining her ring finger. 'I wish I had a little sherry.' She smiled. 'A drink might help me get through the day.'

'I'm thankful you're letting me choose a dress. But it's too much.'

'No, it's your special day.'

Despite her generosity, I remained aware that we weren't really friends. 'I didn't mean to make you sad. If you prefer to be alone—'

She rose from her bed and rushed to me. 'No, don't leave.' She took my hands in hers. 'Can't you see? I envy you – you're marrying the man you love. And a handsome one, I must admit.' Her face reddened. 'I have no wedding, no marriage, to look forward to because the Führer will not set a date while we are at war. His duties are too important. There's too much work to be done for Germany. The Reich's leader shouldn't concern himself with such trivial matters as . . . love. The excuses are always the same.' She released my hands and returned to the bed, sinking upon it in despair.

For an instant, I pitied her and wanted to reach out. I understood how she must feel; however, my concern vanished almost as quickly. How could I pity a woman who was infatuated with a tyrant? Eva insisted on traveling the dangerous path she had chosen. She might have been blinded by Hitler, blissfully unaware of what was going on in the world, but she also chose to ignore the war and its horrors for the sake of a man she loved. Was she also in love with the promise of power?

She called for one of her servants. A middle-aged woman well schooled in deference entered the apartment. She bowed to us and took my measurements upon my host's orders. The dress was to be sent to Munich for alterations. Eva seemed in a better mood by the time I was ready to leave.

'Before you go, I have something to show you.' She pointed to the cedar chest at the foot of her bed. She knelt before it and opened it carefully, with reverence, as if she was revealing a secret. I looked inside. Eva lifted a gorgeous white wedding dress that lay atop leather-bound diaries and a silverware case. She held the silky ruffled bodice against her and looked in the mirror. 'This is what I'd look like as a bride. Do you like it?' She nodded her head and laughed like the Eva I had known before.

She did look lovely, her oval face and brown curls set off by the dress. 'It's beautiful,' I said. Again, I pitied her but wondered how she could continue to live so blithely in her fantasy, unable to see the truth of what was going on around her. She was like a horse with blinders on, unable to see beyond its own narrow vision. I was certain the Führer would never marry her, but I couldn't say that. Instead, I said, 'May the man you wish to marry recognize your beauty.'

She kissed me on the cheek. 'I seek nothing more.' She carefully folded the dress and replaced it in the chest.

I thanked her and left her apartment feeling as if I had spent my time with a ghost. Hitler would never marry

Eva. She would die as lonely as the day she came to the Berghof.

The morning of our wedding a British bomber flew over the Berghof, and, for a time, we believed our afternoon ceremony would have to be delayed. Hitler was alerted and he ordered the fog machines to be activated. A thick haze covered the residence and its surrounding buildings for several hours. Everyone dutifully took their place in the bomb shelter. Hitler stood at the top of the stairs looking into the milky sky while the rest of us waited below. No bombs were dropped and the all clear was sounded.

Karl and I were married at four in the afternoon on June 14 in the Great Hall. After the artificial fog cleared, the sun shone gloriously on the Obersalzberg. Puffy white clouds, their wispy tails catching on the mountaintops, traversed the blue skies. Hitler ordered the Hall's gigantic window lowered so the lovely Alpine air could flood the room. About one hundred guests attended our civil ceremony: Cook, workers from the kitchen and greenhouses; quite a few of the SS officers, including the Colonel who I knew still didn't trust me. He stood off in the corner, sizing up the attendees, looking like a disgruntled bulldog. Hitler, smiling and shaking hands, greeted many of the guests. The only other notable Party dignitary who attended was Speer, who looked reserved but handsome in his suit and leather boots.

Karl and I stood at the south end of the Hall near the large fireplace. We looked over the guests toward the spectacular view of the mountains whose colors shifted in the afternoon sun. The couches and chairs had been cleared from the sitting area so we could stand above the guests seated below. A Party judge officiated our simple Nazi ceremony, which made no mention of God or religion. We were marrying under the auspices of National Socialism. Eva, looking radiant, stood to my right while Hitler stood to Karl's left. My handsome soldier wore a proud smile, mirroring the love I felt for him. Nothing mattered to Karl except our vows. From the corner of my eye, I saw the Reich's leader smile and nod as the ceremony proceeded. He was like an amiable doting father.

Karl and I kissed, a brief promise of what was to come and our marriage was sealed. The nuptials had taken twenty minutes.

On Hitler's orders, a table for frosted cakes and iced champagne had been set up near the west wall. Valets dressed in white tuxedos served the chattering guests. Everyone agreed that our wedding was the most festive event at the Berghof since we had returned late last year. Such compliments gave me little comfort, but I tried to act like the happy bride, despite my knowledge that our lives were in danger and that our future was tenuous at best. I greeted everyone with a smile and a kiss. I even made my way to the Colonel, who sulked in the corner. His eyes were fixed and cold, but I extended my hand and he shook it. 'Congratulations, Frau Weber,' he said with frost in his voice. I smiled and kissed him on the cheek, all the time feeling revolted by my actions.

Hitler didn't stay long. Eva was by his side the whole time snapping photos when she could. Even Hoffmann, Hitler's portly photographer, was there taking 'official' snapshots.

Karl saluted as Hitler approached. The Führer kissed my

on both cheeks and then shook Karl's hand. He gave us congratulations and presented us with two engraved silver wedding rings inscribed inside with his name. He left us with these words: 'Long life, my son and daughter. May you have many children for the Reich.' Eva dabbed at tears as they walked away. Karl and I looked at each other as they departed, aware that the rings were a beautiful token given by a brutal dictator. Neither one of us, I was certain, wanted our feelings for Hitler to spoil what little happiness we might have on our wedding day.

That night, we moved into a small married couples' apartment away from the Berghof and the SS dormitory. As darkness fell, we made love as if it were our last night together. We knew our joys were fleeting and our life together might end at any moment.

In about a month, we left for the Wolf's Lair. The routine was the same – traveling by train at night, arriving in Rastenburg in the morning. Hitler was ensconced in his private train with a few of his senior officers, adjutants, valets and security staff. The cooking staff and other workers followed in a second train. Eva was not aboard either one. I assumed she would stay on at the Berghof for a time before returning to her home in Munich.

Karl and I traveled in a separate sleeping compartment, which was cramped and uncomfortable. He tossed and turned and kept me awake during most of our travels. I asked him what was wrong, but he wouldn't tell me. Only when we arrived at the Wolf's Lair did he feel free to talk. He spoke to me as we walked to our small room near the west end of the compound away from Hitler's security zone.

'It's happening soon,' he whispered.

I walked on as if his words held little importance, although they'd shaken my world. 'Valkyrie?'

'Yes.' Karl kept his focus on the residence in front of us. 'We won't be able to talk once we get inside. It's dangerous to talk anywhere now. We think the Gestapo knows.' He grabbed my elbow. 'Slow down a little.'

I did as he asked, my heart beating frantically in my chest.

'It could be any day now – circumstances may change, but for now it's been decided.'

My feet stopped as if mired in cement. I had to keep my wits about me. 'This week? What are we going to do?'

Karl took my suitcase and lowered it to the ground. He placed his beside mine. 'Let's act like we're in love. Give me a kiss.'

I smiled, but said, 'This is no time to joke. I do love you.'

He took off his cap, placed it on top of his suitcase and then gathered me in his arms. 'This is the perfect time to laugh. You haven't kissed me.'

I looked past him and saw a few security officers strolling down the path. I kissed Karl as they walked by us. We broke off our embrace as a cloud obscured the sun and cast a shadow over us. The forest around headquarters was dark enough as it was; now we seemed cast into a netherworld of green and brown, the vegetation creeping around us, the camp smothering us in its dim stranglehold.

Karl looked about in every direction and didn't speak until he was satisfied no one was near. 'The success of this action depends on one outcome – Hitler's death. Everyone has finally come to an agreement. He must die now.'

'What about the others?' I asked.

220

'Time's running out. If we don't act now we may never have the chance. There've been so many attempts. Something is always wrong. Hitler has left the room unexpectedly or hasn't shown up for an appointment. Himmler and Göring aren't there. No more excuses. We can't wait any longer.

'A new government will be established by those who have conceived the plan. The Wehrmacht will have no choice but to follow the orders of the new leaders. We expect resistance, but Göring and the others will be arrested and Germany will surrender to the Allies for the sake of the people. If Valkyrie fails for any reason, you must look out for yourself, Magda.'

A wash of emotions filled me. I saw the face of an avenging angel, one who would be destroyed or fly away after the plot had been launched. I was frightened by Karl's words, happy and sad at the same time. Happy that these terrible times would come to an end; sad that we had so little time together before the world might come crashing down upon us. I touched his face, thrilled to see his smile and the life in his hazel eyes, which shredded the gloom around us.

'You must save yourself no matter what happens to me,' he continued. 'If I die, you must go on. If we are separated, we must contact each other only if it's safe. We have no say in these matters until Hitler is dead or the Reich is defeated.'

'Where will I go without you?' I asked, my voice catching.

He grabbed my shoulders and looked fiercely at me. 'Listen to yourself. You are strong, Magda – I knew that from the moment I met you, even when I saw your pictures. You will know where to go, what to do. Perhaps you'll have more than one life to save.' He reached down and rubbed his hand over my belly.

My throat tightened and a jolt coursed through my body. 'A baby? How can I?—'

'—You must go on. We will find out soon enough whether fate rips us apart.' He picked up our suitcases and we started again toward the residence.

'How do you know – about a baby?' I asked.

'As we stood talking. It came to me.'

I sobbed for a few moments and then composed myself as best I could. I took my suitcase from his hand. 'I'm not an invalid.'

We entered our small room, which contained nothing more than a bed, a small desk and a chair. It did have a window, which looked east through the forest. I couldn't see the Führer's bunker, the mess hall, the theater, or any of the other buildings, the surroundings were so well hidden by the deep green of the trees. I could only look into that wash of deep emerald and wonder what was to become of us.

On July 20, the bomb exploded.

The blast shook the camp. I was sitting with Else and a few of the other girls on a wooden bench outside the mess hall after the breakfast tasting, but before the afternoon lunch. The day was pleasant, if not a little hot. At first we thought the explosion might be from one of the thousands of land mines surrounding the Wolf's Lair, but this sound was different. We'd heard the mines explode at all hours of the day and night when a poor animal accidentally stepped upon them. This blast sounded heavier and closer.

It was followed by frantic shouts – not screams – none of them from women. A plume of smoke ballooned in the west, pushing its grayish veil in the air. My heart jumped and I clutched the bench's rim. I thought of Karl and whether he might be dead. I knew the conspirators had launched Valkyrie.

Else sprang from the bench and ran toward the smoke. I wanted to follow, but I couldn't. I remained locked upon the bench. She ran several meters toward the sound and then motioned to me and the other girls. 'My God, I think someone has killed the Führer,' she shouted over the chaotic din.

Cries of help filled the air. People ran blindly in all directions, toward the blast and away from it. I imagined the worst: Karl torn limb from limb, lying dead upon the grass, or crumpled in a bloody heap with other bodies. We didn't know where the blast occurred. 'Führer, Führer,' soldiers cried out in voices choked with emotion.

I rose slowly from the bench and walked toward the commotion. My legs took me forward, in a trance, like a somnambulist. I picked up speed as I stumbled along the path, past the cinema, the rail tracks and the garages. I could go no farther because the SS kept me away; they forced all who came to turn back. We stood as outsiders, as if we were prisoners looking through a fence. The acrid air smelled unlike any I had ever breathed; it was bloated, thick with chemicals and the signature of fire. I parted the smoke with my hands and tried to see past the fence.

Images manifested before me in visions similar to walking into a darkened room. Black-and-white spots appeared before my eyes; blurred shapes formed out of nothingness. As I looked through the smoke, my eyes beheld a nightmare.

Officers, coughing and hacking, streamed from the conference room where the bomb had exploded. Some leaned on each other, while others hobbled on one leg. Their clothes were bloody and shredded and hung like rags from their bodies. Two men dragged another man from the room. They held the body by its arms and legs while it swung limply like a hammock between them. They dropped him on the ground.

Karl appeared in the doorway, a cloth over his mouth.

I collapsed against a tree, relieved that he had not been killed. But I was unable to tell if he had been injured as he stepped out of the building. There was no blood on his clothes. He ran to the man on the ground, ripped away part of his shirt and swabbed the fabric over the man's face. The gesture was redolent with pity and pain, from one soldier to another. I could see it in Karl's arched form, the sway of his back over the body. *Why did this have to happen? Why did you have to die?* These were the questions I knew he was asking himself.

'The Führer is alive,' a soldier shouted. Those standing around me moaned and cried out with joy. Karl looked away from his merciful task when he heard the words. His wide eyes caught mine and I gasped. His mouth was pulled back in an expression of terror and disbelief – one I never imagined I would see from him or would ever want to see again.

The message he sent was clear. The Führer *was* alive.

Karl's life was in grave danger.

Then I saw Hitler! He was surrounded by a swarm of officers with only the top of his head visible. When the crowd broke, I knew he had been injured. He cradled his right arm with his left and instead of walking in his usual firm manner he staggered. His pants were in tatters. The men whisked him away through the crowd. I didn't see him again that day.

Cook wandered up to me with tears in her eyes. 'Is it true the Führer is dead?'

I shook my head.

Cook wiped away her tears and smiled. 'Thank God. Heaven has again smiled upon us. Germany will live another day.'

I found out later that four hours after the explosion Hitler toured the shattered conference room with Mussolini. He promised to destroy the conspirators.

I could hardly look at Karl that evening after tasting. We took a walk to get away from our tiny room. The camp was quiet, deathly still. The energy that usually lingered in the Wolf's Lair air had disappeared. No one talked except in whispers. There were no smiles at the dinner table. When Karl and I looked at each other, we knew a hurt, a loss greater than we could ever have imagined, was about to rip us apart.

'He must know by now,' Karl whispered as we walked on the path near the railroad car siding. Hitler's ornate train sat on the rails, dark, silent. He slammed his hand into his palm. 'Von Stauffenberg must know Hitler's alive. Surely he heard the radio address. If he's initiated the coup, he and the others will be rounded up like cattle.' Karl's voice contorted in agony. 'It will only be a matter of time before the Gestapo comes for me. Things could not have gone worse. The conference room was destroyed by the blast. No one should have lived. The stenographer dead. Brandt, Korten, Schmundt, almost. But Hitler survived. Perhaps providence *is* on his side.'

I wanted to crumble at his feet or, better yet, pretend that none of this was happening. Perhaps it was all a bad dream and Karl would awaken me with a kiss. If I drifted away I no longer had to face the truth. In order to pull myself back, I had to face the fear needling me. I had to be strong for Karl's sake.

'Do you think they will come for me?' I asked.

'I've kept your name out of it. No one knows. Von Stauffenberg met you the day I was going to . . .' He was afraid to speak the words. 'He was intrigued by your courage, but I made him swear never to involve you in the plot. I can only pray he keeps his word.'

'Then I believe I'm safe.'

'But I'm not.'

'Karl . . .' I could go no further and I collapsed against him. He remained strong and firm. He never moved while I cried against him. I could not cry out for fear of raising an alarm, although I wanted to shriek to the heavens.

'Hush,' he said. 'It'll be all right.' He stroked my hair. 'But you know I must leave tonight.'

I looked into his eyes.

'I will find you,' he said. 'I will search every city in Germany if I have to. Go about your work, protect your father and, if I'm right – our baby.'

I sobbed against his chest.

'We've said our vows and we have our rings,' he said. 'One day we'll meet again. I promise.'

He took me by the hand and led me back to our room. We turned off the light and lay next to each other on the bed, holding and caressing each other until blessed sleep took away my fears.

A few hours later, my nerves startled me awake and I shot up in bed. The room was as dark as a cave and I could see nothing but dim shapes. I ran my hands over the sheets and found the bed empty. Karl had vanished like a whisper. I switched on the lamp. Nothing was taken from our room; it was as if he were already dead. His clothes hung in the closet; his toiletries still sat on the shelf. A note lay at the foot of the bed. It read: *I love you.*

I held it to my chest and sobbed until the night dragged me away again.

# THE FÜHRER BUNKER

## BERLIN

# CHAPTER 15

A knock awakened me from a fitful sleep.

Karl had been gone for less than four hours.

I opened the door to find the Colonel staring at me. His uniform was bedraggled and a cigarette hung from his parched lips. He looked as if he had been up most of the night. I fought back the fear that jumped inside me. Karl had warned me to be strong.

I suspected the Gestapo and SS were already rounding up suspects in the bombing plot. Perhaps Karl had been far enough down on the list they hadn't gotten to him until now.

The Colonel sat stiffly in a chair and smoked his cigarette while I sat on the bed in my dressing gown.

'Where is he?' he asked.

I looked him in the eye and said, 'I don't know.'

He tapped his fingers against his thigh and smirked. 'You know where he is – you must. You will tell me or—' He broke off his sentence, as if a fresh way to torture me had come into his mind.

'Or what?' I asked casually. I was not afraid because the Colonel, with his first question, confirmed that Karl had escaped the Wolf's Lair. Then I remembered my father in Berlin and Karl's prediction of a child. I had only been thinking of myself. A spike of fear shot down my back. I wondered whether the Colonel sensed my discomfort.

He puffed on his cigarette and blew the smoke toward me. 'You put on a brave face, but you must be terrified.' He paused and looked at me as no man had ever looked at me before, with eyes that bored through my skin to my soul. His gaze was unearthly, chilling in its feverish intensity. 'You will be more terrified once you see the severity of your circumstances, because I control your fate.' His mouth distorted the words so they became powerful and cruel.

'Would you have me tortured? Killed? The woman who saved the Führer from being poisoned?'

He laughed, assured and confident. 'You can only play that hand so long, Frau Weber. The cards become torn and dirty. The Führer tends to forget good deeds when you are a traitor to the Reich.' He leaned back in the chair and crossed his legs. 'You're a very attractive woman. No wonder Captain Weber was taken by you. But you're different. I can't put my finger on it, but I will.'

'I've done nothing wrong. I don't know where my husband is, but I'm sure he would never be involved in a plot against the Führer.'

'I'm not so certain. We have reports that numerous officers were involved in this vile assassination attempt. Von Stauffenberg and several others have already been executed, unfortunately against the Führer's orders.'

I suppressed a gasp. 'I met the Colonel once. He seemed a loyal man.'

'He was anything but. The Wehrmacht is filled with traitors. You only have to ask the Führer his opinion about the fools who are aiding the enemy, filling our soldiers with lies and sabotaging the war effort. We have idiots for generals. But, in time, all the traitors will be eradicated. That is my job. I can tell you these things because your words against me will never be heard.'

I got up from the bed. 'I have work to do. Cook is expecting me.'

'You are no longer a taster until we get to the bottom of this treasonous mystery. I'm removing you from the Wolf's Lair.'

I stared at him and said harshly, 'I want to speak to Cook. In fact, I demand to speak to the Führer. He blessed my union with Karl. He won't stand for such an action against me.'

The Colonel puffed on his cigarette and then crushed it out on the floor. 'The Führer has given me full rein in this investigation. He and the cook know where you'll be going. They agree it's for the best.'

'I don't believe you.'

'It makes no difference what you believe. Be ready in one hour. Pack a few things — only the necessities. Don't try to sneak anything out. My men will check your bag.' He rose from the chair and bowed slightly. 'Oh, another matter. Give me your papers and your Party pin. You won't be needing them anymore.'

He was taking the two items that ensured my security in the Reich — both given to me on orders from Hitler. I took

233

them from their place on the desk and handed them to him.

The Colonel saluted and said, 'Heil Hitler.' I watched as he closed the door and wondered what was going to happen. An armed SS man stood outside the door blocking any way I had of getting out.

An hour later, I was escorted out of headquarters by two men, who walked beside me holding my arms. They whisked me away so secretively no one saw me when they put me in a car. Shortly, I was on a train at Rastenburg Station accompanied by members of Hitler's security forces. My importance as a prisoner was assured, at least in the Colonel's eyes. I had no idea where I was going. I was allowed to take one suitcase and a coat. That was all. Any personal possessions I cared about, photographs of my family and those taken at my wedding were left behind. I assumed they would be destroyed. I hid the stuffed monkey my father had given me as a child under my bed. If the photographs and other personal items were lost, there would be little on earth to confirm my existence. It would be easy for the Gestapo or the SS to eliminate me without a trace.

The train headed west, toward Germany. After several hours, we arrived at parallel train tracks in the flat, wooded countryside of Eastern Poland. A second train sat next to ours, filled with people. Their faces, pressed against the windows, watched me as I departed my train. A deep and vacant sadness filled their eyes.

One of the security men handed me a paper and spoke, the only words he said during our journey together. 'Keep this with you. It shows your destination.'

The day was sultry and hot and I slipped on the greasy tracks as I walked between the guards. The man who'd spoken to me caught me by the arm and helped me to the steps leading to the second train. I turned from my perch on the steps and looked at him. He smiled and brought his hand up as if to wave. Then he walked back to the train with another guard.

Armed soldiers stood on the couplings between the cars. They looked at me as if I were their property. One directed me to the right with the barrel of his rifle. I walked into a car crammed with men, women and children. The men were dressed in rumpled suits; the women, in summer dresses. Still, the smell of unwashed bodies filled the car and I reached for a handkerchief in my coat. I placed it over my nose and looked about for a seat. None was to be found. A young man, with black hair and glasses, sitting on a bench saw me. He stood and offered me his seat next to a young woman, whom I supposed to be his girlfriend or wife. I thanked him and collapsed in the narrow space between the woman and a metal partition.

The train jerked into motion and chugged slowly down the tracks. The young man stared at me. I felt uncomfortable under his scrutiny. He spoke to me in Polish, and not knowing much of the language, I answered in German that I didn't speak Polish. He immediately switched to German. The woman, whose feet rested on two brown leather suitcases, peered at me. She wore a plain gray dress. Despite her drab clothing, she was handsome, with dark hair and eyes.

'Where are you headed?' he asked.

I still held the paper the security man had given me. I opened it and peered at the official document emblazoned with the Nazi insignia and signed by the Colonel. 'It says, "Bromberg–Ost."' The name meant nothing to me.

'My wife is headed there as well.' He loosened his tie, unbuttoned his jacket and sat on the floor in front of us. His body swayed with the erratic movements of the train. 'Perhaps you can be friends.'

The woman spoke up with sudden intensity. 'I want to be with you,' she said in broken German.

The man sighed. 'I'm afraid we have no choice, my dear.' He pointed to the nearest guard, who stood at the end of the compartment casually stroking his rifle and smoking a cigarette as he looked out upon the countryside. Turning to me, the Polish man said, 'Allow me to introduce myself. I am Erik and this is my wife, Katrina. We are teachers.'

'Teachers?' I asked, incredulous at their occupation. I knew what I was suspected of, but I would never have guessed that I would be seated next to teachers. What were their crimes?

'We are political subversives,' Erik said as if it was a common title. 'That's what the Nazis tell me. We've been accused of communist leanings and teaching students about radical governments apart from National Socialism. So, I am being sent to Stutthof and my wife to Bromberg–Ost. That's why we find ourselves on this train. For telling the truth.' He looked at me intently, studying me from head to toe. 'Why are you here?'

Of course I couldn't tell them the truth. I didn't want them to know that I had come from the Wolf's Lair or that I had been in service to Hitler. So much of my life was built around lies. I hated lying, but I had no choice. 'I'm not certain. There are no charges against me. An SS Colonel came this morning and told me I had to leave in an hour.'

'Are you Jewish?' Erik asked.

'No.'

236

'Then you are a traitor,' Katrina said.

Erik shook his head and scolded her. 'Hush. We don't need to start rumors. Who knows what the Nazis are up to?' He took off his glasses and rubbed his nose. 'At least we are blessed to be on a decent train.'

'What do you mean?' I asked.

'We can at least breathe and sit. We've heard about the other trains: people crammed into cars like animals, so tight they can't move. They defecate upon one another, suffocate or die standing up. They travel for days with no food or water.' He added with pride in his voice, as if honored by his captors, 'This train has been reserved for intellectuals and powerful businessmen. Some are Jewish, some not. If the Nazis don't like you, it doesn't matter. I hear Stutthof is no playground.'

The photographs Karl showed me flashed into my mind. The mounds of bodies, luggage, books, glasses, shoes, all discarded, thrown upon the ground as so much human waste. A wave of nausea washed across my stomach.

Katrina burst into sobs. Several men in the car looked at her and then turned away, unmoved by her tears, stoically resigned to their condition. I stretched my arm across Katrina's shoulders and held her.

'How could this happen?' she asked. 'Why? Because we told the truth, we are under arrest?'

She spoke loudly enough that the guard heard her. He stepped into the car. 'Shut your dirty communist mouth.'

Erik attempted to soothe her, entwining his fingers with hers. After a time, Katrina regained her composure. I was shocked at how much the world had changed, how naïve I had become since my service to Hitler began. I seemed on the verge of experiencing the horrible reality I had first witnessed in Karl's photos. For the first time, I truly understood why many Germans defended Hitler. All the Nazis' tricks – the political fervor, the propaganda, the myth of superiority – played to the common man. Few knew such atrocities as these existed.

The train bounced along, and we said nothing for a long time. My stomach growled and I remembered I hadn't eaten since dinner. Soon the rocking and the heat lulled me to sleep. Erik dozed with his head against his wife's legs.

We were jolted awake when the train came to a halt about three in the afternoon at the station called Stutthof. Two armed guards came through the car and looked at everyone's papers. Those who were destined for this stop were told to get off. I looked out the window. I saw little except woods spreading across a plain, which reminded me of the countryside around Hitler's Wolf's Lair. In the distance, I could barely make out a formidable two-story brick building with many windows and a sloping roof that reminded me of a French château. There appeared to be a clearing beyond it. A row of armed SS guards stood outside the train herding people down a pebbled pathway.

When it came Erik's turn to leave, Katrina clung to his arms, sobbing and swearing in Polish. One of the guards stepped up beside them and threatened to ram his rifle butt into her stomach. Erik ordered his wife to let go. She released his arms, letting her fingers drift down, her body shaking with sobs.

'Be good, my dear one,' he said. He kissed her on the forehead and said, 'We will meet again soon.' He looked at me. 'Good-bye . . .'

I had forgotten to tell them my name. 'Magda.'

'Good-bye, Magda. May God keep you in His graces.'

The guard grabbed Erik by the shoulder and shoved him down the car. Katrina collapsed on the bench and buried her face in her hands. I sat beside her, shaking with my own fear, feeling inadequate and scared.

I looked around the car and saw that only ten women were aboard. We were all bound for Bromberg-Ost. No one spoke as the train pulled away. We all stared at one another blankly as if our lives were over.

About three hours later, we arrived at Bromberg-Ost. We gathered our luggage and filed out of the train. A few male guards stood near the platform, but I was struck by the presence of a number of SS women. One of them, a strong blonde with muscular arms, 'welcomed' us to Bromberg-Ost. She explained that we would be treated well during our stay. Most of the SS women reminded me of Dora at the Wolf's Lair. They had a creased, hardened look, displaying a typical Nazi resolve that showed in their condescending attitude and strident gait. They were so rigid it appeared they might break if they had to bend. One was prettier and younger than the others. She was more fashionable, too, wearing a tight skirt and smart leather shoes.

We stood in line to be processed. Katrina quivered behind me. The middle-aged woman in front of me whispered that this was a concentration camp for women, under the jurisdiction of Stutthof. Most of the prisoners sent to Bromberg-Ost were there for political reasons. 'We have a better chance of survival here,' she said. Her words did not comfort me.

When it came my turn, my luggage and my silver wedding

ring were taken away. 'You will not need it,' the sturdy blonde said. I was taken to a room, bare except for a wooden bench, and ordered to take off my clothes. The pretty SS officer whom I'd seen near the platform gazed at my body as I stripped. 'You are strong and well fed,' she said. 'You will be a good worker.' She handed me a striped uniform jacket and a coarse skirt. 'You will get more clothes when we find out what job is best for you,' she said.

The female guards then showed us to the dormitory where we would be staying – about thirty of us to the room. My bed was near the door on a two-tiered platform, a rough wooden board that stretched out from the wall about five feet. We would be sleeping together, side by side. My 'pillow' was a filthy piece of flattened fabric with a little cotton stuffed inside it. An old woolen blanket was pushed back toward the wall. I probably wouldn't need it much during the summer, but I also didn't know how long I would be held prisoner here.

One of the guards explained the rules and regulations: We were to be in bed at nine and up at five. We would have breakfast and dinner in the mess hall. Lunch, she said, might be taken on the job or not at all depending on how well we completed our assigned tasks. She told us where the latrines were located, but encouraged us not to use them at night. The few male guards at the camp would be on watch then. There was to be no smoking, drinking or sexual activity. All work was to be completed in the name of the Reich, for 'Work makes you free.'

'When I blow the whistle or knock on the door, you should fall into line and be ready to do whatever I ask,' the guard added with a flourish before she walked out the door.

We newcomers were left alone with twenty others who were camp veterans. I leaned against the railing of my bed and tried to understand what had happened to me. Katrina, her head hung low over her chest, sat on the bench in the center of the room.

The room was bare except for the tiered beds and the bench. The four windows, two on each side of the cabin, were flung open so a bit of breeze filtered inside. The air was stuffy and smelled of decaying wood and unwashed flesh. The women who shared the room had little to say; there was no welcome or greeting. Exhausted by their day's labor, they sat on the bench or crawled into their sleeping area for a nap. This hour must have been one of the few during the day they were left alone. I could easily see how they would welcome a moment's peace. Their faces were haggard and worn by their daily trials, their hair tangled and unkempt.

The cabin sat in gloom, despite the summer's long hours of sunlight, for it was sheltered in the deep shadows of the trees. I tried to talk to one of the other women, but she was too tired and waved me away. When she rolled over on her bed, I noticed an insignia on her jacket, a yellow triangle with the tip pointing up under a red triangle with the tip down. In effect, it formed a two-color Star of David. The badge meant nothing to me.

I sat on the bench in the middle of the room and stared at the walls. My body felt numb with shock as I tried to digest the horrible conditions I'd been thrust into. I wanted to run, but there was nowhere to flee. Suffocating feelings of loss and hopelessness filled me.

About thirty minutes later, the same guard came back and gathered us for dinner. The mess hall was not much better than our cabin, although the space was larger. Rows of crude wooden tables and benches filled the room. We entered through the front door and stood in a serving line. Our evening supper consisted of a thin soup with few vegetables and no meat served in a battered tin cup. We had one crust of bread each as well. I sat at the table with Katrina and marveled how fast and how far I had fallen – from the freshest produce and chef's dishes created in Hitler's kitchens to the watery dregs of camp. Even though I was hungry, I had no appetite for the soup.

'How are you feeling?' I asked Katrina.

She stirred her beat-up spoon in the broth and said, 'If I don't get out of here, I will not live through the winter.' She turned to me and her dark eyes showed the hollow look of life draining from her body. 'Most of us will be dead after winter.'

I spoke sharply to her, but in a subdued voice because I did not want others to hear. 'If you feel you have nothing to live for, you *will* die. You must be stronger than they are.'

She looked at me piteously, as if she were a cowering dog about to be struck. 'How do I do that?' She looked across the room at the other sad women and then lowered her head. 'How can I possibly win a battle against the SS?'

'Think of Erik. Think of him every waking hour and in your dreams. Live for him, if for no one else.' I thought of Karl and tears gathered behind my eyes, but I was determined not to cry in front of Katrina. She needed my strength. We all needed one another's strength, but as I studied the other women in the hall I knew that finding courage would be difficult. The Nazis had created efficient ways to break our spirits.

We had not been at the table long when a guard told us to finish eating or 'return to your room.'

My stomach was unsatisfied, but I took my soup to the prisoner who collected the dishes. She looked into my cup and said, 'You will not last long if you waste food. Three days from now you will drink every drop.'

I suspected she was right. 'Not tonight,' I said, and handed her my cup and spoon.

Katrina and I returned to the room. No guards accompanied us, but I could see it was useless to consider an escape. The camp was surrounded by a tall electrified fence. One touch and I would be dead.

My arms and legs had grown numb with fatigue. I crawled on top of the hard board that served as my bed. I fell into a dreamless pit of sleep until the morning whistle awakened me. It was time for work.

Breakfast, more like slops of gruel, had the same watery consistency as the soup from the night before. The muscular woman who had greeted us then assigned the newcomers to their jobs. Her name was Gerda and I learned she had been at Bromberg-Ost since its inception. I was assigned to tend the camp garden through the fall. Katrina was to be shipped off during the day to a nearby munitions plant. There was no time to shower, Gerda told me. I would be lucky to get one a week at the communal stall, maybe more, 'if you are a good girl.'

I had a few minutes to visit the latrine before I was expected in the garden, a fairly large plot of land on the north side of the camp. I furtively said good-bye to Katrina, wished her good luck and walked to the patch of tilled soil. Roll call was taken. Three-quarters of the land was in direct sunlight, the other quarter was in shade, so various kinds of vegetables could be grown. Tomatoes and asparagus were coming to their peak. I was instructed by a guard to pick the tomatoes and clip the asparagus plants that were ripe. When I was done with that, the guard told me to hoe the ground for fall plantings.

The day was hot and humid. Mosquitoes and biting flies buzzed around my head. The guard became angry and waved her pistol at me as I swatted at the insects. 'Do your work,' she screamed. 'No bug would find you worthy of a bite.' My exposed neck, arms and legs were covered with red welts by the time we were allowed to stop for lunch. Again, the fare was soup, probably the same we had been served the evening before, with a tiny piece of bread. The tomatoes and asparagus were not going into our stomachs, but into the mouths of our captors. This time I finished my meal.

For four hours in the afternoon, I broke the ground with the hoe. The land was dense, with small rocks. I could dig down no more than three inches before the hole filled in with stones. I told the guard this, but she scoffed and said I was not doing my job. Others before me had completed this work without complaining, she said. She shoved me aside, warning me to get back to digging the furrows.

By five in the afternoon, my back was aching and my arms were like limp strands of noodles. I could barely hold up the hoe. My jacket and skirt were stained with sweat. The bugs continued to flit about my face and neck, biting me into a red pain of aggravation. Finally, those of us who worked the garden were allowed to return to the cabin for a few minutes' rest before dinner. I collapsed on my bed. Katrina was not in the room.

I'd drifted into an achy sleep when a tap on my shoulder awakened me. The woman I'd attempted to start a conversation with the night before leaned over me. She put a finger to her lips and then whispered in my ear, 'You must keep this to yourself, but I have a potion that will stop the bugs from biting. It has camphor in it. It doesn't smell good, but a few drops spread on your exposed skin will keep them away. You must be itching to death.'

I lifted myself on my elbows and looked at her. 'Thank you. It's been a hard day. A potion is just what I need.'

'Wait a minute.' She trundled off from my bed near the door and went to hers, which was halfway down the room. She reached under her grimy blanket and pulled out a small brown bottle. She returned, took off the cap and placed her fingertip over the opening. She shook it and then spread a few drops from her finger on my neck and arms. The camphor burned into my stung flesh, but after a few minutes the itching subsided under its cooling balm.

'You're very kind,' I said. 'I'm Magda.' I stuck out my hand and she meekly took it in hers.

She smiled. The middle tooth was missing from her lower jaw. 'I'm Helen.'

'Why are you here?' I asked.

'I could ask the same of you,' she said.

My eyes focused on her red and yellow badge. 'I believe I am a political prisoner, although no one has charged me with such crimes.'

Helen patted her badge as if she was proud of her insignia. 'I am a political prisoner as well – and a Jew. That's why I have two stars. The yellow is for "Jew"; the red is for my politics. The Nazis accused me of being a communist.' She laughed. 'And they were right.' Her eyes lit up. 'I suppose I shouldn't have told you that. You could use it against me.'

It was my turn to laugh. 'Your secret is safe with me.' I was about to ask about her interment at the camp when the guard blew the dinner whistle. We lined up and filed out the door. Tonight, I would be sure to eat. Katrina had arrived back at the camp during my brief nap. Together, with the older woman, we trudged to the mess hall for more soup and bread. This time, the broth had a slice of carrot in it, but the bread was moldy.

When we finished, Katrina and I walked back to the camp with the older woman. I asked Katrina about her day.

'It was hard work,' she said, holding her hands gingerly at her sides. 'I smoothed ball bearings all day. You have a quota to meet. If you don't, you get taken off the line and disciplined.'

'Disciplined?' Helen asked. 'The word is "beaten." That's what happened to me.' Helen opened her mouth and pointed to the place where her tooth was missing. 'I was struck by a guard who was unhappy with the way I scrubbed floors.'

'You clean the cabins?' I asked.

'That's my job. I'm lucky to have it.'

'I don't know how long I can last,' Katrina said. 'My hands were raw by the end of the day.'

I felt sorry for her, but I wanted her to survive. 'Remember your husband,' I said. 'Be strong for him.'

When we reached the cabin, Katrina opened her palms and showed us the lacerations on her skin. I doubted she would be able to work the next day. I looked down at my own hands and noticed the watery welts rising from the

246

skin between my thumb and forefinger. They would be painful blisters by morning.

I crawled into my bed while a few of the women sat on the bench and talked. Even with the lights on and the sustained chatter, I had no trouble falling asleep. I also slept through lights-out.

Later that night, through the haze of sleep, I felt a pair of eyes staring at me. I had no watch and there was no clock on the wall, but the time must have been past midnight. I jerked awake, startled by the presence looming over me.

'Don't be afraid,' a female voice whispered. 'Get up.'

I shook the fog from my head and stared into the darkness. The dark form of a woman appeared in the bleak shadows. 'Who are you? Where are we going?'

'You'll find out soon enough,' the woman said. 'I could have you removed, but if you come willingly it will be much better.'

I had no doubt about her sincerity, so I crawled from my bed as best I could, my stiff arms and legs aching. I slipped into my shoes when my feet touched the floor.

'Come with me,' the woman commanded. 'We can talk outside.' She led me to the door and down the path away from my cabin. After we had walked about fifty meters, she lit an electric torch. A pistol dangled from her left hand. I recognized her as the young, pretty guard who had told me I looked 'strong and well fed.' She motioned for me to follow her into the deeper shadows under the trees. When we stopped, she stroked my hair and face. 'I am Jenny,' she said. 'I can make life easy for you.'

I knew no good could come from her offer. 'How?'

She put the torch on the ground and leaned against a

tree. The light cast sharp black streaks across her face. A moth flitted around its glow. 'You are pretty. You and Katrina, but Katrina is too weak for what I have in mind. You are strong willed and will survive no matter the cost.'

I shuddered as she touched my face and I pushed her hand away.

'You have a choice,' she said. 'Why not trade pain for pleasure?'

I was afraid to ask what she wanted.

She pulled a pack of cigarettes from the waistband of her skirt. 'Do you smoke?'

I wanted to turn away, run from her questions, but there was nowhere to go. 'No.'

She laughed. 'Do you have any vices? Drink? Marijuana?' She leaned so close to my face I could see the sparkle in her eyes. 'Men?'

'What do you want?'

'The German soldiers need your service.' She laughed again, this time softer with a hint of sadness. 'I have given them as much as I can, but they grow tired of the same body. No man will ever admit it, but it's true. Every man, married or not, looks for more. He cannot be satisfied with one woman.'

'You disgust me,' I said, and then walked away. Glancing back, I saw the pistol rise in my direction.

'Don't ever walk away from me again unless you are ordered to,' Jenny said. 'I will not hesitate to shoot you if you disobey me.'

I turned. 'Murderer.'

She lowered her gun. 'Believe me, no one will care if you are dead. No one will notice that there's one less prisoner in the world. If you don't consent another will take your place – perhaps Katrina after all. I will give you twenty-four hours to make a decision. I will come to you at the same time tomorrow night. I suggest you make the right choice.' She turned off the torch and pointed to my cabin. 'Go back to sleep. Tomorrow's work will be harder than today's.'

I walked away slowly never turning around. If she was going to shoot me, she would have to fire into my back like a coward. *The pictures Karl showed me from the Eastern Front. It seems years have gone by since I saw them. Men, women, even children, lined up on top of a ravine. Then shot in the back. The bodies dropped one by one into the pit until it was full. The dirt covered them until there was nothing left, not even tears.*

When I was sure I was far away from Jenny, I ran until I reached the cabin door. Out of breath, I grabbed the handle, but I couldn't pull it open. Every horror of the past two days crashed down upon me and I collapsed, sobbing, on the damp earth, my body and soul cast into the hell of Bromberg-Ost. There was no way out. Whatever God there was in heaven had deserted my country, my family and me.

# CHAPTER 16

Jenny was right – the next day's work was harder than the day before. My muscles ached. My blistered hands throbbed in pain with every swipe of the hoe, as if glass shards were being thrust into my skin. Some relief from the heat came from the dense cloud cover over the camp. The air, however, clung to my skin like a damp washrag. The hours dragged by like days as I was forced to break open the rocky earth in muddy furrows.

I noticed a curious thing at dinner. Katrina and another woman who had been in the cabin were missing. I didn't dare ask one of the guards what had happened. I got my meal – this evening a brown mush supposedly made of chick peas, which smelled raw and earthy – and sat next to Helen. Like most of the other inmates, she ate slowly, saying little, her head drooping over her bowl. She looked up at me with barely a hint of recognition when I sat next to her.

'Have you seen Katrina?' I asked after a bite of the sticky mess on my plate.

She shook her head.

I got the sense she didn't want to speak to me. 'Do you know what's happened to her?'

Helen turned and glared at me. 'We don't speak of such things. It's forbidden.'

I stopped stirring my mush and let the spoon settle against the side of the bowl. Helen resumed her eating, unwilling to talk. 'Let me tell you something,' I whispered. 'I know by your silence that something terrible has happened to Katrina. I have no idea what, but if you won't tell me, I will find out from someone else. We are killing our own people. It must be stopped.'

We sat silent for a while, both of us eating our meager portion. When Helen had finished, she said, 'The guards are listening, watching, for any excuse to be rid of us. You haven't been here long. It's dangerous to talk.'

'We are surrounded by danger. We must live with it or die. What happened to Katrina?'

Helen sighed. 'You are foolish. I will deny that I told you anything.' She pushed her bowl away. 'The guards make selections. Gerda, Jenny — they make the decisions about who goes and who stays. Katrina and another woman were sent away to Stutthof this morning. They were not in shape to work. Katrina was complaining about her hands; the other woman had trouble with her legs. She could hardly walk. They won't be coming back.'

'How do you know?'

Helen looked at me as if I were an idiot, her eyes wide with wonder. 'They never come back. Have you heard of the showers at Stutthof?'

I shook my head.

'Hundreds, maybe thousands, are sent to take showers and they never come out.'

'They disappear?'

'Yes, like Katrina. And then the camp smells of burning flesh.'

I thought of the picture Karl showed me of the prisoner pushing a corpse into what looked like a giant oven. The prisoner in the photo looked as dead as the body. The only way I could keep from being overcome by the full horror of this revelation was to think of Karl. The hope, the faint prayer, that existed in my mind of seeing him alive one day was all that kept me from dissolving into tears. I hoped Katrina felt the same way on her way to Stutthof.

We were participating in our own destruction. How could everyone in Germany look the other way? I wondered if those living in the cities or on farms outside the camps could smell the odor of burned flesh. Did they look to the skies as gray flecks of ash rained down upon them? How could they not know what was going on; and, if they did, why didn't they care? Where were the people who needed to rise up in horror and indignation at what our government was doing?

I walked back to the cabin alone, apart from Helen. I was in no mood for conversation. I took my time getting ready for bed. When I crawled in, I did not fall asleep because I felt an itchy nervousness as if ants were crawling over my skin. I lay awake, imagining the seconds ticking away, as I waited for Jenny.

True to her word, she arrived in the middle of the night. When she touched me, I still had no idea what to do.

thought of Karl and wondered what decision he would want me to make. I recalled our conversation when he told me that I should do everything possible to stay alive. My father would have said the same.

I didn't speak to her until we were outside, standing in the darkness. 'I will go with you.'

'You are wise,' Jenny said.

I smelled liquor on her breath, not strong, but subtle as if she had taken a few nips of vodka. She lit a cigarette and told me to follow her. We walked through the camp to the showers, where she ordered me to undress and bathe. I slipped out of my jacket and skirt, put them on a hook and stepped into the shower. Jenny watched me, smiling as I stripped.

'The Colonel will be pleased . . . except for the bug bites,' she said, with an arch laugh. 'I told him I had a treat in store.'

I started because I immediately thought of the Colonel who had banished me from the Wolf's Lair. Then I realized he was probably not the same man. There were many colonels in the army. I cringed at what Jenny had in store for me; however, the warm, soapy water running over my body felt good because it had been days since I had been able to wash so thoroughly.

'You will do anything he asks,' she said. 'Whatever pleasure he wants, you will give. Don't speak unless he speaks to you. I will be outside the door, with this . . .' She patted her pistol, which was strapped in a holster underneath her arm.

I spent a few extra minutes in the shower until Jenny began to fidget. I turned off the water and she handed me a towel. She stepped back quickly to avoid getting water on her leather shoes. Jenny was dressed in a black skirt, white blouse and sweater. She wore a red scarf around her neck;

she looked as if she were going out for the evening. The other guards never wore anything as provocative as Jenny. She looked lovely, her long hair falling in waves, her face beautified with makeup.

When I had finished drying myself, Jenny handed me a salve and powdered makeup to put on my body to cover my bug bites. She then gave me a white robe and told me to put it on. 'It's a short walk. Carry your disgusting clothes until we get there.' She squeezed her nose with two fingers as if to block the smell. Then, she ran her fingers through my hair and caressed my shoulders. 'You're almost presentable now. This way.'

The evening seemed cooler after my shower as the air played over my skin. We didn't have far to walk until we came to a cabin near the entrance of Bromberg-Ost. From the outside, it looked deserted, as lifeless as a vacant building, but behind the blackout shades I detected the yellow glimmer of candlelight. Jenny stopped in front of the door. 'Return here when you're finished. I'll be here to take you back. The Colonel is in the back bed – waiting.'

As I pulled on the handle, I reminded myself that I had no choice if I wanted to stay alive. I took a breath and stepped inside. My eyes took little time to adjust to the light. A few candles cast their flickering shadows across the room. No air stirred, and the room smelled of ammonia and stale sex. This was the camp brothel. There were seven beds in the room, three on each side and one on the back wall. All were empty, aside from the far one. A man sat on the bed. He was naked except for a towel draped around his middle. He motioned for me to come forward. I tightened the belt on my robe.

This Colonel was not the one who had sent me here. The man in front of me was in his mid–forties, handsome, with dark hair, graying at the temples. His body was mature, his chest and arms covered with black hair. As I walked toward him, he opened his legs and the towel parted down the middle. I stopped.

'Come forward,' he said. From his tone, I knew he had been in the brothel many times. 'I won't hurt you.' He patted the bed. 'Sit down beside me. Let's get to know each other.'

My nerves quaked under my skin. I shook violently, but I took my place beside him.

'You're new to this,' he said. 'I've never seen you.' He turned toward me. 'What's your name?'

'Magda,' I replied. I wasn't sure I should tell him.

'Magda – pretty. Like you.' He placed his hand on my leg and then rubbed his palm up and down over my robe. 'You need to relax, enjoy yourself. I can make you happy. If you make me happy, life will be much easier.' He reached for me with his left hand, took my face gently in it and turned it toward him. 'You're shaking. I can command you to do what I say, but if you give in it's so much nicer.' He pulled his towel open with his right hand. 'Look,' he commanded, forcing my head downward.

'Stop, please,' I said. 'Give me a few minutes.'

He relented and leaned back on the bed, his naked body displayed for me. 'Would it be easier if I asked others to join us? Is that what you'd like? An orgy? Jenny can arrange it. In fact, she'd be happy to join in.' He laughed.

I felt myself crumbling. 'No, it wouldn't be easier. It would be easier for me to die.'

He chuckled. 'Morals have no place in a brothel. Think

255

of it as a moment's pleasure. Over and then gone forever.' He took my hand and placed it on his stomach. 'Tomorrow night you won't even remember what I looked like. You won't remember the feel of my . . .' He forced my hand lower, driving it into his pubic hair.

I ripped my hand away from his.

'I see this is going to be difficult. Perhaps force is the only way.' He shot up in bed and was about to call out for Jenny.

'I'm pregnant,' I blurted out.

He stared at me, his eyes wide with amazement. He slowly pulled the towel across his waist. He sat for a time, studying me, trying to tell whether I was lying. 'I will talk to Jenny about this. She can't get a man worked up and then throw a bucket of cold water on him. It's not right.'

'I'm married to an SS officer,' I said.

The Colonel's eyes snapped to attention and a wave of disbelief coursed through them. 'If that's true, what are you doing here?'

The truth seemed to be better than lying – at least a half-truth. 'I don't know. I wasn't told what my crime was. I was sent away from the Wolf's Lair where I worked for the Führer.'

He inched away from me. 'You worked for the Führer? What is your name?'

'Magda Weber. I'm married to Captain Karl Weber.'

He buried his face in his hands. 'My God. I know Captain Weber. I knew him before he was asked to serve at the Berghof.' The Colonel screamed for Jenny.

She pulled the door open and jumped inside, her pistol pointed at me. 'What's she done? Should I kill her?' she shouted as she rushed toward us.

'Put that away before you shoot someone,' the Colonel said. 'Get some clothes for this woman and take her to the guards' dormitory. Keep her there overnight and make sure no harm comes to her. I'll make a phone call in the morning.'

'I don't understand,' Jenny said, and looked at me as if I had stabbed her in the back.

'That's all,' the Colonel said. 'Just do as I say. I'll tell you tomorrow.' He lay back on the bed. 'Send in another woman — someone more suitable.'

Jenny pulled me off the bed and shoved me toward the door.

'Remember,' the Colonel commanded. 'Be good to her.'

When we were outside, Jenny waved the pistol in my face and said, 'I don't know what you did, but if there was any trickery involved, I will personally kill you. I don't like to be made the fool.'

I bowed my head, saying nothing.

'Whore,' Jenny said, and spat at my feet. She did not say another word as she led me to the guards' dormitory.

Gerda woke me early the next morning. She told me I could shower at the dormitory and then get ready for the Colonel, who wanted to see me. She gave me a blue dress, clean underwear, stockings and shoes. She had even recovered my suitcase. A few things of no real importance were missing; it had been riffled through; the clothes left inside were wrinkled and messy. Gerda handed me a cup of coffee. The brew smelled delicious and I savored each sip. For the first time in days, I felt like a human being.

Gerda took me to an empty office and told me to wait. The windows looked out on the common grounds, which sparkled like green diamonds in the early morning sun. Past the common, the detention cabins spread out like dominoes to the far ridge of trees.

I saw the Colonel as he approached. He walked as stiffly upright as a stick with legs, his eyes never wavering from the view in front of him. I tried to judge his mood, which was much different from the night before. He seemed somber and subdued, as if whatever he had to tell me would be bad news.

I put my coffee down on the desk and stood up when he came into the room.

He brushed past me. 'Sit down.'

I sat and waited for his decision on my fate.

The Colonel took a seat behind the desk, took off his cap and placed it in front of him. The death's-head insignia the skull and crossbones, caught my eye. He leaned back in his chair and said, 'Tell me what you know about the plot to kill the Führer.'

I didn't flinch from his intent gaze. 'Nothing. I was at the Wolf's Lair when the bomb exploded.'

'Captain Weber is missing. You have no idea where he is or if he was involved in this heinous plot?'

'No.'

He put a finger to his lips and sighed. 'He will be found and executed if my hunch is correct. Others, in the Gestapo believe he was involved. Too many are involved.'

For the first time, I looked away from him and out the window toward the common, where I saw the prisoners begin their lonely marches for the day. 'If my husband was involved in this, he never shared such information with me. But it is ludicrous to believe he would play any part in this plot. He is loyal to the Reich.'

The Colonel pounded his fists on the desk so hard the pen and pencil on it flew into the air. 'I don't believe you! You're lying!'

I turned to him. 'If I'm lying why would I tell you the truth about who I am? Did the SS or the Gestapo tell you that I saved the Führer's life? Or that it was the Führer who wanted Karl and me to be married?'

His face turned sour with a scowl, as if I had deflated his argument. 'No, I heard it from another – your boss,' he stated calmly. He picked up his cap and stared at it. 'When you pledge your life to the Führer you make certain sacrifices. I was told you have made those sacrifices. I believe you.'

The anxiety I carried drained from my body. 'Thank you,' I said.

'I didn't just talk to the Gestapo. I talked to the cook at the Wolf's Lair as well. She vouched for you.' He pointed to his cap. 'See the death's-head? Every SS man is sworn to obey the Führer and the Reich, to give up his life if necessary. The cook told me that no one knew where you were. The Colonel who sent you away told no one he was transferring you to Bromberg-Ost. Your boss was furious that such a loyal and devoted worker would be taken away from her without so much as a word. She went to the Führer and asked that you be returned to the Wolf's Lair. He remembered you saved his life.' He leaned forward and tapped the top of his cap. 'For your sake, I hope you are loyal to the Reich. I hope your husband who has disappeared is as devoted to the Führer as you are.'

I answered with a gut-wrenching lie, but I had to speak. 'I am loyal to the Führer. And so is my husband.' Memories of Karl rushed into my head and tears welled up in my eyes. I put my head down and sobbed.

'No more tears,' the Colonel said. He rose from his chair and lifted my shoulders. 'The cook is sending a car for you. It will arrive this afternoon. In the meantime, you must stay here. I will have Gerda look for your wedding ring. I hope it hasn't been sent to be melted down.' He gathered his cap in his hands, wished me luck and walked out of the room.

I was alone for about an hour before Gerda returned to the office. 'You may have breakfast in the kitchen,' she said. 'We didn't know you worked for the Führer.' She studied me as if I were an actress, a star in my own right. She was in awe of someone so close to Hitler. I knew she was also suspicious of me, a woman who worked at the Berghof and the Wolf's Lair only to end up in Bromberg-Ost. It made no sense to her.

'An SS Colonel wanted to see me punished,' I said to satisfy her curiosity.

She looked at me with more questions in her eyes.

'I'm not sure why myself,' I said, 'but the Führer understands the situation. That's why he is calling me back to the Wolf's Lair.'

'I see,' she said, and the muscles in her thick neck tensed. She opened her clenched fist and revealed my silver wedding ring.

A rush of feelings swept over me and I was overjoyed that my connection to Karl had been restored. I put the ring back on my left hand.

'Follow me,' Gerda said. 'The car won't be here until the afternoon.'

I spent the next few hours in the mess hall with the

kitchen staff. Some were guards and Party workers, the rest prisoners from the camp. Everyone stared at me, including Jenny, who happened to walk through the hall. She said nothing, only glowered at my betrayal of her plans for me to be a brothel woman. After lunch – a sumptuous feast of pork, potatoes, green beans and cake for the guards and officers, as opposed to the meager offerings for the camp inmates – I walked back to the office where the Colonel had questioned me.

About two in the afternoon, I saw a black Mercedes touring car pull up outside the gate. Gerda came to the office and asked me to follow her. I was 'processed,' the gate opened and I stepped out to freedom. The SS driver opened the car door and we sped away. Escaping Bromberg-Ost was as simple as that. As I reclined in the seat, I looked at my ring as it flashed like a silver star in the alternating patterns of sun and shade coming through the window. I wondered what had happened to Katrina at Stutthof. Was she dead? I suspected so. Would Helen, the communist Jew, meet the same fate? I would never know, and that haunted me. I wished I could save her, but to ask such a favor from the Reich would have been impossible.

The driver kept the car rolling at a high speed. He said little to me and seemed in a hurry to get back to the Wolf's Lair. After three hours, the car was in the wooded plains of Poland. We arrived in Rastenburg about six. After we passed through security, the driver left me near Hitler's private rail station. I didn't know whether the room I'd shared with Karl would still be waiting for me, so I picked up my suit-case and walked to the mess hall. Cook, I thought, would be in the kitchen, in the middle of dinner preparations.

As I entered it, a hush descended on the staff. Everyone stared at me – the marked woman returned from her imprisonment. Cook stood at a table in the far corner of the kitchen. When she saw me, she rushed toward me with open arms, hugged me and inquired about my well-being. The staff watched our reunion with interest and then slowly returned to their work.

'Magda, I must talk to you,' Cook said. I could tell from her tone that something serious had happened. She walked me to her small office near the entrance. We sat knee to knee in the two chairs crammed inside. Oddly, the surroundings of cookbooks, inventory lists, the fancy spices, our intimacy, felt comforting after my long days and nights at Bromberg-Ost.

'The Colonel has been relieved of duty,' Cook said. 'The Gestapo has taken him away.'

I was shocked, but relieved to be rid of him. 'Why?'

'No one knows,' Cook said. 'So much has happened since von Stauffenberg's attack on the Führer. It's insanity here.' She tapped her fingers on her small oak desk. 'If I smoked, I would have a cigarette. A glass of wine would do me good.' She looked at me with furrowed brows. 'I want you to be strong – the Gestapo wants to talk to you. I only know this because I spoke with the Führer personally to arrange your return. I told him you would never raise a hand against the Reich.' She paused and the concern in her eyes deepened to sadness. 'He's not well. He usually takes his meals alone, but sometimes he dines with his secretaries for company. His left hand shakes and he walks with a stoop. He is not the man he used to be before the blast. I've been told his rages are more pronounced than ever. No one crosses him.'

Cook's words set my nerves on edge.

'Even Eva spoke highly of you,' she continued. 'Usually she has no say in these matters. But the Führer knows you and believes you had nothing to do with this crime; otherwise, I would not have been able to free you. Many have been rounded up and executed for the bombing – I've heard hundreds have already been arrested. You are fortunate.'

'Thank you,' I said, and reached to touch her hands. She took mine in hers and we sat for a moment as the tension in her body flowed into mine.

'Bromberg-Ost was horrible,' I said. 'The prisoners are treated worse than farm animals. I heard rumors of—'

She withdrew her hands from mine with a look of disgust. 'Magda! Please. Never speak of such things. It isn't allowed. Whatever you saw must be a mistake. If the guards act like criminals they will be punished. The Reich would not allow such atrocities to happen. Tell no one what you experienced.'

A knock interrupted us. A young man, a valet, opened it and motioned for Cook. 'Wait here,' she told me as she left.

I waited for thirty minutes before the door opened again. A middle-aged man with thinning black hair stepped inside. He wore a dark suit with the Party pin attached to the lapel.

'Frau Weber,' he said, and sat down across from me. He held a black dossier, which he placed in his lap. 'I would tell you my name, but my identity isn't important.' He smiled, showing perfect white teeth.

Something in his character unsettled me. He was formal and businesslike, not harsh or overtly threatening like the Colonel. However, I judged he would have no difficulty in slitting my throat and watching me bleed to death. He would draw the knife across my neck gracefully, as if committing the deed were an art. He struck me as a cold, calculating killer.

He withdrew a black eyeglass case from his jacket and placed it on top of the dossier. 'Let me say, you are a lucky woman. Others have not been so fortunate.' He opened the case, pulled out his glasses and slid them on. 'The Führer, in his wisdom, has judged you innocent of the crimes claimed by the Colonel.' He opened the dossier, flipping to the first page, and said, 'You will have no further interaction with the Colonel, rest assured. He has been sent away.'

'To where?' I asked. 'How can I be certain he won't return?'

'You needn't worry. That's all I can report. The matter is of no consequence to you. Perhaps in the future . . .'

He looked down at the typewritten lines and read, '"The Reich reports the death of Captain Karl Weber."'

He continued to read, but my ears refused to hear the voice that droned on. I felt myself slipping from the chair into the void. A strangled scream poured from my mouth, but it seemed to have come from somewhere outside myself, from some distant point in the universe. I tumbled through the darkness until the man caught me and lifted me back in my chair. I refused to believe what I'd heard.

'Frau Weber!' He shook my shoulders until I looked at him in horror.

'He's dead?' I repeated the question over and over until it became a violent protest.

'Yes! I must ask you to compose yourself.'

I steadied myself against the chair and held on tightly to its wooden seat. It rocked underneath me like a boat in a tempest.

He returned to the dossier. 'Regarding the death of your husband, I can tell you his body was found in the outer perimeter of the Wolf's Lair yesterday. A note was found nearby. Captain Weber was a suicide. His body was taken away for burial.'

A dark veil of tears formed in my eyes. 'Where was he taken? How did he die?'

He took off his glasses and put them in the case. 'Unfortunately, that is all I can tell you. The matter is closed. You may return to your duties.' He stood and with a stiff voice said, 'Heil Hitler.' I heard the door open and close and he was gone.

I cupped my face in my hands and cried until I felt a gentle touch upon my shoulders. Cook sat across from me and held on to my arms until my eyes were devoid of tears and only dry, heaving sobs remained. She took my suitcase and led me across the grounds to my old dormitory. There, Dora and Else waited for me. I collapsed like an iron weight upon the bed. I heard them talking, but what they said made no sense. I didn't care. Nothing mattered anymore. My husband was dead.

My period was late and I suspected I was pregnant. But one morning a sharp pain struck my stomach and I rushed to the bathroom. When I lifted myself from the seat, I looked inside the toilet. The water was cloudy with blood and a whitish fluid. Karl's prediction had come true: I had carried his baby; but I lost it after his death.

# CHAPTER 17

If one can live like a corpse, I did so for the next four months. It was deep in the fall before I experienced my days and nights as something other than a morass of pain. The business of living returned slowly like a picture formed by a jigsaw puzzle, constructed day by day, hour by hour, piece by piece. On some days I could see through the haze that floated through my head; on other days I was overwhelmed by depression and tears.

I came to hate the routine at the Wolf's Lair, and, frankly, I didn't care whether I would be poisoned. Cook tried to cheer me up with her jokes and her lighthearted banter about food, but I remained a joyless soul. Most nights, as I tasted the Führer's dinner, I wished for death, some blessed relief from the monotony of my useless existence.

I dreamed about Karl and what must have happened to him. Rumors circulated throughout the Wolf's Lair about his suicide, but most people were too kind to speak of it. I knew when something was being said about me – the hushed voices, the eyes turned away, those actions indicated gossip. Even Dora, who I suspected knew the most about Karl's death, remained silent.

One evening in late September, outside the movie theater, as the wind blew fiercely through headquarters, two SS guards stood puffing on cigarettes. They smiled as I passed, the wind fanning the smoke from their nostrils. One of them mentioned my name, so I ducked around the corner of the building hoping to hear their conversation. Their words carried on the swirling air and I made out 'land mine,' 'pieces of his body,' 'coward.' I waited in the shadows until they were gone; then I went back to the dormitory and confronted Dora. She lay on her cot, reading a book, her long frame barely fitting the mattress.

I threw my coat on my bed. 'What happened to my husband?' She looked at me as if she couldn't believe I'd asked the question. 'I'm sure you know. Everyone in headquarters knows but me.'

She rose on her elbows. The only noise in the room was the infernal swoosh of air through the vent. She shook her head. 'Are you sure you want to hear the answer? Most war widows don't want to know how their husbands died.'

I sat on my cot and stared at her. Dora was no friend, nor would she be an ally. 'I deserve to know,' I said. Since we had little invested in our friendship, I suspected she would tell me the truth.

Dora put her book aside and sat up. 'Very well, I will tell you what I know, but if you mention this to anyone I will deny I told you anything.'

I nodded.

'Captain Weber blew himself up with an explosive pack in the outer perimeter.'

I cringed at the image in my mind, but I retained my composure. I also knew the land in that area was dotted with mines. 'I can't believe it,' I said.

'It's true. I received a firsthand report.' Dora leaned forward. 'Cook found out, but I don't know how. She was afraid to tell you. Of course, no one should speak of such matters.'

'My husband would never do such a thing. I know Karl. He would not kill himself. Is that why I heard officers whispering he was a coward?'

'Most likely. He took the easy way out. Are you so certain he wouldn't commit suicide? What if your husband was implicated in the plot to kill the Führer?'

'Impossible.'

Dora dropped her voice to a whisper. 'I only know what I've been told. It seems the Colonel was blackmailing officers, whether or not they were involved in the bombing. That's why he was taken away. He cast suspicion on many men – and a few women. I assume he tried to get you to confess, but failed. The Gestapo, of course, must investigate every possible lead.'

I shook at her words. 'The Gestapo officer indicated there was a note. Do you know what it said?'

'I never saw it, but your husband proclaimed his innocence – and yours as well. Apparently, he knew he was in for a rough time. To be accused is as damning as the deed itself.'

I didn't have to think hard to figure out what atrocities might occur at the hands of the secret police.

Else came into the room and offered her cheerful smile. She greeted us, but neither Dora nor I answered. When Else perceived our sour moods, she undressed for bed, crawled under the blanket and closed her eyes. Dora returned to her book while images of Karl ran through my head. I had kept his hope for our future close to my heart. That was why it was so hard to believe he had killed himself. I wondered how I would spend my remaining days at the Wolf's Lair.

The first snow fell in late October. Cold, damp air weighed down the day. First, the rain came, turning the tree bark black with wetness. Ice pellets followed for several hours before the snow fell powdery in the gray dusk.

Cook came to me that morning and asked for my help. Of all the people at the Wolf's Lair, I considered her the one person I could trust – a friend of sorts. We went to her office to review food inventories. We stepped inside and she closed the door.

I looked at the journals on the desk. The ink ran in lines over the pages like waves. I rubbed my eyes and said, 'I think I'm going crazy. Time away from the Wolf's Lair would do me good.'

Cook sighed and put her hand on my shoulder. 'We would all be better off away from here.' She sat near me and grinned. 'Would you like some vodka? I keep a bottle hidden, but you must never reveal the secret of my small stash. The Führer would not be pleased if he knew his cook had a drink now and then.'

I chuckled. 'I've only had it once before – at a birthday party. The host gave me a small glass.'

'Well, that's all you'll get here.' She reached into a cabinet

I'd opened many times before. She shuffled boxes and books around and then lifted a piece of wood, like removing the cover to a secret panel. Glass glinted in the dim light. Cook reached in and pulled out a bottle of Russian vodka. 'Contraband. Imagine having this in the Wolf's Lair as our mortal enemies approach. One could get strung up for having a bottle, but I don't worry too much. I wipe off my finger-prints. If someone asks, I'll answer, "How would I know how it got here?"' She took two small glasses from the cabinet and poured the vodka. 'To us.' She tipped her glass against mine and poured the liquor down her throat in one gulp. I took a sip. The drink burned on my tongue and my first response was to cough it up, but I forced it down and a fuzzy, warm ball settled in my stomach. 'You grow to like it,' Cook said, 'especially on a cold night.'

I ran my tongue over my lips. 'It's not bad.'

Cook attempted to fill my glass, but I stopped her with my hand. 'I shouldn't. Dora might smell it on my breath.'

She nodded, but her eyes flickered with anger. 'To hell with Dora. She needs a drink to loosen up. Most people here do . . .' Her voice faded and she poured herself another shot. Her face soured. The joy she got from the bottle dissipated. 'The situation is bad, Magda. The Führer rarely sees anyone but his military staff, whom he constantly berates for their ineptitude.' She tipped back the glass and swallowed her drink. 'He keeps to his room. The doctor tells me he complains about his stomach and takes constant injections to keep up his energy. He looks like an old man.'

'And the war?' I asked.

'We are losing. The Red Army is on our doorstep. I'm

certain it won't be long before we must leave the Wolf's Lair for safer quarters.'

'If I could leave now, I would.' I leaned back and drained the vodka.

Cook put her glass on the desk and sighed. 'You must leave now. The Eastern Front is falling fast. The Reds could be here in a few months, perhaps a few weeks. It's for your own good. Even the SS officers are secretly telling others to leave.'

Her suggestion caught me off guard. A hole opened in my heart as I pondered being pushed out of headquarters into the war. Suddenly, I realized how charmed my life had been despite my incarceration in Bromberg-Ost. I remembered my days at the camp and the women like Katrina and Helen who were left behind. Perhaps their liberation might come soon. There was nothing I could do about their plight.

News of the Red advance shook me. Karl had begged me to stay alive for my sake, and for the sake of our unborn child. But had I survived — and also failed in my desire to kill Hitler — because of my own selfish desire for safety? Without Hitler's protection, I was destined to be an 'ordinary German,' caught in the cross fire of approaching armies. Those around Hitler felt protected, safe from harm, despite the war. The Propaganda Minister continued to feed lies to the Reich's citizens: The army would win the war and Hitler would protect his people. What about American and British troops? How far were they from Germany? I had no idea of their positions. How safe was my father in Berlin, a targeted city?

'The others have gone to a farmhouse outside of Rastenburg,' Cook said. 'It's near here, but safer than headquarters. You can still come to work. A car will pick you up.'

I held out my glass; I wanted another shot of vodka. Cook poured a bountiful dose. 'What about you? Are you coming?'

She shook her head. 'I will stay at the Wolf's Lair. My place is by the Führer's side, no matter what happens.'

The look on her face echoed the resolve in her voice. I could not argue with her. I wanted to tell her that staying at headquarters was suicide. I wanted to tell her about the plots to kill Hitler, the way prisoners were treated at the camps, to get the truth out, but I knew she wouldn't listen because such things shouldn't be talked about. I understood, but despised, her loyalty to the man she admired above all others. Hitler inspired that kind of loyalty in his personal staff. Perhaps it was his paternal attitude, his kindness and attention to their needs, that kept them in line. Why would they believe what Karl and I knew was true? They had no idea what was happening in the East or in the camps.

'The car will take you to the house after tasting tonight,' Cook said. 'It shouldn't take long the way he eats these days. I don't see how he can live on milk and apple cake, but I suppose it helps his stomach.'

I returned to the dormitory and packed my bag once again. Oddly enough, when I searched under the bed, I found my stuffed monkey. It had been moved from the room Karl and I shared. It had lain on the floor since my unfortunate trip to Bromberg-Ost. I pulled it out, patted the dust off its furry body and put it in my suitcase. I vowed it would never leave my side again. The family mementoes had disappeared, however.

Cook was correct about tasting. It had become a perfunctory affair with little worry about Hitler being poisoned. Why poison the man when the end was near? Surely other staff members at the Wolf's Lair knew how badly the war was going. Of course they could say nothing.

A few hours later, Else and I left for our new home.

The wooden farmhouse lay less than ten kilometers northeast of the Wolf's Lair. The couple who owned the property was provincial but maintained a fierce loyalty to Hitler. Nazi insignia draped the mantle. Swastikas covered the pillows and the rugs. Peter and Victoria were true Prussians and intensely proud of their Germanic heritage: He stood tall and thin, while his wife was shorter and stout. He reminded me of pictures I'd seen of Otto von Bismarck when he was middle-aged. Peter wore his hair combed to the left over a long face accented by a russet beard and mustache. Victoria met us at the door and promptly offered me a bowl of goat stew. I accepted and reveled in the taste of her cooking. The stew was hearty and full of potatoes, cabbage and onions. I suspected quite a bit of their home-grown food ended up at the Wolf's Lair. Perhaps the Nazis provided the couple with a stipend in appreciation of their 'sacrifice.'

The rectangular house was filled with rustic furniture. Everything that Peter and Victoria owned came from the land, even the hand-crafted cuckoo clock over the fireplace. Else and I were not the only tasters at the house. Four other women also resided there. I had rarely spoken to them at headquarters, except to exchange greetings and small talk. The six of us shared a long cabin, with comfortable bunks and warm bedding, attached to the main house. Several cats sat on the window ledges and a yellow retriever had free run of the house.

We enjoyed our accommodations, in addition to our trips to the Wolf's Lair. This respite in the farmhouse was much more comfortable than our cramped quarters in the Wolf's Lair. An easy sense of familiarity and warmth pervaded the home, but winter was setting in and the mid-November evenings were growing longer and colder.

One night, whispering awakened me. I shot up in bed, horrified that something was terribly wrong.

'Magda, do you hear it?' the voice asked.

I peered into the darkness and Else's stricken face came into view. She clutched the railing and stared at me. I was in the bunk on top of hers.

'For God's sake, Else, what's wrong?'

She pointed to the single window near the center of the cabin. I slipped out of bed as quietly as possible and tiptoed to it. The room was freezing in the deep of night and the cold wooden planks stung my bare feet. I opened the curtain and peered out. The dark tree line came almost to the house. Past the frosty window, a light snow fell, but I heard nothing.

'Listen,' Else whispered. She cocked an ear toward the window. 'It's been going on for about a half hour now.'

I was beginning to think Else had lost her mind. A few seconds later, light flashed through the dark branches, its yellow-whiteness fractured into shards by the thick trees. Then a soft rumble rolled to my ears. I knew what we had seen and heard wasn't lightning and thunder. It was far too cold for a storm. We waited a few more minutes, transfixed by the falling snow. I shivered and walked back to my bed to grab a blanket. Else continued to watch at the window.

She looked as small and vulnerable as a child. I stood by her side and shared my blanket. Another explosion split the sky.

'Cannon fire,' I said. 'The Reds are getting close.'

The shelling continued for another half hour before ceasing. Else and I trundled back to bed, but it took me a few hours to fall asleep, thinking all the while of the advancing Red Army.

The next morning, the other tasters, except for Else and me, had left by the time it grew light. At breakfast, Peter mentioned the shelling and shook his head in disgust. 'The Wehrmacht will push back the enemy invaders,' he said. 'There is nothing to fear.' Victoria seemed less convinced as she paced in the kitchen. Dark circles had formed under her eyes from a bad night's sleep. She said to me after Peter left the table, 'I'm afraid of what might happen.' She clutched a towel in her hands and absent-mindedly wrung it. 'The Führer says we should protect ourselves from the Asian horde at any cost. They will burn our homes, kill our men and rape us.'

Else's face went white and she cried out. I had not seen her so visibly upset since the day we arrived at the Wolf's Lair.

I was also shaken by the advance, but I wanted to be strong for Else. 'You can't believe everything you hear,' I said, trying to put on a good face. 'The Reich will prevail.' I didn't believe those words, but they seemed to cheer up Victoria, who returned to her duties in the kitchen. I dried the dishes as she washed. Else tidied the table and brought the plates to us. She frowned as she worked; cleaning was an unsatisfactory distraction against the black thoughts of the day.

The snowfall ended by late morning. The sun peeked through the high gray clouds and cast long shadows through the trees. I read in the living room and Else played with the two cats until it was time to get ready for work. The SS car arrived about three to pick us up. The returning tasters departed from the car with long faces. The SS driver leaned against the long black sedan and lit a cigarette. As Else and I were getting into the car, he said, 'This may be one of your last days at headquarters. The Reds are within twenty kilometers. The situation is grim.'

I stepped out of the car. 'Else, gather your things – you may need them.'

'You don't have time to pack,' the driver said. 'I'm on a schedule.'

'It will only take a minute,' I said. On the way to the door, I told Else to cram as much as she could into her bag. 'If anyone asks, say we have orders and leave it at that.'

We took about five minutes to get everything together. It didn't take me long because I had never really unpacked, feeling we wouldn't have long to stay at the farmhouse. I threw my stuffed monkey into my bag and closed it. Else had a few more things to pack than I, but she did so quickly and soon we were able to leave. We didn't say good-bye to the other tasters or Peter and Victoria – we headed straight for the car. Our irritated driver hit the accelerator, spraying mud and rocks as he sped away.

When we arrived at the mess hall, we placed our bags in Cook's office. She also seemed dismayed by the approaching Red force and struggled to keep her distracted mind on cooking. 'You were right to bring your bags,' she said. 'The order to evacuate may come at any time.' Her eyes clouded. 'All we have built and fought for will be destroyed.'

I wanted to tell Cook about the pictures I'd seen, the information Karl had gathered about the camps and the atrocities, but I knew the time for the truth had passed. Her illusions would be shattered soon enough.

As Else and I were about to taste the evening meal, the thud and shock of cannon fire vibrated through the building. The brick and wooden walls shook from the blast. The hall was not a bunker. Cook and I looked at each other and Else took a deep breath. A wave of fear washed over us as another blast hit only a few kilometers away.

'Leave,' Cook told us, 'go to the farmhouse. You will be safer there. I have much to do.'

'I don't want to go,' Else said. 'Can't we stay here?'

'Where do you think the shells and bombs will land?' Cook asked. She took Else's hands in hers. 'Get out now. I pray I will see you in the future.'

Cook ordered a young SS officer to take us back to the farmhouse. We gathered our bags and followed him to the car. Once we had departed from the checkpoints, the man accelerated the sedan down the road. As we traveled the short distance, I saw bursts of orange light to the east, followed by thunderous rumbles. The shock waves hit the vehicle with such force the car shook, like a gigantic invisible hand was pushing against it.

Else shivered in the seat and I tried to console her, but I was having a hard time being brave. 'Hurry,' I shouted to the driver, and looked frantically to the east. My throat grew dry from fear.

As we drew near the house, the driver slowed the car.

'What's wrong?' I asked.

He pushed back his cap and pointed ahead. Flames licked the sky and black smoke billowed from a spot deep inside the forest.

'It's the house,' I said. 'We have to help them.'

'I don't take orders from you,' he said. 'We could be ambushed. I'm turning around.'

I slammed my hand on the back of the driver's seat. 'Do you really want to be responsible for the deaths of four members of the Führer's staff? Could you justify your actions to your superior officer?'

He turned his head toward me. Even in the dim interior I could make out the expression on his face. He looked like a child who had been scolded. I guessed he was hardly over eighteen. He scowled, then faced the windscreen again and said, 'I will go another half kilometer. You can go on foot from there.'

Else tugged at my coat. 'Don't be a fool, Magda. The Reds may be here. Please, let's turn back.'

Else had always been protected since I met her, first by Minna, and then Cook and me. 'We'll be all right,' I told her. 'The other tasters may need our help.' I ordered the driver to proceed.

The young man turned off the sedan's headlights and inched forward. The smooth Mercedes engine purred in a whisper. We swayed over potholes, crunching the rocks in our path. The artillery fire had slowed, but the flames in front of us soared higher in the air.

'Here,' the man said. 'This is far enough. If you wish to—'

A spray of bullets splintered the windshield. One pierced the young soldier's head. His blood spattered backward in warm droplets as he fell on the steering wheel. I screamed for Else and tugged at her arm. She fell limply against my side, her eyes lolling. Blood seeped from a hole in her coat. I screamed again and struggled to open the door. I sat on the right side of the seat nearest the woods. I pushed it open and tumbled into the forest, falling across a log. Fortunately, my heavy coat protected my body. The cold and the snow that fell upon me from the branches above added to the shock coursing through me.

Men's voices, from in front of the car, carried down the road. I cut deeper into the forest, feeling nothing but panic pushing me forward until I came to a small outcropping of rocks. I hid behind it and listened to the approaching men over the wild thumping of my heart. They spoke Russian and I didn't understand what they were saying. I heard the sedan doors open and slam shut. The men laughed and shouted what sounded like curses. The voices then disappeared down the road we had taken to get to the farmhouse.

I shivered in the darkness and pulled myself up from the ground. The fire, spewing orange flames into the sky, still burned a hundred meters away. Its heat warmed my face when I looked toward it. I stumbled through the forest toward the house, away from the men on the road. The closer I got to the fire, the brighter the woods shone. Dark branches glistened in the light. The snow covering them had begun to melt, creating cold drops, which fell upon my shoulders and head.

Soon I reached the edge of the forest. The light was so bright I needed to shield my eyes with my hands to see into it. I gasped. The farmhouse was consumed by flames. Large columns of fire and smoke swirled into the air, dropping sparks and ash to the ground.

In front of the house, spread across the narrow strip of earth between the door and the woods, lay six bodies in a neat row: the four tasters and Peter and Victoria, the owners. Their heads pointed toward me, facedown in the snow. Blood pooled around each of them, shining red on the slushy coating of ice. I crept close to the tree line in order to remain hidden from view. The women's arms were outstretched over their heads while Peter and Victoria lay on the opposite ends of the row, their hands at their sides. It appeared that each had been shot in the back of the head. The yellow dog, snuffling at the bloody snow, circled close to his master.

I put my hand over my mouth to stifle a scream. Peter, Victoria and the tasters were Party members, but they didn't deserve to die in this fashion. Then I remembered the photos Karl had shown me from the Eastern Front that corroborated the rumors of atrocities against the Poles, the Russians and the Jews. My heart sank under the weight of the advancing army's capacity for retribution, to take 'an eye for an eye, a tooth for a tooth.'

I fell to my knees on the wet ground, pulled my coat up to my mouth and sobbed. If only I had listened to their protests, the young officer and Else might be alive. I trembled from the realization that I was responsible for their deaths. But I had only wanted to save the others! Now they lay dead in front of the burning farmhouse that had sheltered me for several days. I couldn't cry out in shame or in horror.

Memories of Karl flooded my mind. I had to have strength

to go forward without him, but I wondered how long I could maintain his wish for me to live. His final note to me, *I love you,* hung before my eyes. He *wanted* me to live and I wanted to honor his intention.

I looked at the fire for several minutes, watching the flames grotesquely illuminate the bodies. Suddenly, the right hand of one of the women jerked against the ground. I didn't know whether she was alive or if it had involuntarily contracted, but I knew I couldn't leave my hiding place to save her. She would bleed to death on the cold earth if she was not dead already.

I struggled to make sense of what I saw. In the distance, like sound traveling through fog, men's voices carried in the air. Gunshots rang out, some rapid fire. There was shouting, cries of pain and then silence. I knelt at the base of a large tree and pondered what to do. I couldn't go back to the car; the sedan was useless. I couldn't stay in the forest overnight, for I would freeze to death. My only option was to find shelter and warmth.

An unpleasant thought crossed my mind. An outbuilding stood several meters behind the house on the edge of the forest. Perhaps it was far enough away that it had not been destroyed. It was my only hope for survival through the night.

I circled through the thick woods, pushing aside branches and brambles, skirting around the house until I arrived behind it. The latrine still stood and the heat from the blaze extended well beyond it into the forest. I opened the door and stepped inside. The stench was overpowering, but the odor was a small price to pay for survival. A quarter moon was cut into the door. I stood for several hours watching the fire and breathing in as much fresh air as possible. Finally, exhausted, I sat between the door and the toilet and put my head down to rest.

I awoke to a watery light that seeped in through the cracks in the door. My watch read nearly eight. I pushed myself up and rubbed my neck, which was stiff and sore from the long night. I looked through the quarter moon. The fire smoldered, sending smoke and waves of heat into the air. I couldn't see over the pile of ash and rubble, but I knew what lay beyond it – the bodies.

I opened the door and listened. The woods were quiet; not even a winter bird chirped in the frosty morning. A spark from the fire hissed and popped now and then, but the world was strangely calm, as if death had laid its hands upon the land. I stepped out of the latrine and skirted around the rubble feeling as alone as I had ever been in my life. The sky was sullen and gray; the Earth, a bleak ball spinning through the cosmos. I looked down at my muddy shoes and torn stockings. My leg had scratches, some of which had bled and scabbed over. My coat was spattered with dirt.

When I rounded the smoldering debris, the bodies came into view. They were still there, the faces, grayish–blue and contorted, frozen now into the ground. The blood had pooled and soaked into the ice creating rusty brown patches around their heads. The dog had disappeared. The sedan was not visible from where I stood, but I knew it was only a few hundred meters down the road. I took one last look at the bodies and then walked toward the car. I had not walked far when I heard the grinding gears of a truck. I darted into the woods and hid behind a large pine. As the truck appeared,

I breathed a sigh of relief. Wehrmacht soldiers filled it, their heads peering over the metal guards of the open bed.

I ran into the road, waving my hands. The truck ground to a halt. Some of the men peered over the top of the cab and aimed their weapons at me.

'Stop,' I shouted. 'I'm Magda Ritter, a taster for the Führer.'

One officer, from the Wolf's Lair, recognized me. He ordered the men to keep their weapons sighted on me.

'I'm alone,' I said. 'The others are dead.'

The officer looked into the woods and then opened the door. Several soldiers jumped out of the truck. The officer questioned me and I told him my story from the time the sedan had been attacked.

'We were on patrol,' he said. 'I'm sorry we were too late.' He looked down the road. 'There was intense fighting through the night. The Reds have temporarily fallen back, but our efforts won't last. The Führer has ordered the evacuation of the Wolf's Lair. You must come with us or you'll miss the train to Berlin.'

I pointed toward the house. 'What about the bodies?'

'The dogs will make short work of them,' the officer said.

I started to object, but he raised his hand and said, 'We have no time to bury them. The Reds will have to do it. They killed them.'

A soldier extended his arm. I grabbed hold of it and he pulled me up into the bed. We turned in the road and headed toward the sedan. Its shattered windscreen glinted like a fractured mirror. I screamed for the driver to stop because I wanted to retrieve my luggage.

'Quickly,' the officer ordered one of his men.

A soldier jumped down. I pointed to the bag, which lay

in the open trunk. My luggage had been searched, but I could see my few belongings were still inside it.

I didn't want to look inside the car, but I couldn't help but see the back of the young soldier fallen over the steering wheel. Else's body lay slumped in the backseat. I could not see her face, but her hands were folded across her chest as if she were attempting to stop the bleeding from her heart.

The soldier returned with my suitcase. The truck sped off, careening down the road. The men peered over the top of the rails, their weapons poised as if the Reds could attack at any moment. I sat on the slats and folded my collar around my neck. A cold wind cut through me. I shed a silent tear for Else and the others and wondered if I would make it out of the Wolf's Lair.

# CHAPTER 18

In less than twenty-four hours, the atmosphere at the East Prussian headquarters had descended into chaos. I sensed the desperate energy in the air as the truck pulled up to the garage near the railroad siding. Rows of suitcases and files lay on the ground awaiting their loading onto one of Hitler's private trains. SS officers, scribbling in notebooks, bent over them. A soldier helped me down from the truck. I felt relieved to be back.

Cook stood nearby. She looked intently at the officer who had questioned me earlier. He shook his head and Cook's face flushed red. She cried out and ran toward me with outstretched arms.

'Damn barbarians,' she wailed. 'I hope they rot in hell!' She dabbed at the dried blood on my face and then collapsed against my shoulder, spending the remainder of her tears. I comforted her as best I could and then told her my story. I cried describing Else's death in the car.

'We have little time,' Cook said after I finished. 'The train leaves at noon and we must be on it. Meet me here at eleven forty-five.' She turned and strode toward the mess hall.

I grabbed my suitcase and walked to the dormitory. Along the way, I passed many men scurrying like ants whose anthill had been stepped on. Dora was in our room packing her things. She looked at me with a sour face and said, 'You smell like shit.'

I threw my bag on my cot in disgust and said, 'I spent the night in an outhouse.'

She stared at me blankly.

'All the tasters are dead,' I said.

Dora returned to her packing. 'Better for them than what we have to go through. Imagine the Reich falling.' She slammed her suitcase lid and turned to me, her thin face quivering. 'I can't believe it.' She repeated those words several times before collapsing on her bed. The overhead light cast stark shadows across her face. 'We can't give up. The Führer will not allow the Wehrmacht to fail.'

'The war will be over soon,' I said, 'and Germany will be defeated.'

She glared at me. 'How dare you say such a thing? You ought to be hanged for treason. People like you and your traitorous husband are the reason we are losing the war.'

Enraged, I wanted to slap her, shake her, until I dislodged her blind obedience to the Party, but I'd said enough. Confrontation would only fuel the fire.

I turned from Dora and opened my locker. Nothing important was inside, a few hairpins and a pair of ruined stockings. I only had a few dresses in my suitcase. The one I was wearing would have to be thrown away. I took a dress out of my bag, left for the showers and immersed myself in soapy hot water until my body was scrubbed and clean. When I returned to the room, Dora had gone. I changed into fresh clothes and left my bloodstained dress lying on my cot, a souvenir for the Russians or the encroaching forest, whichever arrived first.

Cook was waiting for me on the train platform. 'I had to leave so much behind,' she explained, and wrung her hands. 'It will be a new life in Berlin – if not our last.' Her eyes grew hazy with thought. 'I'm afraid of what the Allies will do to us, Magda. The Reds, if they get to us first, will slaughter us in the streets like pigs.'

'You will be safe with the Führer,' I said. Even now Cook failed to see who had brought such destruction upon our heads. She would never blame her Führer for the unfolding catastrophe.

'You're coming to the Chancellery with us, aren't you?'

I looked down the siding at the men and women evacuating the Wolf's Lair. Few words were spoken. Most stood with lowered heads or stared at the train with vacant eyes. Dora, her suitcase by her side, stood at the end of the platform.

'No,' I said. 'I have to find my father. I haven't heard from him in months. I don't even know if he is alive.'

Cook turned to me and put her hands on my shoulders. 'Remember this: Come to the bunker if you must and I will let you and your father in.'

I shook my head.

'Don't be foolish,' Cook said. 'You may have no choice if you want to survive.'

I thanked her for her kindness, but in my heart I wanted nothing more to do with Hitler or his staff. I wanted to find my father and start a new life with him if that was possible. So much was up in the air. The enemy might kill us all. I thought about Karl. He leaned over me, his face filled with joy. We were making love on our last night together. His body lingered over mine and he touched my face as only someone who loves you can do. My heart ached for Karl, but he was dead. *He* wanted me to survive, but without him, life seemed impossible. Yet every time I felt overwhelmed, I remembered my pledge to him.

An SS officer walked in front of those waiting on the platform. He explained that only a small number of us would be allowed to board – there would be several trips between the Wolf's Lair and Rastenburg Station using all of Hitler's private trains. He selected Cook and me to depart on the first. Others, including Dora, would have to wait until later.

Cook and I boarded and settled into seats by the window. Looking out from the ornate car, the world seemed rather commonplace and colorless. My life would never be the same. I would be an ordinary German and my service to Hitler would be a memory. An autumnal melancholy hung over the Wolf's Lair as the November clouds settled in gray sheets over us. Time had stopped for an instant. The bare trees, the bunkers in the distance, the railroad siding, would remain in my memory as they were at this moment. Nothing could change that. As I watched, a stooped old man approached the train. He was surrounded by SS officers and military generals, who seemed to be pushing his frail body forward. The brash, vibrant Adolf Hitler had crumbled before our eyes, a shell of his former self. The assassination attempt had wounded him, physically and psychologically, more than anyone knew. Perhaps self-loathing had led to his weakened condition, or perhaps he'd been consumed with hate because of Germany's failure to win the war. I was uncertain which was true.

After several minutes, the train pulled away from the siding and we rolled through the forest toward Rastenburg. Cook patted my hands. We were bound for Berlin.

I left them at the station the next morning. Several SS cars were waiting to whisk Hitler and his staff to the Reich Chancellery. I hugged Cook and kissed her on the cheek.

'Remember, you can always come to the bunker,' she reminded me.

I thanked her and watched the sleek cars drive away. Hitler was in a large touring Mercedes far from where I stood.

I looked out upon the city. Berlin lay shattered. We had been lucky to even complete the journey. Whole neighborhoods were reduced to rubble. Cook and I had observed the destruction from the train. One soldier who accompanied us said Berlin reminded him of Hamburg after the bombing in 1943 and the horrendous casualties suffered there. My eyes were unprepared for the destruction in front of me.

The overcast had lifted, but the intermittent sunshine did little to lift my spirits. I picked up my bag and was glad I had so few possessions, for my only means of transportation to my old neighborhood, Horst-Wessel-Stadt, was by foot.

I walked through blocks pulverized to shattered brick and ashes. Charred storefronts lined the streets like burnt matchsticks. Vendors conducted what little commerce they could from donkey carts. I was hungry, so I purchased a half-rotted apple from a man wearing a ragged coat. He apologized for the bad fruit, but said I would not find a better meal anywhere else. I suspected he was right.

The trip took more than two hours, taking me over chunks of masonry spilled into the street, burned-out vehicles, homes reduced to cinders. My father had written that he had moved in with a man and his family. They were both workers at the plant. When I came to the man's street, which was not far from where I grew up, nothing was left. The homes were gone, the trees blasted into splinters, the sidewalks littered with bricks and trash. I sat on my bag in the early afternoon sun overwhelmed by the destruction. A few people passed by, but no one spoke. Life had been drained from them; they were more desperate than I. I wondered if I'd been too quick to reject Cook's offer. At least I would have food and shelter at the bunker.

After a half hour's rest, I got up and continued on to my old neighborhood. I recalled the nights the bombs fell, the blazing heat, my attempted rescue of Frau Horst, finding my mother's shoe in the street. I wouldn't have recognized our block at all except for a wooden marker nailed to the corpse of a bomb-blasted tree.

I inched my way down the block, stunned by an overpowering sense of loss. It was as if my past had been obliterated by bombs. Even though the Allies had dropped them, I knew the true perpetrator of this destruction. He was now safe and warm in the Chancellery while the rest of Germany suffered.

I'd found what I thought to be the crumbling steps of my old home when I heard a small voice call my name. I turned to see a woman in a gray coat and black shoes. Her hair was stringy and long and fell out from under the white kerchief wrapped around the top of her head. She looked like an old peasant woman.

'Magda?' she asked with caution.

I did not recognize her at first. Then she smiled, rushed toward me and hugged me.

'Oh, Magda, you're looking well,' she said. 'Much better than the rest of us.'

I asked her name as cautiously as she did mine. 'Irmigard?'

'Yes, don't you recognize me?' Her smile turned to a frown and she looked down at her tattered coat and stockings. 'No, of course you wouldn't. You remember me as we were in school.'

'Don't be silly,' I said, trying to soothe her feelings. 'It's just that I haven't seen you in so long.' I put my bag on the ground and looked at her creased and ash-streaked face. I wanted to ask, 'How are you doing?' I wanted to make polite conversation, but I sensed that neither of us was in the mood for such pleasantries.

'I'm gathering bricks,' Irmigard offered without my asking and then chuckled. 'You have to laugh sometimes about how difficult life is. Who would have imagined that the daughter of a respected jeweler would be collecting bricks for sale? They're in such short supply they're like diamonds – more precious than the real gem. People need them to rebuild their homes.' She pointed to a creaky wheelbarrow on the other side of the street that held her prized possessions.

'Where are you living?' I asked.

Irmigard extended her thin arm in the direction of a row of buildings a few blocks away. 'They're damaged, but enough of the floors and ceilings remain that several families are living there. Our home was bombed to pieces. We are lucky to have a place at all. My father pays a little rent to the owner, who lives on the first floor with his wife. Sometimes they stay up all night guarding the building. My father has a gun.' She put a finger to her lips. 'Please don't tell. You know it's illegal, but we have no other way of protecting ourselves. But if we get bombed again, we don't have much to lose.'

A cold wind raced past us and Irmigard wiped her nose on her coat sleeve. 'Where are you staying?' She looked at the ruins of my home in front of us. 'I was sorry to hear about your mother.'

The thought of my mother's death crippled me with pain. 'I never found her body. My father was sick in the hospital and there was no time to search. I was working for the Führer.'

Irmigard squinted as the sun broke out from the clouds and shone on her face. 'I heard you were working for him.' She spoke flatly as if she wanted to hear no more about Hitler. She looked at me inquisitively because I hadn't answered her question.

I shook my head. 'I don't have a place to stay. I thought I could find my father. I wanted to be away from my job and everything associated—'

'—You must come home with me.' Irmigard cupped her hands. 'It will be like old times when we used to talk after school.'

'I shouldn't. I must look for my father.'

'You *can* look for him, but you must stay with us if you have no place to live.' The look in her eyes told me she would be overjoyed to have my company. 'You have no reason not to. The house isn't pretty, but we've made it comfortable inside and we get a few vegetables now and then. If we're lucky we even get a soup bone with a bit of meat on it.'

I looked at her unkempt face and saw something I had not seen in a long time. Pride. This school chum who had been part of my life so long ago was filled with pride and determination. She made me feel proud to be German. That was something I had not experienced since Karl had shown me the atrocities. My feeling was so different from the resplendent puffery of Eva and her friends and the obsequious pandering of the military men who surrounded Hitler. 'All right,' I said, 'but I'll pay for my room and board and help you gather bricks if you help me look for my father. I've saved a few Reichsmark.'

Irmigard grasped my hands. 'We will be the best of friends. Come, let me take you to my family. I'm sure they will be happy to see you.'

We crossed the street to get her wheelbarrow and the two of us, talking and laughing, pushed the heavy bricks down the cratered streets to her home.

Irmigard's family welcomed me as if they were my parents. Her mother, Inga, met us on the steps of the derelict building. Irmigard led me up to the third floor where she lived with her mother; her father, Frederick; and her younger sister, Helga. Her father, a man over fifty with graying hair, was repairing a watch as he sat in the sun in front of a broken window. He had cut the tips off a pair of cloth gloves so he could keep his hands warm, yet retain the agility of his fingers. Helga – fourteen years old and pretty, with long blond hair – was reading a book in a chair that had no legs. I'd met her a few times before when she was much younger.

All the windows on the front of the building were broken; a strong northwest wind poured into the room. Irmigard showed me the French doors they pulled shut at night to close off the space. The room, about seven meters wide, served as a dining room and bedroom. Scraps of wood and small branches littered the floor around a stove attached to the wall. A door at the back led to a small bathroom, which wasn't working because there was no running water. Still, the apartment was better than living on the street, or in a hut, as was the condition of so many Berliners.

That evening, as the family gathered around a small oak table, Irmigard's father said a prayer – not for Germany or Hitler, but for peace. We sat in dim candlelight because the electricity was out. Inga cooked over the woodstove using the meager kindling for heat. We dined from chipped bowls and cracked plates that had been washed with rainwater. The meal consisted of two scrawny carrots, divided among the five of us, and a weak soup made with a ham bone. I felt guilty taking this small amount of food from their mouths, and I vowed that I wouldn't stay long under their roof. As scant as the meal was, I felt fortunate I didn't have to worry about being poisoned.

'The Nazis will come for me soon,' Frederick said during dinner. 'They will put a rifle in my hand and expect me to shoot the enemy. Soon there will be nothing but old men like me and the Hitler Youth defending the streets. The Führer is only prolonging our agony.'

Inga put her hands to her face and shook her head. 'My God, surely they wouldn't ask you to fight. *You* – who can barely walk up a flight of stairs! They will kill you!'

'Momma, don't say such things,' Irmigard said.

Her father lifted his spoon and tapped it against his temple. 'I've been thinking. I doubt the war will carry on for much longer. But if it does, I'm not going to kill another man. I'll surrender and that will be that.'

'How did this happen?' her mother asked. 'The Führer brought us prosperity, order and respect and now the world is falling apart. We can't go on like this for much longer or . . .' Her voice trailed off and she looked down at the watery soup in front of her. Her words were strangled by her sobs.

The rest of us sat quietly pondering our fate as Frederick talked about the end of the war and of the 'good days' to come. Inga wanted to be cheered by her husband's words, but she would melt into melancholy when she looked at her sad children.

We didn't stay up long after dinner because there was nothing to do and barely enough light to see in front of our faces. Two mattresses were stacked against the wall. When the dishes had been soaked in the rain bucket and dried, Irmigard's mother pulled the bedding down from the wall and placed it in front of the stove. No wood was left to heat the apartment, but the French doors were closed and the temperature was tolerable. We gathered as a family on the tattered mattresses. Fortunately, we had plenty of blankets. Mother, father and daughter shared one mattress while Irmigard and I took the one farthest from the stove. Frederick gave us an extra blanket and wished us good night. Soon we were all huddled together for warmth as the November chill enveloped the room. Irmigard and I talked in whispers until we could go on no longer and we both fell asleep.

Several hours later, I was startled awake by bombs shattering another neighborhood in Berlin. I looked around, but I was the only one aware of the blasts. I listened for an air-raid siren, but heard none. The building trembled slightly and through the cracks in the French doors I saw flashes of light. I shook Irmigard awake.

She flinched and rubbed the sleep from her eyes. 'What's wrong?'

'It's an air raid,' I said. 'We need to get out of the building.'

She sighed and lowered her head back on the dingy mattress. My eyes had adjusted enough that I could see the outline of her face. 'This happens most nights and nearly every day. We have nothing to worry about.'

'How can you be sure?' My stomach turned over when another bomb struck nearby.

'There are no citywide defenses now. If the raid was targeting us, we would have heard the little siren on our block. That's all we have. Mr. Schiff, down the street, sounds the alarm. Go back to sleep.' She turned away and pulled the blankets over her head.

Irmigard's nonchalance shocked me. I couldn't believe she was so accustomed to the bombings that she could sleep through them. I tried to fall asleep, but the rumbles reminded me of my mother's death and the shelling at the farmhouse, and I could think of nothing but the bodies lined up in the snow. When I would drift off, my eyes would snap open with the image of blood frozen on the icy ground.

I thought of the question Irmigard's mother had asked at dinner: 'How did this happen?' I knew the answer, but I didn't have the courage to say it to her family. Not yet. With the world exploding around us, I felt every German would know the answer soon enough if they didn't already.

I stayed with Irmigard and her family longer than I had intended. We celebrated Christmas and New Year's together, although there was not much joy to go around in early 1945. We were thankful to be alive. When the snows fell, Irmigard discontinued her hunt for bricks. Any meager income for the family came from her father.

For Christmas, we clipped a small branch off an evergreen and decorated it with bits of glass and paper – the only ornaments we had. Frederick had finished some clock work and earned extra food and candles as payment. We lit them and stood around our tiny tree and sang carols. I found myself looking down at my wedding ring, glinting in the candlelight. A lump rose in my throat. I was beginning to accept Karl's death. That thought was shocking, yet comforting at the same time. I wanted to give up my dream of seeing him alive.

New Year's Day promised to be dreary and dull, with all of us enclosed in the room trying to warm ourselves by the tepid stove. However, Frederick revived our spirits when he pulled a bottle of champagne from behind the legless chair in the front room. The bottle was already chilled by the air. We all questioned how he had come by the champagne, but he wouldn't tell us. He said it was a gift from God. We celebrated our good fortune with a toast in our chipped porcelain cups. Even Helga drank with us.

In mid-January, Helga caught a bad cold, which we first thought was influenza. We found wooden slats and a small mattress and dragged them up the stairs because her father felt it would be best for her to sleep apart from the family. We placed the mattress in front of the stove. A kind neighbor down the street gave us a few aspirin, which we administered to her. Fortunately, Helga's fever broke after a few days and she recovered despite the frigid weather.

I, who had been fed so well during my days with Hitler, found myself growing cold and tired from hunger. In three months, I lost about ten pounds, maybe more, and developed the gaunt look in my face displayed by all of Irmigard's family.

Irmigard and I asked everyone on the street if they had seen my father, Hermann Ritter. A few knew his name and pointed in the direction of our old house, but most shook their heads and continued on in their shell-shocked way. I ventured to the neighborhood where he had last lived. Even there my inquiries were met with vacant looks. Finding a working telephone was nearly impossible, but a friend of Irmigard's knew where there was one. She led me to a printing business that had somehow escaped major damage from the bombings. I gave the gruff owner a few Reichsmark for a call, in the optimistic hope of finding my father. I dialed Aunt Reina and Uncle Willy in Berchtesgaden, but the line was disconnected. After the call, I realized how difficult it must be to maintain telephone service between northern and southern Germany as the infrastructure crumbled under the crushing weight of the conflict.

The monotonous days, long nights and the tedious burden of coping with the war dragged on through the winter. No one seemed to know what was going on, although there were rumors that the Reds had broken through the Eastern Front in mid-January and were advancing through Poland toward Berlin. All we heard was the occasional radio broadcast about how the German people should resist the 'Red Horde,' and fight to the death in the streets. Death would be preferable, the Propaganda Minister said, to the rape and murderous torture perpetrated by the enemy. I wondered whether the Wolf's Lair was still standing or lay in ruins, either by the Red Army advance or on Hitler's orders. I suspected the latter.

In mid–March, we were all at the apartment one late afternoon. The days were growing longer and the barest hint of spring was in the air, enough so that we could open the French doors on the few warm days. We heard the tramping of feet up the stairs and then a rough knock on the door. Frederick answered it, but before he did, he hid the gun behind a loose wall panel.

He opened the door to find several Wehrmacht soldiers in the hall. One of them thrust a rifle in his face and said, 'The Red Army is on the way. Be prepared. If you are called, you will train with us in the streets. You and your family will help put up barricades and dig trenches if they are needed.' The soldier saluted and the group rushed down the hall, presumably on to the next family they could find.

Frederick turned to us. 'I told you this would happen.' He smiled and then sighed. 'There's nothing to do but give in. We have no other choice. If we resist, we'll be shot as traitors.'

We all looked at one another sadly and realized how dire circumstances had become in the city. Three days later, another group of soldiers knocked on the door. We watched from one of the broken windows as Irmigard's father stood in the rain with his rifle and the soldiers barked orders at him and a bedraggled crew of men and boys. He looked up at us once and waved. The Wehrmacht officer struck his arm with the butt of his rifle. He never looked at us again.

The women were asked to haul water and rations for the men digging the trenches. We did so and even lifted shovels full of dirt. We all came back to the apartment exhausted. Helga, because she was young and pretty, was able to collect a few extra rations from the soldiers. We were grateful to have the additional food.

One night as we were all sleeping, a different sound crept into our ears. It was not the drone of Allied bombers high overhead. This time, unlike past nights, everyone woke up, the sounds were so unfamiliar. These were faster, smaller jets and they roared over the city. In the distance, to the east, shelling broke out. I recognized the sound from the farmhouse. The Red Army was on Berlin's doorstep.

The Wehrmacht could not stop them. Soon they would be at our door.

# CHAPTER 19

The bombings continued night and day. Many times we thought we'd have to evacuate the humble home Irmigard's family had made. We were jolted awake in our beds or forced to take cover during the day. Protecting ourselves was not an easy task because most buildings around us were already destroyed. At night, we would flee down the stairs to a clearing decimated by bombs and hope the devastated area wasn't in the line of fire.

According to spotty radio reports from the Reich, the attacks came from all the Allied forces, including the Red Army. Rumors spread that the Allies were racing toward Berlin in a rush to capture the city. Frederick participated in mock drills on the street as the Reds approached. These exercises, conducted by Wehrmacht and SS officers, became increasingly frequent and militaristic as conditions around the city worsened.

'Such nonsense,' he told us one evening at supper. 'As if

a bunch of amateur street fighters can hold off a well-trained army.'

We, the women, were forced to build barricades with our bare hands. The material was easy to come by: Burned timbers, broken bricks and stones, carts and destroyed car parts were plentiful. However, the work was backbreaking and lasted until our fingers bled and our arms quivered with exhaustion. The army constructed one barricade down the street from our building. It was piled high with building debris and scrap metal. Irmigard even contributed the last of her bricks because she could no longer sell them. Any notion the city could be reconstructed by the Reich faded under the reality of our harsh existence.

On Hitler's birthday in April, the bombings ceased, creating an eerie calm in the skies. Our respite was short-lived, however, for the heavens opened up with a rain of rockets launched from the outskirts of Berlin. These weapons were more terrifying than bombs because there was little advance warning as the missile screamed toward you. The Red Army was relentless in its shelling. What little was left was blasted to pieces as we prayed for our safety and covered our ears against the thunderous explosions.

On the evening of the twenty-third, Inga called us to the front windows. She wore a housecoat and her hair was drawn back in a ponytail. Although it was near seven and growing dark, I cautioned her against standing in the open. The sky was inky blue in the east while streaks of pink painted the western clouds. Frederick was at the barricade below with several soldiers and an SS officer. The officer barked orders and the soldiers fired at an unseen assailant to the northeast. I sensed something was about to go terribly wrong.

Suddenly, several grenades landed in front of the barricade. They exploded in powerful blasts, throwing shattered rocks, metal and dirt high into the air. We watched as the shrapnel fell, the smoke cleared and our soldiers peered cautiously over the top of the barricade.

'Look,' Inga said. She pointed out the window toward the next street. Five Wehrmacht soldiers were running toward the barricade. As they neared the corner, they were cut down by machine-gun fire. They fell in the street like limp dolls, their weapons flying into the air. Several soldiers in uniforms I didn't recognize raced around the corner toward the barricade. The men were ragged looking and dressed in gray, with rifles slung in front of them. I assumed they were Reds.

'My God, he'll be killed,' Inga screamed. 'Freddy, Freddy, look out!'

Bullets spattered above our heads, filling the air with dust. We dropped to the floor. 'Are you all right?' I asked Inga.

She nodded and shook the dust from her head. 'What's going on? Can you see anything?'

I told the others to remain on the floor while I peered over the top of the casement. Another round of gunfire broke out. The Reds had made it to the front of the barricade and were crawling up it. One was about to throw a grenade when a Wehrmacht soldier scampered up the pile of rubble and started firing. He was cut down, but not before he had killed his opponent. The German fell atop the barricade while the enemy fled from their dead comrade. I ducked, closed my eyes and listened for the explosion. The blast shook our building and Irmigard and her sister began to cry.

'Be quiet,' I said. 'We don't want the Reds to know we are here.'

Again, I peered out the window. The advancing soldiers had retreated for a moment. Only the bottom half of the dead Russian's body remained on the street. The SS officer shouted orders at Irmigard's father. The officer wanted him to top the barricade as the soldier had done. Frederick shook his head, threw down his rifle and ran toward the apartment building.

The SS officer ordered him to stop, but Frederick ran on. The officer aimed his pistol and fired twice.

The bullets struck Frederick in the back. He stumbled down the street and then collapsed on the sidewalk. His head smashed against the curb. I knew he was dead.

'What's going on?' Inga asked. She reared up as if to look below.

I pulled her back. 'It's too dangerous here,' I said. 'We have to get out of the building.'

'Why?' Irmigard asked.

'The Reds are on our doorstep. We only have a few minutes.' I crawled toward the other room, encouraging the others to follow.

Another explosion shook the building. Then gunfire rang out followed by hideous moans of pain.

Irmigard, her mother and sister, collapsed on the floor. Inga wept, for she knew her husband was dead. The soldiers below cheered and shouted in Russian. Their cries echoed through the broken windows.

When we got to the room, I closed the French doors and cradled Inga in my arms. She pushed me away.

'I want them dead,' she said in an angry whisper. 'I want them *all* dead. The Germans, the Reds, the Americans . . .' She sank against my shoulders and cried out, 'My husband is gone.'

I had no time to console her. 'Don't look down the street,' I said. 'Grab your coats and head for the stairs.'

For a moment, everyone realized the seriousness of our situation and that mourning would have to wait. We gathered our coats and were about to go down the dark hallway when we heard voices below. The Reds were climbing the stairs.

I pushed them back into the room and quietly closed the door. 'Get under the blankets and don't make a sound,' I ordered. They scurried to the bed as I stood near the door.

The soldiers made no attempt to knock. One kicked the door open and shined his torch into the room. I stared back through the blinding glare. The disheveled appearance of the beds was not enough to fool the soldiers. Five of them burst into the room. They were hardened men, two of mixed descent with Asian eyes. The torches gave them a ghostly look adding to the horror I already felt. One of them poked the bed with his rifle and Helga screamed. He ripped off the blankets, exposing the women.

I could not understand what they were saying, but they made it clear what they wanted by their gestures. Four of them spread out through the apartment while one stood guard with us, his rifle aimed and ready. There was not much to see or find in the three rooms, so soon they were back.

The soldier holding the rifle on us lit a cigarette and pointed to the front room beyond the French doors. He seemed to be in command of the others. He talked to the men and they laughed. One of them took a swig from a flask he carried in his pocket. The other four men walked to the front of the apartment and extinguished their torches.

They were silhouetted against the windows that allowed a dim light to seep in. Rockets would sometimes hit many blocks away and their flashes exploded through the room like lightning. Slowly, the soldiers took off their breeches, leaving only their shirts on. Their hands moved below their waists, massaging themselves, as they waited for us.

The men wanted Helga first. They made that clear with their calls. Inga grabbed her daughter and wouldn't let go. She screamed for mercy as the man with the rifle attacked her. The commander struck Inga in the back with his rifle and sent her plummeting to the bed. Irmigard and I attempted to hold him off, but it was no use. He swung his rifle in a deadly arc that would have killed us had we not jumped out of the way.

One of the half-naked men came from the back room and grabbed Helga, calling her a 'Nazi whore,' in German. Those were the only words I recognized.

Helga, her eyes wide with terror, fought against them as much as she could, but it was no use. The other soldiers dragged her, screaming and sobbing, away. The men closed the French doors and for a time it was quiet. The commander stood near the doors with his rifle pointed at us. Inga sobbed on the bed.

Then Helga screamed and we heard her cries of pain for ten long minutes before they turned to muffled moans. Irmigard and I looked at the door, unable to do anything but sob. I tried to think of a way out, a plan to get us away from these beasts, but my head was too filled with horror and pain to think.

Then, after another long wait, the door opened and Helga was roughly pushed through the door. Her blouse was torn and blood dripped down her legs. Inga grabbed her younger daughter in her arms. They huddled together on the bed.

Irmigard was taken next.

Then the soldiers came for me.

The French doors closed and it was dark. Rough hands covered me. Teeth bit at my neck. Breath that smelled of cigarette smoke and liquor filled my nostrils. My dress was ripped open on top, the bottom thrust over my waist. Then the night became a haze of blinding red pain. Four of them took me in turns as the others watched. It didn't take them long, although it seemed as though hours had passed.

When they were through, they shoved me out of the room and I collapsed on the bed with the others. All the time, the commander kept his weapon pointed at us.

A short time later, the four men came out, pulling up their pants, laughing and jeering. 'Heil Hitler,' they sang to us, and raised their arms in the Nazi salute. When they were finished mocking us, the five soldiers slung their rifles over their shoulders and fled down the stairs.

'I'm going to kill them,' Inga said. She rushed toward the panel where Frederick's gun was hidden.

I'd forgotten about the weapon and screamed at her to stop. 'What can you do? Kill one of them and the others will kill us. Let them go.'

She stopped, leaned against the half-opened door and cried.

I pulled myself up from the bed and winced in pain. I lit a candle and its meager yellow light spread across the room. 'We need medical attention.'

Irmigard stared at me and said, 'There's no doctor in this neighborhood.' She rocked her sister in her arms. Helga's eyes were vacant and black. She stared at the ceiling and said nothing.

I could only go one place for help – the Chancellery.

Irmigard and I tended Helga as best we could. We dipped rags in cold water from the wash bucket in order to staunch her bleeding. The bloody cloths turned the water pink. I rested with my friends for a half hour before I got off the bed. At first I thought it might be better to walk to the Chancellery in the morning when I could see the enemy, but after thinking about it I decided to take advantage of the darkness.

I told Inga to get Frederick's gun, but to use it only as a last resort. I doubted the same soldiers would come back again, but conditions seemed to be worsening by the minute. There was little she could do against armed men. Firing the weapon would likely get her and her daughters killed. I looked out the front windows to see if I could spot any enemy soldiers. I only saw a young man and woman, dark hooded figures, running down the street toward the east, a dangerous direction. They looked like Germans running toward the enemy. I would be heading west.

The view from the window was like a nightmare. Artillery rockets shook the ground as they exploded near us. Many of them buzzed overhead, dangerously close to the apartment. Buildings burned on the horizon; several a few blocks away were engulfed. To the east, a flamethrower split the air with its orange fire. Its powerful stream shattered any window left unbroken. The liquid fire cascaded through the structure like a hellish waterfall. Far off, screams echoed through the night.

It took every ounce of my courage to leave the apartment, even though it offered no real safety. I washed up as best I could and changed into another dress. I threw my things, including my stuffed monkey, into my suitcase. I would have to leave my bag behind because I was in no condition to carry it.

'Wait here,' I said at the door. 'I'll send for a doctor. If you have to leave, don't go far – at least tell a neighbor, anyone, so I'll know where you are.'

Helga stared at the ceiling, unresponsive to my words. Irmigard thanked me and blew me a kiss. Inga nodded and said, 'Pray for us.'

I closed the door and stared at the dark staircase. I let my eyes adjust to the light and walked slowly down. With every step, my legs and abdomen throbbed. The building's door was shattered and wrenched open. Anyone could walk in, but not a living soul was in sight. Frederick's bloody corpse lay in the street, his left arm stretched into the air as if he were reaching for heaven. There was no time for tears. I hoped that Inga and her daughters would not see his body in the morning. Perhaps some kind stranger or German soldier would carry him away before the sun rose.

I ran left down the street. Each step felt like a knife had been stuck in my groin. I had no choice but to walk on, to run if necessary. The Reich Chancellery was several kilometers away; how many I wasn't sure. I was certain, however, the trip would take me several hours, and, at my slow pace, I would be lucky to get there by midnight. Of course, there were soldiers to worry about, too. The Russians could capture and rape me again. The Wehrmacht might fire at me, a shadowy figure in the night, mistaking me for the enemy.

I passed mountainous piles of rubble and the shattered shells of buildings, which rose like charred, blackened skeletons from the ground. Some were white with ash. I'd only gotten a few blocks away when I faced a barricade of battered trolley cars. I lifted my foot to the step of one of them and grabbed hold of the railing. I could see through the car – blazing ruins and empty streets filled with debris lay on the other side.

I stepped up, but in the process my right leg caught on a jagged piece of metal. A sharp slicing pain cut across my flesh. Instinctively, I reached down and felt for the wound. Warm, slick blood dripped from my fingers.

A hand caught me by the back of my coat and pulled me down from the step.

'Where are you headed?' a Russian soldier said in perfect German. He wore a long coat that brushed the ground. He pushed his cap back with the barrel of his pistol and then pointed the weapon at me. A fiery orange light flickered across our faces.

'You need a doctor,' he said, looking at my bloody leg.

'I'm looking for one,' I said. 'Your men have raped me and two other women. One was very young.'

His eyes shifted from one of hostility to concern. He asked me to open my coat. I complied and he searched me. Satisfied that I wasn't carrying a weapon, he said, 'The men get carried away. They realize any hour may be their last on earth and they take advantage of the women.'

'Take advantage?' I asked incredulously. 'They nearly killed us. The young woman was a virgin.'

He leaned against the battered side of the trolley. 'War spawns hellish creatures. Go ahead, find your doctor. I wish you luck. There are German troops on the other side of these cars. If I were you, I'd walk with my hands up.'

'You're letting me go?'

He nodded. 'Of course. We're not all rutting beasts. We're looking for a particular monster and when we find him . . .' He took a white scarf from his coat and wrapped it around the cut on my leg. He started to speak, but his words died as if he had spotted a threat across the street. He slid around the corner of the trolley, dodged past a shattered doorway and disappeared.

Somehow, I trusted him. I lifted myself up on the trolley, my legs aching in pain, walked through the shattered car and climbed down the other side. I raised my hands over my head and walked down the littered street. In a few seconds, I was surrounded by a few old men, some boys from the Hitler Youth and an SS officer. The officer looked at me blankly and then searched me. He asked my name and wanted to know where I had come from.

I told him my name and said, 'About a kilometer to the east.' I pointed in the direction. 'I was raped by the Russians.'

'Pigs! Attacking our women.' He escorted me down the street to the relative safety of a crumbling building. The other men and boys dispersed back to their hiding places and barricades.

'I must get to the Chancellery. I work for the Führer.'

The officer laughed. 'You?'

'Do you have a torch?' I asked.

He shook his head. 'I have a cigarette lighter.'

'Strike it,' I said.

He did. I took off my ring and showed him the inscription on my wedding band.

311

'My God,' he said. 'I'll get you there as soon as I can.' He shouted orders to the men and then walked with me. We ducked at a street corner as a Russian shell flew over our heads and struck several blocks away. He pointed to a brown lump about a hundred meters to the east. When we arrived, the officer pulled the netting off what looked like a pile of dirt and revealed a small vehicle, a cross between a motorcycle and a small tank. He instructed me to get in the rear seat while he drove. My stomach turned over many times on the bumpy journey, but in twenty minutes we were at the garage bunkers of the Chancellery.

The two officers on duty at the bunker did not believe my story until I told them to get Cook. They knew immediately who she was. The soldier who had brought me left me with them. One was kind enough to offer me a seat in the cold hallway as the other went to deliver the message. The garage bunker was a vast complex on the west side of the New Chancellery on Hermann Göring Street.

I doubled over in pain at one point and the remaining officer rushed to my side. He asked if there was anything he could do.

'Get me to a doctor,' I said. Points of light swam before my eyes, and despite the cool, clammy air, heat rose from my skin. The blood from my cut had pooled reddish brown on the Russian soldier's scarf. I shivered on my wooden chair.

It seemed hours before I heard Cook's familiar voice. She rushed toward me, shouting my name. 'Why didn't you tend to this woman?' she yelled at the officers. 'She works for the Führer.'

The men cringed and made their excuses. Cook waved

them away with her hands and said, 'I will take her to the Führer, no thanks to you.'

She lifted me from the chair and I leaned against her. 'It's a long walk, Magda, but you can do it. Think about pleasant things. Better yet, you can tell me what has happened since we last saw each other. Talking will keep your mind off your pain.'

Cook didn't know I had been raped. As we walked through the long corridors of bunkers, I told her of my stay with Irmigard and her family and my efforts to find my father. Many soldiers milled about, and it seemed an equal number were laid out on gurneys awaiting operations. Moans filled the air along with the smell of antiseptic. 'We can't stop here,' Cook said, and shook her head. 'These bunkers are only going to become more crowded as the wounded come. I'm taking you to the Führer's personal physician. You remember him.'

I did remember a pudgy doctor. He was responsible for giving Hitler his daily doses of vitamin injections and morphine. I never liked the doctor's obsequious attitude or his pandering to his boss. However, given the circumstances, I would be happy to see him. The pain grew worse as we drew closer to Hitler's underground headquarters.

We continued through the seemingly endless tunnels of unkers until we came to a connecting corridor. I huffed and held on to Cook tightly as we turned left down the narrow passageway. An SS officer rose from behind his desk as we approached the Vorbunker. This was the first air-raid shelter Hitler had built under the Old Chancellery. Cook nodded and the man let us through this security checkpoint.

'I saved a bed for you in the sleeping quarters,' Cook said.

'You'll feel right at home. It's close to the kitchen.' Sh
managed a smile. We turned again down a broader passag
until we passed through a dining area. My room was off i
I collapsed on the bed, relieved to rest again. Nothing suite
me better than to sleep, but Cook wouldn't hear of it. Finall
I told her my story of the Russian soldiers and my rape. Sh
listened with tears in her eyes.

When I finished, she said, 'Stay here. I will get Dr. Haase

I didn't know Dr. Haase. Hitler had dismissed Dr. Morel
the fat physician who had been with him for years. Driftin
in and out of sleep, I lay on my cot until the rat-faced docto
snapped his fingers over my eyes. I jumped awake.

'Please leave us,' he said to Cook.

Cook stroked my hand. 'Be well, my Magda. I'll be outsid
the door.' She left the room.

The doctor pushed up my dress and pulled down m
bloody underpants. He shook his head. 'The cut on you
leg is the least of your problems. You're bleeding internall
I'm sending for a nurse.' He called out to Cook, who poke
her head in and then ran to follow his instructions.

I focused on my surroundings. I didn't want to look at th
doctor or feel his fingers upon me. The room was sma
crowded with iron bunk beds and devoid of color. A few bar
bulbs lit the room. A constant hum filled my ears, like th
low whirring of machinery. The bunkers at the Wolf's La
seemed like a palace compared to those in the Vorbunker.

In a few minutes, a nurse appeared with a syringe in h
hands. My arm stung briefly and then I lost consciousnes
I awakened several hours later dressed in a clinical gow
Cook sat by my side, but I wanted nothing but sleep. A fe
other women slept on beds nearby. I lifted my head to sa

a few words, but the anesthetic's effects were too powerful. My head dropped back to the pillow and I fell asleep.

When I woke up, I had no idea whether it was day or night. The room was empty. I tried to move my legs, but they were unresponsive. My heart quickened in a panic. I drifted in and out of consciousness until Cook appeared at my side.

'You mustn't move,' she said, and pointed to my legs. 'They're strapped to the bed. The doctor doesn't want you to walk for a few days so the healing process can begin. Then you should be fine. I'll get you some food later.' She smiled and reached over to hold my hand. Despite her allegiance to Hitler, Cook again displayed her worth as a friend. She sat and stared at me with sad brown eyes.

A horrible thought struck me and I rose up on my elbows.

'The women I left behind,' I said. 'They need a doctor. Someone must go for them. I'll tell you where they are.'

Cook shook her head. 'It's impossible, Magda. Every available physician is here at the bunker, aiding wounded soldiers and the people who are defending the city. Besides, no doctor could make his way to the neighborhoods now. It would be suicide. They would be cut down by the Red Army.'

'I made it.'

'You were lucky. You had a much better chance coming west to the Chancellery than those trying to travel east. The enemy is drawing closer by the hour. Our casualties increase by the minute.' She paused and then dropped her voice to a whisper. 'There's something else . . .'

I stared at her.

'Dr. Haase says you will never be able to have children. Too much damage was done.'

315

I lay back on the bed as tears gathered in my eyes. But there was more going on in my battered body than sadness. A red-hot anger surged through me.

'Where is he?' I said to Cook.

She looked at me as if I had lost my mind. Perhaps I had. 'Who?' she asked.

'Hitler.' I spit out his name and didn't care if anyone heard my blasphemy.

Cook stared at me, horrified. 'Magda, you're ill. I'll get the doctor.'

'I'm not ill! He's the cause of all this! He's the one who should be punished!'

Cook leaned over and put her hand on my forehead. 'You're not making sense. Calm yourself.'

I pounded the cot with my fists and pulled against the leg straps until I thought my feet would snap off. Hot stabbing pain shot through my abdomen. I held on to my stomach and thrashed on the bed until I couldn't move. Exhausted, I melted into tears.

The doctor did not come, but a nurse came with a sedative. She administered the shot and the light above me turned hazy and weak until it faded to blackness. One thought filled me as I slipped into unconsciousness: *No matter what it takes, I will kill Adolf Hitler.*

# CHAPTER 20

The next few days slipped from my memory. I wasn't sure how many hours had passed. I recalled doctors and nurses observing me, changing the bedding on the cot, my gown, my dressings, Cook feeding me although I wasn't hungry.

Then, like a patient emerging from a prolonged fever, I felt better, well enough to get up on my feet. I took small steps around my room and stuck my head out in the corridor. A few people said hello to me. Others gave me a glance and then looked away. Cook and I talked when she brought me my meals; however, she never mentioned my ravings about Hitler or wavered in her steadfast friendship. She told me Berlin was about to fall – everyone knew it and was making plans to flee the city. Hitler, she said, was not convinced and planned to stay to the end. She and several members of the staff, including Hitler's valet, wanted to remain as well.

I asked her if a doctor had been sent to Irmigard's. Cook shook her head. I could tell from her expression that as much as I wanted them to be saved there was nothing Cook or I could do.

The hours droned by in synchronicity with the hum o the generators. If there were bombs falling, rockets smashing into the Chancellery, we didn't hear them. There could have been hand-to-hand fighting in the garden above. We wouldn' have heard it. It was as if we lived in a tomb sealed from the world with no hope of finding our way out.

One evening, I felt strong enough to take a meal in the canteen. The room was next to the kitchen in the Vorbunke and, as I was eating, I spotted a woman I recognized from the Berghof. At first I thought my eyes might be playing tricks on me, as if the lingering effects of my medication had affected my vision, conjuring a ghost before me. She wore a plain blue dress with long sleeves and glided around the kitchen in her usual breezy manner, smiling and talking to the staff. I recognized her voice immediately. The woman was Eva Braun.

I was dressed in a surgical gown. Cook was trying to find clothing for me, but dresses were in short supply.

Eva spotted me and walked toward me with a friendly look. She pulled out a chair from across the table and sa down. She grasped my hands. 'It's so good to see you, Magda I heard about your misfortune. I'm glad you're feeling better

I didn't know what to say. How could she engage in small talk when her world, indeed our world, was crumbling around us? But Eva always blithely ignored reality in favo of clothes and parties. She was the fiddler while Berlin burned. I was surprised to see her in the bunker because she usually spent her time away from Hitler at her home in Munich. Her face was more careworn than the last time I'

318

seen her. The opulent jewelry and clothes of the past had disappeared in favor of a more modest appearance.

'How long have you been here?' I asked.

'For a few weeks,' she said, and looked at me with a piteous smile. 'Why don't you come to my room? I have a few dresses I can give you. The gown doesn't suit you.'

I finished my meal while Eva talked about her parents and her sister. When I was done, she led me out of the canteen to a passageway door that led to a rectangular flight of stairs. These steps descended even deeper into the earth until we came to an SS checkpoint. We were in the Führer Bunker. The atmosphere was similar to the Vorbunker, only more claustrophobic. One heard the constant whir of the generators, the passageways were garishly lit, the ceilings were low, a series of small rooms branched out from the corridor. A dog barked from what seemed a great distance away. I heard the muffled whine of puppies.

'Blondi,' Eva said. 'I keep my dogs away from her. I would never allow them to mix.'

'Blondi has puppies?' I asked.

'Oh yes, he had her bred. I think there are five. I don't pay that much attention to them.'

We stopped in the narrow corridor between two doors. The scent of diesel oil and disinfectant hung in the air. 'Everything is within walking distance here,' Eva said, and tried gamely to smile. 'The closet is next to my bedroom. Unfortunately, so is the bathroom.' She opened the closet door and peered inside. The light was on. There was room inside for a small chest of drawers and a rack for her dresses and furs. She thumbed through the rack and said, 'Pick out a few. I'm sure I won't need them all.'

'Really, I shouldn't.'

She touched me on the shoulder. 'Magda, we all know what's happening. Let's make the best of it. Take them as a gift. If they don't fit, I'll have them altered. Believe it or not, I can even work a needle if I have to.'

I thanked her but felt guilty looking at her clothes. I stepped inside and peered at the rack. Ten beautiful dresses, mostly navy and black, were gathered on hangers. They were all monogrammed with an *EB* on the collar. I inspected them one by one until I got to a beautiful white gown, the one she had shown me at the Berghof.

'You can't have that one,' she said. 'I'm wearing it soon on my wedding day.'

I jumped back as if I had touched fire. 'You're getting married?'

Eva laughed and her voice sounded like sparkling champagne. 'He held out as long as he could, poor thing. Now he has no choice but to marry me.' She giggled like a schoolgirl. 'You must come – be a witness. Perhaps my Matron of Honor.'

I shook my head, astounded at the thought.

'No, really, you must. Who can I ask here? One of the women in his SS guard? They all have faces carved from concrete. A nurse? One of his private secretaries? They're just as bad as the SS.' Cupping her hand over her mouth, she stifled a laugh. 'I shouldn't make fun.' She grabbed my hands and squeezed them. 'Please tell me you'll consider it. My wedding would be incomplete without a Matron of Honor.'

'You're very persuasive,' I said. 'Thank you for asking. Of course I will.'

In reality, all I was thinking about was how to murder

Hitler. How ironic it would be to kill him on his wedding day, the 'happiest day' of his life. But how would I do it? It would take much more planning than just thinking about it. And what to do with Eva? Kill her, too? No. There would be no need. Once Hitler was dead the remaining members of the Reich would spring into action. The SS would come for me and I would be gone soon after. In a way, I felt sorry for Eva for being such a fool. I could see how she drew people to her with her kind dispensations, her invitations to celebrate life in the midst of war. Men and women were flattered to be part of her social circle, to perhaps get close to Hitler; however, her experience must have been as shallow and hollow as having tea in the sun on the Berghof terrace. I was convinced she knew nothing of the massacres, the concentration camps, the atrocities committed by the Reich. She was not stupid. Her greatest fault was that she was blind to everything except her own perception of life.

I took three of the dresses – two black and one dark blue – and said good night. Eva accompanied me to the staircase and the SS checkpoint that led back to the Vorbunker. Before we reached it, she looked back in the direction of her room. 'Poor, poor Adolf,' she said. 'They've all deserted him. He's all alone now. He only has Blondi and me.'

I thanked her for the dresses and left her in the passageway. On the way to my room, a woman wearing an expensive silk dress appeared in the corridor. Three young girls dressed in a similar fashion accompanied her. They stared at me as if I were a specter. I must have looked a fright in my surgical gown, unkempt hair and plain face. Later, I asked Cook who they were. 'Don't you know?' she asked with astonishment. 'That's Magda Goebbels and her children. They're here to ride out the storm.' Her husband, the Propaganda Minister, was also in the bunker, but I hadn't seen him. Cook told me that a few days earlier he had read a proclamation of his allegiance to the residents of Berlin. A printed copy of it lay on a kitchen table. I picked it up:

*I call on you to fight for your city. Fight with everything you have got, for the sake of your wives and your children, your mothers and your parents. Your arms are defending everything we have ever held dear, and all the generations that will come after us. Be proud and courageous! Be inventive and cunning! Your leader is amongst you. He and his colleagues will remain in your midst. His wife and children are here as well. He, who once captured the city with 200 men, will now use every means to galvanize the defense of the capital. The battle for Berlin must become the signal for the whole nation to rise up in battle.*

The madness had descended deep into the earth.

One evening I asked Cook what day it was. She told me April 28. I had no idea how to tell time other than by asking people. There were no clocks or calendars on the walls. The hours in the bunker vanished in a monotonous litany. I'd left my wristwatch and suitcase in Irmigard's apartment after the attack. I thought of her family and wondered whether they were alive. I prayed that they were.

Here, all six of Goebbels's children, five girls and a boy, were in the bunker. The whole family had been personally invited by Hitler. Since my first spotting, I had come to notice them more often. They seemed a game lot, and stood out from the crowd of usual officers and staff. The eldest daughter appeared more reserved and sulky than the rest. I assumed she missed her freedom and her friends because she was older. Life inside the bunker was less of a game for her than for the younger children.

That evening, the Goebbels boy wandered by me in the corridor. From his appearance, I judged him to be about eight or nine years old. His hair was darker than his sisters' and I spotted the resemblance to his father, particularly in his thin lips. He was growing into a lean young man, although he still carried some childhood softness around his belly. He brandished a wooden revolver at me and asked me where I was going. He was pretending to be a soldier, but his severe tone undercut the playfulness of the game.

'Who are you?' I asked, knowing all along.

'I asked you first,' he said. 'Do you have your identification papers?'

'You only have to ask the Führer. He will tell you who I am.'

His eyes widened and he holstered his gun. 'You're a friend of Uncle Adolf?'

I would never claim that I was Hitler's friend, so I answered, 'I work for him.'

His shoulders drooped. 'Everyone works for Uncle Adolf. I have no chance to catch spies or traitors. Did you see the man they dragged in today?'

I squatted against the wall to be closer to his face. 'No, who was he?'

'Eva Braun's brother-in-law,' he said proudly. 'He worked for Uncle Adolf, too, but they demoted him. He was drunk. Maybe they'll shoot him.' He smiled.

I'd heard that Eva had a sister and that she was married, but I knew nothing more about the man. I pointed to his toy weapon. 'Where did you get your gun?'

He took the painted replica out of the holster and handed it to me. 'I'm Helmut Goebbels and my father gave it to me. He ordered me to protect my mother and sisters while he works with Uncle Adolf. My father is very important.'

I looked at the realistic ridges on the grip, the sight, the trigger, of the replica. I handed it back to him and said, 'You're doing a good job for your father.' Then, it struck me that I might ask him an 'innocent' question of importance. 'Are there other guns like yours in the bunker?'

His eyes narrowed and I wondered whether I'd given myself away. 'Well . . . because you work for Uncle Adolf, I guess I can tell you.'

The walls rocked from a muffled explosion. They'd become more prominent within the past day. When I had first arrived at the bunker, I'd heard nothing. The Russians were only a few blocks away from the Chancellery now and the shelling was constant. Helmut looked to the ceiling and the teetering lightbulb overhead.

'My mother says the Red Army is coming. It makes her sick to her stomach. She tells my sisters that we may have to leave the bunker soon. That makes them happy, especially my oldest sister. She wants to go home, but I know my mother will never leave Uncle Adolf.' He patted the gun at his side. 'This doesn't shoot bullets, but my father said he would give me a real gun if I needed one.'

Another shell shook the walls. They were dropping on the Old Chancellery over our heads.

Helmut continued, oblivious to the artillery. 'I'll have a

gun. Ever since the traitors tried to kill Uncle Adolf, he doesn't allow guns around him. Only a few SS men have them. He knows they are loyal.'

I could have questioned his naïve assertion that Hitler's staff was unwavering in their loyalty, but I left it alone.

Down the corridor, near the stairs that led downward to Hitler's bunker, a stooped figure shambled by like a hunchback. Helmut saw him, too, shouted his name and darted after him without another word to me.

The figure stopped and turned. I gasped, looking into the face of evil. He'd aged a lifetime since I had seen him. His shirt was falling out from the waist of his pants. His hair shone gray in the dim light, his face lined with dark ridges. He stopped, turned his head toward me and stared. The light in his eyes had vanished. His left arm shook. He didn't raise a hand or smile in acknowledgment. I wondered if he could see me at all.

His grotesque face terrified me. I wondered if I really needed to kill him, because, in actuality, he was already dead, a walking corpse holding court in his tomb. He grabbed Helmut's shoulders and ambled away, using the boy like a cane.

That evening, as I lay on my cot, I wondered whether I should give any more thought to killing Hitler. After seeing his ghostly figure in the corridor, I knew his time was short. However, there was nothing in my religious upbringing that would cause me to lose sleep from murdering a tyrant. I had been raised Lutheran, but my devotion was lax. My father rarely went to church; my mother attended sporadically on Sundays and on religious holidays. I sometimes went to church with my mother, but only because she wanted me to go. I had little desire to be instructed in the ways of religion. Some satisfaction would be gained, posthumously of course, of having my name in history books as the 'woman who killed Hitler.'

That night, Eva tapped my shoulder. I had fallen into a deep sleep, despite the reoccurring blasts, and her touch startled me. She carried a torch. I rose up on my elbows and asked in a groggy voice, 'What's the matter? Is something wrong?'

She shook her head. Then I saw the tears in her eyes. 'My brother-in-law is dead. The security forces took him up to the garden and shot him. I begged for his life, but Adolf wouldn't hear of it. He called him a "drunken, womanizing fool." My sister is about to give birth, but it made no difference. I said, "You are the Führer."' She sat on the edge of my cot and hung her head. 'Poor, poor Adolf. They have all deserted him; they have all betrayed him. But it's better that ten thousand others die than *he* be lost to Germany. My sister will have to live without her husband.'

A spark of life returned to her eyes. 'Adolf and I are to be married in about an hour. You must dress. I want you to be there, Magda.'

'What time is it?'

'A few minutes after midnight. Come as soon as you can. We are to be married in the small conference room. I'll let the guard know you are invited.' She rose from my cot and stole out of the room.

I climbed out of bed and reached underneath it for the box that held my things. I'd not had a real bath in days, only given myself quick splashes of water from the kitchen faucet. The only bathtub was in Hitler's apartment and only he, Eva and the Goebbels family were permitted to use it.

I pulled out one of Eva's blue dresses and put it on. It fit well enough that I could wear it. I washed at the kitchen sink, making myself as presentable as I could for the wedding. A butcher knife glinted on the counter and I considered taking it, but then discarded the idea. I had no way of concealing it. Besides, I didn't know how many people would be at Eva's wedding or how close I'd be able to get to Hitler.

I left the kitchen and walked through the darkened canteen to the passageway that led to Hitler's lower bunker. At the bottom of the stairs, the SS guard let me pass after I told him my name. I noticed he wore a holstered pistol. I went past the conference room where Hitler held his daily briefings and found myself at the door of the smaller room. Neither was large; the more expansive of the two contained a table in its center. I pictured the generals and officers crowded around it as Hitler issued orders for his crumbling offensives. Everyone knew Berlin was falling. The Führer was an 'emperor with no clothes,' but no one laughed at him. What little power he had was near its end.

The door stood open. Eva saw me and waved me in. She was wearing the white dress she had shown me a few days earlier. Her face was reddened with blush and she looked somewhat pretty, although nothing like the woman of her carefree days at the Berghof. Hitler, attired in a dark suit and matching tie, sat in a chair looking glum and preoccupied. He wore the Party pin on his lapel. Goebbels, with his thin, mousy face, stood nearby, his hands folded in front of him. His expression was as stern and uncompromising as I'd seen in all the pictures taken of the Propaganda Minister. The skin underneath his eyes was lined with black from lack of sleep. Martin Bormann, looking like a bulldog, occupied himself with a paper that lay on the table. It was the marriage certificate for Adolf and Eva.

Hitler nodded at me but did not speak. I stood next to Eva. She grabbed my left hand with her right in a strong but cold grip. I looked down at my fingers and noticed the silver wedding band given to Karl and me by the Führer on our wedding day. Eva wore no such ring.

Soon an SS man appeared at the door accompanied by a grubby man dressed in civilian clothes. His jacket, shirt and face were streaked with dirt. Goebbels introduced him as Herr Wagner, a Berlin Councilor and a member of a fighting unit not many blocks away from the bunker. Goebbels had pulled Wagner from the streets to conduct the wedding.

The civil ceremony did not take long. Hitler and Eva swore they were of Aryan descent and had no hereditary diseases that would make them unfit for marriage. Hitler signed the certificate and then handed the pen to Eva. I watched as she started to sign her name as *Eva Braun*. She laughed, slapped her hand in jest and then wrote: *Eva Hitler, born Braun*. The couple kissed quickly and then took turns shaking hands with everyone in the room. Hitler said nothing to me as he took hold of my hand. No words were needed. His vacant look and weak handshake told me everything I needed to know about his condition.

'I am so happy, Magda,' Eva said to me as she led me to her husband's private apartment. This room contained a sofa and small table. A pretty Dutch still life hung on the wall. Hitler's desk was also in the room and above it was a portrait in an oval frame.

Eva pointed to the picture of a stern-looking older man

in a powdered white wig with a starburst silver medal pinned to his dark waistcoat. 'Do you know who that is?'

I shook my head.

'Frederick the Great,' she said. 'Adolf stares at it for hours, as if the old warrior is talking to him.' She sighed. 'Pointless. All of it is pointless. A dead King of Prussia cannot save the Reich. How I wish he could.' Her eyes filled with tears.

Hitler walked into the room followed by his small entourage. Eva wiped her tears away and stood by him. I wanted to express my hatred, my overriding wish to see him dead. Despite my loathing, I was struck by his precipitous personal decline. Perhaps it was the late hour, but he had always worked late into the night; perhaps all his illustrious illusions had finally shattered. He was a noxious shadow of his former self. His chalk-colored face sagged from his months of living underground. His wrinkled suit and stooped gait mirrored the collapse unfolding over us. As the Reich's leader crumbled underground so did Germany above.

Others appeared at the door, including Cook, Frau Goebbels and the secretaries, all invited by the groom. The room grew warm from the bodies crowded inside and I moved away from Eva and Hitler to be closer to the passageway where I could breathe.

Hitler's valet brought champagne and the guests drank a toast to the bride and groom. A small gale of laughter and clinking of glasses died, and everyone looked to the Führer. He sat on the couch eating a piece of iced cake. Crumbs fell from his mouth onto the lapels of his suit. Eva frowned but said nothing to chastise him, as she would have in her days at the Berghof.

When he finished eating, he said, 'Now is the time to

remember better days.' He wiped his fingers on a champagne towel and leaned back against the couch. 'My life has always been devoted to Germany and the Party. How wonderful it was in the early days when every man, woman and child rose up in pride to answer the call of National Socialism.'

Everyone's eyes, except Bormann's, glazed over. We were in for a long harangue about the 'good old days' of the Party and reminiscences of the Führer's rise to power. He talked for nearly an hour. No one could do anything but hold their champagne glasses and listen as he pontificated about his youth, the glory of the early years and the terrible fate now befalling the Nazis. Finally, he lowered his head and stared at his hands. His guests remained silent, waiting to be dismissed.

He took another piece of cake and put it on a napkin in his lap. 'There is one final thing to say on my wedding night.' He paused. His watery eyes took in everyone in the room. He shook his head as if he could not believe the cascading decline of his power, the shells exploding over his head, the destruction of his 'lightning-war' army, was happening to him. 'It's over,' he finally said. 'National Socialism is dead, never to be revived. Who would have the courage to lead such a movement but me?' His lips parted in a sardonic smile and he stared at Goebbels and Bormann in turn. They stood unflinching under his gaze.

'Anyone who wants to leave the bunker should do so,' he said.

'Never, my Führer,' Goebbels said, and saluted. Those assembled echoed this sentiment and saluted as well. I stood in the passageway with my arms by my sides.

Hitler held out his hands, as if pleading with the gathering.

'You are released. Do not suffer with me. Everyone, except you, my loyal friends, has betrayed me. Even the German people have deserted me.' He clenched his fists and pounded them against his chest. 'They haven't the will to survive – they haven't the backbone to stand up to our enemies. I have overestimated their worth from the beginning. They deserve to be crushed.' He sagged back on the couch like a deflating balloon.

Bormann shouted, 'Yes, my Führer.'

Rage boiled through me. I wanted to strangle Hitler. He *blamed* the German people for his tyrannical failings. In one stroke, he discarded my father, my mother and my aunt and uncle who loyally supported him, even the innocent children who died in the streets in his name. No remorse flowed from the Führer. No apology sprang from his lips. Only blame. The devastating downfall was the result of the Wehrmacht. The soldiers were cowards who valued their lives more than their country; his generals and military officers were idiots who knew nothing of strategy and tactics. Who could blame the poor Führer when all of Germany was at fault?

'It will be a release for me to die,' he said. 'And so I shall – here, with my wife by my side. She has chosen the same fate.'

Magda Goebbels burst into tears. Her husband rushed to her side until her blubbering subsided. Several of Hitler's secretaries wiped their eyes as well.

As the gloom and depression of the suicidal confession spread over the room, several of the guests slipped away from the oppressive atmosphere. The wedding party was over. Hitler rose from the couch taking care to wrap his cake in a napkin. He tucked it in his right pocket and walked past me, staring straight ahead as if in a trance, as I stood in the passageway.

Eva patted me on the shoulder. 'Thank you for coming, Magda. I suppose I won't be seeing much of you from now on.' She watched as the other guests disappeared in the passageway. 'Leave as soon as you can. Get out of Berlin and head south toward Munich. The Americans will be there. They will be more forgiving than the Red Army.'

A secretary, Frau Junge, passed by and stepped into the adjoining room with Hitler.

'She's a loyal one,' Eva said. 'Junge will be here until the end.' She attempted to smile, but her mouth turned quickly into a frown. 'Adolf is dictating his last will and testament. It won't be long now.'

Eva kissed me on the cheek. 'Good-bye, dear Magda.'

She walked to her room and left me with the valet and Dr. and Frau Goebbels, who sat on the couch in disbelief, stunned by their Führer's decision to die in Berlin.

I, however, silently rejoiced.

The next morning, I sat on my bed and cried. No one came to my aid. I doubted that anyone cared, or if they did they were too tired and depressed to bother. I felt the effects of the bunker existence – the lack of fresh air, the walls closing around me, the same faces every day, a routine that never varied as the hours hung over me like those of a clock winding down. One of the SS men told me I shouldn't worry about being outside; one couldn't see the sun anyway because of the smoke. The Russians were firing artillery cannons point-blank as they advanced. Berlin was burning to the ground. Now shells struck above us relentlessly and the ground shuddered. The attack came faster and with more ferocity as the hours dragged on.

I pulled myself together and thought about how I could get south to Munich and Berchtesgaden. The journey seemed impossible; however, I would worry about it when the time came to evacuate – if I got out of the bunker alive.

Shortly after eleven that same morning, Cook rushed into my room, her face wild and flushed. 'Mussolini is dead,' she said. 'The Führer is distraught. His best friend is gone.' She sat on my cot for a time, her arms bouncing wildly at her sides as if she didn't know what to do. 'I'm not leaving him, Magda. Neither is Frau Junge. We will remain until the end.'

I grasped her hands. 'You should leave with me. We can travel to Berchtesgaden. It will be safer there. We can stay with my aunt and uncle if we can't get to the Berghof.'

She looked at me in amazement. 'What about your father and your friends in Berlin?'

I shuddered. 'I have no idea where my father is or if my friends are still alive. I can't face the Russians – again.' The finality of losing my father crushed me. I, like everyone else in Germany, had lost so much. Cook leaned toward me and we both hugged. It was a simple gesture born of loss.

After a time, Cook said, 'I must go. He's not eating, but I still make his meals.' She hugged me. 'Please say good-bye before you leave.'

I nodded, lay back on my cot and remained there for about twenty minutes until I could rest no longer. I got up and paced the room. I needed to see the sun, breathe the air again, before I was captured or killed. My chances of escaping the bunker seemed slim.

Cook had told me about an emergency exit on the west end leading to the bombed-out garden behind the New Chancellery that Speer had constructed. Several people, including Eva, had gone there to get a breath of air. I left my quarters and crossed through the canteen to the passageway leading to the lower bunker. I walked down the stairs. The guard gave me a quick glance and waved me through as if my presence didn't matter. He, too, knew the end was near. The central passageway was long and led past the conference room and Hitler's quarters. Beyond them, I saw a figure stooped in shadow near a door.

'Kill her,' I heard him say. 'I don't want her captured by the Russians any more than Eva and I want to be. The Italians have made a mockery of my friend – strung him up like a pig on a hook. I will not allow this to happen to her . . .' He struck his fist against the wall.

He stopped, suddenly aware of my presence, and glared at me with his sunken eyes. The crisp, astute Hitler had transformed into a slouching cave dweller, a grotesque monster of the underworld. He held up his hand for me to stop, leaned toward the door and pulled it partially shut. 'What are you doing here?' he asked.

'I was hoping to get some air,' I said.

'Only those who have permission can leave the bunker by this route.' He turned away from the door. 'You might get killed.'

A man stuck his head out of the room and said, 'It's done. The poison was quick as lightning.'

'Leave me and take the puppies,' Hitler ordered. The man stepped back inside and a few moments later came out with a box. As he passed, I heard the muffled scratching and

334

whining of the young dogs. He proceeded down the passageway toward the stairway leading up to the exit. Hitler shuffled inside. Soon muffled sobs filtered into the passageway.

I stole forward hoping to see whose death had elicited such a response from Hitler. The door was cracked. The light inside the room was harsh. Hitler knelt on the floor, his chest heaving over the black-and-tan creature that lay silently on the floor. Blondi had been poisoned.

I heard the exit door open. Then five loud shots echoed through the passageway. Soon the man returned. I stepped back into the shadows, moving away from them. 'The puppies are dead,' the man told Hitler. 'You no longer have to worry.'

I walked quickly, hoping to get away from what I'd witnessed. Death offered its cold hand everywhere in the bunker, even for the dog who meant so much to Hitler.

My confinement clawed at me. I walked back to the Vorbunker and toward the long connecting hallway that led to the series of tunnels running east – west under the New Chancellery. The SS guard asked me what I was doing. I was in no mood to lie. I told him I was going crazy in the bunker and needed to take a walk. He nodded, smiled sadly as if he knew what I was going through, and waved me on.

I remembered little from the night of the attack on Irmigard's apartment. When I'd arrived, Cook had led me to the Vorbunker. Now I saw the horror that had been thrust upon the German people. Medical facilities had been constructed in several rooms. The smell of blood and flesh permeated the corridor. Several doctors moved from table to table as if animated by ghostly puppet strings. Their aprons were stained red and splattered with human tissue.

One of the doctors shouted orders to a nurse who looked

lost amid the daunting task confronting her. A hundred patients, many with severed limbs, burns or open wounds, waited for them. Perhaps there were more than a hundred. The wounded lay like mannequins on the tables, covered by bloody sheets or naked in their pain. A doctor cut through the right arm of a soldier just below the shoulder. He held up the limb and then threw it into a metal tub overflowing with severed legs, arms, hands and feet. My stomach churned at the bloody sight as the stench of death filled my nostrils.

The doctor who had performed the amputation called out to me, 'Can you help us?'

At first, I didn't know what to say. I stared at him.

'We need your help,' he pleaded. 'People are dying.'

I looked down the passageway. Rows of silent refugees, some of whom were decorated Party members who apparently thought they had a right to escape what others were suffering, sat on the floor looking crushed and sullen. They had not offered to help the doctors. I wondered why. Perhaps they had seen enough blood or they had no taste for the tragedy unfolding around them. I started to walk away from the makeshift hospital and then stopped. A strange question filled my head: *What if I'm able to find out about Irmigard and her family?* I turned and wound my way through the maze of tables to the doctor who asked for my help.

# CHAPTER 21

A tortured hope also arose in me as I walked to the doctor. What if Karl wasn't dead and he was here in the bunker? As remote as that possibility was, I clung to it for an instant.

But any hope I had of finding Karl among the hundreds of wounded was soon dashed. I looked at each of the faces filled with pain. He was not among them. The doctor shrugged when I asked him about Irmigard and my old neighborhood.

'I'd say their chances of survival were slim,' he said. 'We haven't been able to get east for weeks.'

I had little time to chastise myself for asking such questions. I shook off my sadness and asked the doctor how I could help.

I changed bandages, scrubbed bedding in a washtub, held men's and women's hands as the doctors cut into them. Many times I had to look away because my stomach, and heart, could not bear their screams. Anesthesia was in short supply and only the most seriously wounded were given a dosage. One man administered whiskey, with the doctors' blessings, to those half-crazed with pain.

'I want to die,' one soldier who had lost both legs from a Russian shell told me. Another less seriously wounded echoed a similar urge to end his life. I tried my best to cheer them up, making no mention of the Reich. Rather, I told them how important they were – how they were needed on this earth. As I visited others, Hitler and his suicide pact came to mind and I marveled at how the mood of the soldiers and citizens had fallen into utter despair, mirroring the Reich leader's psyche.

As the hours passed, the toil of struggling with the wounded, and lifting bodies, exhausted me. I found an empty chair and collapsed in it for a few minutes. One of the doctors saw me and said, 'Thank you for your help. Get something to eat.'

'What time is it?' I asked.

'After nine in the evening,' he replied.

I walked back to the Vorbunker and wiped the blood from my hands. Gore spotted my dress. I bumped into Cook in the passageway. She grabbed me by the arm and dragged me along. 'We're to meet the Führer,' she said. She rushed us along until we came to the large conference room in the lower bunker. Hitler stood inside, hunched over a large map of Germany spread out across the table. His two secretaries, who had been summoned as well, stood across from him. As we entered, he took off his glasses with his shaking left hand and placed them on the table. He wore the tan uniform jacket. I'd not seen him in it since we'd left the Berghof.

All of us lined up in a row and waited for him to speak. A sad smile crossed his face and he said, 'I want to thank you for your loyal service to your Führer.' He put his right hand into his jacket pocket and walked toward us with an unsteady gait. He kept his left hand on the table for balance. 'The others will know soon, but I am releasing you from your oath . . .'

He continued to speak, but we could barely hear his mumbling voice. Yet we all knew what was to come. Still, I thought of killing him.

His fingers shook in his pocket, knocking the fabric in and out in frenzied punches. Finally, he withdrew his hand and opened it. Four cyanide ampoules, their copper casings glinting in the light, rested in his palm. He gave us each one.

'I wish I could have presented you a better going-away gift,' he said. 'If the Russians break in, you may prefer this to a forced captivity and their beastly ways.'

His eyes drifted from us and focused beyond the walls, as if we were not in the room. We were left standing with the poison in our hands as he shuffled off to his quarters.

Frau Junge wiped away tears and we dispersed.

'I have no intention of using this,' Cook said as we walked away. I held mine in my hand, unsure of whether I should use it on myself or Hitler. At my bed, I put the capsule under my pillow and lay down. The next thing I knew I was awakened by shouting and laughter. I got up and, bleary-eyed, staggered toward the canteen. At least twenty of Hitler's staff, including officers, were holding a party. A pile of records sat next to a phonograph. The music blared through the room and mixed with the raucous clinking of glasses. Several green champagne bottles floated across the crowd, passed by eager hands.

A drunken SS officer approached me, unfazed by my

unkempt appearance and blood-spotted dress, which I had slept in. His pants were wet with champagne and his exposed chest showed through his open shirt and uniform jacket. He collapsed against the door and put his hand on my shoulder. 'Want to dance?' He swayed erratically with the music.

I was afraid he would topple over upon me.

'Live a little. We only have a few hours left.' He pointed to the ceiling. 'The bastards are only a few blocks away. Maybe over us now. Screw them.' He winked and put his face close to mine. His breath smelled of a horrid mixture of cigarettes and champagne. 'How about it, how about a little screw? What have you got to lose?'

I knocked his hand away. 'Thanks for the offer, but no.' I attempted to move past him, but he grabbed my arm. I kicked him in the shin and he winced in pain.

'Little bitch!' he yelled. 'You'll get yours.' He stumbled backward away from me.

I took a deep breath, moved into the canteen and looked for a familiar face. I saw Cook and Frau Junge, who sat at a table on the far side of the room. I pushed past the revelers, many of whom could barely stand up after drinking numerous libations. Expensive chocolates and pastries sat on the tables as well. Someone had raided what remained of Hitler's palatable luxuries. I joined the two women at the table. Cook offered me a glass of champagne. I shook my head.

'Who knows when you may have this opportunity again?' she said. 'I wouldn't turn it down.'

'No,' I said. 'I want my wits about me.'

'Why?' Frau Junge asked. 'The end has come. It's only a matter of time before we're taken out of here – dead or alive.'

'I have unfinished business.'

They both looked at me as if I had said something heretical. Cook sighed and said, 'We all do.'

A nurse and a soldier danced past us, knocking into our table. We held on to its edge with our hands to prevent it from tipping over.

'Drunken fools,' Frau Junge said. 'They have no respect for the Führer.' She took a sip of champagne. 'Who would want to leave this life in such a state?'

Magda Goebbels appeared at the far end of the canteen, attired in a white dressing gown. She glared at the crowd and shouted, 'Shame. Shame on all of you. The Führer can't sleep. Neither can my children. Have some decency.'

The revelers laughed and continued their party. She turned away, disgusted by the display. Soon Hitler's valet appeared and repeated what Frau Goebbels had said. He begged the crowd to quiet down so the Führer could sleep. His pleas were ignored as well.

Cook leaned toward Frau Junge and said, 'We have been loyal and true to the Führer. Let's drink to his health.' They clinked their glasses and then looked at me because I refused to join in.

I got up from the table. 'I've had enough of this spectacle.' I left them and walked back to my room. Sleep did not come because the party continued until five in the morning. It broke up when the shelling became so intense no one could hear the music. The earth moaned and shook around us like an erupting volcano.

About two hours later, Eva came to my quarters. She wore a pretty blue dress, the color of her mood. 'Come, walk with me,' she said.

341

No one could rest because of the explosions, so I decided to join her. By now my face had become familiar to the SS, and because I was walking with Eva, no guards questioned us. We walked through the Führer Bunker toward the exit where Blondi and the puppies had been killed.

'I want to see light,' she said. 'These days have been hell, but it'll soon be over.' She turned into the passageway leading to the exit staircase, shook her head and laughed like the 'old' Eva, the one at the Berghof, her voice bubbling like a brook. 'Actually, it's a great relief to know it's going to be over soon.' Eva climbed the stairs slowly, savoring each step. I followed.

She pushed open the door, which could only be opened from the inside. The shelling had let up for a moment. A nightmarish vision of scorched earth lay in front of us. Fractured trees littered the ground. Even though it was April 30, no leaves shaded the Chancellery garden. Instead, a pitted landscape of shell holes and destruction lay in front of us. The New Chancellery was in ruin, its grand structure obliterated by bombs and shells. Huge stone blocks lay in tumbled piles at its base. A thick pall of smoke hung in the air, giving the morning sky a hellish red-orange hue. Fires burned so close to us, we could barely make out the sun's disk through the noxious clouds.

Eva stepped out. I didn't stop her. 'Look, Magda!' she exclaimed proudly. 'I'm outside and the Russians don't know it.' At that moment, a shell streaked over the bunker and landed a few hundred meters away. The blast rocked Eva off her feet. I called for her to come back inside.

She did a pirouette around a crater. 'Death can wait a few minutes.' She pointed to the tortured earth. 'That hole may be where we are buried. It's a bit in the open. I hope they do a good job of concealing our bodies.'

I looked at her incredulously and knew she was losing her mind. She was talking nonsense. I stood near the door to the desolate garden. 'Come back inside, Eva. It's too dangerous.' Another artillery shell streaked overhead, but struck farther away this time.

She hung her head and walked slowly back to me. 'I guess we must – but let me linger a bit at the door.'

I stood behind her as she craned her neck and viewed the destruction. 'I have a favor to ask you,' she said, her face turned away from me. I drew close to her side, so close I could see the sparkle in her eyes as she talked.

'Adolf and I are to die when the time is right,' she said. 'Our bodies are to be burned. The men will take care of that.' She looked at me and smiled. 'You've been so loyal to us and to the Führer. I want you to make sure we die. I want it to be quick. Adolf agrees there should be someone in the room with us to make sure our orders are carried out. So, dear Magda, you must end the reign of the Third Reich. You must make certain we are dead.'

I grabbed the railing to steady myself I was so stunned by her words. Her request repulsed me, yet gave me a thrill of satisfaction. Hitler would take the easy way out and not answer for his crimes. By committing suicide, he could let blame fall on his generals, the soldiers and the German people for *his* defeat. He would die a martyr's death, at least in his eyes. And Eva, who concerned herself with nothing except her blind devotion to the Führer, would join him in their death pact.

Smoke swirled toward the door and the shelling suddenly

picked up again. Eva slammed it shut, plunging us both into the bunker's netherworld. Explosions again rocked the Chancellery garden. One of the blasts shook us violently on the steps.

I turned, ready to descend back into the bunker. Hitler stood at the bottom, attired in a red dressing gown and slippers. He looked up at us without a smile, his face garish and sagging under the glare of a lightbulb. Perhaps he wanted a look at the sun himself. Without acknowledging us, he turned and disappeared down the passageway.

As I watched him, I knew fate had decided the course of my life.

I would kill Adolf Hitler.

# CHAPTER 22

Eva came to me about two the next afternoon. Her husband, the secretaries and Cook were having a meal. She had no appetite, she confessed. Her dogs had been killed.

Not long after, we joined staff members in the large conference room. Eva introduced me to Hitler's pilot, Hans Baur, several generals and Otto Günsche, a member of the Liebstandarte and a personal adjutant, who was at Hitler's side when the bomb exploded at the Wolf's Lair. No one recognized me as the wife of Karl Weber, or, if they did, they didn't care. Goebbels and his wife were in the room as well as Bormann. Much the same happened as the day before, although Hitler did not dispense cyanide.

While these farewells were going on, Eva pulled me aside and led me to the sitting room between Hitler's study and bedroom. Here, Eva said, they would end their brief marriage. On a table lay two cyanide capsules and two pistols. An open bottle of champagne and two glasses also sat upon it.

'Stay here,' she said. 'We'll be back soon.'

I sat on the couch, running my fingers over its flowered pattern. As the minutes dragged by, I got up and looked at the paintings in the study and sitting room. Eva had left the connecting door ajar. The room had been rifled through and most of Hitler's papers and books were missing. I assumed they had been destroyed by a staff member. I returned to the sitting room and sat again on the couch. I picked up one of the pistols and studied it. I read the engraving on the weapon, a Walther 7.65mm. I assumed it was loaded. The cyanide in their copper capsules sat nearby.

The door to the study opened and Eva came into the room. She was wearing her blue dress from the morning. She collapsed on the couch and wiped tears from her cheeks. She looked at me with an uneasy smile and poured a glass of champagne. She took a sip and said, 'It's so hard to say good-bye Magda.' She rested the glass next to her on the couch. 'Interruptions, always interruptions. Now we can't even die without being interrupted. My life with Adolf has been one of constant delay. "Duty calls, my dear Eva. Perhaps next month, perhaps next year." Waiting and waiting for what? A consummation that never happened. For years, he couldn't make love to a woman because *the Führer* was too important. Germany was his mistress. Now that we're married, it's too late. He's not physically able.' She laughed and took another drink. 'I shouldn't tell you these things, but I guess it doesn't matter. If you record my words for history, they will ask, "Who was Eva Braun?" No one will believe a word I said.'

I started to answer, but we heard someone enter in the study. Eva held a finger to her lips. I recognized the voices as those of Magda Goebbels and Hitler.

'You must leave Berlin!' Magda pleaded hysterically. 'I

you die, we will die also — the children as well. There will be no life in Germany without you.'

'Nothing you can say will dissuade me,' Hitler said. His tone was flat, complacent. 'You have the choice of leaving or staying. Why would you kill your children? Think of what you're doing. I must end my life here — for Germany's sake.'

Magda burst into sobs. 'Then it is over for all of us.'

'There is nothing more to say,' Hitler said. 'Please leave us and attend to your children and husband.' The door to the study opened and then closed.

My stomach knotted as I thought of the murder of six innocent children, particularly the boy, Helmut, I had met in the hall. Hitler was as responsible for their deaths as he was for any soldier or concentration camp prisoner. I tried to think of a way to keep the children alive, the tragedy in abeyance, but my mind raced with other thoughts as well.

Hitler walked unsteadily into the sitting room and closed the door. He wore his dark uniform jacket with the Iron Cross pinned to his chest. He looked at the floor with sullen eyes and then at me. He walked past and the smell of death filled my nostrils, as if his flesh were already putrefying from decay. His left arm shook as he lowered himself onto the couch.

'Frau Weber,' he said. His voice was faint, restrained, a fragment of its former power. 'Eva has told you why you are here?'

I nodded.

'Then let's be on with it. The barbarians are at our door.'

'I will die first, Adolf,' Eva said, 'but for a moment's pause. Let's toast to a lifetime in eternity.'

'Millions will curse me tomorrow, but providence would

have it no other way,' Hitler said. 'For many years the Fates were on my side. Now I have to face reality. There is no way out except by an honorable death.'

Eva poured champagne for both and they drank. She kissed him on the cheek and said, 'Good-bye, my love.' Before I could react she had the capsule in her mouth. The glass crunched between her teeth and a metallic gasp, like the sound of a grate closing, escaped from her lips. Her face contorted and she drew up her legs involuntarily against her chest in pain. The odor of bitter almonds filled the room. She died, frozen on the couch, as if she had suddenly been struck dead by some divine power.

I walked to the table and grabbed both pistols. I pointed one at Hitler's head and said, 'I am here to give you an honorable death. You are right – there is no way out.'

Hitler lurched forward but then fell back on the couch.

My body shook so violently I dropped the other weapon near the door. I held the remaining pistol with both hands and steadied my aim. 'You think you are powerful, but you are a coward.'

'I'm far from it.' He leered at me. 'Kill me now.'

'Death can wait. It will not come before I say what millions have known but were afraid to admit. Many, many soldiers, including your closest staff members, have wanted you dead for years. I am sorry that they failed. Perhaps the war would have ended sooner, but there was always the question of who would take your place. The death of one devil could spawn a bigger demon. But Germany no longer has to worry about that.'

He put his fists up to his face and shouted, 'Traitors, all traitors.'

'No! You are the traitor. My husband, my mother, perhaps

even my father have died because of your false pride, your hollow words. I saw firsthand the horror of your camps. What good was the Reich? It was nothing but an illusion perpetrated for your gain.'

His face flushed and he threw his champagne glass past me. The crystal shattered against the door. 'What I did, I did for the good of Germany. You are a small-minded traitor like the rest. If the people hadn't failed me, Germany would have been the most powerful country in the world. I should have you arrested and executed.'

'Go ahead,' I said. 'Shout for the SS. They can't hear you. I will shoot you between the eyes before you get to the door.' I smiled and drew closer to him, the pistol still pointed at his head. 'You think Germans love you. A few may – the bullies you surrounded yourself with: Goebbels, Bormann. But the common people whom you disparage for their lack of courage, the people you supposedly loved, despise you. If you walked into the street now, they would string you up like Mussolini. They would stone you and spit on your corpse.'

He reached for the cyanide capsule. 'I will hear no more of this.'

I waved the gun at him and swiped the ampoule from his reach. 'Don't touch that! It won't be much longer.'

He withdrew his hand.

'My husband wanted you dead. He knew, as others did, what suffering you caused for all you deemed as enemies. Those you murdered were honest people, caring people with families who had done nothing wrong other than being named enemies of the Reich. Your Reich. They were less than your vision of what German perfection should be and they died. For, after all, they were the cause of Germany's problem – sinful, decadent money-grubbers who had ruined us for a thousand years. At least they died with honor. They were so much stronger than you could ever be. I hope those you murdered, those you executed, those innocents who died because of your maniacal dreams, will spit on you beyond the grave. They deserve some measure of revenge. In the beginning, they believed your hollow words. That was before you betrayed their trust – as you crushed them to fulfill your quest for absolute power.'

I leaned close to him because I wanted him to hear my words. 'You will be despised as the most evil man in history. The mention of Adolf Hitler will bring shame upon this nation – not glory. Your name will be reviled as long as man inhabits earth.'

He bowed his head. 'Your kind has brought Germany to defeat. Look at the destruction that surrounds us, the deaths on every corner. If the people had stood with me, Germany would have been invincible. Think on that as you return to the ashes.' He thrust his hand for the capsule and, this time, I did not stop him. He slowly put it between his teeth.

'For good measure,' I said, and knelt beside him. I put the pistol to his right temple. 'There is no way out.'

He bit into the capsule and I pulled the trigger. The blast knocked my hand backward. A hole opened in his head and blood poured from the wound. Hitler slumped on the couch, his eyes still open in death. Then, he fell, his head crashing against the table. My hands, the couch, the carpet and the wall behind him were slick with his blood. Even Eva's body carried some of the stain of his death. I looked at the crimson flow and marveled that it had been part of him. I was proud I'd killed him. For a few moments, I reveled in the gore around me, as if I had gone mad. The blood didn't bother me; it would wash away down the sink. But for now, I wanted to feel its warmth as it flowed down my hands. Time was against me, however.

I threw the pistol on the floor in front of him, wiped my hands on my dress and put the other pistol back on the table. I rushed to the door of Eva's adjoining bedroom because I knew it wouldn't be long before the others would investigate the gunshot. I sat on her bed until the blood began to dry on my dress. I heard rustlings in the sitting room, but no one came into her bedroom. After an hour or so, I peeked past the door. The bodies were gone. Someone had carried out Hitler's orders to dispose of his and Eva's remains.

As I walked back to my quarters, I passed the Goebbels children sitting on the staircase between the upper and lower bunkers. Helmut, who recognized, me, shouted out, 'Did you hear the shot?'

I shook my head.

'It was a bull's-eye.' He clapped his hands together.

I collapsed against the wall, shaking uncontrollably at the enormity of what I had done. My knees gave way and I slid to the floor in a heap.

One of the older daughters rushed to my side. 'Don't,' she said, and clutched my hands. 'We'll be out of here soon. My mother and father said so.'

I sat trembling for several minutes before I managed to say good-bye to the children. I wondered if there was anything I could do, because I feared what lay in store for them.

Cook told me later what happened to Hitler and Eva.

They were carried out, as he had instructed, dumped into

a shallow depression, their bodies doused with gasoline and set on fire. The men had little time to make sure the Führer and his bride were never discovered. The shelling continued even as the pallbearers tried to ignite the makeshift grave. Throughout the day and into the evening, a few of the Party faithful renewed their pledge to make sure the bodies were burned into nothingness. Eventually, the disintegrating corpses were covered with earth from the garden – their graves surrounded by rubble, garbage and the detritus of war.

Rumors circulated wildly about what was to come next. Communications had been cut days before, but we knew from firsthand reports the Russians were only a few hundred meters away engaged in fierce hand-to-hand combat with the last defenders. Now that Hitler was dead, many of those who'd vowed to stay with him to the end were planning ways to escape. No one wanted to be captured by the enemy. I was told by Baur, Hitler's pilot, to travel north or west to areas held by the British and the Americans. I didn't know if this would be easier than Eva's suggestion to travel south to Munich. However, Bormann and the Goebbels family were still in the bunker. None of us wanted to make a move as long as they controlled the last vestiges of the Reich's power.

That night I slept fitfully. I'd ended Hitler's life, something I had dreamed of, but never dared believe would come true. Deep within me, I mourned the loss of my soul. I felt my humanity had been sucked away, and I would be doomed to Hell for being a murderer. My victim's face came into my head. I had pulled the trigger, the bullet had blasted a hole in his temple, his blood poured forth from the wound. Every time I closed my eyes his face appeared.

I also thought of the Goebbels children and their fate in the bunker.

The next morning, I knocked at Magda Goebbels's apartment. She and the children slept near me. She opened her door a bit and peered out. Her face was white and cracked like a thin sheet of parchment. She nodded, but her eyes looked as lifeless and dull as a cold, gray sea. I started to speak, but she closed the door. I could not see it, but I heard the sound of a chair being hastily pitched against the knob. I left, quite certain I could not sway any decision she or her husband might make.

All of us waited patiently the afternoon of the first day of May for any word from Goebbels or Bormann. None was forthcoming. We sat in the bunker like stranded fish in a shrinking pond.

That evening, Cook asked me if I would help her deliver food to the Goebbels children. We each took two trays, four in total, and carried them to Magda's apartment. I had told no one of her deadly threat, not even Cook. Again, Magda appeared at the door, and when she saw who was outside, she opened it only enough to let Cook hand her the trays.

I spoke hastily as the last one was delivered: 'I know what you are doing.'

Magda's eyes blazed for a moment and then softened. 'My family is none of your concern.'

She attempted to close the door, but I held it open. 'I know, but please reconsider.' She put the tray down and stepped outside the door.

'Keep your voice down,' she said, and tears swam into her eyes. 'Now that the Führer is dead life is not worth living.' She choked with sadness and regret. 'Everything we stood for is in ruins; everything beautiful, noble and good has been destroyed. Our children deserve better than to live under barbarian rule.' She pointed to the door. 'I could not ask for a better ending than to follow in the footsteps of the Führer. Neither could they.'

Cook now understood what was happening and she begged for the children's lives.

'Nothing can change my mind,' Frau Goebbels said, 'and if I have to use force to carry my plan out, I will. My husband and I have sealed our fates.' She stepped back inside and closed the door.

That was the last I saw of Magda Goebbels. About three hours later, Cook and I were walking in the lower bunker when we heard shots. Soon a few SS men and orderlies flew down the passageway coming from the emergency exit to the Chancellery garden. I asked what had happened, and one of them told me that Goebbels and his wife had committed suicide. Their bodies had also been set afire in the garden.

Cook and I passed the Goebbels apartment. The door was closed, but I opened it and peered inside. The children, all six of them, slept like angels in their beds. The girls, dressed in white, wore ribbons in their hair. I nudged one and her arm felt cold and stiff. I called out for Helmut and he did not answer. I went to the oldest girl, Helga. Her face was bruised and shards of glass lay across her lips as if she had been forced to eat a cyanide capsule. The other children looked as if they'd somehow ingested the poison. The deathly almond scent drifted in the air.

Cook gasped upon seeing the children and backed out of the room. I shook my head and regretted I could not ave them. Another pillar of the Reich had fallen and, as was common throughout the Nazi reign, innocents had paid the price as well.

With Goebbels dead, we were instructed to gather in groups and evacuate the bunker. I was placed with Cook, the secretaries and others in the first group to leave. Wilhelm Mohnke, an SS Brigadeführer, was to lead us. We had nothing but the clothes we wore. I put on my coat because it was night and the air was chilly. I put the cyanide capsule in my pocket.

Mohnke issued his orders. The four groups were to head north to join a group of German soldiers. The plans called for all of us to gather at the Kaiserhof underground station, proceed to Friedrichstrasse and then travel to another station farther north.

We left the bunker around eleven. Passing through the tunnels and then to the basement of the Reich Chancellery, we finally found our way out by crawling through shattered windows.

Cook and I held on to each other as we ran across the rubble-strewn Wilhelmplatz. The shelling and street fighting still raged and flames flared into the sky. I nearly twisted my ankle on the large chunks of debris that lay in our path. We descended into darkness once again when we reached the train station.

'Stay close to me,' Cook said.

I found myself shivering in the tunnel, imagining all kinds of horrors, from rats to armed Red troops. I clung to Cook's coat as we plodded along the center of the tracks. Those carrying torches cast a shaky light ahead. Members of our group pitched in and out of shadow. A few lagged behind.

The rays from their torches bounced over us and the[y] disappeared in the murky distance. Above, shells explode[d] showering dirt and rocks from the tunnel's arch upon o[ur] heads.

'Magda.' Cook said my name breathlessly, as if it mig[ht] be the last time we spoke. 'If we are separated, be sure [to] go west. Baur told me he had flown over the America[ns] near Magdeburg. You must cross the Havel River at Spanda[u.]' Her words corroborated what the pilot had told me earli[er.]

It had been years since I visited Spandau. I knew th[e] general direction to take, but doubted I could make it alo[ne.]

Mohnke and the others shouted they had reached an ex[it.] One of the soldiers tried to get to the street, but was driv[en] back by the shelling. We went on. Cook and I ran side [by] side, holding on to each other's hands. We stumbled throu[gh] the tunnel, dodging the debris that appeared out of nowh[ere] before us. We were puffing along when I felt Cook's ha[nd] slip from mine. She cried out in pain and disappeared in t[he] darkness.

I called for her. 'What's wrong?'

'I tripped on a timber,' Cook said. 'I'm finished.' A soldi[er] came near us and cast his torch down. Cook's leg was bleedi[ng] and puffy. 'I think it's broken,' she said. 'You must go [on] with the others.'

'I'll stay until help comes.'

She pushed me away. 'Don't be a fool. No one will com[e.] You have a chance to escape. The enemy will arrest me a[nd] that will be that.'

'We need to move on,' the soldier said, and waved h[is] torch in the direction of the others far ahead. The gro[und] was splitting apart.

'Go on without me,' I said. The soldier nodded and ran after the others, leaving us in the dark. A few stragglers, or perhaps others from the groups leaving the bunker, passed by. Their steps sounded on the wooden tracks; I felt the cool sweep of air from their bodies rush past mine. Then, all was black and silent. Far down the tracks, where the soldier had tried to climb out, the artillery flashed like lightning. Cook's pain-filled face appeared for a split second.

'Leave me, Magda.' She thumped her fists against my coat. 'Go, or I'll have a soldier drag me into the street and shoot me like an injured horse.'

'You don't mean it.'

'I do! Leave! You can't save me, but you can save yourself. I want you to go. I will never forgive you if you don't.' She paused, clutched my lapels and then said in a voice twisted by agony, 'I will never forgive myself if something happens to you.'

I was about to repeat my conviction to stay by her side when Karl's words came into my head. The strength and resonance of them shocked me. 'Remember to stay alive, Magda. Whatever you do, stay alive,' Karl had spoken to me in a train tunnel under war-ravaged Berlin. My body trembled and I struggled to hold back tears.

'I don't want to go,' I told Cook.

She was silent for a moment; then her cold hands grasped mine. 'You must. You have your life ahead of you. Mine is half-gone – and the rest doesn't matter.'

I held her close to me, kissed her on the cheek and struggled to my feet. I turned and the tears I had been holding stung my eyes. Behind me, the exploding shells lit up the exit again. I ran away from Cook toward the direction of the light,

leaving her alone, on the tracks. I decided to get above groun
rather than travel with the others.

A large pile of rubble at the exit made it almost impossibl
for me to get by. Several minutes passed as I crawled ove
the concrete and twisted metal. I cocked my ears trying 
hear any sound of approaching shells. Finally I darted int
the street and was met by another hellish vision of fir
crumbling buildings and destroyed vehicles. Gunfire echoe
down the streets, but the *pop-pop-pop* sounded far away. 
took a chance and turned left – what I thought would 
to the west. I dashed across the street, dodging rubble ar
garbage, and ended up scrunched in a deserted doorway. M
heart beat heavily in my throat. I stepped backward to re
and bumped into something.

I screamed, but I might as well have been screaming in
the wind.

'Where are you headed?' a man asked. His voice was fille
with concern and compassion. There was no hint of weal
ness behind it.

I turned. 'My God, you scared me to death.' I could s
his strong face in the fiery light of war. He was clothed 
black and unshaven, with a dark growth of beard.

'There's no need to be afraid. I'm on the run – like yo
He smiled.

'I'm sorry, but you startled me.' I leaned against the wa
trying to catch my breath.

'A shell is coming,' he said. He pushed me into the corn
and held his body over mine. It exploded in the middle 
the block. Rocks and debris hurtled past us.

I had heard nothing. 'How did you know?'

'I can sense these things,' he said. He backed away fro

e, brushing the dirt from his shoulders. 'You can feel the
bration in the air. Are you looking for the Allies?'

I nodded.

'Everyone is. I'm going that way myself.'

'I don't know who you are,' I said. 'Why should I trust you?'

'My name is Karl. We can do this together. Who are you?'

I stared at him as the light flickered on his face. An over-
>wering sense of calm rushed over me. 'Magda Ritter.'

'Magda. A pretty name.' He pointed to the street. 'If we
ant to escape we should go before it gets light. We'll have
better chance.'

'Are you a soldier?'

He shook his head. 'No, I'm a German who never believed
the Führer or the waging of war. I was away for a time.
n no fortune-teller, but I always knew it would end up
e this.'

I wanted to believe him. There was something in his eyes
at spoke of safety and warmth. Of course, his name brought
> memories of my husband, but Karl was a common name
r German men. My intuition told me I had nothing to
ar. 'Let's go then. I was told I need to cross the Havel.
ow far is it to Spandau?'

'About eighteen kilometers. We can cross the bridge before
wn.'

I wondered how he knew about the bridge Cook had
ld me about. Perhaps it was common knowledge gleaned
>m a web of underground communications.

He grabbed me by the hand and pulled me into the street.

The next few hours passed in a haze as we wound through
e deforested woods of the Tiergarten, across shattered streets,
t through courtyards, even going back to the train tunnels

359

briefly to get to our goal of Spandau. Scenes of desolati
continued in the hours ahead: burned-out buildings, ent
blocks leveled from the bombing. Now and then we saw peo
scramble for cover as more shells fell. Misery and destructi
accompanied us everywhere on our journey. Karl said
considered the dead to be the lucky ones.

About five in the morning we reached the Charlott
Bridge over the Havel River with a few other refugees w
appeared out of nowhere. I wondered whether we mig
not be shot crossing it. I stopped, uncertain what to do.

'Go ahead,' he said. 'I'll wait here.'

'Aren't you coming?'

He touched my face with his hand and said, 'It would
a pleasure, but I have work to do. There are others w
need my help – just as you did. More are coming.'

A strange sadness filled my heart and I hoped he wou
change his mind.

'I can't,' he said as if he could read my thoughts. 'Go n
while it's still safe.'

'I can't persuade you?'

He shook his head and waved me on.

I walked across the bridge, turning to look back now a
then. He stood on the east side of the Havel staring at r
When I'd crossed, I turned and waved to him. He wav
back, a dark figure a hundred meters away.

Spandau lay abandoned before me, its streets lifel
drained by war. From somewhere in the distance, shou
words filled my ears. I immediately recognized them
Russian. Terror shot through me and for an instant I thou
of running back across the bridge to Karl, but when I turn
he had disappeared.

Daylight grew stronger by the minute, although the city still lay in shadow. I ran past the deserted storefronts, darting through the empty streets, heading west. The Russian voices receded the farther I ran from Spandau. Soon I came to a narrow road lined with abandoned farmhouses. The landscape reminded me of photographs I'd seen of World War France – blasted houses with blackened windows staring out at me like lost souls. The vile stench of rotting cattle and horses rose into the air. After about an hour on the road, I heard the sputter of an approaching vehicle. I ducked into a grove of trees and flattened myself against the ground. I dared not look up for fear of being caught. When I finally got the courage to lift my head, the vehicle had passed and the world was deathly silent. I walked for another hour, keeping close to the road. I passed a sign propped against a tree that read: *Staaken*. Nothing living had crossed my path until I noticed a raven sitting on top of a barn. The black bird eyed me suspiciously. As I drew near, it flew off in a wide circle to the west.

I left the road, went to the barn and pulled open the door. There was nothing inside except a rusty tractor and leather bridles. The horse stalls were empty, but hoofprints remained stamped in the dark earth. I rested for a few minutes in the hay of one of the stalls. My legs ached, my stomach growled and my throat was parched with thirst. I forced myself to get up. The only food I found was a cup of chicken feed sitting on a windowsill. I couldn't eat it; it was so dried up it would crack my teeth.

I lay down on the hay, fell asleep and awoke late in the afternoon. The sun's slanting rays filtered through the cracks in the siding. Sleep had done little to revive me; if anything

I felt worse. Lack of food had made me weak and trembli
I tried to get up, but my legs wouldn't carry me. My crack
lips cried out for water. I lifted my head and my body sw;
in blackness. My breath left me and my head dropped ba
to my straw pillow.

I awoke on a rickety cot in an underground room illur
nated by candles. The air was close and humid and brou;
back unpleasant memories of the bunkers.

A boy of about eight stared at me and then called upsta
'She's awake, Mamma.' A thick-legged woman wearing tc
hose and black shoes trundled down the stairs. She frowr
at the boy and scolded him with her eyes.

'I told you not to wake her,' the woman said.

'I didn't,' the boy protested. 'She woke up by hersel
was watching her to make sure she was all right.'

'Thank you,' I said, forcing the words out. 'Where am

'Staaken,' the woman said. 'My son found you in a b;
about a half kilometer from here. He was looking for
cat. My husband carried you home.'

I pushed myself up on my elbows. Apparently, I was i
room underneath a farmhouse. Shelves filled with g
containers of food lined one wall. I pointed at them.

'We've been feeding you,' the boy said. 'Don't y
remember?'

I shook my head.

'You're not all we've been feeding,' the woman said. '
give food to the Reds. They leave us alone, but they alw
come back for more.'

I must have flinched or shown pain in my face, for
woman responded, 'They've never looked down here. As

362

as they know, it's a root cellar. They eat in the kitchen and then leave. Most of them are headed east to Berlin anyway.' She shook her head. 'We can't stop the soldiers from coming down – if you're running from them.'

'What day is it?' I asked.

The woman wiped her hands on her apron. 'May fourth.'

'The last I knew it was the morning of May second.'

'It'll be suppertime soon, if you feel well enough to eat upstairs.'

'I don't want to put you in danger. I'll leave as soon as I can.'

The boy stepped toward me. 'Don't leave. It's been exciting with you here.'

Above us, the sound of an engine grew closer. I huddled next to the damp wall.

The woman bent over me and touched my shoulder. 'Don't be afraid. I recognize the sound. It's the Americans.'

'Americans?'

'Yes. They drive by in their military vehicles at least once a day. I think they're meeting with the Russians near Spandau.'

I sat up and put my feet on the ground. 'When they come back, I must leave.'

The woman nodded. 'Whatever you like. We don't need an extra mouth to feed.'

washed at the cistern and then had supper with the family as the sun set. The husband had been working the fields all day, now that the fighting had stopped near Staaken. He was late planting, but hopeful some crops would grow.

The farmer and his family were people of few words and was glad. I could tell the boy was the most curious of the three, but he was not allowed to speak at dinner. I didn't want to tell this family my story for fear of putting them in danger with the Russians. I said only that I was looking for my husband, an SS Captain, who might have been captured by the Americans.

I helped the woman with the dishes after the husband and boy had gone to bed. About ten thirty we heard the sound of the engine again. She looked toward the road and nodded. I grasped her hands and thanked her for saving my life. The vehicle was approaching fast and I didn't want to miss it, so I pushed open the door and ran into the road. The headlights rushed toward me. I planted my feet firmly and waved my arms. A stout-looking green car skidded to a stop in front of me.

A man in a uniform I'd never seen before stuck his head out of the passenger window.

I walked toward them. The driver opened the door and pointed a pistol at me. I kept my arms raised. The two men looked around excitedly as if they might be ambushed.

'Shit. What the hell are you doing?' the driver said in German.

'I'm giving myself up,' I said.

He scowled. 'You and the rest of Germany.'

'I worked for the Führer,' I said in German and repeated my words in what little English I knew.

Past the glare of the headlights, I saw their stunned faces. The soldier got out and walked toward me. The driver never dropped his aim.

'Prove it,' the soldier said in German.

I took off my wedding ring and showed it to him.

'Holy shit . . .' He spoke to the driver in English and then continued in German. He told me to keep my hands up while he patted me down.

The driver shouted instructions in English.

'He wants us to get in the jeep,' the soldier told me. 'There're Germans around here who still think the war is going on.'

'Isn't it?' I asked.

He pointed to the jeep. 'Climb in, sister. If it isn't over already, it soon will be.'

At 10:44 p.m. on May 4, 1945, I was taken into custody by officers of the American army Ninth Division. After midnight, I sat, shivering and disoriented, in an army camp near Magdeburg on the Elbe River. I was happy to be alive, but deeply saddened for my country.

# BERCHTESGADEN

## SUMMER 1945

# CHAPTER 23

Freedom came through the price of blood. The Allies had leveled the Reich. Germany stood humbled and divided because the world wanted our nation enslaved. No people on earth wanted to see Germany, or the slightest specter of fascism, rise again. Meanwhile, Germans dug through the rubble trying to rebuild their lives. Along the way, many were felled by disease and hunger. Retribution also played its part in the continuing deaths. Many women killed themselves after being raped by enemy soldiers. Families starved on the streets. Hitler, in many ways, was right when he predicted that Germany would suffer terrible consequences for losing the war. He had taken the easy way out while those left behind suffered.

At first I was numb and unsure what to do. How much could I tell the Americans who held me? Who would believe me if I told them I killed Hitler?

My wedding ring was the talk of the camp.

The Major who took it off my finger whistled when he

saw the inscription. Soon I was in front of a sour-faced General who had little patience for 'Nazi scum,' as he put it. All of this I learned through the German interpreter. I broke down and told him everything – how I came to be a taster through my stay with Aunt Reina and Uncle Willy, how Karl Weber shared information about the Party that changed my life. I told him of the bomb plot, how Karl sacrificed himself to end the horror ensnaring our country. I even gave him details about my rape by Russian soldiers and my final days in Berlin. I left out one detail about my stay in the bunker – the murder I committed. History would be better for not knowing.

Other Americans wanted to question me, too, and made a strong case for it by citing my familiarity with the Berghof. A few weeks after my 'arrest' at Magdeburg, I was picked up by a Lieutenant Colonel in the U.S. Army and transported to a camp near Munich called Dachau. I spent several days there answering questions from American authorities. Spring was in full bloom now and the days were pleasant, but the presence of death hung over the camp like a shroud. There were rumors among those being held of a 'massacre' by the Americans of German guards. Everyone feared they would be lined up against a wall to receive a similar fate. The noxious odor of rot lingered over the camp. It hadn't been that long since the prisoners who died here had been buried.

I sat in a room with a military policeman, an interrogation officer and a young soldier who was a typist. The officer who spoke perfect German as well as English, lit cigarettes one after the other while the typist puffed during breaks in my testimony. The smoke drifted through the room in a checkered haze. They wanted to know about the layout of the Berghof, who was there, how much information I was privy to and what Hitler did on a day-to-day basis. I answered their questions as best I could.

Apparently, my 'closeness' to Hitler made me somewhat of a celebrity. The interrogation officer had taken my stated wish to end Hitler's life, and Karl's collaboration with the bomb plotters, as amusing sidebars in a worldwide story filled with tragedy. Such admissions didn't 'cut mustard' with him. There were too many lies being told, he said, too many to sort out.

I lived in a large barracks with other women prisoners of war. In a way, it reminded me of Bromberg-Ost, only with better food and a nice view of the surrounding scenery, and, except for the rumors, no clear threat of death or mistreatment. I was a model prisoner and soon the American soldiers and guards took a liking to me. They smiled and laughed when we talked, even though there was a strict non-fraternization order between soldiers and German nationals. The Allies wanted to ferret out the Nazi criminals from the populace at all costs. Being a friend to a German woman was forbidden.

In mid-June, the interrogating officer came to me one morning. 'We're going on a trip,' he said. 'I think you'll enjoy getting out.'

I was suspicious, but any chance to leave the camp was a relief, even though conditions there were better than in most German cities.

'Where are we going?' I asked as I grabbed my jacket.

'Berchtesgaden,' he replied.

My heart jumped and then sank in my chest. Where was

he taking me? I thought of my aunt and uncle and wondered if they had made it through the war. I had not spoken to them in years, yet I dared not ask the officer to take me to their home.

The officer escorted me to a jeep driven by a military policeman. I sat in the seat next to the MP while the officer relaxed and smoked in the back. The day was luminous and the clouds whisked by overhead. The sun warmed me and, for the first time in months, I felt like a human being, despite my incarceration.

The driver turned the jeep south and we sped down the road. Sometimes we were blocked by troop convoys or had to cut across fields because of damaged roads. At one point when the going was particularly slow, the officer leaned forward and said, 'British army intelligence has corroborated your testimony to us. We know a great deal about you.' He smiled and then leaned back in his seat. I wondered why he had told me this.

We entered the northern edge of the Alps and then turned toward Berchtesgaden. The memories of my stay here came flooding back to me. We traveled on roads scarred by war, and I instinctively knew where we were headed. Soon the Berghof appeared high above us. I could tell it was different; it was no longer the white, pristine structure I remembered. We drove past the guardhouse, now occupied by American soldiers. The driver parked the jeep and we walked up the pitted driveway. The blasted face of Hitler's mountain retreat came into view. Bomb craters scarred the ground; the trees had been stripped bare by the blasts. We turned the corner near the naked linden tree given to Hitler by Bormann.

The gigantic window, part of the Great Hall where my

wedding was held, looked out on the landscape like a great hollow eye. A GI stood outlined in its frame, a lonely sentry admiring the view to the north. The roof had been blown off, the wood burned in a massive fire, the masonry blackened by the blaze. The east wing, which had contained my quarters and the kitchen, lay in jumbled ruins from a direct hit.

Stunned by the destruction, I stood near the stone staircase leading up to the Berghof. I felt no sadness, only regret at the waste Hitler had brought upon the land. He had walked these stairs so many times: getting into his car, welcoming foreign dignitaries, taking his daily walk to the Teahouse. Now the cracked steps, the blackened stones, were emblems of the defeated Reich.

The officer tapped my shoulder. 'Tell me, Magda. What was it like here?'

His question opened a torrent of emotion like blood flowing from a deep cut. I took a steadying breath and started my story. We walked through the rooms still smelling of ashes and destruction, and I told him everything I remembered about the Berghof. Part of our tour included the tunnels where Hitler's record collection lay untouched. Much of the Berghof had already been stripped bare by the conquering forces. Graffiti covered its walls, a reminder of man's innate desire to trumpet his victories.

We spent several hours at the Berghof before we returned to the jeep. The MP took us to Berchtesgaden for lunch, where we ate American rations because the restaurants were dark and deserted. We sat in chairs outside the one that had served me before I went to the Reichsbund. There, my life had changed. I looked down the street and saw the façade of my aunt and uncle's house. I didn't want to bring up their names again.

'What are you looking at?' the officer asked.

I shook my head. 'Nothing.'

'Your aunt and uncle's home isn't far from here. I'd like to talk to them as well.' He lit a cigarette and blew the smoke toward the street. 'I'm sorry to surprise you like this, but we have our reasons.'

The wind, suddenly cold, gusted across our table and I buttoned my jacket.

'What do you want with them?' I asked. 'They belonged to the Party, but my uncle is a policeman and minor bureaucrat. He's had no direct contact with Hitler.'

The officer looked down at the table and then at me, his blue eyes hard and inquisitive. 'Your aunt is a fervent supporter of fascist governments. We know that about her. We'd like you to ask her to tell us more about what happened here – regarding the Party.'

I looked away from him. 'I doubt she will talk.'

'Maybe you can persuade her.'

We sat there for a few more minutes finishing our canned lunch. The officer rose from his chair and said, 'Let's go.'

I had no choice.

When we arrived, I was afraid to knock on the door. I wasn't certain why, but a sense of dread filled me. The officer urged me on. I knocked, and a few moments later my aunt answered. She wore a simple housedress. The Nazi jewelry had disappeared from her attire. She gasped in surprise and covered her mouth with her hand, but when she saw the American officer and the MP, her eyes grew cold.

'Why are you here?' she asked me.

'They wish to talk to you,' I said.

Aunt Reina hesitated for a moment and then opened the door. She drew me close and whispered in my ear, 'They must stay in the living room.'

The officer observed our whispering. 'No secrets.'

My aunt turned and led the three of us into the room. We took seats around the fireplace. The pillows, the rugs that had been embroidered with swastikas, were gone. The room was plain and dull in the afternoon light. The large portrait of Hitler that had hung in the dining room also had disappeared.

My aunt sat across from us on the couch. With no display of emotion she said to me, 'Your uncle is dead.'

I started toward her, but the officer stopped me. The shock of my uncle's death stunned me. Despite my aunt's politics, I felt sorry for her. She had lost the man she loved.

'He hanged himself when he learned of the Führer's death,' she said. 'He had talked about it for days – an American occupation, the fall of the Reich. I begged him. "Governments come and go," I said.' Her eyes moistened and she took a handkerchief from her pocket.

By killing Hitler, I was partially responsible for my uncle's suicide, an irony that struck me hard. But I couldn't dwell upon it. One way or the other, Hitler would have ended up dead.

The officer nodded politely to my aunt and said, 'I need to ask you some questions about the Party structure in Berchtesgaden.'

Reina chuckled. 'Go ahead. You won't get much because I don't know much.'

I heard footsteps.

The officer and the MP jumped up and withdrew their pistols.

I turned my head and saw a man's legs on the stairs. He wore a loose-fitting pair of black pants and scuffed shoes.

My aunt rose from her chair. 'Go back! I told you to run, to get away when you could!'

'Come down slowly,' the American officer said, and kept his pistol poised on his target.

The man came down with his hands up.

'I'm tired of running,' the man said.

I fell to my knees and sobbed. The man on the stairs ran toward me.

'Halt,' the officer shouted.

My husband stood before me. My legs buckled and Karl rushed toward me. He pulled me up and, weeping, I fell into his arms. Time stopped as I collapsed in his embrace.

'I told you,' he said as he covered my face with kisses. 'Never give up.'

I put my head on his chest, thinking I was clutching a phantom. I felt the flesh and blood of his shoulders and chest, but it was hard for me to believe he was alive. 'I did it for you,' I whispered. 'I survived because you told me to.'

'I never doubted you.' He cupped my face with his hands for a time and then said, 'Step aside for a moment, my love. I have unfinished business.' He opened his jacket slowly to show the Americans he was unarmed. Then he held out his hands. 'I am SS Captain Karl Weber. I am surrendering to you.'

'Do we have to use restraints, Captain Weber?' the officer asked as he patted my husband down.

Karl shook his head.

'I'll take you at your word,' the officer said. 'Please don't try to escape or we may have to shoot.'

Karl saluted the men. 'No, sir, I will not. I want to be with my wife.'

We left my aunt's a half hour later after the officer made radio contact with the camp. We traveled back to Munich. Karl was immediately whisked away by the Americans and it was two long weeks before we saw each other again. We sat across from each other at a long wooden table. Karl was dressed in camp clothes and looked tired, but otherwise seemed in good health. We held hands as we talked.

'I still can't believe you're alive,' I said. 'I pinch myself every day and thank God for this miracle.'

'I believed,' he said. 'I had to believe; otherwise, I couldn't have gone on.'

I looked at him, full of the questions I needed to ask in the short time we had together. One, in particular, troubled me. 'Who died in that terrible blast and fire? I always felt in my heart you wouldn't commit suicide.'

'Franz. He never recovered from Ursula's death.' Karl sighed, his face tinged with melancholy. 'He was wounded at the Eastern Front – not badly, but enough to knock him out of service for a few weeks. Then, when the bomb plot failed, he knew we would both be implicated. The morning I left, I met him near the dark field where von Stauffenberg stopped you. Franz asked me to switch papers, which I did.

He said he had a plan to save our lives. I had no idea what he intended to do. Franz kissed me on the cheek and I should have known what was going to happen.

'I had formulated a plan to get to the railroad siding undetected and walk down the tracks. The guards knew me and let me pass through checkpoints. Everyone was in an uproar. I told them the Führer had given me orders to search for traitors. The last obstacle I faced inside the perimeter was the electric fence. I was able to find a tree with branches extending over it, one that had not been cleared. I climbed it and then jumped to the ground. The forest, Hitler's hiding place, worked to my advantage. If I hadn't been on my way, I would have turned around and tried to stop Franz, but I was already far away from Rastenburg when I found his note.'

'Note?'

'Yes, it was stuck in his papers. He explained in detail how he was going to kill himself by blowing himself up. It was better that he died than I, he said, because he knew you and I could go on together. There was no hope for him. The body must not be identified, he said; otherwise, the Gestapo would be on my trail. That's why his death was so horrific. He doused himself in gasoline and set himself on fire. The fire burned over him until it ignited the bomb he carried. He succeeded; otherwise, they would have questioned you.'

Karl's jaw quivered and he wiped a tear from his eye. 'I tried every trick I could to disguise myself. I had to destroy his papers and the note. They could never be found upon me, or I would be a dead man. I shed my uniform as soon as I could.'

I stood up and looked past the American guard to the light that filtered through a window at the end of the barracks. Far off, thunder rumbled over the mountains. 'Night and day, I wondered if you were really alive. Every time I thought about giving up, you came into my head. A man took me to Spandau from Berlin. His name was Karl. When we got there, he disappeared, just like you. I thought he was an angel sent to guide me, perhaps your spirit in another man's body.'

Karl clasped his hands. 'No, I've been in the south for a long time. I remembered your aunt's and uncle's names from our early days together. It was a struggle to get to Berchtesgaden. I slept in barns and fields some nights. Sympathetic farmers would welcome me now and then. I even worked a few days for some of them. When I arrived, I told your aunt and uncle I was married to you. I showed them our wedding ring and they took me in. I lied about my involvement in the plot to kill Hitler because your uncle would have turned me in. I pretended to be a spy for the Reich and a good Nazi. I begged them to tell no one I was here. I told them we had been separated when the Wolf's Lair fell, and that you were still in service to the Führer. They were happy to know that.'

'What happened to my uncle?'

'Your aunt and I tried to reassure him that Germany would go on without Hitler, but he didn't believe it. I could see what was happening, but I couldn't stop it. He hung himself from a bridge. The Nazi flag was draped around his body.'

I lowered my head as I paced, shamed by my uncle's actions. 'He would be alive today if it hadn't been for that evil man.' I hadn't told Karl everything about my days in the bunker and I wondered how he would react. I couldn't broach the subject. 'Where did you stay before you traveled south?'

'I made my way to Berlin and stayed there, before conditions became intolerable. I took clothes I found in abandoned buildings and stood in breadlines. Many days I went hungry because it was too dangerous to be seen. I had to be careful because people were hung for stealing. One time, I took the coat off a dead man. He didn't need it anymore. The hardest part was avoiding soldiers. I hid most of the time until I knew I had to leave.'

I sat again on the bench and studied Karl's face: It was leaner; worry lines spread outward from his mouth and eyes, furrowing deeply into his skin. Both of us had lived a full life in the year we'd been apart. I wanted to ask him another question, but was afraid to hear the answer. He looked at me as if he knew what I was going to ask.

'I looked for your father,' he said. 'I never found him.'

The guard approached and spoke to us in broken German. Our time was up. We had to return to our respective 'homes.' I held up my hand, a signal for a moment longer.

'I have something to tell you,' I said to Karl. 'How much do you love me?'

'You know the answer. Enough to wait a lifetime.'

I trembled and held on to his hands. 'I was raped by Russian soldiers. I can't have children. If that's what you want, perhaps—'

He looked at me sadly, but thwarted my words with a finger to my lips. After a few moments, he said, 'I married you. I've taken you for life. Nothing you say can change that.'

The guard signaled he had had enough of our delays and he made us leave the table. We looked at each other as we were led away.

Two years later, Karl and I were released by the Americans. On that day, we started our second life. Our first night together we made love and talked until dawn. I told him everything.

# EPILOGUE

*Berlin, 2013*

Did I kill Hitler? Now you know the answer. I only wish it could have been sooner.

Before the Soviets began the blockade in 1948, I traveled to Berlin and made my way through the sector to my old neighborhood. The block where my family had lived was still in rubble. I asked a few people if they had heard of my father, but they shook their heads and looked at me blankly.

I made my way through the streets to Irmigard's old apartment. Three families were living there because the building still had walls and floors, although there was only the woodstove and no running water, much as it had been when I was there. I asked if I might see the room where Irmigard's family had lived. A nice woman and her young son welcomed me in. The apartment looked the same, only the current residents had brought in their few belongings.

'I lived here early in 1945,' I said.

'What's your name?' the woman asked.

'Magda Weber. Ritter was my maiden name. Are you from this neighborhood?'

'No. We came looking for my husband, a soldier, and ended up here. We were fortunate to find this shelter.' She frowned and then sat in a rickety chair. 'It isn't much, but it's all we have.' She paused and studied me. 'If you lived here you must know something about this place. What happened? Every day I wonder because I feel their presence.'

I looked at her with alarm. 'Who?'

'Spirits of the dead. The war has caused so many to walk the earth, so many horrible stories remain untold.'

'I would tell you, but—' I pointed to her son.

'Rolf, go into the front and stay until you're told.'

The boy reluctantly left us and closed the French doors that had muffled our screams that terrible night. I told her the story and she wept.

'The house is filled with tragedy,' she said. 'Rolf,' she called out, 'bring out the suitcase that was left here.'

The doors soon opened and the boy dragged a beat-up suitcase across the floor. The woman lifted it to a table so I could inspect it. Her eyes glistened with tears. 'It was buried in a corner, covered by a bloody mattress. Your name is written in pen inside. I kept it, thinking that one day the owner might return.'

'Thank you,' I said, and clasped her hands. 'What happened here was no more tragic than what happened to others.'

'It had been rifled through,' the woman said apologetically. 'I hope you will pardon me. I pushed everything back inside and closed it.'

I hugged her and then opened the lid. I had forgotten

that years ago I'd written *Magda Ritter* in blue pen on the inside. My watch had disappeared, but a few dresses and some undergarments still remained. And beneath them lay my stuffed monkey. It had remained in Berlin waiting for my return. I clutched it to my chest and cried.

'Mother,' Rolf said, 'the lady is crying over a toy.'

The woman nodded and said, 'It's much more than a toy. You will cry someday – over a memory.'

I've cried many days over memories. I never found my father. I heard that Cook had been captured by the Russians. She disappeared from my life after I left her on the tracks beneath Berlin. Karl died in 1995 from an aneurysm. We, of course, had no children, but we spent many happy years together. I went on with my life and never remarried. No man could replace Karl.

As I consider what happened to me as I approach the end of my life, I give thanks for what I've learned. I want to share my knowledge with others. What happened in Germany in those terrible years must never happen again. As much as humanity strives for good, cruelty remains.

I, Magda Ritter, was one of fifteen women who tasted food for Hitler so he would not be poisoned by the Allies or traitors to the cause. As far as I know, only two attempts to poison him were made – one by Ursula Thalberg, the other in the Great Hall. He lived much longer than he should have.

As I said in the beginning, so it is in the end. The secrets I held so long inside needed to be released from their inner prison. I have been punished enough by the past. Now that you've read my story perhaps you will not judge me as harshly as I've judged myself.

# AUTHOR'S NOTE

The idea for *Hitler's Taster* came from an Associated Press news story of April 26, 2013. The report, by Kirsten Grieshaber, chronicled the life of Margot Woelk, a taster for Adolf Hitler. Ms. Woelk had kept her previous profession a guarded secret until she turned ninety-five. She told the reporter that for decades she had tried to shake off the memories of her days with Hitler but that 'they always came back to haunt me at night.' *Hitler's Taster* is not an account of Ms. Woelk's life, although I based several scenes in the novel on her experiences. Nor is the novel intended to be a veiled biography of her life.

I have been interested at various times in reading about the Nazi Party, Adolf Hitler and World War II. When I told a colleague about my intention to write *Hitler's Taster,* she said she hoped I would refrain from turning it into a celebration of fascism and the German dictator's life. I assured her that I had no such intention. I've met so many people who have been fascinated by Hitler – not because they admired the man who was responsible for the death of millions but because they, like me, wondered how this terrible tragedy could have happened. And, more important, how we could prevent a similar occurrence from happening in the future. Unfortunately, as we know, history repeats itself. What were the factors that led to the rise of fascism and its embrace by most of the German people? How did Hitler fool the world? These are complex questions that historians, sociologists and psychologists have struggled to answer. I make no pretense at providing answers. If I, as an author, have allowed the reader to remember, to never forget, then I have succeeded in my task.

Most will read this book as a novel, a fictional account of a life in a significant time period. Others may read it as history. And it is to those latter readers that I issue a caveat: *Hitler's Taster* is not intended to be a strictly historical account of the Third Reich. For example, Joachim Fest in his book *Inside Hitler's Bunker* (2002) makes the astounding statement that the circumstance of Hitler's suicide in the Berlin bunker 'has by now become impossible to reconstruct.' Was a third party involved in his death? Historians have speculated on such a possibility. That question opened up my novel for me. It allowed me to place Magda in the bunker with Hitler.

I researched *Hitler's Taster* to the best of my ability; however, historical accounts and timelines do vary. The reader should know I made every attempt to marry history with fiction. In reconstructing the day-to-day life at the Berghof I relied on many sources, some of which differed. I inserted real people, now dead, among my characters. Hitler had a knack for keeping company with those who served him personally. A major character in the book, Cook, is a composite of several hired by the leader of the Reich. Hitler had many cooks who served him with varying degrees of success. My main model was Constanze Manziarly, but she was not serving at the Berghof when my heroine, Magda Ritter, arrives in the late spring of 1943. Such is fictional license.

The timeline of Hitler's stays at his various headquarters and travels is well documented. The Nazis were, if anything, meticulous in their detail. Again, I have tried to honor history, although there may be, for the sake of fiction, occurrences where action and timeline don't necessarily coincide. For example, I placed Hitler in the Berghof during Christmas 1943. Other sources say he spent an unobserved holiday at the Wolf's Lair during that time. Some historical details were difficult to track down. I advanced the timeline somewhat for Bromberg-Ost, a concentration camp for women. Try as I might, I found no photos and little information about this camp, except for details about female guards who were later hung for their crimes.

Many readers may ask the question: Did the rank-and-file SS, Wehrmacht and German citizens know about the death squads, the camps and the corresponding atrocities? The answer is open to debate. Several books have questioned whether all Germans were complicit in the Nazi undertakings. Or were they just blithely unaware? Certainly high-level officials and some officers within the Party knew what had been ordered, but to indict *all* officers, Party members and nationals is misleading, I think.

From that viewpoint, I also wanted to portray the plight of the German people during this time. Not all of them were fervent Nazis. The SS 'conspirators' and other officers who spearheaded the July 1944 bombing at the Wolf's Lair knew details about Reich activities that were not available to the German people. Had the public known what was going on, the propaganda machine perpetrated by Joseph Goebbels might have taken a very different turn. But even today, historians disagree on why the attempt was made on Hitler's life. Was it because the war was going badly and the officers wanted to save their necks, or because they knew about and abhorred Hitler's atrocities? History favors the former supposition.

Many assassination attempts on the Führer's life failed or were never carried out. Some were 'lone wolf' plots; others were hatched by groups. My research indicated that a major factor in these attempts was the intention of killing not only Hitler but other major targets as well. Many conspirators were concerned about who would take over the government and, therefore, failed to act. Some plots were quashed over this important consideration. I used this idea as a fictional element in *Hitler's Taster*. This factor had faded considerably by the time von Stauffenberg came into the picture.

In the creation of this novel, I would like to thank my editor at Kensington Books, John Scognamiglio, for believing in this book; Evan Marshall, my agent, for steadfastly steering the course; and editors, Traci E. Hall and Christopher Hawke, both of the brilliant red pen, for their invaluable suggestions in plotting, emotion, nuance and choreography. As always I rely on my beta readers for their astute observations: in this case, Robert Pinsky and Mike Deaton.

I have read too many books on the Third Reich over the years to cite them all, but a listing of a few major works in my library is necessary. There are also many invaluable Web sites, too numerous to mention, that aided me in the writing of *Hitler's Taster*.

*The Rise and Fall of the Third Reich.* William L. Shirer.

*Inside Hitler's Bunker: The Last Days of the Third Reich.* Joachim Fest.

*Inside the Third Reich.* Albert Speer.

*Until the Final Hour: Hitler's Last Secretary.* Traudle Junge, edited by Melissa Müller.

*He Was My Chief: The Memoirs of Adolf Hitler's Secretary.* Christa Schroeder, with an introduction by Robert Moorhouse.

*The Hitler I Knew: Memoirs of the Third Reich's Press Chief.* Otto Dietrich, with an introduction by Robert Moorhouse.

*Night,* Elie Wiesel.

*The Holocaust Chronicle.* Publications International, Ltd.

Of significant help with photos useful for historical reconstruction was *Third Reich in Ruins* at www.thirdreichruins.com.

Lest we forget, this book should serve as a remembrance for all who lost their lives in World War II. We tend to forget that the events portrayed in this novel occurred only seventy-five years ago, a blip in time. We can only hope and pray that God's grace and our diligence will deliver us from similar events in the future. Another global war would surely lead to annihilation; therefore, we must maintain a constant vigil against those who would use their power to destroy.

A reading group guide

# HITLER'S TASTER

## V.S. Alexander

About this guide
The suggested questions are included
to enhance your group's reading of
V.S. Alexander's *Hitler's Taster*

# DISCUSSION QUESTIONS

1. Magda describes what her life was like as a young woman in Germany. The Reich wanted women to be mothers as well as workers. Do you think she was happy under these restrictions?
2. Early in the book, Magda witnesses a couple being arrested on a train. What do you think their crime was?
3. Magda has little choice but to accept the job as a taster for Hitler. If you were in her place would you have continued or left the Reich's service?
4. Cook teaches Magda about poisons. What do you think your reaction would have been to such training?
5. Eva Braun tells Magda a secret. Do you think Magda was correct in her understanding of the secret?
6. Karl shows Magda the pictures of the atrocities committed in the East. Would you have believed him?
7. Hitler loved his dog and acted as a father figure to many on his staff. Do you believe that he held any goodness in his heart?

8. How did Magda change in the course of the novel? Do you think she became a stronger woman?
9. Would you have pulled the trigger?
10. *Hitler's Taster* is written from the viewpoint of a German woman. Much has been written about 'ordinary' Germans and their role in World War II. What do you think? Has the novel given you a new perspective on the war?